DEBORAH MOGGACH

FOOL *for* LOVE

THE SELECTED SHORT STORIES

TINDER
PRESS

Versions of some of these stories previously appeared
in the collections *Smile* and *Changing Babies*.
All other stories are newly published in volume form.

Smile first published in Great Britain by William Heinemann Ltd in 1987
Changing Babies first published in Great Britain by
William Heinemann Ltd in 1995

Page 335 constitutes an extension of this copyright page.

This collection first published in Great Britain in 2022 by Tinder Press
An imprint of HEADLINE PUBLISHING GROUP

First published in paperback in Great Britain in 2023 by Tinder Press
An imprint of HEADLINE PUBLISHING GROUP

1

Cataloguing in Publication Data is available from the British Library

ISBN 978 1 4722 9001 4

Typeset in Sabon LT Std 10.75/14.5 pt by Jouve (UK), Milton Keynes

Printed and bound in Great Britain by Clays Ltd, Elcograf S.p.A.

Headline's policy is to use papers that are natural, renewable and
recyclable products and made from wood grown in well-managed
forests and other controlled sources. The logging and manufacturing
processes are expected to conform to the environmental
regulations of the country of origin.

HEADLINE PUBLISHING GROUP
An Hachette UK Company
Carmelite House
50 Victoria Embankment
London EC4Y 0DZ

www.headline.co.uk
www.hachette.co.uk

Contents

Contents

Introduction

Have you noticed how, in TV dramas, people always park right outside the place they're visiting? There's always a space. And they never have to fuss around with parking meters either.

I felt the same wave of nostalgia when re-reading my stories for this book. They were all written a while ago, and are of their time in some ways. Language, references and politics change and evolve, just as finances do – in one of them, I notice, you could buy a whole house in Fulham for £68,000. In another, 'The Wrong Side', the police were still driving those white Rovers. People smoked in cinemas, watched videos and listened to cassettes. Women wore shoulder pads. #MeToo, climate change and trans rights were not even glimmerings on the horizon and as I read the stories I felt protective about my characters, who had no idea how the world would change, and no idea how they would cope with it, just as we ourselves had no idea at the time.

Human nature, however, never changes. Nowadays we might be on Instagram but we feel the same joys and fears, the same jealousies and resentments. Many of these stories focus on that Ground Zero: domestic life. Time and again I return to families, children, and the eternal battleground of marriage, and these stories strike me as true now as when they were written.

What was personally fascinating was how re-reading them was like revisiting a diary of my past. I've never kept an actual diary, which is something I regret, but many of these stories were triggered by a past event, or a situation that I'd long since forgotten, and it was strange to have them swim back into focus.

In my experience, short stories are triggered by two seemingly disparate images, which jolt an electric charge. 'Changing Babies' was commissioned by a magazine as a Christmas story, and sprang from something that happened in my local swimming baths, where I was taking my son for a lesson. There was a plastic crib in the changing room. A little boy asked his mother what it was for, and she replied, 'It's for changing babies.' I could see that the boy was confused by this – did it mean that if he was put into it, she'd change him for another child? In my story, his parents were recently divorced and he confused the Christmas image of baby Jesus in his crib with his own anxiety about what would happen to him.

'Hot Tickets' was inspired by a newspaper story about a famous production of *The Blue Room*, starring Iain Glen and Nicole Kidman, which was so notorious that seats were being re-sold for a huge amount of money (£500 in those days was a fortune), and I linked it with a woman looking for love – a recurring theme.

Marital break-up and internet dating, of which I'd had plenty of experience, popped up again and again, though the women concerned grew older, just as I did. Usually it's been a tiny scrap of my own life which has spawned a very different story. 'The Wrong Side', for instance, was inspired by holidays in France with my first husband, which were actually the happiest times in our marriage. I just used the power of the passenger, sitting on the left seat, the lookout side when driving in France, to build up a totally different plot.

'Smile' dated from the seventies, when I'd been waitressing in the Swiss Cottage Holiday Inn whilst pregnant, and had to wear a smiley badge even though I was feeling nauseous. I wove that into a story about an errant father. 'Sunday in the Park with Henry' dated from long-ago memories of seeing John Lennon and Yoko Ono at the Albert Hall, where they messed around in a sack and the audience went wild. This was woven into my stumbling into picnic rubbish on Hampstead Heath, and amongst it I spotted a mobile phone. 'Snake Girl' dated from my time living in Pakistan, where I had a brief chat with an airline pilot. He seemed a lost soul, and later I made up a story for him. 'Some Day My Prince Will Come' stems from glimpsing an old boyfriend in the cinema, each of us with our children, and speculating on how it would have been if we'd stayed together, how those particular children would never have been born but replaced with others, who now had no chance of existence.

These stories rest like holograms over what actually happened – in fact, they have become the truth. Some, however, are entirely fictitious. The Whistler story was simply inspired by the painting of his mother, which now hangs in the Musée d'Orsay, in Paris.

On the other hand, some characters became so rooted in my brain that I couldn't get rid of them and they migrated from novel to short story. Buffy was a boozy old actor with many ex-wives who starred in two of my novels and still hung around, like a guest at a party when everyone's gone home. So I wrote 'Twin Beds' to give him one last outing.

It got more meta than this. In one of those Buffy novels, *The Ex-Wives*, a character reads one of my stories in *The Times*, where it actually appeared. It was called 'How I Learnt to be a Real Countrywoman' and described how somebody put rare newts into a pond to stop a motorway being built. This idea also pops up in another of my novels, *The Carer.* I'm a dedicated recycler of plastics, bottles and plots.

'Making Hay' is another story which re-invented itself in a longer form. It was triggered by the sight of a coach parked near my home in London. I seem to remember some women boarding it, wearing dungarees. Maybe this was a figment of my imagination, but from it grew a short story where a coach driver who'd always scoffed at the CND found himself taking a load of women to a protest at Greenham Common. That very week he'd been diagnosed with leukaemia, so I explored his feelings of imminent extinction with their fears of the world blowing up. When I'd finished the story he, too, hung around, so I gave him a whole novel to himself, *Driving in the Dark*. He was a slightly altered character in this version, which described how he stole a coach from its depot and drove across England, searching for his unknown son, the result of a one-night stand.

It gets weirder. For the novel was optioned for a TV drama and when I started to adapt it, I found it had gone dead on me. I simply couldn't turn the characters into creatures of drama; they remained stubbornly inert on the page. So I picked one of them, a peroxide blonde called

Shirley, who lived with an Elvis impersonator in a trailer park outside Spalding, and wrote her a story all to herself, called 'Stopping at the Lights'. Re-energized, Shirley started to breathe again and when I put her back into the original narrative this warmth spread to the other characters, who also sprang to life. The TV drama was never made but it was an interesting process, which I'd recommend to any writer in the same fix.

When thinking up an idea, writers usually know, by instinct, what form it will take. Do we want to dip into a life or explore it at length? Short stories are like chamber music compared to the full orchestra of a novel, but there are no rules. They may take place over several months, even years, or simply five minutes. Whatever their time frame the writer has to be ruthless; every word counts so one has to cut, cut, cut. One just hopes that, though brief, they suggest a world beyond their pages. A world all the more tantalizing for not outstaying its welcome.

So I'll stop now. I won't outstay my own welcome. I just hope you enjoy them, in all their variety, as much as I enjoyed writing them.

Deborah Moggach. Kent, November 2021

Twin Beds

T. S. Eliot was wrong. It's December that's the cruellest month, certainly for those whose life has been somewhat chaotic on the domestic front. During the past few years, with the departure of his third and final wife, the looming prospect of the festive season had filled Buffy with dread. Upon which of his exes or children could he foist himself? In his more paranoid moments, he pictured phone calls between them where hostilities were briefly halted as they bargained over who would take him in for the day, like a neighbour's parcel from Amazon. There was nothing like the pitiless glare of Christmas to show up the fault lines of one's past and to remind a chap that he came first with nobody. Sometimes Buffy had the urge to release his extended family of their obligations, and crawl off to some obscure hotel and the company of paper-hatted strangers.

Well, now he had a hotel of his own so could do just that. Why not stay put? Myrtle House, left to him in an act of astonishing generosity by his old friend Bridie, was a ram-shackle B&B situated in the town of Knockton, on the Welsh Borders. He had been living there since the summer. A more unlikely career change was hard to imagine, especially at his age, but he had taken on the role of proprietor with surprising ease, principally because the main task of running the place was done by Voda, his sturdy second-in-command.

She was also at a loose end this Christmas, due to her boyfriend being banged up in jail. Her brother, Aled, was carrying on with a woman who lived up in the hills and he was planning to spend Christmas with her.

'That leaves us,' Buffy said, watching Voda change the sheets. 'We could go to that place on the bypass, the one with the Carvery. They do an Xmas special for £16.99, there's a sign outside.'

Voda shook her head. 'The council closed it down last week. They've been using contaminated meat products.' She straightened up, wiping her forehead. 'I know. Why don't we get people to come here? People in your position, who nobody wants.' Buffy opened his mouth to object but she carried on. 'Three nights, turkey and all the trimmings. We could play charades, you being an actor and all. Well, you were once. I could put it on the website, see if we get any response. Double rates, of course, due to the time of year.'

'Nobody'll want to come here.'

Within an hour they had fifty-three replies. It was a comfort to know there were so many other desperate people out there. All day, Voda's laptop pinged with incoming mail. A few couples had requested bookings but most of them were singles. The problem was how to winnow them down, there being only five bedrooms.

'We'll just have to choose the names we fancy,' said Buffy. 'As I did with the horses in my gambling days.'

The preparations were surprisingly enjoyable. As Voda nailed up the holly, Buffy felt a tender obligation towards the waifs and strays who would be seeking shelter under its berries in this difficult time. That he and these strangers had no emotional baggage made it so breezily simple; why couldn't families be like this? No guilt, no resentment, no tearful meltdowns, and what's more he was making a financial profit – the opposite of Christmases past in every respect. His various offspring had sent him gifts and cards, their lengthy rows of kisses effusive with relief. He felt a surge of festive cheer. A turkey had been ordered from the butcher's where mulled wine was served to the waiting queue of country folk, their cheeks flayed by the gales. Fairy lights festooned the high street, and in the windows of Audrey's shop tinsel draped the bedroom slippers. How different it was to the crass materialism of London and the Flanders Field of family life!

And now it was Christmas Eve and the guests were arriving. James and Tik were a couple, who were to occupy the only double-bedded room. James was a debonair chap – grey hair, well-cut suit, with an old Etonian air of entitlement. Tik was a comely young consultant haematologist.

'Tik's got no family here and I can't possibly foist him on mine,' said James. They had apparently been together for years and lived in St James's, a fact that still struck them with the freshness of a joke. Buffy felt a stab of envy as he heard them chattering in their room. It was as if they hadn't seen each other for years. They usually went abroad, they said, but the Olympics had brought on a surge of patriotism and they planned to explore the surrounding hills in their state-of-the-art hiking boots, their Christmas gifts to each other.

Brendan, another guest, had just arrived. He was an old

hippy and said he knew the hills like the back of his hand, due to living in this area in the seventies.

'London was doing our heads in,' he said, 'so a bunch of us freaks headed west and this town was where the petrol ran out.' Apparently, they had raised goats and taken lots of LSD; his eyes moistened at the memory. He said that he'd come to revisit old haunts while his partner spent Christmas in Australia with her parents, who disapproved of him as an unreconstructed stoner.

Darkness had fallen and they were drinking tea in the lounge. The fourth guest had joined them – Patricia from West Wittering. She was a good-looking woman of indeterminate age – jeans, pearls – and a tense, waspish manner. Brendan was warming his feet on the fender and Buffy caught her glancing at the holes in his socks.

'There's a book in my room that I'm longing to read,' she said to Buffy, 'but it's propping up one of the bed legs.'

'How frustrating, I'm so sorry,' said Buffy, 'I'll swap it with another one the same size.'

'Still, it's nice to see that nothing's changed. I used to come here with my husband. It was run by a game old trout, I've forgotten her name.'

'Bridie,' said Buffy.

'Such a charming place,' she said, looking up at the cracks in the ceiling. 'So shabby-chic.'

Was she being ironic? Buffy had no idea. They were all of them starting from scratch, and he found this exhilarating. Freed from the weight of family expectation, they were chatting with the conviviality of strangers. As Voda sliced the Christmas cake, he gazed at the people warming themselves at the fire. Already he felt bonded with this disparate little group, and he hadn't even had a drink yet.

The doorbell rang. That would be the last guest, Hugh Plummer. The dog bounced around, yapping, as Buffy got up.

A balding middle-aged man stood at the door, with his suitcase. The sound of carols drifted from the church.

'Come in, come in,' said Buffy, leading him along the hallway. 'Fancy a cup of tea or do you want to settle into your room first?'

The man didn't reply. He had come to a halt at the open door of the lounge.

'What on earth are you doing here?' He stared at Patricia.

Patricia put down her cup of tea with a clatter. 'What are *you* doing here?'

Hugh sat down heavily on the sofa. He looked at the other guests. 'She's my ex,' he said.

There was silence as everybody gazed at the two of them. Even Brendan removed his feet from the fender.

'What's happened to your little friend?' said Patricia.

'She's in a panto, in Wick.'

'Why haven't you gone there?'

'It's the top of Scotland and I had to work today, and tomorrow there are no trains, and on Boxing Day she's got a matinee and an evening performance, so I'd hardly see her anyway.' He stopped. 'Hang on, why am I telling you this? It's nothing to do with you.'

'It is, actually,' Patricia said. 'Because it means you're here.'

'So are you.' He looked at her, his eyes narrowed. 'Where's whatshisname?'

'Having Christmas with his ex. They always do that, for the children's sake. Her chap goes back to *his* ex, too.'

Hugh raised his eyebrows. 'How awfully civilized.'

'Some people can be.'

Hugh grinned. 'How *is* Thingy? Still enjoying the wacky world of accountancy?'

Patricia looked at the other guests, whose heads were swivelling like the onlookers at a tennis match. 'I'm sorry,' she said. 'This is very awkward.'

'Don't mind us,' said Buffy.

'Have some cake,' said Voda. ''Scuse fingers.'

'You must have different surnames,' said Buffy. 'Or we'd have spotted it when we did the bookings.'

'Look, we'll behave ourselves,' said Hugh. 'We don't want to ruin everyone's Christmas.'

At dinner, Buffy put them at opposite ends of the table. That wasn't far, however, seeing as there were only seven people there. James and Tik, their voices bright with artifice, told amusing stories of their former Christmases in various hotels around the world as the exes eyed each other across Voda's fish pie. The air was heavy with expectation. Both Patricia and Hugh were knocking back the wine. What might erupt – a screaming match or maudlin reminiscences? Buffy had form in this situation. In his experience matters were on a knife-edge and could go either way.

Apparently, they had been married for fifteen years, a marriage that collapsed when Hugh met a younger actress on a train who was having problems with her mobile. 'I looked her up on *Spotlight*,' Patricia whispered. 'Ferrety little face, half his age of course.' She herself had recently got together with a man she'd met on *Guardian* 'Soulmates', who was kind and caring and, indeed, an accountant. All this Buffy learnt when he helped him take out the plates. She promised that hostilities would be halted over the Christmas period, for everybody's sake.

And for a while both she and her ex were as good as their word. The trouble began after Buffy had uncorked the dessert wine, inadvisable in the circumstances. Brendan, his voice blurred, was droning on about the days he played in a band and the various substances he had ingested. He started counting them out on his fingers.

'Ks, Qs, acid, speed—'

'I can't believe you called me a ball-breaker.' Patricia glared at Hugh across the table.

'Not now, Pat,' he muttered.

'You always said you liked feisty women. I suppose you're happy now you've found yourself a doormat.'

'She's not a doormat!'

'You really think I'm bossy? I only did things because you were so useless. Remember when we got lost on Offa's Dyke because you looked at the map the wrong way round?'

'We laughed at the time,' Hugh said, gazing at her in the candlelight. 'Don't you remember? And we came back here and played Boggle with Bridie?'

There was a silence. Suddenly Patricia's eyes filled with tears. She drained her glass and set it down on the table. 'Where did it all go, Hughey? What happened to us?'

Hugh paused. 'You started wearing tracksuit bottoms.'

'They were comfy.'

'Exactly.' Hugh, who was perspiring, mopped his head with his napkin. 'You stopped trying.'

'Only because you stopped looking.'

'And then someone came along who made me feel—'

'Don't!'

'Any more apple pie, anyone?' asked Buffy.

'Anyway, *you're* happy now,' said Hugh. 'With Thingy.'

'His name's Gerald.' She reached for the bottle and refilled her glass. 'Yes, I'm happy, thank you. He's kind and considerate and he's very nice to the dog.'

'That's all right then.'

'Yes.' She broke off a piece of crust and put it into her mouth.

'*That* used to drive me mad too,' he said.

'I just like the outside bits.' She looked up at him, her eyes glittering. 'It feels odd to have Christmas with you and not give you a present.'

It was nearly midnight and the guests had disappeared upstairs. Buffy and Voda sat slumped in the lounge, exhausted.

'Did you take the giblets out of the turkey?' asked Buffy. 'In their little plastic bag?'

Voda gave him a pitying look. 'Yes, Buffy.'

She still wore her grease-spattered apron, her dreadlocks tied up with string. The clock struck twelve. Buffy looked at her dear, blunt face, sheeny with sweat.

'Happy Christmas,' he said.

'You too, with knobs on.'

As the chimes died away they became aware of a muffled

sound in the room above, the room in which Hugh was staying.

Buffy and Voda exchanged glances. It was the dragging scrape, and thud, of twin beds being pulled together.

*The **Christmas truce** was a series of widespread, unofficial ceasefires that took place along the Western Front around Christmas 1914, during World War I. Through the week leading up to Christmas, parties of German and British soldiers began to exchange seasonal greetings and songs between their trenches; on occasion, the tension was reduced to the point that individuals would walk across to talk to their opposite numbers bearing gifts. On Christmas Eve and Christmas Day, many soldiers from both sides – as well as, to a lesser degree, from French units – independently ventured into 'no man's land', where they mingled, exchanging food and souvenirs. As well as joint burial ceremonies, several meetings ended in carol-singing. Troops from both sides were also friendly enough to play games of football with one another.* (Wikipedia)

Darkness had fallen. Christmas dinner was over, the table strewn with dirty dishes and discarded paper hats. In the lounge, a game of charades was in progress. Buffy was performing the ridiculously easy *Brokeback Mountain* to a smattering of applause.

The day, so far, had been a success. Buffy had feared that Patricia and Hugh, the sort-of-adulterers – if that was the word, what *was* the word – would have some sort of public meltdown. Fascinating though this would be, it would have driven a bulldozer through the festive spirit and no doubt reminded people of exactly what they had hoped to escape by 'Spending Christmas with Strangers'. In the event, the lovebirds had emerged with the some-what glassy defiance of guilty teenagers, their behaviour muted by crippling hangovers, and behaved with exem-plary politeness both to each other and to the assembled company.

And something had happened to the atmosphere. The previous night's showdown had bonded people together, like an audience at the theatre, and given them something to whisper about in the hallway. Were the exes going to get back together again? After all, there was a flush to their cheeks, they looked pretty happy. Or was their romp in the sack just an aberration, a final huzzah for old times' sake before they returned to their partners?

Actually, it was only James and Tik who were interested. Voda wasn't the curious type and Brendan had slumped into silence, having finished the stash of weed that he car-ried around in a dog-poo bag. If he had been pleased by Buffy's lax attitude to the *No Smoking* sign in the hallway, a regulation at this sort of establishment, he had given no sign of it and had lit up with a druggie's bleary defiance. Buffy didn't mind. He was fond of a gasper himself. Besides, he felt sorry for Brendan whose glory days were so obvi-ously in the past. And the poor chap's attempts at *Mary Poppins* were pitiful to a professional such as himself.

James was just getting to his feet, miming *book*, when there was a knock at the door. Buffy got up to answer it. A gale was blowing. Standing there, her hair whipping around her face, was a woman Buffy vaguely recognized.

'Do you have a room?' she yelled.

'But it's Christmas.'

'Exactly!' She pointed to a sign in the window. 'It says you have vacancies.'

'Oh dear, does it?'

'I'm desperate!' she shouted. 'I've got my spongebag.'

Buffy ushered her into the hall. The woman was obviously mad, but the wind was blowing the paperchains off the ceiling. He shut the door.

'Don't you recognize me?' she said. 'I'm Carol, from Cats in Crisis. You know, the charity shop in the high street. You bought a teasmade last month.'

'Oh yes, it seems to be missing a knob.'

'I can't bear it,' she said. 'I had to get away.' She wore a smeared apron under her coat. 'The house is a tip and everybody's quarrelling and I've been up since dawn cooking the bloody turkey and all the trimmings with nobody lifting a bloody finger and the grandkids' toys are broken and Colin's drunk and the baby's yelling and his parents are telling my daughter-in-law she's bringing them up all wrong, and his awful uncle and aunt are describing every single course of every single meal they had on their last cruise and I can't bear it, *I can't bear it*!'

'I do see your point,' said Buffy.

'I want to sleep for a week. Nobody'll miss me.'

'Come and have a glass of port.'

Buffy led her into the lounge and introduced her to the other guests. Voda, being local, knew Carol's shop. In fact, she had dumped a bagful of her boyfriend's clothes in it only the week before.

'I've been having a clear-out while he's in prison,' she said. 'Those Bermuda shorts did him no favours.'

But Carol was gazing, puzzled, at Brendan. 'You look familiar,' she said. 'Were you in The Adders?'

Brendan nodded. 'For my sins. Drums.'

'My uncle ran the King's Head in Llandrod. You used to play there.'

Brendan scratched his goatee. They could almost hear the rusty cogs in his brain, turning. Slowly his face cleared. 'You worked behind the bar, right?'

Carol nodded. 'I didn't half fancy you.'

Everyone looked at the portly Brendan, his grey, receding hair tied back in a ponytail, his reading specs on a cord round his neck.

'Do you remember, you took me to Builth Wells on the back of your motorbike.'

Brendan stared at her. 'That true?'

There was a long pause as they looked at each other. Carol reddened but that might have been the heat from the fire. 'Did we . . .?'

'I'm trying to remember, love.'

'I was pretty stoned at the time.'

'What with?' Brendan asked with interest. 'Qs, Es—'

'Everyone knew why you were called The Adders, of course.' Carol laughed. 'You 'ad her' she pointed round the room, 'and her, and her.'

He burst out laughing – a throaty, smoker's laugh. 'You sussed that out?'

'Course. It was so simple then, wasn't it? We put flowers in our hair. We were going to change the world.'

'Not me, I wasn't.'

'No. That's what made you so attractive, I suppose.' She

paused, searching his face for a clue. 'I think we did it, you know.'

'I'm sure it was very nice.'

'I'm sure it was.' Suddenly she clapped her hand to her mouth. She looked at the people sitting around the fire. 'This is so embarrassing. I have six grandchildren. My husband's a parish councillor.' She stood up. 'It was a mad idea, I'm going home.'

Patricia said: 'Don't. I heard what you said in the hall. Have a night of freedom.' She paused, glancing at Hugh. 'You can take my room. I've sort of moved into another one.'

So Carol stayed. Later that evening, they all settled in front of *The Best Exotic Marigold Hotel*. Carol had already seen it twice and Brendan, who hadn't, grimaced at the wrinkled thesps on the screen and hummed 'I Hope I Die Before I Get Old'.

'You *are* old,' Carol whispered. 'So am I.'

The others shushed them up. Leaning closer, she whispered to Brendan: 'You haven't got any *stuff*, have you? It's forty years since I had any.'

Brendan gloomily shook his head. 'Finished it.'

Voda leaned towards them. 'You can get some from Wickett's Farm,' she whispered. 'My brother's there, with his girlfriend. She supplies half Powys, socking great polytunnel.'

Brendan's face lit up. 'How far?'

'Three miles, I'll give you directions.'

Brendan was already pulling on his shoes. 'Coming, Carol?'

Buffy was asleep when they returned. Far off, the clock

struck midnight. The dog jumped off his bed, yapping, as footsteps creaked up the stairs.

Through the wall, in Brendan's room, he heard thumps and murmurs as the two of them blundered against the furniture. Carol laughed – a shrill, stoned giggle. Then Buffy heard a scraping sound as the twin beds were pulled together.

In the morning, Carol was gone. She had left a cheque on the hall table, weighed down with Buffy's BAFTA, and had presumably returned to her life. Patricia and Hugh had checked out separately, presumably to do the same. Buffy, walking the dog around the block, ruminated on the unexpected Christmas presents that had been given and received. *A dog's for life, not just for Christmas*. In the case of humans, the opposite appeared to be the case. As a veteran of the marital merry-go-round, he was glad that Myrtle House had played its role in this. Those staying in a hotel were freed from responsibility, existing in a limbo with strangers who they would never see again; that was part of the allure, and worth every penny. *This never happened*. What thrilling words for those encumbered by domesticity and family life!

It was a cold, wet morning but children were out on their new bikes. Buffy paused as his dog lifted his leg against a recycling box, crammed with empties. There were couples exempted from these ruminations. Some of his acquaintance, including James and Tik, seemed freed from the normal recriminations and guilt. Even when faithless, they seemed at heart faithful. The lack of children and a high disposable income played a part in this, but that couldn't be the whole answer. James and Tik had been together for years but they seemed utterly content – better than that, delighted with each other's company, chattering away as if they had only just met. How did they manage this? Theirs seemed such a clear stream compared to the muddy, churned up sediment of the married life.

He couldn't ask them this, of course, and now they were leaving. Buffy arrived through the back door to find them settling the bill with Voda.

'We've had a wonderful time,' said Tik, carrying the bags down the hallway. He turned to James and kissed him. 'See you next year,' he said.

'And you, Tikki my love.' James opened the front door.

Picking up his case, he walked across the street to where a large, black Range Rover waited. A uniformed driver greeted him, took his bag and put it in the boot. James waved at them and climbed into the passenger seat. As Buffy stood there, staring, it drove off in a cloud of exhaust smoke.

A taxi drew up. Tik shook Buffy's hand and picked up his case.

'Sorry to be dense,' said Buffy, 'but what did you mean, *see you next year*?'

'We only meet at Christmas.'

There was a silence. Voda came downstairs, staggering under a bundle of sheets.

'You don't know who James is, do you?' said Tik.

'No,' said Buffy. He glanced at Voda who shook her head.

'If he's on the TV I wouldn't know,' she said. 'Coz I never watch it.'

'That's what we hoped,' said Tik. 'That's why his people booked this place, in the middle of nowhere.'

'It's not nowhere,' said Voda. 'It's Knockton.'

'Is he some sort of celebrity?' asked Buffy.

Tik considered this. 'In a manner of speaking.'

'I'll look him up on the internet.'

'That's not his real name, of course.' Tik went to the door. 'You've given us a wonderful Christmas, Mr Buffery, and I would really appreciate your discretion. Ridiculous, isn't it, in this day and age?'

And he was gone.

Buffy followed Voda into the utility room. He watched her as she jammed the bundle of sheets into the washing machine.

'Well, fancy that,' he said.

'Fancy what?' she said, turning the dial to *Colourfast Cotton*.

'Everything.'

'Oh, it's normal for Knockton,' she said. 'Get used to it.'

Just then they heard the creak of the stairs. Somebody was descending very slowly.

They had forgotten about Brendan. He stood in the doorway, swaying slightly. He wore a crumpled Glastonbury T-shirt saying *Your tent or mine*.

'Merry Christmas!' he said.

'That was yesterday, Brendan,' said Voda.

He looked at them both, frowning. 'Was it?'

Blind Date

It's unnerving, this dating business, when you're in your fifties. A woman like me loose in the world. A woman sitting in a themed pub, fiddling with the fringe of her scarf. That's how he will see me, this man, also loose in the world. He catches sight of me, maybe first in the mirror. He spots the scarf – a red woollen scarf, that's how he'll recognize me. And my head is bent over *Private Eye* because both he and I share a sense of humour. We also like log fires, the theatre and long country walks. Who doesn't?

These first dates are daunting. There's so much to find out; it could take weeks, months . . . It's like buildings. You move into a new house and it takes a while to discover what its departing inhabitants knew so well – its jammed sash window, its faulty boiler. My résumé is this: one marriage; two 'long-term relationships', as they are coyly called; no children, no complications there. This sort of information is always established early on, before the second drink (pray God that he drinks). Sometimes you know it's hopeless and then you can relax. But usually it's more subtle than that.

One thing, however, is simple. I want somebody for Christmas. Not just any Christmas – *this* Christmas, millennium Christmas. And the dreaded New Year celebrations to follow. I don't want to be on the periphery of other people's lives. Not this year.

You know the feeling, when it's another family's celebrations? There's a gift for you, of course – a Body Shop set of bath lotions, something perfectly acceptable. And they serve you first: 'Breast or thigh?' But you're sitting just outside the warmth of the fire, and to my mind, there's nowhere quite so lonely.

I want to unwrap my own man for Christmas, all for myself.

I want him to be divorced, if possible. Widowed is too Rebecca-ish; who can live up to a dead wife? Single is too creepy, at our age (50+ said the ad). A divorced man means that he's OK, somebody wanted him, something worked for a while, he's part of the human race. I can see him now, weathered but still attractive, as if grit has been flung in his face but he'll still soldier on. With grown-up children if possible, a ready-made family but old enough to have lives of their own, kindly young adults who are glad to have their father taken off their hands.

And he'll take care of me. I know that's sad, but quite honestly, I'm tired of being alone. Six years, it's been. I want a warm body in my bed, lit windows when I come home from work. Things shifted around from where I left them. I want somebody to stand up to the plumber when he overcharges me, somebody who lifts the decisions off me, who suggests a film and drives me there and knows where to park. Somebody who leaves a party with me and gossips about the people on the way home. I'm tired of stepping out alone, into the dark.

That's the funny thing about the fifties. You're in the dark, pressing your fingers against your face, feeling it like a blind person. Who is this woman? Shouldn't she know by now? And if not – when?

I presumed I would be sorted out, you see. When I was at school, girls in the sixth form were grown-up. Then, when I reached the sixth form, the age shifted further on . . . the thirties, the forties . . . I'm fifty-six and I still don't know what sort of person I am, or who I will become. A whiskery old woman, digging her vegetable garden? A predatory woman, with a freckled, wrinkled cleavage, who stays too long at parties? Shouldn't I know by now? 'Intelligent, humorous' is how I'd describe myself. Log-fire loving, of course. A 'professional woman' – though, to tell the truth, I feel more like an amateur one.

It's December. Outside, fairy lights chase around the Dixons window. I sit there, sipping Chardonnay, and wait.

Maeve's husband was on the loose. He had slipped his leash, yet again. Maeve had to admire his cunning. This time he phoned the Emergency Gas Board number, saying he smelt a leak. When the man arrived and tramped down to the kitchen, out Howard shot through the front door. When he wanted to, he was nippy on his feet. Last time he had ordered a minicab; the time before, a delivery of Coalite. Anything to get that front door unlocked. Despite its other failures, his brain had developed its own special cunning. It was like a stand-by generator, thrumming into life during a power cut.

Until recently he had not been a cunning man. No doubt this was because he didn't need to; he got his way without it. That's what their daughter said. 'He's such a bully, Mum! Don't be so feeble.' He wasn't used to obstructions.

At least, this time, he wasn't wearing his pyjamas.

Maeve thought she knew her husband, but the old Howard

had disappeared, to be replaced by the husk of Howard. His eyes were inhabited by a stranger; it was like coming home and finding a squatter in the house. Sometimes, the familiar Howard returned, briefly, but then he was gone. Where had he disappeared to? Somewhere she couldn't follow.

And it happened so suddenly. Three months ago, he started to throw away his letters; she found them, unopened, in the kitchen swing bin. He started getting dressed in the middle of the night and going downstairs to make breakfast. 'I'm going out,' he said. Where? He looked distracted and irritable, as if he were late for a meeting. 'But it's four o'clock in the morning,' she replied.

She started locking the front door. She did it with a heavy heart. Never, in her life, had she felt so alone. She missed her husband. Where had he gone, her darling Howard with his booming laugh and bracing, un-politically correct opinions? 'Dad, how *could* you?' Jo cried. He loved provoking his daughter; humour had never been Jo's strong point. Provoking Maeve too, but that was part of their long-running marital dance. She had long ago learnt to deal with that – a side-step, a twirl.

She had told nobody, not yet. It seemed too painful, once it was put into words, and too demeaning for him. If she didn't speak of it, she could pretend that he was just getting a little forgetful – aren't we all? (Light laugh.) She went out rarely now; she didn't like to leave him. Her neighbourhood had become a foreign place where people spoke in a language that was becoming unintelligible to her. If to her, how must it seem to Howard? She hadn't told their daughter, not yet; Jo was too busy, Maeve didn't want to upset her. That was how she explained it to herself.

'Where's the blithering key, you pest?' Howard had bellowed. *Pest* was such a funny word, but he used new words nowadays. 'I'm going to find another wife. She won't lock me in!'

Was that where he went? 'What sort of wife?' Maeve tried to tease him. 'Where are you going to find her?'

'None of your business!'

'There's a sale on at the Wife Shop.' Maeve laughed shrilly. 'Discontinued lines, seconds . . . polish them and they'll come up good as new!'

He was found wandering the streets. Strangers brought him home – cab drivers, unknown neighbours into whose houses he'd walked. Once he had crossed town – the dual carriageway, the shopping centre – to look for Williams Hardware Stores, to buy, for some reason, half a pound of nails. When he arrived, he found that it had been turned into a Starbucks. Their town had changed; his old landmarks had gone. Even to her it seemed a strange world now – what must it seem to him?

Maeve wept for him. Sometimes she wept for herself.

Where was he? Should she phone the police?

He's late. I've finished my glass of wine but I'm not going to order another, not till he arrives.

This imaginary man, as yet unmet, has materialized into my perfect mate. He takes me into his arms and laughs at my jokes. We discover that we both loved the William books when we were little. Log fires are just the beginning of what we have in common. Hope still springs eternal, you see. It triumphs over experience. My therapist says, 'You must give yourself permission to be happy.' It's embarrassing, isn't it, when people talk like that? We've discussed my parents, of course; in fact, we talk about little else. She understands the effect my father has had, on my relationships with men. She talks about damage and breaking the old patterns, about empowering myself. When I'm sitting in her room, I *do* feel empowered; the trouble is, by the time I get home it's drained away.

I'm longing for a cigarette but I said 'N/S'. It's best to keep one's options open.

So, I'm sitting here, reading the small ads in *Private Eye* because I've read the rest. And then the door opens and a man comes in. He stands there, startled, like a rabbit caught in headlights; then he gazes around. He's wearing a suit, but his tie is knotted around the waistband of his trousers and he's got such a thick grey beard that it takes me a moment to recognize him. I can almost feel the cogs connecting, clunk . . . grind . . . in my brain before I open my mouth to speak.

'Dad.'

Maeve lifted up the phone and put it down again. It was seven thirty. She should call the police; she should leave a message with Doctor Salcombe. By doing so, she would turn Howard into a Case. She would shunt him into another world, a world where professionals sprang into action. She knew she was fooling herself, by delaying this, but then she had always disliked facing the truth – who wouldn't, in this particular situation?

She was fooling herself about Jo, too. Her daughter's busy life was just the excuse Maeve made to herself. The truth was, Jo hadn't spoken to her father for years. Her hostility towards him seemed to have deepened with age. 'How can you stand him, Ma?' she cried. 'He grinds you down, he oppresses you, he's so bloody selfish!' She lived on the other side of town but it could be another country, so little contact did they have.

Maeve stood at the window, willing her husband to lurch into sight. Opposite, Susie Fanshawe unloaded carrier bags from her car; she had been late-night shopping. Her Christmas tree blazed in the window. Maeve thought: why don't I phone Jo? Because I couldn't bear her pity? Or is it something murkier than that? Because, in my daughter's reaction, there might be a small germ of satisfaction? *So that explains it . . . Dad's always been mad . . .*

This shocking thought energized Maeve. What rubbish! She punched in Jo's number.

'*We're sorry but we can't come to the phone right now . . .*'

Jo said 'we', so people didn't think she lived alone. This phantom protector made Maeve sad. If only Jo could get along with men; her daughter's past was littered with broken relationships. If only she could meet a nice man; there must be one, out there.

He doesn't recognize me. It's taken me a moment to realize this. He's sitting opposite me, drinking from the other glass, the one reserved for my date.

'This used to be the King's Head,' he says.

'It's the Slug and Lettuce now.'

'Used to have a pint with Albert Conlaw.' He looks around and then focuses, vaguely, on me.

'So, what do you do with yourself, young lady?'

'I work for Equitable Life,' I reply, and light a cigarette.

I've always been 'N/S' as far as my father is concerned; this small act of rebellion feels bracing. I'm still stunned with shock. This is an unknown man, sitting opposite me; a *tabula rasa*, wiped clean.

'I've been walking a long way,' he says.

'70+,' his ad would say, *'fond of long walks.'*

'I'm looking for a new wife,' he says.

'Why?'

'Someone who won't lock me in.'

'Where will you find a new wife?' I point to *Private Eye*. 'The small ads?'

'I'm really walking to Cookham's Field.'

I look at him with surprise. 'Isn't it Cookham's Acre?'

'Field!' He's always liked correcting me. And me, him.

'I used to go there when I was little,' I say.

'Buttercups,' he says dreamily. 'So many buttercups.'

He remembers it! Our days together in the buttercup field.

'I used to pick so many,' I reply, 'that my hands didn't meet in the middle.'

'My God, I was happy,' he says.

My heart leaps. I remember us, him and me, the buttercups brushing my shoulders. My father's hand reaching for mine as we walked through the field. How wonderful – how truly wonderful – that he recalls it as a time of joy. It was for me, too.

He closes his eyes. 'Happier than it is possible to bear.'

'Why?'

He glares at me. 'You ever experienced love?'

His voice booms. The people at the next table turn to stare. I don't care. I feel warmth seeping through me. Us in the meadow. I stagger towards him, my arms full. '*Do you like butter?*' he asks, lifting my chin and seeing the light reflected there.

'I'm so glad that you remember it too,' I say.

'Those blessed buttons!' he snorts with laughter. 'A devil to get undone. All thumbs, I was!'

'*We're sorry we're not at home . . .*'

This time Maeve didn't flunk it. She left a message.

'Jo darling – it's about your father . . . he's not well . . .'

He's not talking about me at all. I realize that now; he's talking about my mother.

'That WAAF uniform, a bugger to get inside it,' he says dreamily. 'I laid her amongst the buttercups, I only had three days' leave, I laid her there . . . let joy be unconfined . . .'

He lifts his glass of Chardonnay and puts it to his lips. His hand is trembling.

'Didn't see her till the war was ended . . . and there's this little girl, clinging to her mother's leg . . . *Who's that man*, she said. *Make him go away.* I fought for my country, young lady, but the biggest battle waited for me in my own home.'

He puts the glass down carefully. 'I fought for my country, and then I fought for my wife.'

'Why?'

'Why, young lady?' He glares at me. 'To get her back, of course.'

And who was the casualty of that battle? I want to ask. I don't need to, however, for I know the answer.

He's shivering, even though it's warm in here. I take off my scarf and wrap it around his neck.

'There's no buttercups now,' I tell him. 'It's winter. And besides, Cookham's Field isn't there any more. They've built a Tesco on it.'

'What a century,' he murmurs. 'What a botch-up.'

Malcom Williams, 'N/S, 50+', arrives an hour late. Virgin Trains volunteered no explanation for the delay. He enters the Slug and Lettuce and looks around. No single lady sits there; she must have gone, and who could blame her? The only red scarf is wrapped around the neck of a dotty-looking old man who sits at a table, shuddering with tears. Next to him, a middle-aged woman puts her arm around him and gets him to his feet. Malcolm, on his way to the bar, passes them.

'Come on,' says the woman. 'I'll take you home.'

My mother opens the door. It's Christmas Eve; this terrible, thrilling century is drawing to a close. Its battles have been fought and, just for now, an amnesty has been declared. My arms are laden with carrier bags but when I set them down, I feel as light as tissue paper, as light as an Amaretto wrapper floating to the ceiling.

'Darling!' she calls out to my father. 'It's Josephine. She's home for Christmas. New Year, too. Isn't that nice?'

My father shuffles along the corridor. He wears his best suit and a lopsided bow tie.

'It's Jo,' she says. 'Our daughter.'

'Yes, yes!' he replies testily. 'You think I didn't recognize her?'

I glance at him. He ushers me into the living room. The log fire blazes.

'Come in, dear girl,' he says. He looks me directly in the eye. 'I've poured you a glass of Chardonnay.'

New Year's Story 1

Playing the Part

It was Derek who had the idea. These friends of ours, they were going on holiday and they asked if we'd keep an eye on the place, feed the cats and so on. When they got back, they were ever so grateful and gave us a bottle of sherry. Later Derek said to me, 'Why don't we take it up professionally?' House-sitting, he meant.

Derek had retired, you see, and where I worked, serving dinners, they'd all been sent back into the community and I was out of a job – so we were footloose and fancy free and we still had some mileage left in us. Pastures new, we thought. So we put the advert in the *Daily Telegraph* and it just took off from there.

Reliability, that's what we offered. Peace of mind. Honest, respectable couple, no family ties, not any more. House-sitting's a word-of-mouth business and the word spread. We live in a fearful society, you've only to open the newspapers. Remember the old days, when we left our doors on the latch? Nowadays we lock ourselves up in these fortresses, don't we? In fact, that's what we call our business: Holding the Fort.

It's mostly the wealthy, of course, who use our services; one booking led to another and soon we had a list of customers as long as your arm – regulars, and new ones who'd

28

heard about us, in particular our love of animals, because pets was our speciality.

You might think it an odd sort of carry-on, living like vagabonds in other people's homes. But I love it. I love travelling round the country in our Ford Fiesta, stopping one week here, two weeks there, in unfamiliar surroundings. The places we've stayed in – you wouldn't believe – Georgian splendour in Sussex, penthouse in Chelsea with his 'n' hers Jacuzzis. Derek, being a Yorkshireman, disapproves of ostentatious wealth but I find it fascinating. Who would believe women needed so many shoes? And I like looking at their family photos. Derek says I'm snooping but I'm just curious, it's what keeps me young at heart. I'm pretending I'm someone else, and when the fortnight's up we pack our bags and steal away like ghosts; we even take our rubbish with us.

People ask us – don't we ever get lonely, just the two of us, always on the move, cut off from our family and friends? We're like portable electrical appliances, plugging ourselves into a new location then disconnecting ourselves when we leave. But we'd be a lot more bored at home, sitting staring at each other across a gas fire. And there's plenty to keep us busy. Derek's a worrier, he takes his responsibilities seriously. But in all these six years we've had no real disasters – thefts, major breakages. Not, that is, until last month.

It was the winter holiday and we were booked into a house in London – a Mr and Mrs Allsop, new clients, who were going on holiday to Florida. We arrived there on Boxing Day. It was a big house in Holland Park – porticos, pillars, blinding white paint – built to intimidate tradesmen. I *was* intimidated, but Derek's immune to grandeur. If it was Buckingham Palace he'd just say, 'Must be a bugger to heat.'

The Allsops were packed up, bags in the hall, ready for the handover. He was a shrunken little fellow, a distinguished barrister I believe, and she towered over him. He gazed at his wife as if he'd won her at a fair – one of those fluffy toys you don't know what to do with once you've got them home. She was a lot younger than him, though not that young, and she had Big Hair – a puffed-up, blond helmet. I thought: imagine sitting behind *her* in the cinema.

Mr Allsop showed Derek how to work the burglar alarm – they always show Derek, not me. With good reason, actually. Mrs Allsop led me down to the kitchen. I thought she was going to talk me through the appliances, but I heard a groan as a dog climbed to its feet.

'This is Torts,' she said. 'He and my husband go back a long way.'

I knew there was a dog, of course. As I said, we do pets. Torts, however, was a particularly repulsive creature. He had one of those bashed-in faces, as if he'd been in a collision, and was largely bald. He lumbered towards me, claws scrabbling on the marble floor, and shoved his snout up my skirt.

'He's a Schronishwapeki,' she said, or words to that effect. 'They're very rare.'

I'm not surprised, I thought, as I extricated him from my nether regions. He growled at me. Strings of saliva hung from his black, frilled lips.

'He's got a bit short-tempered in his old age,' she said. 'And I must warn you, he has a bladder problem.'

Sounds just like my husband, I thought.

She showed me his pills and his ointments. 'This is for his skin infection and these are for his arthritis. Good luck!'

Torts and I disliked each other on sight. Once I had rejected his amorous advances, he spent the next few days hurling himself at my ankles; usually he missed, skidding across the polished floors. He seemed to harbour some grudge against me, a grudge whose origins were too mysterious for either of us to understand. When I took him out, he had to be dragged along in a sitting position. Passers-by, watching us, snickered behind their hands. Once, in the middle of Holland Park Road, he refused to budge, bringing the traffic to a standstill. Back at home he lay slumped in doorways, tripping me up and emitting silent, noxious farts.

He did, however, gain one fan. Our street was largely deserted – blinds down, no sign of life. It was that dead week between Christmas and New Year. On Tuesday, though, I was hauling Torts back from his walk when a young woman emerged from the next-door house and uttered a cry.

'What a darling dog!' she said, hurrying over. 'I have a dog back home and I miss him so badly.' She wore dark glasses and a headscarf.

'Where's back home?' I asked.

'Beverly Hills.' She stroked Torts' head; it was bumpy with warts, but she didn't mind. 'Dogs – they're so, like, unjudgemental. They accept you, they don't want a piece of you.'

'I wouldn't bet on that,' I laughed, as Torts bared his teeth.

Then I realized – his fangs were bared in a ghastly grin. As she stroked him his hindquarters trembled, and his breath grew hoarse.

'It was great meeting with you,' she said. 'Gotta go, I have a matinee.' And she disappeared into a waiting car.

Back in the kitchen Derek was struggling with a tin opener. We were having a can of soup for lunch. We always bring our own supplies, of course, and top up at the local shops.

'Can't find a decent sliced loaf,' he grumbled. 'Shops round here, it's all this arty-farty bread full of nuts and whatnot. Plays havoc with my dentures. And have you seen the price on them? Daylight robbery.'

Mrs Allsop's shelves were full of spaghetti made from squid-ink, and stuff like that. Bottles of oil with bundles of twigs in them. To distract Derek, I told him about the woman next door. 'She's American,' I said. 'She took a shine to Torts.'

The next day I saw her in the street and asked her in for a cup of tea. To tell the truth, I was longing for some company. So, it turned out, was she.

'London's such a big city,' she sighed. 'Everyone's so polite . . . they're kind of hard to get to know.'

'Not in this establishment,' said Derek. 'Here, you take us as you find us.'

Derek, like the dog, had perked up. Now the girl had taken off her dark glasses, she was really very pretty. She didn't want normal tea and asked for a herbal infusion.

She told us she'd split up from her husband in LA and was feeling lonely. 'It's like – every man I meet – it's like he has problems with personal relationships.'

'Torts likes you,' I said.

'I mean, the guy who plays Hamlet, I'm getting a lot of negative energy from him.'

'Come to Yorkshire!' said Derek.

'*Alas, poor Yorick*,' she added.

'Pardon?' I asked.

She told us she was acting in *Hamlet*, that's why she was in London. She was playing Ophelia. She wasn't happy, here in her rented house, dodging the paparazzi. Though she had an assistant and a minder they were just employees, and the cast didn't seem too forthcoming. 'I guess it's because of, like, who I am.'

'Who are you?' I asked.

There was a silence. The only sound was Torts' wheezing breath as he sat at her feet. He gazed fixedly at her.

'You really don't know?'

She told us her name. It sounded vaguely familiar but I couldn't place it. Derek, of course, hadn't a clue.

'I'm sorry,' I said. 'We don't go to the cinema much – we're not supposed to leave the premises for more than three hours out of twenty-four.'

But she said it was such a relief; at last she felt like a normal person. We had a lovely chat. We discovered, in fact, that we had a lot in common. She grew up in a trailer and we live in a trailer, too, when we're back home. 'And I still live in one,' she said, sipping her tea. 'Like, on location. That's my home from home. I'm kind of rootless, just like you.'

'And *I'm* like an actress,' I said.

'Steady on, Marjorie,' said Derek.

'It's true,' I said. 'These houses we sit, they're like stage sets, and here we are living another person's life in them. Except nothing that dramatic happens.'

Words that I regretted, later on.

*

On New Year's Eve, Derek and I shared a bottle of sparkling spumante and were tucked up in bed by ten. It was a huge four-poster thing and I pretended to be Ophelia, dying. *Out, out, brief candle*, I thought, but maybe that was the wrong play.

New Year's Day dawned rinsed and shiny; there was a hopeful feeling in the air, though the streets were littered with bottles and there was a smashed car outside Europa Food and Wine. I dragged Torts to Holland Park where, in a sudden rush of energy, he dashed after a squirrel and disappeared into some bushes.

Fifteen minutes passed and he still didn't emerge. Finally, I pushed my way into the thicket. The dog lay there, dead.

It had happened: the house-sitter's worst nightmare. Trembling, I went home and broke the news to Derek. My husband's good in a crisis – he's a Yorkshireman, he takes the practical view.

'Come on, lass, let's collect the body,' he said.

We searched for a carrier bag and decided on one saying Sotheby's, because it was heavy-duty, with poppers. We also found some bubble wrap. Wordlessly we walked to Holland Park and I pointed out the thicket. When the coast was clear Derek plunged in and emerged with the bulging bag.

'Aaah,' he groaned, 'feel the weight of him.'

On the way home he was caught short. My husband has a prostate problem. In rich people's houses there are always plenty of lavatories – a perk of the job – but now we had to hastily look for a café. We found one, and Derek disappeared into the gents.

The place was crowded with people shouting into their mobile phones. *Is that Mr Allsop? Know what's happened to your dog?* My cup shook when I tried to lift it to my lips. What were we going to do? How were we going to face them?

I was so distracted that it was not until we rose to leave that I noticed something missing. The bag had gone.

When we returned, our neighbour was just leaving the house. We told her what had happened.

'It was a Sotheby's bag,' I said. 'They probably thought there was something valuable inside. A bronze statue or something.'

'He weighed a bloody ton,' said Derek.

'I'd love to see their faces when they opened it up,' I shrilled hysterically.

'You'll have to bury him,' she said. 'Those poor people, they'll need a focus for their grief.'

'But we've nothing to bury!' I cried.

'Leave it to me.' She put her hand on my arm. 'I'm an actress, hey? That's why I'm playing Shakespeare. That's why I've come to this city, so people can see I'm not just a flaky movie star, I'm a serious artiste! Trust me.'

The next day, the Allsops returned. I heard their cab stopping in the street and phoned next door. By the time they'd got their bags indoors our new friend was ringing the bell.

Mrs Allsop stared at her. 'Are you who I think you are?'

'Hi.' The film star shook their hands.

Mrs Allsop sat down heavily. 'You! In our house! Pinch me, Bernie.'

'I've brought you two tickets for my show,' she said. '*Hamlet*, you know? It can't compensate for your loss, but maybe it'll help you through your grief, for as the Prince of Denmark says, *how weary, stale, flat and unprofitable seem to me all the uses of this world,* when we have suffered the loss of one we love.'

'Come again?' asked Mr Allsop.

She was wonderful, our film star. It was as if a light had been switched on inside her. She told them how she had missed her own dog, and how she used to play with Torts in the garden. 'We were pals, him and me.' Her eyes filled with tears. 'So – I was throwing the ball when suddenly *he raised a sigh so piteous and profound as it did seem to shatter all his bulk and end his being.*' She paused. 'He died happy, I want you to know that.'

Dazed, they followed her into the back garden. A fresh grave was dug in the flower bed.

'*He is dead and gone, lady,*' she said. '*At his head a grass-green turf, at his heels a stone.*' She snapped off a twig of something and flung it on the grave. '*There's rosemary, that's for remembrance . . . I would give you some violets, but they withered all when my father died.*'

The Allsops stood there, transfixed. Mr Allsop blew his nose. Mrs Allsop wiped away a tear, though I could tell she was faking it. The dog belonged to her husband's past life, with his former wife. I'd looked through their photos, you see, I knew all about them by now. The present Mrs Allsop hated Torts even more than I did.

And as I gazed at Mrs Allsop the Second, her head bowed in sorrow, I realized that she, too, was a very accomplished actress.

New Year's Story 2

Hot Tickets

I've always liked neurotic men. They talk, for a start. And it's not about football or computers. They talk about themselves. If you love somebody, what could be more interesting than that? I can spot a neurotic at a hundred paces, across a crowded room. In the midst of others they stand alone, watching the proceedings with a mixture of belligerence and panic. They look like little boys, lost in the playground. No wonder I want to rescue them.

I met Jeremy at a party. It was a reception for some poetry prize so, in the neurosis stakes, he was amongst strong competition. When I offered him a tray of canapés he asked: 'Are they without meat or fish in them?'

'Try the quiche wedges,' I said.

'Or eggs.'

My interest quickened. Veganism is a promising sign. His face was pale and sensitive and his fingers nicotine-stained.

'You must be a poet,' I said.

He nodded. 'Though God knows why I'm here.'

There was an existential ring to this – why are we all here? What's it all about? I was becoming strongly attracted.

'I'll go and find you some crudités,' I said.

The speeches happened next, and the prize-giving, and

when I returned the crowd was dispersing. I found him in the cloakroom, in a state of agitation.

'I've lost my coat,' he said.

How helpless he was! How needy! As we searched for his coat, I gazed at the frayed hole in the elbow of his jumper. He was a damaged person and only I could stitch him up. I longed to lay his head on my lap and stroke him better. You see, I haven't had children yet, and my maternal urge is powerfully erotic.

I found his coat and we started talking. One thing led to another and within a month I had moved into his flat. It was a pigsty, but I soon sorted it out. Jeremy wrote his poetry and I got a job working at one of his stepfather's establishments.

Jeremy hated his stepfather. Frank was a tycoon – a property baron and a famous foodie. He was a stylish, grizzled man who featured heavily in the Saturday supplements and who referred to London as a world-class city. He owned a string of restaurants and I waitressed at one of them, a former slaughterhouse that had become a fashionable eatery. It was through one of my customers that I got hold of the tickets. Two seats for *Hamlet*.

'Know who's playing Ophelia?' I said excitedly. 'It's what's-her-name, you know, she was in that film with Harrison Ford.'

'Which film?' asked Jeremy.

'And she played a serial killer cop in that other one, and she was married to what's-his-face, but they got a divorce – you know who I mean—'

'No.'

'She's famous!'

I gave up. Jeremy doesn't go to Hollywood movies. He

rents videos of obscure Croatian films which you can't do the ironing to, because you have to watch the subtitles. Besides, that day he was feeling particularly vulnerable. On the way home from his therapist, the tube got stuck between stations and he had a panic attack. He'd had a difficult birth, you see, and always freaks out in tunnels.

I was thrilled, however. These were hot tickets, the hottest in London. Hamlet was being played by our latest home-grown superstar, whose brooding good looks were plastered over every magazine from the *Sunday Telegraph* to *Loaded*.

And I needed a night out. I was worked off my feet during the festive season. The Slaughterhouse was heavily booked for parties and on New Year's Eve, the place was crammed with merrymakers, swigging back their champagne and shouting 'Happy New Year' down their mobile phones. Waitressing is exhausting work. You surrender yourself up to other people's needs. I'm good at it, because of my strong maternal instincts, but by the time we closed at four in the morning I was shattered.

When I got home, my wallet bulging with tips, Jeremy had fallen asleep under an outspread copy of Primo Levi. I gently removed his glasses and climbed into bed.

'My mother's hair smelt of cigarettes,' he murmured. 'When she came home from her lovers, I used to climb into bed and say, *you smell of grown-ups*.'

'Happy New Year,' I whispered, cradling him in my arms. He clung to me. I was needed, you see, at work and at home, and I thought that was happiness.

The next day we went to lunch with Jeremy's mother and stepfather. I had to drag Jeremy there, of course. Frank cooked us Thai food. He was king of his kitchen, which gleamed with stainless steel and Sabatier knives. Jeremy eyed the blades. During lunch, he stayed mutinously silent, so I babbled.

'We're going to see *Hamlet* on Thursday,' I trilled. 'Aren't we lucky?'

'Know how much those tickets are worth?' Frank asked me. 'Five hundred pounds.'

'Five hundred pounds!' I gasped.

'On the black market,' he said.

Jeremy turned to his stepfather. 'Can you only think in terms of money?'

'We'll have the flat back then,' said Frank.

'Boys, boys!' Jeremy's mother turned to me with a glazed, desperate smile.

But I was distracted. 'Five hundred pounds *each*?' I asked.

That night Jeremy and I had our first quarrel. It started with the tickets. I said we should sell them, but Jeremy said that was tacky. I accused him of being a prig and said that if we had a thousand pounds, we could buy a bed. My bones ached from lying on his terrible futon. I said we could buy a bed *and* go to Amsterdam for the weekend. He said this was a perfect instance of the corrupting power of money, that we were happy until we knew how much the tickets were worth and look at us now.

'It's only money,' he said.

'You can afford to say that,' I replied. 'Whenever you're in trouble your stepfather bails you out.'

Jeremy's voice rose. He started railing against Frank, saying what a control freak he was, how could his mother live with such a monster?

'*In the rank sweat of an enseamèd bed*,' I said. '*Stewed*

in corruption, honeying and making love over the nasty sty.'

Jeremy stared at me. I'd been re-reading *Hamlet* in my tea break.

'At least Frank didn't pour poison into your father's ear,' I said.

We made it up in bed. Jeremy was a good lover – tender and emotional. I had vivid dreams and woke up the next morning in a state of anticipation. It was my day off. Instead of serving tables, I was going to watch *Hamlet* and Jeremy, either out of remorse or sexual contentment, was bringing me breakfast in bed.

And then disaster struck. Sainsbury's was crowded that morning, trolleys jostling, and when I got to the checkout, I found my shoulder-bag was gaping open. My wallet had gone.

It wasn't the credit cards that upset me, though my hand trembled as I dialled the numbers. It wasn't the loss of all those things you can't remember you had in your wallet until you miss them, like your library card and people's scrawled addresses. It wasn't even the cash, £60 of it, mostly tips for which I had worked myself to the bone.

No, what devastated me was the loss of my tickets.

Jeremy put his arm around me; for once our roles were reversed.

'Harry Enfield's on TV tonight,' he said. 'You like him, don't you?'

'But I want to see *Hamlet*,' I cried. 'I've been looking forward to it for weeks!'

How could anyone do this to me? The tickets would

mean nothing to a thief. For all I knew they had been flung, with the ransacked wallet, into some gutter.

Then I read the newspaper. *'Beg, borrow or steal a ticket,'* it said.

That was when I had the idea. I rushed into the bedroom where Jeremy was gazing at his computer screen.

'Let's go to the theatre,' I said.

'What?'

'Everybody's heard of this show, even thieves. We'll go there and catch them! I know our seat numbers, they're D12 and 13. If somebody's sitting there, we nab them, and if the seats are empty, we see the show!'

Jeremy gazed at me with pity. 'Darling, you're suffering from post-traumatic stress syndrome. Have a glass of wine.'

'Where's your spirit of adventure?'

'They'll have thrown away the tickets. And it's freezing outside. Think of my sinuses.'

He wouldn't come. 'You're hopeless!' I said as I stormed out. 'You're just like Hamlet, you're always whingeing and dithering and making objections, *to be or not to be*, no wonder Ophelia went mad.'

In the tube, I brooded. I knew I was being unfair – Jeremy's arguments were perfectly reasonable – but tonight I didn't want reason. I wanted a man to brandish his sword for me, to slash away disappointment and doubt. I wanted a *man*.

At the theatre there was a queue, waiting for returns, but no criminal type trying to sell them tickets. The play was about to begin. Heart thudding, I marched towards the door to the stalls.

'Tickets please,' said the usher.

'The thing is, mine were stolen,' I said. 'So, if I could just peek in, I can see if the seats are taken and if not . . .' I stopped.

He was gazing at me with the same pity I'd seen on Jeremy's face. 'Nice try,' he said. 'Next!'

I had guessed this might happen. The solution was simple. I would wait for the interval and get in for the second half, mingling with the crowd. Nobody inspects tickets then.

So I went to an Italian restaurant and ordered some fettucine. It was nice, being served for a change, but I suddenly felt lonely. Where was Jeremy, when I needed him? Sinuses indeed! Maybe it was my fault. Maybe it's a neurosis in itself, to be drawn to neurotics.

Back at the theatre the interval was over. 'Please return to your seats!' I made my way to the stalls. Arriving at row D, I plucked up courage and had a look. One of my seats was occupied by a young man.

To be honest, until that moment I didn't believe my plan would work. The young man was pretending to read his programme. Edging along the row I sat down beside him. My heart was hammering. I fixed my eyes on the stage – or what I could see of it. In front of me sat a woman with Big Hair.

'Do you want to change places?' the man whispered.

I jumped.

'I shouldn't be here anyway,' he said, and stood up. Awkwardly, we changed seats and sat down. I didn't thank him – how could I thank a man who had stolen my wallet?

Act IV began. I couldn't concentrate, of course. Hamlet

appeared on stage. '*Oh, from this time forth, my thoughts be bloody,*' he said. My thief shifted in his seat, craning to look around the woman's hair. His leather jacket creaked. No doubt it was stuffed with credit cards. What had he ordered on mine? A CD player, a lavish meal-for-two?

Ophelia entered, wearing a nightgown. Her hair was tangled, her eyes wild. She looked as disarrayed as I felt. I hardly recognized her as the famous film star. '*Young men will do it, if they come to it, by Cock, they are to blame,*' she crooned. What was I going to do – accost him when the curtain fell? Call the police? '*I cannot choose but weep,*' she sighed.

It was the strangest sensation, sitting next to the man who had robbed me. Time passed and the stage became heaped with bodies. I thought of us all, casualties of love and of crime. How muddy were human relationships, compared to the clean thrust of a sword. *I shouldn't be here*, my thief has whispered. Did he feel guilty for what he had done? Surely criminals are strangers to remorse? – they have to be, to perform their crimes. How simple it must be, to ne'er be sicklied o'er with the pale cast of thought.

The play ended, to thunderous applause. We got up to leave. In front of me, the woman with Big Hair said to her companion, 'Don't be sad, Bernie, we'll buy a puppy.'

Should I call for help? As we shuffled out, I kept close to my robber. 'Wasn't that amazing?' he said as we emerged into the street.

'Where did you get your tickets?' I blurted.

'Ha! You've found me out.'

'Did you really think you'd get away with it?'

'I just wanted to see her close up,' he said. 'I've seen all her films. Remember her in that thing, what was it called . . .'

'Have you no conscience?' I demanded.

'But there was nobody sitting in the seats.' He looked at me. 'I'm sorry if they were yours but there was nobody in them. It's not such a crime, is it?'

I laughed bitterly. 'Obviously not, to people like you.'

There was a silence. We stood there, in the freezing cold. Taxis slewed to a halt and loaded up with people.

'What do you do with all those Organ Donor cards?' I asked. 'Do you ever think of all those dying people who can't have other people's livers?'

He stared at me.

'Or hearts,' I said.

He gazed at me, puzzled. I started to feel uneasy. He didn't look like a thief but then who does? If we knew what they looked like, then it would be simple, wouldn't it?

'I think we've got our wires crossed,' he said. 'I mean, I was just sitting in the Upper Balcony, miles up, and saw these empty seats. So I came down for the second half.'

We burst into laughter. I apologized. He bought me a drink. We fell in love and lived together happily with the three children my maternal urges had been clamouring for, all these years. I'd found my real man, at last. He didn't steal my wallet; he stole my heart.

It didn't happen like that, of course. We stood there talking until the lights for *Hamlet* were switched off. Then we shook hands, went our separate ways and no doubt told the story, with amusing embellishments, to those with whom we lived.

And I lived with Jeremy for another year. We parted in the end but that was another story, and far less shapely than fiction.

Joyce's Big Lie

Joyce looked after holiday homes. The owners arrived in July and left, like the swallows, in September, for the rich are migratory creatures and are always somewhere else.

Just for a few short weeks, however, they were here, in the fashionable seaside village of Gosford Haven, and Joyce was at hand to make it all run smoothly. Before they arrived, she hoovered and dusted, she filled larders, she re-stocked the wood burning stoves and trimmed the rows of pricey olive trees in their terracotta pots. Sometimes she put on the electric blankets because even in July, and even in Cornwall, it could be bracing, the ocean pounding against the harbour walls, reminding people of their puny existence in this huge indifferent planet we inhabit.

That's why they came here, the rich, to be reminded of this as they surfed, and strode over the cliffs, and drank their Prosecco as the sun sank over the turbulent sea. Then they could retire to their warmed beds, in rooms Farrow and Balled in blue, decorated with shells and trails of bladder wrack, dragged up from the beach by their loud and entitled children, who actually spent most of their time crouched over computer games in their darkened bedrooms.

What valiant efforts they made, these parents, to bond with their offspring! They bought them kayaks and fishing rods. They picked up their towels without complaint – sodden towel after sodden towel, how could there be so many? Sooner or later, they even stopped nagging them to play Scrabble, old-fashioned family fun, and the box would be returned to the cupboard in which it languished, year after year.

Joyce was sorry for the parents, who tried so hard. She knew about their lives because she chatted to the teenage children, loitering in the cobbled streets. They were over-indulged, no doubt about it, but that was the rich for you. They were another species.

And now it was September and they were leaving. Outside the cottages the vast 4x4s blocked the alleyways as they were loaded up to drive back to Notting Hill, or Wandsworth, or wherever they came from. The fathers would be returning to venture capitalism, or bond trading, or whatever they did. The children would be returning to boarding school, because that was where they seemed to go. This seemed a curious thing to Joyce. Why have children if you're only going to send them away?

One by one, the lights were extinguished in the charming fisherman's cottages clustered around the charming harbour. The shutters were closed as they returned to their long winter's sleep, and the final bin-loads of empties crashed into the refuse truck and were driven away to the dump in St Austell. The last Master of the Universe was spotted on the cliff-top, where you could get a signal, bellowing into his mobile phone, and then he too was gone.

And as the visitors left, the villagers emerged, blinking in the light, to reclaim their territory after the summer invasion. The true villagers didn't inhabit the charming fisherman's cottages, of course; no way they could afford one of those. They lived in the bungalows next to the public toilets.

That's where Joyce's parents lived, and where she had humiliatingly returned after her divorce. Forty years old and she was back with Mum and Dad; how tragic was that? Back in her bedroom which she thought she had left for ever, with its view of her father's greenhouse and his celebrated tomatoes. She simply couldn't afford to buy anywhere round here; house prices had shot up since Gosford Haven had become the uber-fashionable place to be, Kate Moss had been spotted, and that hot guy from *Poldark*, and the dear, smelly old Duke's Arms, where Joyce used to get drunk as a skunk as a teenager, had been transformed into the Gosford Fish Depot, its walls stripped back to the brickwork like an abattoir and hipster waiters swanning around with plates of calamari and announcing their own names, as if people were interested.

The place had changed, no doubt about it. Joyce, however, felt exactly the same. Her disastrous marriage had dissolved as if it had never been. Now she was alone again, and forty, and looking for love. She had joined a dating site and lied about her age, well everybody did that, didn't they? Thirty-five was hardly a lie at all, just part of the fictional Joyce she created for herself. How could she attempt the true Joyce in three hundred words? The fictional Joyce had a good sense of humour, everybody said that too, and of course she enjoyed long walks but also a night in, watching box sets with a glass of wine in front of a log fire. This Joyce looked a lot more sorted than the real Joyce felt. No doubt all those other people, out in

cyberspace, had this same sense of dislocation when looking at the selves they had created for their possible suitors.

And the big lie was yet to come.

The swifts had gone, the swallows would soon be gone, too.
The crazy golf and fish 'n' chip shop had shut. The nights
were drawing in and Joyce was closing the cottages for their
winter hibernation. She looked after six properties. Some
were left in a shocking state, you wouldn't believe it. The
Fanshawes, at Seaview Cottage, hadn't even cleared away
their breakfast. They'd left in a rush the week before, as if
war had been declared. Muesli was glued to the cereal bowls
and the coffee percolator appeared to have exploded, scattering coffee grounds over the draining board. Sand was
everywhere, even in the rumpled bedsheets. There was also
a mush of pomegranate seeds blocking up the bathplug –
what *had* Mr and Mrs Fanshawe been up to?

Joyce popped the leftover food into a carrier bag, to take
home. This was one of her perks. Into her bag went half-
finished bottles of wine and waxy lumps of Cheddar. As she
worked, she ruminated on her internet dates so far. There
had only been three, all of them more or less disastrous.
How attractive the men had seemed, in their potted biographies. As attractive, no doubt, as her own fabrications.

They had met in the Hollyhock Tea Rooms in St Austell.
First up had been Malcolm, who described himself as a
cheerful, can-do kind of chap. Two kids, divorced, worked
in IT. Over a buttered scone he'd talked her through the
wiring on his Honda 570 and was still at it when she asked
for the bill.

Then there was Graham, who had put on weight since

his photograph was taken. Graham had been in the merchant navy and had bought himself a foreign bride who had proceeded to divest him of his savings and finally of his maisonette in Plymouth. Graham's subsequent bitterness extended to the government, the *Today* programme, traffic wardens, cyclists and small yapping dogs. Though Joyce agreed about the dogs, she suspected this might not be enough for a long-term commitment.

Finally, there was Keith, poor grieving Keith, whose wife had recently died of breast cancer and who showed Joyce photographs of their last holiday together before collapsing in uncontrollable tears.

At this point Joyce had given up. No doubt these men were as disappointed in her as she was in them; she couldn't blame them for raising her spirits and then dashing them again. What a miracle it would be if the click of the keyboard could deliver up the man of her dreams. Nowhere was there such a gap between hope and reality, except in packets of flower seeds.

So Joyce loaded sheets into washing machines and stacked away the patio furniture. In the Bullingtons' kitchen, she treated herself to a Nespresso, the closest she would ever get to George Clooney. *Her* dreams, of course, were more modest. But even these seemed to be dissolving into a sexless future caring for her mum and dad in their bungalow full of clocks, ticking away her future.

The kitchen blurred and she realized she was crying. Surely there was a man out there who would want a woman like her, who was good at housework and who could swim across the bay? Who could sing 'Bohemian Rhapsody' and get all the words right? Whose body was a little thicker around the waist but ready, oh so ready, for love?

All she had was her fantasy life in other people's homes. For once the occupants had gone, their homes were hers for the winter. She had the keys, she could drop in whenever she liked, to make herself a coffee. Joyce had a powerful imagination and throughout her childhood had been accompanied by her invisible friend, Natalie. Now, aged forty, the fantasy had changed. Now, in these empty homes she could create her own perfect family, her own parallel life. Her children would be laughing in the bedrooms, no computer games for *them*, they would be playing Scrabble like children used to do. And somewhere, whistling, was her fantasy husband. Nobody whistled any more, but *he* would. *Their* house wouldn't be empty for most of the year, its sea-views unseen, its kitchen silent. It would be filled with life, and at night, while the winter storms raged, she would lie in one of those big brass beds, naked in her husband's arms.

Of all the cottages, Harbour View was the best for her fantasies. It belonged to the Bullingtons, a banker couple, and their sulky teenage daughter. Its marble bathroom had a Jacuzzi. Joyce sometimes dropped in there, to run herself a bath and sink into the bubbles, scented with the Bullingtons' Badedas. She would lie there and daydream, gazing at the sunshine streaming through the window. When she came home her mother said: 'You smell nice.'

It was almost October and the last swallows had gone. Joyce decided to have one final try online, and logged on to the dating site. And there, miracle of miracles, she found Dennis.

How do you know, just from an email exchange? It was not as if they had a lot in common. He liked Viennese opera, for instance, and she knew nothing about it. But they just felt easy with each other, and cracked a few jokes, and before long arranged a meeting at the teashop in St Austell.

Dennis was a large, jovial man in his fifties. 'Good Lord, Eccles cakes!' he said. 'Haven't seen one of them since I was a boy.'

He looked too big for the dainty tearoom with his meaty hands and booming laugh. In his presence, the other customers seemed shrivelled and spinsterly. Evidently a man of large appetites, he wolfed down an Eccles cake and then eyed up a rum baba, another childhood favourite.

'This internet lark's a funny business, isn't it?' he said. 'I've only just started. How do you feel about it?'

He was the first man who'd asked Joyce such a question.

She found herself telling him about the other men she'd met, and then her life in Manchester with her faithless ex-husband, and from there she found herself telling him about her childhood crush on the harbourmaster's son and how they used to race snails together. Dennis told her about his wife, who he had obviously adored and who had recently died. How easy it was, talking to him! She felt like a sheet shaken loose in the sun.

And before she knew it the place was closing so they went for a walk, still talking, and had a drink in the pub, still talking, and then it was nine o'clock and she had to collect her mother from Mevagissey, because the last bus had gone, so they said goodbye.

*

It all started from there. For she omitted to mention her mother, or the fact that she lived with her parents.

Lying about her age was understandable. Everybody did it. But this was different. As the weeks passed it became harder and harder to tell Dennis the truth. It seemed such an admission of failure, to be back in her old bedroom. How could she bring him home as if she were a teenager again? It didn't bear thinking about. Nor could she face her parents' nosiness. They would cross-question her about this new man in her life and she simply couldn't bear it. And how on earth could they have sex?

For they had met several times by now. She hadn't been to Dennis's place; he lived in Exeter, where he ran some sort of business, and it was two hours' drive away. But he was keen to visit her in Gosford Haven and she found herself offering him lunch.

Looking back, Joyce was astonished at what she did. But was it really that strange, to pretend she lived in another house? After all, she had been living a parallel life for two years, a life so much more vivid and powerful than her own. She chose Harbour View, the Bullingtons' cottage, and gave Dennis the address. Lunch was arranged for the Thursday. She woke that morning feeling strangely calm. Think of it as a lark, she told herself, a piece of theatre. She mustn't allow herself to be spooked.

So she bought some food, and a bottle of wine, and some flowers. She let herself into the cottage, arranged the flowers and laid the table. Her knees had turned to water and her heart was hammering. The madness of it was catching up with her. But it was too late now. To calm her nerves, she said to herself *I know this place better than the Bullingtons do. I've cleaned every inch of it. Perhaps this afternoon, I'll be having sex in their bed, like the Three Bears!*

As she burst into appalled laughter there was a knock on the door. Dennis stood there, holding a bottle of champagne.

'Sorry I'm late, had to take the bus.' He looked around. 'What a great place! Love the blue. Is it Farrow and Ball?'

He kissed her on the cheek and stepped in.

Just at that moment there was the sound of footsteps on the stairs.

Joyce swung round. Trinny, the Bullingtons' teenage daughter, came into the room.

She stared at Joyce. 'What are you doing here?' She wore a rumpled T-shirt. Her hair was tangled; she must have been asleep upstairs.

'What are *you* doing here?' stuttered Joyce.

'I've run away from school,' said Trinny.

'Good Lord.' Dennis turned to Joyce. 'I didn't know you had a daughter.'

There was a silence.

'Er, Trinny,' said Joyce. 'Can you come into the kitchen?'

She ushered her out and they sat down at the table laid for two.

'Don't tell Mum and Dad!' whispered Trinny. 'Not that they'll notice. He's away in Hong Kong and she's gone to some conference, they wouldn't know if I was alive or dead.'

'That's not true—'

'I wish *you* were my mother; you're always here and *you* wouldn't send me away to boarding school.' Puzzled, she looked at Joyce. 'Why *are* you here?'

'I'm so sorry, Trinny. Let's just say, while the cat's away . . .'

Dennis's voice called through the door. 'Is everything OK?'

Joyce pushed back her chair, jumped up and ran out of the back door.

Of course, it was cowardly but what else could she do? She ran down the street, gulping great lungfuls of air. The sea smashed against the harbour wall. Around the corner she collided with a large, shiny Range Rover. A uniformed driver leaned against it, smoking.

It all fell into place. The school had phoned Trinny's parents and they had sent their driver, they probably had one in London; they were bankers, after all. They'd sent their driver to take her home.

'Have you come for someone at Harbour Cottage?' Joyce panted.

The driver nodded. 'I was told to wait here,' he said.

Why was he waiting, and why out of sight?

Joyce was puzzling over this when footsteps approached. It was Dennis.

'Ah, there you are,' he said. 'So, you two have met.'

He was Dennis's driver. Dennis hadn't come by bus at all. It turned out that he was hugely, staggeringly rich. He'd kept this a secret in case it skewed things, in case he met a gold-digger.

Revealing lies to each other can be more intimate than sex. Over lunch they both confessed, before cracking open a bottle of the Bullingtons' brandy.

How Are You?

Her husband used to say: 'I never knew we had so many friends until we built the swimming pool.'

It was true. The moment the sun came out the phone used to ring. 'Diana, how are you?' people would say. 'How's Malcolm? Haven't seen you for ages.'

'Come round for tea,' she would reply, 'for drinks. Have a swim.'

'A swim?' They would sound surprised, as if this was the last thing on their mind. 'What a wonderful idea.'

She had liked it, actually – summer arriving, swallows arriving, her neighbours arriving with their costumes on already under their clothes. That was what the pool was for – that and Malcolm's heart. Their doctor had recommended swimming – cardio-vascular exercise – and Malcolm, who had just retired, said: 'I've always wanted a pool. Better late than never.'

When people rang now, they said: 'Diana, how are you?' Their tone was different. 'How *are* you, Di?'

Eight months had passed, and the phone calls were less frequent, but the tone was always there. She heard it in the village, in the post office, in Sainsbury's. They would break off their conversations and turn to her. 'Di?' Their voices low and sympathetic. 'How *are* you?' When she left there

56

was a respectful pause; then, when she was nearly out of earshot their conversation would resume – low at first and then gathering normality like a train gathering speed.

It was June – the first hot week of summer. Nobody had phoned yet, inviting themselves over obliquely for a swim. Maybe the idea of splashing about in a pool seemed too trivial for a house of grief, maybe they didn't want to intrude. They didn't understand that it made no difference; she felt just the same, surrounded by other people. Nothing made any difference. It just seemed a waste; she had had the man around to clean the pool and check the filter, whatever men did. When he left, she took off her clothes and sank into the water. It closed over her head, warm as tears.

Her most regular visitor was her daughter, Meredith. In the early weeks, Meredith had come to stay a great deal, to keep her company, but to tell the truth her presence had been a mixed blessing. Her daughter's bullying protective- ness was so tiring.

'Don't see anyone you don't want to see! Why should you go to the Taylors' for drinks?'

'I don't mind,' said Diana, 'they're just being kind.'

'They're so ghastly. Such ghastly Tories.'

'Even Tories can be kind.'

Meredith would try to rally her, dragging her round the house. 'Let's wash these sofa covers, they're filthy, where's the zip?'

Sometimes, Diana felt like a patient who had taken an overdose; her daughter was the nurse, marching her up and down and slapping her cheeks to keep her from sliding into unconsciousness. Meredith, never the most intuitive of women, didn't understand that most things were simply beyond Diana's reach – literally so, sometimes, when she couldn't get things from the top shelf. Malcolm had put them there; Malcolm knew how to do it. And then there was everything else – the screw-tops she couldn't unscrew, the rusted lightbulbs she couldn't replace. Everything.

'He kept you in a doll's house. It's like Ibsen,' said Meredith, who taught Communication Studies. 'He kept you from learning how to cope.'

'I didn't want to learn,' said Diana. 'He did it.'

Her daughter just snorted. Diana couldn't tell her the truth – that even after eight months, when she should be getting better, it was such an effort to do anything at all. On the bad days she had to concentrate through each moment, just to get to the end of them. The nearest sensation was the pain of childbirth; the way you couldn't be distracted. And then there were little things which suddenly walloped her, as if she had been hit with a sock full of sand. When her son, for instance, had helped her sell Malcolm's Rover and she saw the tax disc so confidently paid up until May. He had presumed he would live that long; don't we all?

But her son had long since returned to Zurich – he was a banker – and that just left Meredith. She had had a difficult relationship with her father, and his desertion, through dying, seemed to inflame her rage against men in general, as well as him in particular. When she was little her nickname had been 'Merry', but it was hard to imagine anyone calling her that now. Soon after the birth of her son, Luke, she had grown into a big, troubled adult. Recently she had ballooned in girth.

Meredith and Luke arrived on Saturday morning. 'How are you?' asked Meredith, dumping down her stuff in the hall.

Diana said: 'I was thinking yesterday, people ask me this but with this peculiar emphasis. How *are* you. Before your father died, they'd say how are *you*? What's the significance about this? In the old days they were interested in me, and now they're interested in the process, the *areness* of it? You should know, you teach communication studies.'

Meredith sniffed. 'The house smells funny. We must find you another cleaning lady.'

'You haven't answered my question.'

'It's a denial of communication.'

'What, not answering my question?'

'No, what they're doing. They just want you to say *I'm fine*.' Her square face, framed by shorn hair, looked at her mother. 'You're not eating properly. You look thin.'

'I'm fine,' said Diana.

They went out into the garden. Meredith looked at the vegetable patch. 'I'd better get cracking on that,' she said.

'Somebody's given me some runner bean plants. I've been meaning to put them in.' Diana thought: one day, surely, I'll feel hungry enough to want to eat beans again. Surely, by the time they are ripe.

The poles still stood, from last year. Last year's withered plants, beige tatters, clung to them. Malcolm had tied the strings and she hadn't been able to bring herself to untie the knots his fingers had worked on. No wonder she never got anything done.

'We can dig a new bed for them over there,' said Meredith.

'That's where Norman's buried!' cried Luke. Norman,

their dog, had been run over two years ago. 'Will he be a skeleton by now?' asked Luke.

'Go off and play!' said his mother.

Luke picked up a worm. 'Wonder how many worms it took to eat him?'

'Luke!' said his mother.

'It's all right,' said Diana. It was true. She only minded things when another person was there; to mind on their behalf was so tiring.

Luke, slashing at nettles, wandered off. He was nine. For Malcolm, Luke had stopped at eight and a bit. Malcolm knew nothing of his grandson's new compulsion to buy lottery scratch-cards; the new mannerisms he had, of rubbing his nose and saying, 'wicked'. This made Diana feel strange, but it had its advantages. On his last visit, Luke had bragged about how some boys in his class had been caught glue-sniffing and Diana had felt an unexpected jolt of relief, that her husband had been spared being upset by this. He had been spared eight months' toil of terrible newspaper stories. He had died, innocent of the knowledge of the Oklahoma bombing. He need no longer worry about how Luke was going to grow up in a household without a father of his own. Wasn't that something?

'Don't do that,' said Diana to her daughter. 'Come and have a swim. Enjoy yourself.' She nearly added: enjoy yourself, because you don't know how long you've got.

Meredith didn't swim, however. She sat beside the pool reading a book called *You Don't Listen: Men and Women Talking*. Luke jumped in and splashed around. 'There's lots of dead things in here,' he called. 'Some of them aren't quite dead.' He rose up from the shallow end, a struggling insect on his finger.

'See how many you can rescue!' called Diana.

Meredith, who was a vegetarian, said: 'He's always killing things. I try to tell him it's wrong, it's all bloody testosterone.'

'He's a bit young for that.'

'No male is too young for that.'

'So you want him to be a New Man,' said Diana. A wave of loneliness hit her. She thought: I don't want a new man. I want the old one back. To hide her face, she went back to the house to fetch some drinks.

She walked into the kitchen. Sometimes, she felt as if she were underwater, so slowly did she move; it was like pushing against the current. She poured out some wine for herself and some orange juice for her daughter and her grandson. The fact that Meredith didn't drink suddenly irritated her. Her daughter was training to be a counsellor but Diana thought that she would do a lot more good if they could simply crack open the gin bottle and get sloshed together.

She opened the ice-making compartment. The door fell off, clattering on to the floor. 'Blast!' It always did this. Only Malcolm knew how to wedge it closed on its stupid plastic hinge. 'Time for a snort,' he'd say, looking at his watch. 'Gin and tonic, old fruit?' He'd yank open the ice-making compartment, push out some cubes and shove it back, kicking it with his foot. Sometimes he didn't refill the tray with water; it used to drive her mad. 'Malcolm!' she'd yell. 'There's no blithering ice!'

'Are you OK?' Meredith stood in the kitchen. Diana clambered to her feet; she seemed to be sitting on the chair.

'I'm fine. Put the door back, will you?' She turned away, pulled off some kitchen roll and blew her nose. 'Bloody house,' she said. 'There's all these little things, not quite big enough to get a builder in for.'

'We have to do it ourselves,' said Meredith, shoving back the door. 'Women have to learn to live without men.'

Diana thought: but I don't want to! She said: 'Where's Luke?'

'In the pool.'

'Should he be there alone?'

'He's fine.' Meredith took the tray. 'I'll carry that.'

The phone rang. It was Francine, Meredith's girlfriend. Diana felt another spasm of irritation. Couldn't she have Meredith to herself, just for a few hours? She got irritable so easily nowadays, the slightest thing set it off. People made allowances in the first few months but she really must try to pull herself together. A weeping widow – they could cope with that. But most of grief's manifestations were so unattractive – irritability, slow wits, resentments against all second-rate people in the world who stayed alive.

She looked at Meredith's broad back; she wore a T-shirt and baggy trousers. 'Shall we go ahead and make an offer?' Meredith was discussing a flat she was buying with Francine. Diana knew she should be more interested in this – an involved mother discussing curtains. But she only thought: in a few months Meredith and Luke will be living in a place Malcolm's never seen. Each day, of course, brought more of these things. Soon she was going to have to buy herself a new car, her Renault was falling to bits, and start driving around in something that had no connection to him whatsoever. I must ask him what sort of car to buy, she thought. Then she realized – how stupid!

She carried the tray into the garden and walked down to the pool. Luke lay floating in the water. He was face down, motionless.

Diana placed the tray on the grass – look, quite calmly! She kicked off her espadrilles, strode to the pool and jumped in. The water closed over her head. She surfaced, spluttering, and lunged towards her grandson. She grabbed his shoulder; they bumped together and sank. He struggled – he was surprisingly strong – and when he surfaced, he yelled: 'Help!'

Diana felt her clothes ballooning around her. Luke's wiry arm grabbed her. 'Hey!' she spluttered, pushing it off.

She swam to the edge and heaved herself up the steps, gasping for breath. Luke pulled himself up behind her.

'Mum!' he called. Meredith was running across the grass. 'I saved Granny! She jumped into the pool!'

Diana tried to speak but she had a fit of coughing.

'She was trying to drown!' he gasped.

Meredith grabbed a towel. She rubbed Diana briskly. 'Shall I take off your dress?' she asked. 'Are you all right?'

'I wasn't trying to kill myself,' said Diana, catching her breath. 'I was trying to rescue Luke.'

'Why?' asked Luke.

'You were drowning.'

'I was counting worms,' he said.

'What?'

'I was counting all the dead worms lying on the bottom of the pool.'

Meredith's hands stopped. There was a moment's silence,

then Diana found she was making a noise. For a moment she didn't recognize it; it felt like a rusty door opening in her chest. She was laughing.

Even Meredith smiled. Luke gazed at them dispassionately. Diana grabbed the towel and rubbed her hair vigorously. Suddenly she felt full of energy; refreshed by her dip in the water, she felt more wide awake than she had felt for months.

'You're shivering,' said Meredith.

'I'm fine,' she said. 'I just thought, I've lost one man, I don't want to lose another.'

Luke got up and slid back into the pool. Diana lay on the grass and let the sun warm her through her wet dress. Meredith said: 'Yesterday a car stopped outside our flat. It was the same as Dad's Rover, and covered in mud. I thought: he's going to get out. He's going to ring the bell and say *I've been on this long journey, look at the milometer. But I'm back now.*'

There was a long silence. In the lilac bush a blackbird sang. Meredith said: 'The reason I didn't want to swim is I've got so fat.'

'Since he died, you mean,' said Diana.

Meredith nodded. 'And you didn't swim because you've got so thin.' She paused. 'How are you, Mum?'

And Diana told her.

An Arrangement in
Grey and Black

Whistler stands in his studio, in his large house overlooking the Thames. He is painting his mother, but she keeps interrupting. She says: 'I don't want to be An Arrangement in Grey and Black, Number One. I'm your mother.'

'Sit still,' says Whistler.

'And Number One! Are you expecting to have any more mothers?'

Whistler shakes his head. 'Only more paintings. Stop looking at me.'

'You have a strange expression on your face,' says his mother.

'I'm just looking at you,' replies Whistler.

'Not like a son, you're not. You're looking at an arrangement of me.'

'I'm looking at your soul,' says Whistler.

'Rubbish!' snaps his mother. 'My goodness, this chair's hard.'

'Turn back, Ma! I'm painting your profile.'

'I know why you're painting my profile,' replies his mother. 'So you don't have to face me.'

There is a silence. Just the stroke, the loving stroke, of brush upon canvas. Outside the Thames flows, the waves stroking the bank. The gardens of Cheyne Walk are bathed in sunshine. Then Whistler's mother speaks again.

'This nice wall behind me, nice patterned wallpaper, you've painted it grey, haven't you?'

'How do you know?' asks Whistler.

'You think I don't know you?' asks his mother.

'You don't know anything about painting.'

'But I know *you*,' she says. 'Nobody will know you, my son, better than I know you. Women will come and go, that woman you call The White Girl—'

'Oh-oh, here we go—' Whistler sighs.

His mother's voice rises. 'Know what really rankles – apart from your flaunting her around London – you know what really rankles? That when you paint her you call her a White Girl and me, you call me an Arrangement! *She's* the one who's an arrangement, and a shameful one at that.'

While his mother talks, Whistler has been gazing at her beaky profile, pale against the wall. He says: 'She's an arrangement too, when I'm painting her. She's not Joanna Hiffernan.'

'Don't mention that name.'

'And as for our arrangement, she perfectly understands that I'm an artist.'

'Doesn't she want to get married?' asks his mother. 'Doesn't she want to have children?'

'The enemy of art, mother, is the pram in the hallway.'

'But you were in a pram once. You are my son. Without me, you wouldn't be here.'

'So I'm your creation?' says Whistler. 'You produced me and I'm producing this painting. And if you're interested, it's going very well.' Whistler strokes the grey paint across the canvas. It isn't grey, of course. His mother doesn't understand about painting. So many pigments are laid on his palette – umber, indigo, green. He mixes them to create the most vibrant of greys. The wall behind his mother is as alive as she is. He says: 'You've been a good mother, Mother. That is your work. Mine is painting. In fact, I *will* have children, here and there—'

'Here and there! What do you mean?'

'Unlike you, however, I'll be a poor parent.'

'How? What will you do?'

'Nothing,' Whistler replies. 'That's the point. I'll shamefully neglect them, my future biographers won't even know how many there are, they won't be printed in the index.'

'How can you talk like that?'

'Because I'm an artist,' says Whistler, wiping his paintbrush with a rag.

'Stuff and nonsense!' snorts his mother. 'That's no excuse for being a bad parent. Won't you even paint your children? Won't you even make them into an arrangement?'

Whistler shakes his head. 'They'll be irrelevant.'

His mother's profile stiffens. 'That's a terrible thing to say.'

Whistler doesn't reply. For a while he paints, in silence.

Outside the window, across the gardens of Cheyne Walk, the River Thames runs glintingly in the sunshine. All is quiet, but for the admonishing slap, slap of its water against the bank. No road has yet been built, no cars and lorries thunder past, filling this room with exhaust fumes. It's 1871. As Whistler paints, his unborn children have yet to experience their sadness.

'I'm a selfish person, Mother.'

'Is that my fault?' she snaps.

'I'm not blaming you,' he says. 'I'm no longer your responsibility.'

'I can't stop being a parent,' she replies. 'You're a grown man but it doesn't stop. When you were little I worried, oh how I worried. I worried you would die in infancy, like your brother Kirk and your brother Charlie. I worried you'd be run over by a tram—'

'Now do you understand why I don't want to be a parent?'

'And still I worry.' His mother shifts in her seat. The black dress crackles.

'Don't worry, Ma. I won't die for another thirty years.'

'What?'

'Sit still and relax,' he says. 'You did your best, Mother, but I'm an artist and all artists are selfish. They have to be, to get their work done.'

'Rubbish!' she snaps.

'I'm ruthless, I'm vain.' Whistler pauses, his paintbrush in his hand. 'Know how vain? When I'm compared to Velazquez, I'll reply *Why drag in Velazquez?* I'll become increasingly touchy and litigious. When Ruskin criticizes my painting *Nocturne in Black and Gold*, know what he'll say? I haven't even painted it yet and already he's sharpening his knife. He'll say, *I never expected to hear a coxcomb ask two hundred guineas for flinging a pot of paint in the public's face.* That's what he'll say, and as God's my witness, I'll drag him through the courts.'

'Why?' asks his mother.

'Because I must defend my art.'

Whistler's mother, who can no longer face her son, stares

into the middle distance. 'You've always been a strange boy. I've never understood you.'

'I care nothing for the past, present or future,' says Whistler. 'I care for harmony.'

His mother snorts. This is the nearest she ever gets to a laugh, for she is not a humorous woman. She says: 'Harmony, huh? So why will you quarrel with everybody?'

'—harmony of line and colour,' says Whistler. 'That's the harmony which will outlive us all. In 1881 you'll die, in Hastings—'

She swings round, startled. 'How do you know?'

'Turn back. How do I know? Because this painting releases us from the here and now. You, Mother, will die, but the true you—'

She interrupts him. 'The arrangement of me—'

'You'll be sent to America. Over the next nineteen years you'll be exhibited in London, Philadelphia, New York, Paris, Dublin, Munich and Amsterdam.'

'I've never been to Amsterdam,' says his mother.

'You will.'

'Or Dublin.' His mother pauses. 'Or Munich.'

Whistler gazes at his painting. He speaks to the canvas, rather than to his mother. 'You'll finally be sold to the French and can you guess where you'll end up?'

'In the cemetery.'

'In the Louvre,' says Whistler. 'I'll sell you to the French, where you'll become one of the most famous portraits of all time, as famous as Leonardo's immortal Mona Lisa. The *Cornhill Magazine* will call me *an amazing natural genius*. They'll say *the qualities of feeling are irresistible*—'

'I'm freezing,' says his mother. 'Can't you light the fire?'

Whistler isn't listening. He stands there dreamily. 'They'll say that *nothing can be truer than the patient fold of the aged hands and the pathetic calm of the aged face—*'

'Pathetic?' she snaps.

His voice rises. 'This is the painting with which I'll be remembered, and with which you'll be remembered too! When you and I are in the past, *this* you, she'll always be in the present tense.'

'She is me, you know,' says Whistler's mother. Her dress rustles in annoyance. It is made of stiff black bombazine.

Whistler puts down his brush. He points to the canvas. 'This painting releases you from the here and now – from this house in Chelsea, from your pride and disappointment in me, from my own bad behaviour. None of it will matter because before too long it will all be over.'

'What about the casualties?' she snaps. 'Your children, your broken friendships, the woman with whom you live and for whom I'm feeling increasingly sorry?'

Whistler closes his eyes. He speaks dreamily. 'She will be *The White Girl* and hang in the Washington National Gallery. People will gaze on her as they gaze on you, and none of this will matter. You lost children to death and I lost children to art, but none of it will matter. Do you understand?'

There is a long silence. Whistler picks up his brush and carries on painting. His mother wants to turn, to look at him, but she keeps her head in profile. She feels her son gazing at her – not at her, at *her* – her white mobcap, her determined chin, the folds of her dress – as he stands at his easel. He is a blur, in the corner of her eye. Today he is not a blurred son. He is a blurred artist. She is an arrangement, but she too must re-arrange her thoughts. *Stuff and nonsense*, she said, but now she is pausing to consider. There is plenty of time to think, sitting here on this chair that seems to grow harder by the minute. Her children have been her chink into the future, her own immortality, but that is something her son cannot understand. A restless stir in the corner of her eye, he is busy making her immortal. *You will always be in the present tense.*

At last he puts down his brush and lights a cigarette. 'It's finished,' he says. 'Come and look at yourself.'

She gets up creakingly – her back, her joints! She walks over and looks at the painting.

'Forget children,' he murmurs. 'Forget reproduction. You will be reproduced, Mother dear, for as long as such things will be possible . . .'

The river flows, glinting in the changing light of the seasons. Its current chases the years and neither of them catch up with each other. Years pass. Only the Thames remains unchanged as London grows taller around it. A hundred years pass, Whistler's children, who entered and left the world unrecorded, are long since dead. Opposite Cheyne Walk, the office blocks have risen and traffic thunders along the Embankment.

Behind the office blocks, in Stockwell, a painter is struggling with her own arrangement. It is a collage. It consists of blown-up photographs of art critics and over their mouths she has stuck sticking plasters – the transparent ones, with just a small oblong in the middle to staunch the wound. The artist's name is Susannah. She is having doubts about it, now it is finished. She stands back, pushing her fingers through her cropped hair. Is its target too small and petty? Should she be helping her daughter with her homework?

For Susannah has a daughter, Blythe, who is fourteen. Blythe is sitting in her bedroom struggling with an essay on *Animal Farm*. Outside the church bells ring. It's Sunday and they are calling whoever is left, whoever still believes in such things, to worship. Susannah has never taken her daughter to church. She has given her no father figure, transubstantial or temporal. Blythe's father decamped at her birth and was last spotted on the beach in Goa, dispensing drugs. Susannah has brought up her daughter alone. She has farmed her out to child minders while she has travelled around making video installations. For several years she has had doubts about her own abilities both as an artist and a mother, for in trying to cope with both of these she feels she has succeeded in neither.

Susannah gazes at her collage. Way beyond her twelfth-floor window, the Thames flows unperturbed. How many artists have painted this river, which has shown a fine disregard both for them and their critics? Who cares, anyway, what the critics say? Susannah has read a book on Turner. The *Literary Gazette*, in 1842, described his work thus: *His paintings are produced as if by throwing handfuls of white and blue and red at the canvas, letting what chanced to stick, stick.*

She looks at the sticking plasters. In the months ahead the adhesive will dry and they will fall off like scabs. Beneath, maybe the wounds will have healed, for what is this painting and does it really matter? Was it worth snapping at her daughter?

Susannah is thinking this when the door opens. Her daughter comes in. She is holding a bunch of chrysanthemums. 'Happy Mother's Day,' she says.

'Is it?' Susannah jumps up and takes them. 'I forgot.'

Blythe gives her an envelope. Susannah pulls out the card.

She gazes at the painting. She gazes at the profile, stark and uncompromising against the grey wall. *An Arrangement in Grey and Black; Portrait of the Artist's Mother.*

'I know it's a bit gloomy,' says her daughter. 'But the others were really, like, soppy.'

'Are you trying to tell me something?' asks Susannah. 'Should I have been like this, sitting here for ever, never going away?'

Her daughter shakes her head. 'I'm not trying to tell you anything.' She looks at the card. 'It's just Art, innit?'

Afternoon Games

This is not an edifying story. Happily married couples should read no further, in case they learn the language of lying. It is an easy habit to acquire; the accommodations I made for myself, in matters of the heart, surprised me. For when I was forty, and long-married, I acquired a lover.

When I was young, I pictured a lover as one of the accessories of maturity, like having a Barclaycard. I dreamed of having, by my thirties, a silver Peugeot coupé, real leather luggage and a silky-knit designer suit. And a lover, preferably foreign. My thirties came and went and none of this happened. Why should it? I was just like anyone else. By the time I was forty I had a husband, a messy house in Holloway, two darling children and a Ford Mondeo sedimented with sweet wrappings and empty cassette cases.

I wasn't unhappy. As the years passed, however, I felt like a grounded aircraft while all other flights are called. I felt, like Peggy Lee, is this all there is? You might think, with some justification, that I was one of the lucky few – loved by three people, warmed by central heating. Had I any idea how brutish and disappointing were the lives of so many people who had started out as hopeful children?

Of course I knew this, but strangely enough it made no difference. Boredom is too simple a word for what I felt. It was more a sense of other possibilities receding into the distance, of my other un-lived lives slipping beyond my grasp. And I had run out of things to say to my husband. I remember when this hit me. It was my birthday and Christopher suggested that we went out to dinner, just the two of us. With a spasm of panic, I thought: what will we talk about? What on earth is left to say?

I blame computers. In the old days, people went out to work. In the evenings the couple, oxygenated by separation, returned to each other. Such a reunion must have been rejuvenating, all those people jostling into one's life. Nowadays most of the people I know work from home. Chris is a graphic designer. Week in, week out he sits in front of his Apple Mac, faxing and emailing, padding into the kitchen to make us carrot and coriander soup for lunch. (See, I have a husband who cooks. How could I be so ungrateful?)

I work, correcting the manuscripts of romance novels, a poorly paid job which acquaints me only too well with the clichés of escapism, of chisel-jawed heroes spiriting women away to happily-ever-after-land, wherever that is. I try to remove these but the editor always puts them back in. She believes in airbrushing the truth.

The truth being that love dulls into familiarity. Not in a predictable decline; there are plenty of dips and swooping highs on the way. Each marriage has its own climate, with blustery springs and Indian summers, sudden heatwaves in February. Some marriages, I'm sure, improve with age. Mine, however, had been eroded by proximity. The couple we once were seemed hardly recognizable. Was it possible that we used to kiss passionately in the car? Now we said: 'Why didn't you buy any anti-freeze?' And nobody was to blame.

So I was loose on the twig, a fruit ripe for plucking,

when I met Anton. Anton – a name, you must agree, that was made for a lover. We met three months ago at a book launch for one of my romantic novelists. My husband, who doesn't like parties, was at home babysitting.

What is your image, when you think of a lover? Silver-haired and suave, like the Italian count in *Darling*? A smouldering Joseph Fiennes sort of person? Anton resembled Walter Matthau, but I've always liked weathered men. He was a good deal older than me, twinkly and creased, and he told me he was there because at one point in his past he had stepped out with the romantic writer.

'Stepped out' sounded delightfully dated, not threatening at all. Already, however, I was feeling strongly attracted. Not to his looks, not yet, but to his experience. 'Summertime' was playing, and we talked about George Gershwin.

'How did he raise money for *Porgy and Bess?*' said Anton. 'Know how he did it? By broadcasting radio programmes sponsored by a laxative chewing gum.'

A spasm shot through me – not of desire, but hunger for knowledge. Here was a man who could tell me things, new things; here was a man with a Past! He'd had so many more years of life, and I could bet they were interesting ones. Words were released in me, too. I think bodies are overrated; love springs from the head, not the loins. Suddenly I wanted to tell him all the things my husband had heard only too often – a new audience for my stories.

'You bear a strong resemblance to my second wife,' he said. 'The same charming pointy chin.'

'How many wives have you had?'

'And you blush! What bliss! Let me take you out to lunch. Do you like Italian food?'

'Everyone likes Italian food.'

'Ah, but do you like expensive Italian food?'

The next day he took me to lunch. At that stage I didn't lie. I told Chris I was having lunch with a man I'd met at the party, and when the children came home I greeted them guiltlessly, though I felt strangely husk-like, as if the beating organs had been removed from my body. I drifted weightlessly from room to room. It was games day and, like a Persil mother, I bundled my son's muddy football shorts into the washing machine. But I wasn't having Persil thoughts.

For Anton had kissed me – the first time a man had kissed me on the mouth – oh God, on my mouth – for fourteen years. Apart from Chris, of course. *And you blush! What bliss!* As we ate supper in front of *The Bill* my whole body radiated warmth, like a storage heater – all that electricity, stored for so many years. Surely my husband could feel it?

'*Why are you smiling?*'

'*I like looking at you.*'

'*Don't!*'

'*Aren't you going to finish that linguine? Can I have some?*'

'*Goodness, you're a greedy man.*'

Couldn't Chris tell that I had made an assignation – ah, the illicit word! – for the very next day?

And so it began. Anton's flat was in the West End, behind Liberty's. Does this seem sophisticated to you? It did to me. I went there in the afternoons. These visits were called 'Meeting my Sister for Tea'; they were called 'Buying a New Attachment for the Hoover'. With a terrible facility, I learnt the vocabulary of deceit. Because my husband worked at home, I had to make up lies. Computers aren't just bad for marriages, they complicate adultery too.

Did I feel guilty? Of course I did. But my afternoons were so hermetically sealed that they bore no relation to my normal life. Anton and – Anton and I – a couple! – we seldom went out. To be precise, we didn't visit the sort of places where we might meet anyone we knew. Fearful of being spotted, we just nipped out for a cup of tea or to look at some paintings; we were like tourists, we did the sort of things one does on holiday, in a foreign city. In fact, London seemed like a foreign city to me. I was a woman who listened to buskers and shopped for a cashmere jumper in Dickins & Jones (Anton paid) – a jumper that remained in his flat, for how could I take it home? For two brief hours our lives were suspended. We lived in a vacuum.

'I'm not really here,' I said.

'You're not here,' he murmured, buried in my hair. 'I can't even see you.'

He did something in the City, a job that was obviously not too onerous to be interrupted. I suspected he was rich, though drained by alimony payments. His flat was filled with paintings, and Bollinger chilled in the fridge. He was certainly generous, as all lovers should be. After all, he had nothing to lose, and I risked everything.

And the risks were huge. Take the carrier bags. Anton had grown up in the suspenders era and loved me wearing fancy underwear. He even liked high heels, which I hadn't worn for years. So on our afternoons of love, I stuffed a carrier bag with such items and smuggled them out of the house. En route to Anton's flat, I stopped at the ladies' cloakroom in Liberty's and changed into my alluring underwear. It was winter, and a cumbersome business – overcoat, elbows bumping against the cubicle door, poppers unpopping and having to be snapped shut – but one must suffer to be beautiful. I was trussing myself up to pleasure my lover, and to be pleasured. Outside, London went about its business. In Anton's block of flats, I pressed the bell to the seventh floor. As I shifted from one foot to another, silk slid against my skin.

I was horribly exhilarated. Here was a man who worshipped my elbows – *elbows* – who kissed, with wonderment, parts of my body that nobody had ever noticed before. That *I* hadn't noticed. A man who asked me about my childhood. 'How big was your garden? Where was your favourite hiding place? I want to picture you. How was your hair cut, when you were ten?'

Nobody had ever asked me this; nobody had wanted to know. I felt focused upon, full beam. I felt like undistinguished scrubland where oil has been discovered – it gushed out, my untapped riches. Anton and I talked so much that when I went to the loo, I left the door open so we could carry on our conversation. What did my husband and I talk about? Whose turn it was to take back the videos?

As the weeks passed, I slipped away from my husband. My soul moved elsewhere and when I came home it was my own neighbourhood that became foreign to me. Our local pub had been smartened up – scrubbed tables, and seared tuna on the menu. As I walked past, I saw the old soaks sitting there, utterly lost, in front of a solitary candle. I knew how they felt; their old surroundings had gone, what were they doing there?

During the day, I moved around the house like an automaton. My son, Ben, had got into the football team. 'We're going to play Tottenham High next week!' he told me excitedly. As I hugged him, the words floated harmlessly away. I was thinking of the red silk basque I had bought that afternoon. See how I was, what sort of mother?

The next Wednesday, Chris was going to visit a client in Nottingham. I rang Anton from the callbox down the road – I didn't possess adultery's vital accessory, a mobile phone. 'We have a whole day!'

That night, I dreamed I was standing on a stage. Chris was in the audience and I was singing, *It's all over now, Baby Blue.* My husband's face gazed at me, bemused. I realized he couldn't hear a word, the microphone wasn't working. I mouthed at him in desperation, I shook the mike, but finally he stood up and left.

Wednesday dawned. From a hundred miles away, I heard my family in the kitchen.

'Mum, the bread's hard!'

'Pretend it's toast!' I called gaily.

'The milk's sour.'

'Pretend it's yoghurt!'

I bundled my basque into a carrier bag and hid it in the hall.

'Mmm, you smell nice,' said Chris, as I went into the kitchen. 'What are you doing today?'

'Getting the car MOT'd.'

'Hope it passes.'

'Oh, there's life in the old thing yet,' I laughed.

Chris swallowed his coffee. 'Good luck in the match,' he said, ruffling Ben's hair. 'You thrash 'em, see?'

'They're a bunch of plonkers,' said Ben.

Chris left for Nottingham. I took the children to school. As they ran across the playground, their little legs thrust a blade through my heart. *I'm not really here!* As I dropped off the car at the garage I thought: how strange it would be, to live in the real world with Anton. I had never met his friends or his grown-up children, we had never been tested by life's MOT. Would either of us fail? If the milk was sour, if the cat was sick in his shoes, would he get irritable? How would he behave in a traffic jam? How would he react to my mother? We were cocooned in the present tense. We couldn't shunt it forward, for the future held only pain.

Maybe I had a premonition, thinking this. I don't know. The cloakroom at Liberty's was closed for redecoration so, clutching my carrier bag, I made my way to Anton's flat.

He threw his arms around me. 'Darling, come to bed.'

'Get in and wait for me,' I said, disentangling myself. 'I've got a surprise for you.'

I went into his bathroom and undressed. Then I reached for the carrier bag.

It's funny how time passes, isn't it? Aeons of it. And it may have been no time at all.

After however long it was, I heard a tap at the door. 'Are you all right in there?'

Anton, a blurred shape in his dressing gown, walked into the bathroom. Now it was *his* voice that echoed, from a far foreign country.

'What on earth's happened?'

No doubt he was gazing at the pair of muddy football boots on the floor. I had picked up the wrong carrier bag.

I sat on the edge of the bath, clutching my son's football shorts. Shuddering, I pressed them against my face to mop up my wicked, guilty tears.

'Chop, chop.' Mr Montague, the games teacher, clapped his hands as he hurried into the changing room. 'They're waiting, Ben.'

He stopped in surprise.

'Why aren't you ready?'

The afternoon was over. It was all over, though Betty was unaware of this. What had happened that day, miles across London, was none of her concern. In the changing room she had put down her mop and bucket.

For she was no longer a cleaner; she was a sex goddess. Inspecting herself in the mirror, she pouted. The basque was stretched to breaking point across her breasts. Her damp cleavage glistened under the bulb that hung from the ceiling. She smiled at her reflection. The high heels, too, were a tight fit; when she posed seductively, she wobbled and regained her balance.

Gazing at herself in the red basque, the black stockings, the strappy stilettos, she chuckled. *Wait till Andy sees me in this. See his face then!*

Sunday in the Park with Henry

The thing is, one feels exactly the same. Everyone says this, as they get older – as they get to, say, sixty. Say, what I am. I feel the same person as when I was nineteen, when we could smoke in the cinema and park anywhere and rent a room for three pounds a week. When Diana wasn't a princess, she'd hardly been born, but she was alive then, and so was John Lennon. Not just alive, but wriggling in the sack with Yoko Ono. I remember this because I happened to be there at the time, at the Albert Hall when he and Yoko were on stage, and things got out of hand, the music grew wilder and people in the audience started taking off their clothes until they were *naked*, and I thought, this is the sixties, I'm here and I'll remember this moment for ever.

Which I do. But I also remember the Stones playing in Hyde Park, Mick Jagger in that silly dress, and though I can picture it in detail and smell the incense, I wasn't there, I'm sure of that. But it's just as vivid, almost more so.

I'm thinking this as I walk across the park this beautiful Sunday morning. How I'm still the same person I was forty years ago. I still like lipstick, and intelligent men, and potatoes. I'm still terrified of spiders. Nothing's been solved, nobody's the wiser. There's just been this huge accumulation of memories, real and imagined. I've lived so many fantasy lives with people I've met, so many men I've been married to in my head and we've had six children and gone to live in the Quantocks, or wherever, in houses I've glimpsed in estate agents' windows, and those lives are so potent I can smell the honeysuckle, drenched by rain, as if I was brushing past it now.

I was up early this morning because I couldn't sleep. Last night I had a disastrous date with a man I met on the internet. A Professional Man, he called himself. I think I prefer the amateur ones. He also said he had a good sense of humour, a sure sign, of course, that he hadn't. After the first sip of wine I knew it was doomed. A shared liking of log fires wasn't enough for a lifetime's commitment.

I only went because my daughter bullied me. She's like Mrs Bennet in *Pride and Prejudice*; she wants to see me settled. She lends me her silky top and pushes me into the unknown, to sit in gastropubs with men whose wrinkles mirror my own mortality. We look at each other with a jolt and think *that's how the world must see ME now*. These men too will be children of the sixties, these men who're thinning on top and who hold in their tummy when they get up to go to the loo – as I do too, of course. We've tried to paper over the cracks but it's like looking round a house with many previous owners; once you move in, you'll discover the dry rot. It's always hopeless, or disastrous, and I vowed this morning that I'd never do it again.

Besides, you can't arrange for love. It'll happen when you least expect it. My friend Annie has fallen for a young Croatian who came to fix her boiler. She spends her evenings in a sort of dormitory, filled with his fellow countrymen, somewhere near Luton Airport, eating cold pasta from plastic bowls. She's blissfully happy.

My friend Julie, however, believes that fate needs a nudge. 'Get a dog,' she says. 'That's the way to meet men. You'll bump into some hunk with a schnitzel, or whatever they're called. Or you could save the money and just get a lead and shout in the bushes.'

The thing is, men of my age have disappeared like the London sparrows. They've run off with younger women, predictably enough their secretaries or else Russian girls who bat their eyelashes and behave like Carole Lombard in some black-and-white movie. Even the notorious adulterers have hung up their spurs and returned to their long-suffering wives.

But that's all right. I'm fine. I don't need anyone. And the park's so beautiful it stops my breath. There's something about September, isn't there? That low sunlight slanting through the bleached grass, that elegiac sense of summer ending but not yet, not just yet . . . I used to think sixty-year-olds were at the November of their lives but funnily enough I've changed my mind now. September's our month. We're still the same people, us Freedom-Passers, but with a certain glow to us, a certain sun-warmed maturity. Our attraction comes from our deeply lived experience and our bodies are fine, go on, have a look and see. Who wants the dumb blonde of May?

Quite a lot of people, I've discovered.

I've walked into the park from the Bayswater Road. The joggers are out early. They pound along, glugging water from plastic bottles. Why does everybody drink water all the time? We never drank any. The Americans, sleek young bankers, push their offspring into those monster three-wheelers that are almost as annoying as the vast 4x4s I bet they drive, clogging up the streets and squashing cyclists.

Oh dear, I'm starting to sound irritable. I'm not, of course. I'm still the same warm, lovely person I've always been. There's just more to be irritable about, isn't there? Newspapers strewn all over the tube, people bellowing into their mobiles. Brainless celebrities I've never heard of hogging the TV, eight thousand channels and nothing to watch except people cooing over their blithering garden decking, and don't even start me on Digiboxes freezing and videos not recording and laptops crashing and printers jamming and great spaghettis of cables all over the place, what are they all for? And charities sending me biros that make me feel guilty and don't work anyway. Why don't they spend the money on world peace? And spam emails offering me *a better sex*. Where did they learn their grammar? A better sex, indeed. Chance would be a fine thing. And parking wardens everywhere but never any police. And nasty dogs all looking like pit-bulls with bowed legs. Where did all the Airedales go?

No, I'm not irritable, not really. Catch *me* being a tut-tutter. Catch *me* growing into one of those whiskery crones who glares at teenagers. Here I am, striding across the park in my silver trainers; us sixty-year-olds, we're the children of the revolution, we're like Joanna Lumley, though not so gorgeous, we're making it up as we go along. Look at us, having affairs with younger men! Sending YouTube clips to our long-suffering children, who're trying to get on with their work. Nobody can call *us* fuddy-duddies!

Actually, my trainers are starting to hurt. As you get older the soles of your feet begin to burn, God knows why. It's one of the things nobody tells you about. Through the trees I can see the Albert Hall. Yesterday was the Last

Night of the Proms. I think of all the music that has been played there since John and Yoko wriggled in their sack. It got so chaotic that the management turned off the power. The music stopped, the lights went out and the audience subsided into a sort of stoned embarrassment. The boy I was with, who had half taken off his T-shirt, put it back on. He's probably a grandfather by now.

I cross the bridge and walk through the area where they've let the grass grow long. I love it here, where it's wild and secret. In places, the grass is flattened where people were picnicking last night. I imagine them lying here as the sun set, lovers lying in each other's arms while the music drifted through the trees and I was stuck in the pub with my Non-Smoking Professional Man, a date that had to be rescheduled because one of his teeth had fallen out. There's a secret glade here, my favourite place of all, where you could be in the country, the birds singing, the traffic a distant hum – I stop dead. The grass is strewn with rubbish. Not just one or two bottles – an explosion of garbage from somebody's picnic. Fag packets, crisp packets, beer cans, chicken bones, half-eaten tubs of coleslaw, half-gnawed ribs, sweet wrappers, plastic bags, a wine-sodden copy of *Heat* magazine . . .

I stand there, seething. All right, I admit it. I *am* a tut-tutter. I feel a flush rising. Not a hot flush this time, though I get plenty of those. A flush of pure, righteous anger. How could they, whoever they are? How could they ruin this place, the drunken slobs?

I pick up one of the carrier bags and get to work. A few years ago, I would have been too self-conscious to pick up somebody else's rubbish but age brings a certain freedom – you no longer care what other people think. Or, not quite so much. Anyway, a little bit less. Besides, there's nobody around, so that's all right.

I start shoving the garbage into the plastic bags. It's still damp with dew, or maybe slime. Cranberry juice still slops around in a sticky plastic bottle. Ants have invaded the coleslaw and a small black slug has left a trail of mucus across a photograph of Paris Hilton. Various celebrities are shown stumbling out of nightclubs but she's the only one I recognize. My daughter says I needn't bother learning their names. In fact, even *she* doesn't know some of them; that's how old she has grown, seemingly overnight, without my even noticing.

As I shove in the rubbish, tut-tutting away, I speculate on whose picnic this is. There's an empty Rizla packet, so they must have been smoking dope. Kids, probably, but not the sort who would be singing 'Land of Hope and Glory' at the Proms.

And then I see the mobile. It's lying on the grass next to an empty bottle of Valpolicella. I pause for a moment. A *mobile*, eh? I pick it up. It's damp; I wipe it on my jumper. It's a sleek, fancy mobile, a newer model than mine. A very nice mobile, in fact.

Well, well. What now? A fly buzzes over the remains of the food. I feel something shift inside me. I should give it back, of course.

My blush deepens. *Of course I should give it back.* If I keep it, I'm transformed from a good citizen into a thief. I stand there, considering. But does this sort of litterbug deserve to get their phone back? Aren't other people more deserving of such a mobile – people like myself, in fact, whose own mobile is so ancient that it hardly works at all? Better still, my son, who's a teacher in an inner-city school and who is spending this sunny weekend stuck in his dingy flat preparing for another term of dodging flying knives, and whose own mobile has packed up completely?

I open the phone and scroll down the list of names. Chloe. Zoe. Bella. Leo. Zak. *Zak!* They're middle-class! No wonder there's a pot of tabbouleh amongst the mess. Besides, you have to be well off to live round here. This makes me seethe even more. I can just picture them, these privileged kids who should know better. Chloe would be lounging on the grass, all long, tanned legs, fiddling with her iPod. Leo, rolling a joint, will be trying to get off with Bella, who's ludicrously beautiful. Zak's parents will be in the media, of course. I've taken a particular dislike to Zak. Zak's got straight A's but that's because he went to private school, like the rest of them. Throughout the future, doors will open for these young people. Blithely, obliviously, they'll sail through life, leaving their rubbish behind for someone else to clear up. Somebody like me.

I know! I could text them all and arrange a meeting in some pub. When they arrive, Zoe and Chloe and Zak, they'll find nothing but a pile of bin bags!

I look at the names again. 'Mum' is at the top. There's her phone number. I have a good mind to ring up Mum and tell her what a litterbug she's got for a daughter; why didn't she bring her up properly? I'm pretty sure the mobile belongs to a girl. My suspicions are confirmed when I click on the Outbox and read the most recent message. It is indeed to Mum. *Please check I switched off my hair straighteners*. Spelt funnily of course, in text-speak. Suddenly I feel a wave of sympathy for my fellow mother, wading through the cesspit of her daughter's bedroom searching for a pair of straightening tongs. I know it, I've been there.

The poor woman is obviously divorced. 'Dad' is a separate entry. Maybe Mum's still reeling from her husband's defection. Dad has run off with his PA, who is, of course, younger and prettier than Mum. He has two numbers: Dad Mob and Dad Work. Maybe I should phone *him*. Maybe it's Dad's fault that his daughter has become such a delinquent. She's deeply unhappy, she's seeking his attention. She feels that *she's* rubbish, discarded by the father who abandoned her.

But then, perhaps I'm wrong. Perhaps it's Dad who's the victim in all this. Mum has fallen for a Romanian minicab driver and chucked him out. Dad's now languishing in a bedsit above a launderette. Maybe I should phone up Dad. We could moan about our divorces. Moaning is very bonding ... quite erotic, in fact. We arrange to meet, so I can hand over the phone, and one thing leads to another ... as Annie says, love comes when you least expect it.

Suddenly, the mobile rings. I nearly drop it in surprise.

Oh God, it's Mum, looking for her daughter who hasn't come home! It's the owner, hungover and groggy, trying to find out who's got her phone!

I dither for a moment. Finally, curiosity wins and I press the answer button.

A voice says: 'Morning, love. Henry's waiting for you. Have you forgotten your appointment?'

My brain whirls. Who's Henry? A doctor? A hairdresser? But hairdressers don't often work on a Sunday. A boyfriend? But you don't have appointments with boyfriends.

I ask the voice. 'Er, what appointment?' And the person tells me.

Fifteen minutes later, I'm sitting astride a big bay gelding called Henry. We're trotting out of a stables, just behind the Bayswater Road, a whole group of us. I haven't ridden a horse since I was a teenager, but it all comes back to me; the years vanish and I'm young again. Look, I can do it! Now we're cantering along Rotten Row and the old muscles are working again, my knees are gripping the saddle and Henry's mane is rising and falling in the wind. His neck is damp with sweat, he's a beautiful horse and I'm rapidly falling in love with him, that fierce, pure passion I felt for horses before boys came along, before love affairs and marriages and divorce. The sun shines, the pigeons scatter in front of our thudding hooves. This is Flora's ride – that's the name of the mobile phone girl, they told me at the stables – but Flora must have overslept, she never turned up and I'm that young girl now, just for an hour, the young girl I've always been, despite the wrinkles. Nothing's changed. The memories come flooding back, how I was so pony-mad that even when I wasn't sitting on one, which was most of the time as I couldn't afford it – even then I pretended to be riding, I cantered through the suburban streets which were transformed into forests and glades, and in a weird way that was just as thrilling as the real thing. Indeed, more real.

We trot past the Albert Hall, where the signs for the Proms are being taken down. I feel a wave of affection for the unknown Flora, whose life I am living for this brief hour. She's got everything ahead of her, the joys and sorrows, and I forgive her the rubbish because I wasn't so perfect myself, especially when I'd smoked a few joints, and hey ho, who cares?

Henry tosses his head and snorts through his nostrils. I wonder what she'll be like when I meet her, this Flora, when I give back the phone. We're united by our love for a horse, the first great passion for girls, the simplest passion of all. But half an hour later, back at the stables, I discover that the mobile has gone. It must have fallen out of my pocket while we were cantering. So, I'll never meet Flora, or Chloe, or Zak. I'll never know my little cast of characters.

Except I do, of course, in my head. That group of friends, picnicking on a golden summer's evening, they're as real to me as the real thing.

Light my Fire

Reg was a large man, built for hauling slabs of marble. He had a beer belly and arms like oak trunks. He was a builder, with premises in Camden Town, under a railway arch. In a haze of dust, he sanded and stripped, assembling fireplaces and installing them for his customers – marble, pine, repro and mock, gas-effect grates or solid fuel.

'A fire's for life,' he joked, 'not just for Christmas.'

It was January, perishing outside, and he was doing a job up in Hampstead – Victorian-style corbelled marble, cost a few bob, but they could afford it judging by the powder-blue Merc parked outside. Mrs Adams was her name, buffed and polished, leather trousers, way out of his league, breathing expense.

While he was chipping at the chimney-breast, the phone rang. 'Darling . . .' her voice lowered. 'He's gone to Pittsburgh . . . oh yes, me too . . . come over right now – what? Oh, it's only someone putting in the fireplace.' She took the phone into the other room.

Reg, just someone, banged the mallet sharply on his chisel. Soot fell, billowing over her carpet.

Next morning there was a maroon Audi parked outside. Mrs Adams opened the door in a state of disarray. 'Oh, it's you,' she said.

She went upstairs. He heard giggles. The waterpipes hissed in the wall. Later, footsteps descended the stairs. A man stood there, gazing at the sooty mouth of the fireplace. Mrs Adams tousled his hair. 'Isn't it romantic?' she lowered her voice. 'Just imagine lying on a goatskin rug . . .' she whispered something into his ear.

'Can't wait,' he replied.

The woman turned to Reg. 'Kettle's downstairs.'

Reg had worked in the building trade for twelve years. He was accustomed to being plunged into the intimacy of other people's lives. Despite the din of his hammer-drill, he was an invisible man. Amazing, what people said when he was in the room; sometimes he doubted his own existence. Mrs Adams was having some nookie. Fair enough. He should be so lucky. But he wondered about Mr Adams, away in Pittsburgh, and the unknown Adams kids, whose school photos hung on the wall.

Because the next Tuesday, when he was cementing in the mantelpiece, she was on the phone again. In the next room, admittedly, but cementing is a near-noiseless activity.

'We can't go on like this,' she said. 'I love you. I want you so much I ache all over.'

Reg straightened up. His back was hurting, an ache that shot down his legs.

'I want to run my tongue down your chest . . . I want to lick you, oh my sweetheart.'

No woman had ever talked to him like that. His ex-wife, in rare moments of affection, had called him 'cuddlebums', but it didn't have the ring. In the last, bitter months she had called him 'gross'. Reg, remembering her, dropped his palette knife with a clang.

'What?' said Mrs Adams. 'Oh, it's all right. Just the fire-place man.'

She still hadn't asked Reg his name.

On Thursday, the fireplace was installed. Reg demonstrated how to light the gas. The flames jumped up, *phut*.

'Feel the heat,' he said. 'Just like the real thing, but look! No mess.'

'No mess . . .' she paused. 'If only real life could be so simple. Switch it off, switch it on . . .' Today she looked terrible – pale and raw.

He pocketed her cheque. 'And it's a great investment, property-wise.'

While he was gathering his tool bags, she picked up the phone twice, then put it down before dialling.

'Is that Goldschmidt and Howland? I want to sell my house.'

Her voice was bright, but when she finished the call she winced, as if she had stomach cramp. Pushing her hand through her hair she looked at the photos. The children returned her gaze, smiling in their silver frames. Outside the trees stood, their arms raised to heaven.

'Freezing out there, eh?' Reg shouldered his bag. '*I'm* off on holiday next week, aren't I the lucky one?'

She didn't ask where he was going.

'Goa's where the action is, my sonner. Goa's rock 'n' roll.' Thus spoke Neville. Goa was cheaper than Spain. It was sun and sand and beach orgies. It sounded all right to Reg. He hadn't had a holiday for years. All hours he had been working, toiling over his acid tank whilst overhead the rumbling trains took people elsewhere, anywhere but here.

Neville was a scaffolder. Reg had his doubts about Neville as a holiday companion. Like a lot of scaffolders, Neville was a randy sod. He lived on a knife-edge, that was why; there was a dangerous air to him that drew women like a magnet. Thin, fit, with a year-round tan, Neville had the grace and sensual appetite of a mountain goat. He treated women like his buildings – something to scramble up and then abandon, no long-term investment to them. Already, on the plane, he was limbering up for action. After consuming three miniatures of Martell, he disappeared up the cabin to chat up a bird in row 23, only to return for a smoke and an unsought update on his progress.

Stepping out of the plane, Reg was hit by blinding heat. The air had a curious smell, a corrupt perfume that filled his nostrils like cotton wool. The bus deposited them at the Baywatch Beach Resort, a concrete building surrounded by coconut palms. Neville was already ensconced in the bar with a bottle of beer and a 'Danish bird', so tall she towered over him even when seated.

'I'm in the erection business,' he said, a line that was lost on her but it didn't seem to matter.

Reg picked his way down to the beach, past the Delighted Dry Cleaners and the Cold Spot Café. Buildings were going up around him, concrete husks encased in bamboo scaffolding. He imagined Neville skimming up them like a monkey. He paused to gaze at the Try Once Tailors. What did that mean – try once and never again? Suddenly he felt a wave of loneliness. Who could share the joke?

On the beach lay oiled bodies. Reg, jet-lagged, fell asleep.

When he woke, the sun was sinking, and he was burnt. Wincing, he pulled down his trunks to inspect his two-tone lower gut: white and lobster-red. He went back to the room he shared with Neville but on the doorknob hung a sign saying DO NOT DISTURB.

Their room faced the street. Opposite was a half-built block of flats and a hoarding depicting a sturdy brassiere: *'Toneform Bras: The Right Tone for Your Melodious Moods'*. Lorries thundered past, swerving round pedestrians and animals. The next day, Reg's swimming trunks blew off the balcony, where he had hung them out to dry. Falling into the street, they were eaten by a holy cow.

Neville had disappeared, presumably with his Great Dane. Not a note, nothing. Reg thought: I've lost my swimming trunks, I'm fat, I'm burnt, I'm alone. For a moment, he succumbed to self-pity. Where were the soothing hands to rub moisturizer into his skin? In London people toasted themselves beside his fires but here in the sunshine there was nobody to warm his heart.

What the hell. Reg rummaged in his suitcase and pulled out a pair of boxer shorts. They were printed with pink elephants – a gift from his ex – but they were his sturdiest item of underwear. He pulled them on. Gathering together his stuff for the beach, he sallied forth to look for love.

Reg was a modest man. He suffered no delusions about his appearance but according to his female friends it was personality that counted, personality and a small bottom. Though he was big, no denying that, he was recognizably tadpole-shaped. A large tadpole, but still. Besides, he was a romantic. Who knew what awaited, just around the corner? Give up on that and you might as well throw in the towel.

Reg walked along the beach, stopping for liquid refreshment on the way. He told himself: this is the holiday that will change my life. He walked a long way, searching for love. He walked past the high-rise hotels, past the sunbathing couples who lay, fingers entwined, cheeks pressed against their outspread paperbacks. He walked through the white heat of midday and into the afternoon. Dreamily he saw a woman rising out of the sea and running towards him, spray flying; running in slow motion, her arms outstretched, calling 'Reg!' He blinked and she was gone.

He walked around a headland and there, in front of him, stretched a wide sickle of sand, scattered with rocks. There were no crowds here – just some hippies and the odd fisherman hauling in his net. No hotels either; only huts. Pigs gambolled under the palm trees. Reg's spirits rose; it was the loveliest beach he had ever seen, a beach from the dawn of time, a clean slate where anything could happen.

One hut stood on the beach, the Step-In Café. Reg stepped in and ordered a beer. '*Most thrilling chilled*', said the label. It was chilled; he was thrilled. For he was sitting in paradise and the detritus of his life – traffic jams, VAT arrears, botched relationships – fell away. He closed his eyes and murmured 'Om . . .' After all, he was in India. His mate Arnold swore by meditation and used to sit in the pub centring his body fluids.

And when Reg opened his eyes she was there, standing in front of him. 'Got a light?' she asked. 'These Indian matches are crap.' Forget the nose-stud, she was a looker, with her long, tanned limbs and tight T-shirt, frayed shorts. And she knew it.

He lit her cigarette but then she was gone, clomping down the beach in her boots. She sat down with some other kids.

Reg got up and approached them. They were passing round the cigarette – it was a joint, dickbrain! Reg said: 'May I join you?'

She barely moved but he sat down all the same. One of the blokes gazed at Reg's nether regions. 'Great trunks,' he said and burst into giggles.

They had drawling upper-class voices. They were on their gap year, they said: travelling rough, travelling round India. Reg had never had a Gap; he had gone straight from school into the building trade.

'I suppose you're staying in one of those sad hotels,' said the girl. 'We watch them each fortnight, the package tourists, herded in and herded out.'

She and her mates slept in huts, they said, or on the beach. The sun was sinking. They lit a fire. On their cassette player The Doors sang 'Come on baby, light my fire'. It seemed appropriate, in the circumstances. Reg tried to think up a joke about stripping doors for a living – he did that as well as fireplaces – but they weren't taking any notice of him, he was invisible.

The girl was moaning about her parents. 'They're so materialistic,' she said, scratching her knee. 'So boring. All they think about is doing up the bloody house. Like, possessions, all that.'

'Where do you live?' asked Reg.

'Here.' She gestured around. 'Anywhere. The universe.'

'I mean, in England.'

'Hampstead,' she said, with a tone of contempt.

'What's your name?'

'Zoe.'

'Zoe what?'

'Zoe Adams.' She got up. 'I'm having a swim.'

She pulled off her T-shirt and her boots. Bare-breasted, she strode into the sea. The others got up and followed.

Reg gathered up his things and went back to the Step-In Café. Ordering a beer, he gazed at the girl's head bobbing in the waves. Behind her the sun slid down, a red disc. He thought of her photo, smiling as her mother put their house on the market. *Ladybird, Ladybird, fly away home, your house is on fire and your children have gone.* Reg felt a surge of power. He may just be a bog-standard package tourist, the lowest of the low, he may look a prat in his underpants, but he knew something she didn't know. *They're so boring, my parents* . . . A few words from him could blow her world apart.

Reg rummaged in his wallet, to pay for his beer. His money had gone.

Reg was not a bitter man. He didn't brood on the skewed imbalance of his lot in life. That he was fat whilst others were thin; that love bypassed him while alighting on Neville, who had done nothing to deserve it; that he had been ignored by Mrs Adams, and both ignored and robbed by her daughter (no doubt when his eyes were closed in the café). Life was a mess; in that respect Mrs Adams had hit the nail on the head.

Out of the mess, however, appeared a shapely equation.

He had been robbed, but he could rob the robber. A few words to Zoe and her blind, superior happiness could be stolen from her for ever. It was in his power.

Reg gave his sunglasses to the bloke in the café, in lieu of payment, and left. He turned away from the sea, however, and walked back through the woods. He behaved decently and for that he was rewarded.

Through the palm trees, in the slanting evening light, he saw a woman of ravishing beauty. A village woman, loading bits of wood into a basket. She smiled shyly at him. Bending down, she tried to lift the load.

Reg moved swiftly. With his hefty arms he heaved up the basket. He deposited it on to the coiled cloth that rested on top of the woman's head. She smiled her thanks and walked away.

This moment of grace was something he remembered all his life. She was the most beautiful woman he had ever seen. Glimpsed briefly, she had walked out of his life for ever. She would use the wood to cook dinner for a family who were as invisible to him as he was to so many others. But he had helped light her fire, and he was satisfied.

How to Divorce Your Son

Muriel

When his wife threw him out, Martin came back home to live with me. Neither of his sisters would have him. Karen was too busy, what with her children and her Open University course and her manic-depressive husband; she couldn't take on Martin's problems, on top of everything else. Besides, she didn't have the room. Janet simply said: 'Not on your life.'

So Martin came back home to Belper; Martin and his computer and printer, and filing cabinet and back-dated copies of *Period Homes* magazine, and mounds of carrier bags. 'I'm back, Mum,' he said. 'You'll have company now.'

Of course, I should have been pleased, one of my chickens returned to the nest. The trouble was, Martin was no chicken, not any more. He was forty-two and had put on a lot of weight, these past few years. He had also lost most of his hair. If he had kept his figure, I thought, maybe his wife would still love him.

Sue had been the dynamic one of the duo. While Martin sat at home in Nottingham, doing his indexes, his wife had climbed the career ladder at Boots, up to management level. En route she had started an affair, the minx, with the Deputy Services Manager; hence my son's expulsion.

For the first few weeks, I was pleased to have him home.

The poor boy, he needed looking after. As time passed, however, I started to get irritated. The trouble was, he got in the way. Wherever he sat, he spread. Newspaper supplements multiplied around him. His discarded anorak tripped me up. He smoked, filling my Crown Derby saucers with stubs, and leaving them balanced precariously on the arms of chairs. And he didn't open the window after he'd used the lavatory.

It was twenty years since I'd had him in the house for any length of time. Like all boys he had been untidy, but now he was a middle-aged man, such habits had somewhat lost their charm. It was my fault, of course. I indulged him and cleaned up after him, I had helped create this large male person who sat around the house waiting for meals. In fact, as the weeks passed, I started to feel sorry for his wife. Loyalty to Martin disappeared and my initial anger against Sue turned to pity – to a rueful, aren't-men-the-end sort of female solidarity. I even started thinking: how could she have put up with him for so long?

The problem was, I had grown accustomed to living on my own. Martin thought I was lonely; he thought I needed him. Apart from unscrewing jam jars, however, I was perfectly able to take care of myself. I'm only sixty-eight, I have all my faculties. I was used to the airy freedom of empty rooms, of eating when I felt like it – cold potatoes from the saucepan or fingerfuls of hummus from the tub.

Martin was simply there, all the time. He compiles indexes for technical books – work about which I find it hard to summon up any interest. It's a dogged sort of a job, but then he has always been like that – a slow learner, compared with his sisters, a kind, diligent boy but cautious.

The image I always remember, from his childhood, is of a holiday beach in Cornwall. His sisters ran shrieking into the water while Martin, facing away from the sea, made his way slowly down the rocks – inching, step by step, backwards.

He never ventured far into treacherous territory. When he left home, he only moved a few miles away, to Nottingham, and brought his washing home on Sundays. He married late, when everybody was starting to give up hope. He was the plodder, good at sums; his sisters used to tease him mercilessly.

But he was an affectionate boy; he liked sitting on my lap, sucking his thumb. And he was still affectionate, though now in a bossier, more claustrophobic way.

'I'm worried about you, Mum. You should look after yourself.'

'But I am. I do.'

He wanted to sort me out. I was trying to read my book one night when he said: 'Why don't you get on the net, Mum?'

'The what?'

'The internet. You can talk to people in their chat rooms.'

'Why should I?'

He tried to show me how to use it, but first I logged into a Volkswagen dealership and then a picture came on to the screen saying *Busty blonde waits for your call.*

The thing was, I didn't want a man around. My husband had been dead for fifteen years and though I missed him, it wasn't how Martin thought. I had grieved for Robert but now I had made my adjustments; solitude had become essential to me. I had also adjusted to losing my children, to letting them loose into the world's treacherous waves. All mothers have to finally release themselves from their anxieties and let their children shoulder their own responsibilities. Distancing is necessary, for the children's sake as well as one's own. And here was Martin, back again when I thought I had waved him off; back again and fussing around.

'You ought to make the best of yourself,' he said. 'That awful tracksuit.'

I tried to resist but, suddenly energized, he drove me to the Berketex Factory Outlet. His wife had been a keen shopper. The main reason she came to Belper, I suspected, was its proximity to her beloved factory shops – Liz Claiborne, Viyella. Travelling around these places buying discount clothing is something of a hobby in Derbyshire. Not one of mine, I have to admit, but Martin was adamant.

Outside, it was a dank January day. I stood under the pitiless lighting, gazing at myself in the mirror. Martin had made me put on a turquoise two-piece, viscose, pleated skirt and patent leather belt. Its shoulder pads shifted when I moved.

'You look years younger,' said Martin.

Strangely enough, I looked years older. Old and stout. A wave of desolation swept through me. I swung round and glared at my son.

'For God's sake,' I barked, 'let me make my own accommodation with death.'

Martin jumped; I never shouted. All next day he sulked. It was like marriage. A crisis had been reached, a point of no return. I knew I could no longer live with Martin; to remain together would erode our love. He was a grown man; he needed a life of his own.

There was only one solution: divorce. What could I cite – adultery? Not on my side, and certainly not in that dress. It would have to be him. I had to find him a woman. The trouble was, he showed no inclination in that direction. He preferred to stay home eating the meals I'd shopped for and cooked – oh, how time-consuming that was, when time was so short. I had spent my life cooking.

Besides, who would have him? This time round my son was a good deal less attractive. Still appealing to me, of course, but I was his mother. For both our sakes, I had to get him off my hands. But how do you get rid of your son when he thinks he's doing you a favour by living with you? And when he has it so easy too?

I had to make a plan.

Martin

Shall I tell you about the final humiliation of my marriage? The proof, if such a thing needed proving, that I could get nothing right?

We were in the middle of the showdown about Keith, her oily colleague and *inamorato*, and life at home had become insupportable, so I suggested a meal out. An attempt at reconciliation, at salvage. When we arrived the restaurant was full, all but for one large, empty table in the middle of the room. There were eight places laid.

'But sir,' said the manager, 'you said a table for eight.'

'Eight o'clock,' I said. 'A table for two, at eight o'clock.'

Beside me, Sue snorted. Our entire marriage was contained in that snort, all six years of it – contempt, impatience, a certain grim satisfaction. The manager, too, looked exasperated. He cleared away the other place settings. Sue and

I sat alone, that vast empty space between us, the other diners watching us with mild curiosity, and I knew it was all over.

Marriage: see under <u>Humiliation</u>. See also under <u>Sex</u>.

Sex: see under <u>Infrequency of</u>. See also under <u>Performance</u>, inadequacy of.

Compiling indexes is the only thing that keeps me sane. Out of chaos, it creates order. There is a certain beauty in it – sorting out priorities, making connections.

Adultery: see under <u>Newman, Keith</u>. See also under <u>Boots, opportunities for liaisons at</u>.

Unlike me, Keith had a full head of hair. He played rugby on Sundays and was obviously a vigorous athlete, both on and off the pitch. I pictured him in his bachelor duplex, disporting himself with my wife. My stomach heaved.

'You were never up to much in that department,' Sue told me, that last, terrible night. What marriage could survive that?

So I returned home on a grey November day. I had known the area all my life, of course. I had grown up in Belper, but now the countryside looked dingy and despoiled, the houses looked meaner. The scars of open-cast mining, gouging out the hillsides, still looked raw even though the mines, like myself, had been made redundant. Some had been landscaped over but that didn't fool me; I could see the bumps of their hidden wounds.

As you can imagine, I was at rock bottom. The only beneficiary of this whole sad business was my mother. She has always been a spirited woman; she puts on a brave face for the world. When I visited her, at weekends, she seemed happy enough. But once I was living with her, I realized how lonely she had been, underneath the bright exterior. She was irritable and restless – a symptom of depression – and couldn't settle. She wore awful old gardening clothes and resisted my attempts to smarten her up; taking her to Berketex was not a success. Since Dad died, she had no focus for her life, nobody to look after. Caring for me put some shape into her day.

And I let her do it. I let her cook for me – huge meals, when I was supposed to be watching my weight. To be perfectly frank, cooking is not Mum's *forte*. Her generation hasn't heard of cholesterol; she cooks fat-sodden food that I'm sure contributed to Dad's final heart attack. On the other hand, I enjoy cooking – I was responsible for most of the meals, when I was married – adventurous food, too, Thai, Indian. I let her care for her little boy, because that's what I will always be, in her eyes.

As the weeks wore on, however, I found it increasingly stifling. Mum asked me about Sue but I didn't want to talk about my marriage, it was too painful. The house seemed more cramped than I remembered, and being back in my childhood bedroom depressed me; I had come full circle, with nothing to show for it. What an admission of defeat!

Of course, I loved my mother. We had always been close – closer than she had been to my moody and rebellious sisters; when they teased me, she always took my side. But now *she* seemed to be the moody one. Suddenly she would blurt out: 'Are you going to sit in front of that TV for ever? I'm going to die one day, watching *Eurotrash*!'

It was almost like being married again. 'Funny how it's all M's,' I said. 'Marriage, Moody . . .'

'What on earth are you talking about?' Like my wife, Mum has never taken an interest in my work.

I thought: we're imprisoned under the same letter. *Martin* and *Marriage*. *Martin* and *Mother*. We're stuck in an M box, in the *Middle* of the *Midlands*, surrounded by exhausted *Mines*, and we will never escape off the page and into real life.

Know why? Because real life is too terrifying.

And then, one day out of the blue, Mum suggested we went to a library function in Chesterfield. 'You do read books, don't you?' She gave a Sue-like snort. 'Not just the indexes?'

Stung, I agreed.

Apparently, some author was coming to give a reading. It was the next evening and Mum seemed in high spirits. She even wore a dress.

'Sandra will be there,' she said. 'Remember Sandra? She was in your class at school. And Lorraine's promised to come. She's mad about books.'

'*Lorraine* – mad about books?'

'She's divorced now. Gary packed in the garage and buggered off.'

Buggered? My mother didn't usually talk like this. But, as I said, she was in a funny mood. We drove into Chesterfield. I've always been a careful driver. As I slowed down at the traffic lights – I was right, they switched to red – Mum shifted restlessly in her seat. She pointed to the floodlit church. It's famous throughout the country for its crooked spire.

'You know the saying,' she chuckled. 'The spire will only straighten up when a virgin gets married.'

Virgin, like *buggered*, seemed a startling word to use. What was up? Of course I knew the local saying; it was one of the things we giggled about in school, though at the time we hadn't a clue what it meant.

When we arrived at the library I looked around in surprise. The audience was mostly women; you would expect that, in a library. But a lot of the faces were familiar to me. Not just Sandra and Lorraine; there was Pauline – or was it Pamela? – whose dad ran the turkey farm. There was Whatshername from primary school who once showed me her verrucas. She had put on weight (join the club) but her hair was now a startling shade of gold and tied up with a diamanté clip.

Mum ushered me from one woman to another. 'Fancy seeing you here,' she gushed. 'Remember Martin?'

Then a man came in, accompanied by the author, and we had to take our seats. He introduced himself. His name was Preston, and he was Chief Liaison Officer or something. I didn't really listen because just then he caught my eye.

Muriel

It was an interesting talk, I'm sure. A local writer was reading from her book about Peak District Rambles. I wasn't listening, however. I was working out which of the unattached girls – they were still girls to me – I would steer Martin towards when the time came for tea and biscuits.

Pauline was sitting in front of him. Divorced, she ran her own hairdressing salon and had two little sons.

'. . . nestling between the swelling hills, the lake plays host to a plethora of wildfowl,' read the writer.

In my mind I was already marrying Martin off. I wanted

more grandchildren and Martin would make a splendid stepfather. Why hadn't Sue produced any offspring? Too busy, one way and another, at Boots? (No more free pots of Night Rejuvenating Cream, I thought bitterly.)

Several of the girls worked at Thorntons chocolate factory, our biggest employer in Belper. I pictured them, one or another of them, coming home to Martin smelling of sugar. I pictured a new life for him, boisterous grandchildren and an unlimited supply of chocolates, all with soft centres.

When I opened my eyes the talk was over, however, and Martin had slipped away. Finally I spotted him. He had wandered over to the far shelves and was leafing through a book. Irritably, I thought: he's probably checking its index. Oh, he was hopeless! I had gone to all this trouble for nothing.

I gave up and queued at the tea urn. It was then I saw Preston, the man who had introduced the speaker, making his way towards my son. They spoke together, he said something, and Martin laughed.

I hadn't seen my son laugh for months. For some reason I was transfixed. My tea slopped into the saucer as I watched my son talking to the man. He was taller than Martin; slimmer too, though he was thinning on top. He had a neat moustache. As they stood there, laughing, a look passed over my son's face. And suddenly I realized.

I set my cup and saucer down, carefully, on an empty chair. At that moment everything fell into place. How could I have been so blind, all these years?

My own son. Suddenly I felt weak and sat down, heavily. The chattering women, the clink of teacups, they receded into the distance. I thought: maybe I have blinded myself to the obvious on purpose. Mothers have always deluded themselves about their children, it's a survival tactic.

'Be a devil, Muriel,' said somebody, 'and have the last biscuit.'

I tried to eat but my mouth was dry. I understood that this was a momentous evening. I needed to gather my wits. Think back to the past, Muriel! Think! It might all make sense.

As it turned out, however, it was not only momentous for me. For over the next few days, when it all became clear, Martin admitted that the evening in Chesterfield library had changed his life, too. For, like his mother, he himself had been blind to the obvious. And he hadn't realized it until then.

Martin

As I said, an index makes sense of things. Mine does, now. *Jowell, Martin: Schooldays, see under Bullying; Mother, see under Complicated relationship with; Marriage, see under Misery and Misunderstanding; Happiness in middle years, see under Preston, see under Joy, see under Relief.*

See under Love.

Changing Babies

Duncan was only little, but he noticed more than they thought. He knew, for instance, when the phone rang and it was his dad on the other end, because his mother always got out her cigarettes. She only smoked when his dad phoned up.

He knew Christmas was coming, but everybody knew that. In the shops, tinsel was strewn over microwave cookers. There was a crib at school, with a baby in it. He had already opened two doors in his advent calendar. Inside the first door was a bike and inside the second was a Walkman. 'My God!' chortled his mother. 'It'll be video recorders next! The Bethlehem Shopping Experience! No baby Jesus at the end, just a credit card hotline!'

No Jesus! There had to be a baby; it was Christmas. He wanted to open the last door, just to make sure, but he didn't dare.

It was his granny who told him the Christmas story. She said that the birth of Jesus was a miracle, and that Joseph wasn't his real father. God was. Sometimes she took Duncan to church. She went up to the altar to eat God's body. Once, when they came home for lunch, she tried to make him do it too. 'Come on,' she said. 'Eat it up, it's good for you. Look, *I'm* eating it. Mmmmm . . . lovely cod.'

Apart from that moment of alarm he liked being with

his granny. She watched TV with him, sitting on the sofa; she wasn't always doing something else. She kept photos of him in a proper book, with dates under his name, instead of all muddled loose in a drawer. She smelt of powder. She wasn't always talking on the phone. Nowadays she came to his house a lot, to babysit. Before he went to bed, she made him say his prayers. When she wasn't there he whispered them, so his mum couldn't hear.

His mum didn't pray; she did exercises. Once he went into her bedroom and she was kneeling down. He thought she was praying for his dad to come home but she said she was tightening her stomach muscles. He often got things wrong; there were so many big, tiring adjustments he had to make. Anyway, she didn't want his dad back. She was always on the phone to her friends. 'He never thought of *my* needs,' she said. 'He's so cut off from his feelings, so bloody self-absorbed. He didn't notice how I was growing, he's just like a child! It would take a miracle to change him.' But Christmas was a time of miracles, wasn't it? That was the point.

His dad had moved into a flat with a metal thing on the door which his voice squawked through. His mother would stand there in the street, shouting at its little slits. His dad's voice sounded like a Dalek's; 'What?' he said. 'What?' He could never hear what she was saying. She never came in. The hall smelt of school dinners. The flat smelt of new paint.

Duncan visited his dad twice a week. He slept on the sofa. Its cushion had a silky fringe which he sucked before he went to sleep. His dad talked on the phone a lot, too. When he had finished he would take him out. If it was raining they went to the swimming baths. If it wasn't raining they went to the Zoo. Duncan knew every corner of the Zoo, even the places hardly anyone went, like the cages where boring brown birds stayed hidden. At school Duncan impressed his teacher, he could recite the names of so many unusual animals. Years later, when he was a grown man, words like 'tapir' and 'aardvark' always made him sad.

Christmas was getting nearer. He had opened seven doors on his advent calendar now. He went shopping with his dad and they bought a very small Christmas tree. They walked past office buildings. Old men sat in the doorways, their heads poking out of cardboard boxes. 'Huh. They've been thrown out too,' said his dad. Motorbikes leaned against the pavement, chattering to themselves. But Duncan kept quiet. He wanted to ask his dad if he was coming back for Christmas but he didn't dare. Instead he searched the pavement for rubber bands the postman had dropped.

They stood at the bus stop. When he was with his dad they were always waiting for things. For a waitress to come, when they sat in a café. For the bus, because his dad didn't have the car.

'At school,' Duncan said, 'we've got a black baby Jesus. Last Christmas there was a pink one.'

He was suddenly conscious of the stretch of time, since a year had passed, and how old he was to remember. What had happened to the pink baby? It couldn't have grown older like he had, it couldn't have learnt to walk; it was just pretend. Had they thrown it away? But it was supposed to be Jesus.

His dad rubbed Duncan's hands. 'Bloody buses,' he said. 'Where's your gloves?'

'I took them out.' They had been threaded through his coat-sleeves, on elastic. 'I'm not a *baby*,' he said.

The bus came at last. They got out at the late-night supermarket. It was called Payless but his dad called it Paymore. They bought some Jaffa Cakes. Back in the flat the phone was ringing. It wasn't his mother; his dad didn't turn his back and lower his voice. He spoke quite normally.

'. . . they've had to re-edit the whole damn thing,' he said. 'Nobody told them at Channel Four. It'll take another four weeks. Frank's incensed.'

Frankincense! The word billowed out, magically.

His father was still talking. '. . . I'd better bring it round myself,' he said, 'by hand . . .'

Duncan had sucked the chocolate off his Jaffa Cake. He dozed on the sofa. To tell the truth it was way past his bedtime, but he wasn't saying anything. He closed his eyes. His father, wearing a flowing robe, knocked on the door on Christmas Day. He would come and visit, carrying gold and frankincense and the other thing. He would come.

Duncan pressed his face into the cushion. He felt his father gently pulling the collection of rubber bands off his wrist.

The next morning he was back home. He opened the eighth door on his advent calendar. A doll – ugh! After lunch, his mother took him swimming. She had threaded the gloves back through his coat-sleeves but he refused to put them on; they flopped at his wrists. 'Next stop, hooliganism!' she said, whatever that meant. 'Glue-sniffing. Truancy. It's all my fault!'

At the pool they had another struggle with his water wings. He said he was too old for them now. She liked him wearing them because it meant he could bob around in the water while she swam to the deep bit, up and down for miles. She said she had to do a unit of exercise a day, which meant twenty minutes. She told somebody on the phone that it was part of her *Cosmopolitan* Shape-Up Plan. 'I'm going to take pride in my body,' she said. 'It's had years of neglect. It's like one of those old churches nobody's been into for years.' She had laughed loudly at this, but he didn't see why it was funny.

He bobbed up and down in the water. A sticking plaster floated nearby. He liked collecting sticking plasters and lining them up on the edge of the pool. In fact he loved everything about the pool. When he came with his parents they used to laugh together and splash each other. They mucked around like children, and the black stuff from his mother's eyes ran down her cheeks. There was a shallow babies' bit and an elephant slide. In the deeper bit a whistle blew and the waves started, which was thrilling. He liked wearing the rubber band with the locker key on it, this made him feel important. There was a machine where you could buy crisps; the bag swung like a monkey along the bar and dropped into the chute. He loved going there. That was why it was so terrible, what happened.

After his mother had swum her unit they got out. She wrapped him in a towel, and he watched her as she stood under the shower, rubbing her head with shampoo. She sang, much too loudly: '*I'm going to wash that man right out of my hair!*' She didn't mind people seeing her bare, either; she was always striding around the changing rooms, wobble-wobble. His dad did too; everything swinging about. When his parents were together, and they all came to the swimming pool, Duncan would run from the men's cubicles to the ladies' ones, depending on which parent was being the least embarrassing. But nowadays he had to stay in one place.

Anyway, this particular day he had got dressed. His mother was drying her hair. In the corner of the changing room he saw something he hadn't seen before: it was a big red plastic thing, on legs, like a crib. He nudged his mum and pointed.

'What's that for?' he shouted.

She switched off the dryer. 'What's what for?'

'That.' He pointed.

'Oh, it's for changing babies,' she said, and she switched on the dryer again.

That night his mum went out and his granny came to babysit. She tut-tutted around the house, as usual. She opened the fridge and wrinkled her nose.

'Jif and a J-cloth,' she said, 'that's all it needs. But they're all too busy nowadays, aren't they? Lord, this yoghurt's covered with mould!' She put all his mum's empty wine bottles in plastic bags and dumped them outside the front door. 'Hope *she* didn't drink all these,' she muttered. Then she sat with him while he ate his supper.

'You've been very quiet,' she said. 'I know what you're thinking about! All the things you'd like for Christmas!'

He didn't reply.

'Come on, poppet,' she said. 'Aren't you going to eat up your lovely fish fingers?'

Later she washed up. Usually the clatter comforted him; Granny putting things in order. Tonight it didn't work. He was thinking about the red plastic crib. Which babies did it change? Any baby that climbed into it? If his mother put him there, what would happen? At school they had taken away the old baby and put in another one. His mother was always changing things. Granny's presents, for instance. Granny gave her clothes and she took them back to Harvey Nichols. 'Eek! What does she want me to look like – Judith Chalmers?' She would come home with something completely different. And only last week she had stared angrily at her bed, as if she had never looked at it before. 'Paisley's so *seventies*!' she had said. She had yanked off the duvet cover and squashed it into a rubbish bag. 'Memories, memories.'

His head spun. When Granny was getting him ready for bed he said: 'Tell me about Jesus in the manger again.'

'I'd read it to you if only I could find a Bible,' she said. She looked through the bookshelves, clicking her tongue. '*The Female Underclass*,' she said. '*Aggression and Gender*. No Bible, honestly! My own daughter!'

Undressing him, she told him the story. He squeezed his eyes shut. 'Virgin Mary . . .' he heard. '. . . wrapped him in swaddling clothes and laid him in a manger . . .'

She took him into the bathroom to brush his teeth. He suddenly saw the carrier bag, from swimming. It sat slumped in the corner, bulging with his damp towel and swimming trunks; the washing machine was broken. The bag had big letters on it: VIRGIN MEGASTORE. He stared at it, hypnotized.

Swaddling clothes . . . Virgin Mary . . . He tried to work it out, but it was all so difficult. He was in bed now, his eyes shut. What was wrapped up in swaddling clothes, lying in the Virgin bag? Did he ever dare unwrap it?

His granny kissed him goodnight. 'Their behaviour beats me,' she murmured. 'Honestly, why don't they grow up?'

'I am growing up,' he said, sleepily.

She laid her cheek against his; he smelt her powder. 'Poor little thing,' she sighed.

In the morning he didn't open the next door in his advent calendar. He didn't want to get to the end. There was something terrible inside the last door, just as there was something terrible inside the Virgin bag.

Granny rang up while he was watching TV. He was watching his video of *The Magic Roundabout*, even though he knew it was babyish. Babyish things made him feel safe.

He heard his mother talking to Granny. '. . . honestly, Ma, the dustmen have just taken away all the bottles I was going to recycle, two months' worth! Haven't you any morals? What's going to happen to the planet?' Her voice lowered. '. . . I know, but I wish you wouldn't interfere. Not in that, either. He's perfectly all right. I'm the one who looks after him all the time, I should know. He's just lost his appetite . . . I know it's all very difficult, you needn't tell *me*, but it's not all my fault, do you know what Alan did last week—'

Duncan climbed to his feet and turned up the sound of *The Magic Roundabout*, very loud.

His mother tried to make him go swimming on Tuesday, after school, but he refused to go. He knew exactly what she was planning. She was going to wrap him up in a towel and put him into the crib. Jesus had no father, just like him. Granny said: 'We're all children of God.'

He heard his mother on the phone, talking to one of her friends. 'I know why Duncan doesn't want to go swimming,' she whispered. 'It's because his father goes and we sometimes see him there. These bloody freelancers, never know where they'll pop up. When he sees his father unexpectedly, he gets really upset.'

It was odd. She never called him 'Dad' any more. She called him 'his father'. It made his dad sound awesome, like somebody in the Lord's Prayer. *Our Father, which art in heaven . . .*

She had got it all wrong, of course, about swimming. Grown-ups got everything wrong. But he couldn't possibly tell her. He started crying, so she took him out to buy a Christmas tree instead. It was much bigger than Dad's. They decorated it with tinsel and bags of chocolate money that made the branches droop, but when she switched on the lights they didn't work. She shouted a rude word. Then she muttered: 'First the washing machine, then the guttering, now the bloody lights. Christ, I need a man!' She looked as if she was about to cry, too. She went to the phone and dialled a number. 'Is Mr Weisman home yet?' she asked. 'I've been phoning him for two days!'

Duncan stopped peeling a chocolate coin. He sat bolt upright. Mr Wise Man?

It was all getting more and more confusing. The next day his dad collected him from school and took him back to his flat. He had put the very small Christmas tree into a flowerpot.

Duncan sat in front of the TV. There wasn't a lot to do in his dad's flat. His dad had bought a box of Snakes and Ladders but they had lost the dice. He pushed his jeep around the carpet for a bit, making noises to encourage himself, but then he stopped. He thought about the Wise Man. He mustn't come! If he came, Christmas would start and it would all be wrong! It was already going horribly wrong. He had to do something about it.

Dad was in the kitchen part of the room, frying sausages. His jacket lay over a chair. Duncan put his hand in the pocket and pulled out his dad's wallet. He wanted to see if his photo was still inside.

There he was. And there was the photo of his mother, holding him when he was a baby. She was smiling. But he wasn't reassured. The room grew smokier. 'Baked beans, or baked beans?' called out his dad.

He pulled out his dad's Access card, and his video club card. Then he pulled out another one. It said: *I would like to help someone live after my death.* He turned the card over. *Kidneys*, it said on the back, *Eyes Heart Pancreas Liver*, it said. *I request, that after my death, any part of my body be used for the treatment of others.*

On Thursday Mr Wise Man still hadn't come. His mother cried: 'My life's going to pieces!'

So was his. When the Wise Man came, he was going to take somebody away. Jesus died on the cross, said Granny, so that the rest of us could live. That's what his dad was going to do; that's why he had the card in his wallet. And then everybody ate him because he was God.

'Why don't you want to go swimming?' asked his mother. 'You used to love it.'

That night he heard her on the phone. 'We've got to settle this, Alan.' Even upstairs, he could smell her cigarette smoke. 'You keep putting it off. What are we going to do about Christmas? Are you going to have him, or me?'

Duncan pulled the duvet over his head. They were going to saw him in half, like a leg of lamb.

The next morning the phone rang. His mother was in the lavatory so he answered it. A voice said: 'Mr Weisman here, chief. Can I speak to your good mother?'

'No!' he shouted, and put the receiver back.

But the Wise Man was going to come. It was Duncan's last day at school and his granny fetched him home. When they opened the door, his mum said: 'Thank God Mr Weisman's coming. He'll be here at six.'

Duncan thought, fast. Then he had an idea. He pulled at his mother's leg. 'I want to go swimming!' he said urgently. 'Let's go!'

And it worked. His mother smiled. 'Darling, I'm so glad!' she said.

Granny said: 'I'll stay here and let Mr Weisman in.'

While they were talking Duncan ran upstairs and dialled his dad's number. He needed to see him, badly. But only the answerphone answered, his dad's voice all stiff and formal, so he left a message. 'Come to the swimming pool. Please!'

In the changing room he scuttled past the crib, fast. And then he was in the water, with his mother. There wasn't pop music today; they were playing 'Rudolph the Red-Nosed Reindeer'. He was bobbing around when the whistle blew and the waves started, tossing him up and down, and suddenly his father was there, his arms outstretched. His parents were shouting at each other but Duncan couldn't hear, there were so many other people in the pool, their voices echoing. They squealed when the waves came, rocking the water and splashing over the sides. Duncan was tossed towards his father, who held him; then he was tossed back to his mother, who pulled him to her. The black stuff was running down her face. Spluttering, he was grabbed by strong arms, then the waves pulled him away.

He was in the changing room now, and his mother was rubbing him dry. She did it so hard it hurt. His dad's voice shouted, from the men's cubicles. 'You can't live without me, Victoria! You know that!'

'Shut up!' she shouted. 'I'm managing perfectly well!'

'You're such a liar!' he shouted. 'I know you inside out!'

'You've never known me! You're too bloody selfish!'

'Me? Selfish?' He bellowed with laughter.

'It takes one to know one!' she shouted.

'I love you!' he shouted.

Duncan cowered; everybody was listening. This was worse than them being bare.

'Look at what it's doing to Duncan!' shouted his dad. 'He doesn't understand. He thinks it's all his fault, he's getting terribly disturbed. He's started wetting the bed again!'

Duncan froze. How *could* his dad say that? He darted out of the cubicle, into the open part. There was a baby lying in the crib; its mother was changing its nappy. He dashed for the exit, but just then his dad appeared, nearly naked. He grabbed Duncan and held him tightly.

Duncan pressed his face against him; he smelt of chlorine.

When they got home Mr Weisman had been. The lights sparkled on the Christmas tree. The washing machine worked; his mother bundled the damp towels into it. She was panting; she seemed out of breath. Later, after supper, she put on her red woolly dress and squirted perfume on her neck. She kept telling Duncan to go to bed, but in a vague way as if she was looking for something.

Later that night his dad came home. Duncan heard his suitcase bumping against the banisters as he came upstairs. Light slid into Duncan's room when he opened the door, just a bit. He stood there for a moment but he didn't come in. The next morning his stripy spongebag was back in the bidet and his computer was back on his desk. On Christmas Eve he helped Duncan open the last door on his advent calendar, and there was the baby Jesus. He had been there all the time.

In fact, his dad didn't just stay for Christmas. He stayed at home for good. When Duncan was older, he sometimes thought of his father's six-month absence, and the way it had ended. And he told himself: the swimming pool wasn't just for changing babies. Not as it turned out. It was for changing grown-ups, too.

Suspicion

He seemed such a normal bloke. That's how they get away with it, I suppose, looking normal. He looked like a real football-playing, I'm-in-sales, make-mine-a-double-scotch sort of bloke. That's what attracted me in the first place. After the waifs and strays I'd been out with he seemed so male. I mean, he actually looked as if he could drive a car.

His name was Kenneth McTurk and I met him when he came in for a glass of guava juice. He'd just been to the acupuncturist upstairs – the café where I work, it's in this building full of ists, reflexologists, aromatherapists, all that alternative stuff that's not so alternative any more since Prince Charles took it up.

He sat at the counter, rubbing his back. 'By Jesus, I feel like a pin-cushion,' he said. 'You seen the size of those needles?'

He had an Irish accent – beguiling, almost female in such a beefy man. He had a ruddy face and sticking-out ears; they gave him a boyish look. He wore a suit – *nobody* wore a suit in our place. He was one of those fidgety men who are always jangling their car keys. He said that he was a martyr to his back, stress-related said his doctor, and why not give acupuncture a whirl? So he had looked it up in the Yellow Pages.

'A load of mumbo-jumbo, my love, if you're asking my opinion,' he said. 'Now would you recommend the carrot cake?' I said it was made with bran. 'I see I've entered a bowel-friendly environment,' he replied. 'I suppose a cheroot is out of the question?'

It was, but the place was empty. So he had a smoke and we introduced ourselves.

'Velda,' he said. 'Now that's unusual.'

'It means wise woman,' I said, and laughed.

The next day, when I was cashing up, he walked in and said he was taking me out for a drink. Well, why not? He made me feel flushed and reckless. As we walked towards his car he stopped at the NatWest, plucked a sprig of fuchsia from its windowbox, and put it in my hair. When we arrived at his car, he blithely removed a 'Doctor on Emergency Call' sticker from the windscreen.

'I know you're not a doctor,' I said. 'What *do* you do?'

'Bit of this, bit of that.' He tapped the side of his nose with his finger. 'Import export.'

Until then I had only seen dodgy men in TV series. I suppose I lived a sheltered existence, me and my cats and the long-running non-event of my love life. Suddenly here I was, sitting in a flash car with an unknown middle-aged man who jumped the lights and filled the air with cheroot smoke. He said the acupuncturist had been a con artist and I said boldly: 'Takes one to know one.'

He laughed and told me about a practical joke he had played on somebody, a bloke he'd once worked with. He had filled the drawers of the chap's desk with water and put some goldfish in them. Did I believe him? Who cares? It was so insanely silly that I fell in love with him, then and there.

He took me to a pub in Kilburn. It was big and noisy. Two fiddlers played, they were called the McDougal

Brothers, and I drank a pint of Guinness – me, Velda, who was usually in bed by ten with a cup of herbal tea. There was a raffle for a fluffy elephant and I didn't want to join in because it was so hideous but Kenneth insisted. 'Fund-raising,' he said.

'Funds for what?'

But he just put his finger on the side of his nose. I hadn't a clue what he was talking about but by then everything was getting swimmy and suddenly there was this furry thing in my arms – not Kenny but the elephant, I had won it – and I was in his car and next thing we were sitting in a restaurant drinking champagne and the next thing I remember it was Kenneth in my arms and my duvet over us and the sound of my cats scratching at the kitchen door where I had shut them away.

A couple of weeks later he moved in. Not that he brought much with him – just a suitcase of clothes. But there he was, a full-grown man, knocking into the furniture and whistling in my bathroom – he even managed to whistle while he shaved; 'My Way' with a buzzing accompaniment. I bought him Typhoo teabags and – proof of my love – bacon for breakfast. I'm a vegetarian, you see. With him in it, six-foot-two, my flat looked stuffy and spinsterly, with its batik hangings and its bowls of pot-pourri, but he said it was so peaceful. He said it was like stepping into another world, a Bedouin tent with just me and him.

'It's a battlefield out there, Velda my love,' he said, lying on the bed with his arms around the elephant. A joss-stick spiralled smoke one side and a cheroot spiralled smoke on the other. 'You've no idea of it.'

He charmed me. He even charmed Mrs Prichard

upstairs, carrying her shopping and flirting with her, though she's eighty-three. He made me feel as if I was the most bewitching woman in the world; my skin blushed, I bloomed for him. He told me I was beautiful, voluptuous, a goddess. He wrote lewd suggestions in the steam on the bathroom mirror. And flowers, oh the flowers! When he arrived late, the nodding heads of them wrapped in fancy paper from the all-night shop in Westbourne Grove.

He often arrived late and left early. Or he would be home for the afternoon and leave after supper. He never got any phone calls and I never met any of his friends, but I didn't mind, he and I were cocooned in ourselves, we had no need of anything. My job at the café was part-time so I fitted in with him. As for his job – well, he was very mysterious about it. He only said it involved a lot of travel and in fact he was away a great deal, days on end sometimes. I wasn't suspicious. Believe it or not, I wasn't even suspicious when I found the handcuffs. Or not for the right reason.

It happened like this. Kenny had been living with me for two weeks and we had just come home from the pictures. I realized I had left my shawl in his car so I found his jacket, which was hanging up in the hallway, and fished for his car keys. In the pocket I felt something heavy, wrapped in a paper bag. I took it out. Just at that moment he came out of the kitchen. I held out the pair of handcuffs and laughed.

'Oh-oh, bondage-time!'

His face reddened. Then he recovered himself and laughed. 'Tie me up!' He shoved a cloth in my hand. 'Here, the killer tea towel! Whip me to a frenzy! I like it, I like it!'

Another odd thing happened that evening. He said he was just popping out for some cheroots. I watched him from the window. Why? I don't know. He crossed the street and walked towards Westbourne Grove. But he stopped at the phone box on the corner, looked around, and went in. I watched him – a small, solitary figure in the illuminated booth. Somebody familiar always shrinks, don't they, when they think they are unobserved. Why was he making a secret phone call? In my area of Bayswater, the phone booths are plastered with cards – *I'm Lorraine, Spank Me! Strict French Lessons!* I remember thinking: suppose he *is* a bondage-freak. That's why he's always popping out. He's ringing up one of them now. Lorraine or someone.

I didn't say anything. He was away too much for me to spoil our short times together by wife-type accusations. The next morning, however, he seemed edgy and abstracted. When I went into the bedroom, after breakfast, he was shoving a pair of muddy trainers into a carrier bag. When he saw me, he stopped, dropped the bag behind the bed and put his arms around me.

'I have to go away for a couple of days,' he said. 'Oh Velda, my lovely, if you knew how much I wished it was you and me alone in the world, far away from all this.'

'From all what?'

'It's dangerous out there, see. A man, he's weak. Maybe he's young and foolish. He makes a mistake maybe once in his life and then he's caught like a fly in a spider's web. They have him there, where they want him. He can run, but he can't hide. He can hide, but he can't run.'

He kissed the tip of my nose and then he was gone, carrier bag and all.

That night there was an explosion in the Territorial Army Barracks in Albany Street, near Regent's Park. Four men were injured – it was a miracle it wasn't more – but half the place was gutted. The IRA claimed responsibility and issued a statement saying it was stepping up its mainland terrorist campaign.

I don't read the newspapers. I'm not a political sort of person. I saw it by chance on the front page of a *Guardian* that somebody had left in the café. Nothing clicked together, not even then. Nothing clicked until the following Thursday.

Kenneth had been back for a couple of days. Was it my imagination or was he changing? He looked fleshier – he was putting on weight. Maybe it was my lentil lasagne. And he snapped at Flapjack, my Burmese, when she was only playing with his shoelaces.

It was early evening and I had to nip out to the shops. Halfway down the street, however, I realized I had forgotten my purse so I went back and let myself into the flat. Kenny was in the bedroom, speaking on the phone. I paused in the hallway.

'Let me speak to Fergus,' he said in a low voice. There was a pause, then he said: 'Fergus, you keep away from that gun, see? Any messing around and I'll be informing the boss. And you know what'll happen to you then, don't you?'

I let myself out of the flat and crept downstairs. I managed to make it to the end of the street and leaned against some railings. My heart hammered against my ribs. How could I have been so stupid? The shock was so great that when I tried to pull the facts together, I had to haul them slowly, as if I were drugged.

The handcuffs. The Republican pub in Kilburn. The

terrorist explosion . . . The long, unexplained absences . . . The phone box and now the threatening telephone call . . .

Funnily enough, I wasn't alarmed, not for myself. In fact, I felt a shameful tingle of excitement. This man I loved was suddenly strange to me. It didn't cross my mind, not yet, that he might be dangerous – that he might be a killer. The whole thing seemed as disconnected and unlikely as some TV drama I happened to have stepped into, the sort of TV drama I never watched anyway, that was happening to someone else.

I was in the late-night supermarket, standing in front of a pork chop. A kidney nestled in the pallid flesh. I thought: I came out to buy some dinner and now a different Kenneth will be eating it. To someone like me a meat counter smells of death; it lurks there, inert, under the cellophane. I knew I mustn't think like this – I mustn't even *start* to think about killing or I wouldn't be able to behave normally when I got home. What was I supposed to be buying anyway? My mind was a blank. Beside me a guy dipped up and down to the beat of his Walkman; a woman shouldered me aside and pulled out a pack of sausages. Trolleys rattled and a tannoy boomed, but it came from a thousand miles away. I had to get through this evening somehow, walk it through like a robot, until tomorrow came, Kenneth left for work and I could start to think clearly.

I went back home and let myself into the flat.

'Light of my life!' He pounced at me from behind and pinioned me against the wall. 'Five minutes you've gone, and it's an eternity!' His breath was hot on my face.

It had been an eternity. I had stepped out of one life and into another. Nothing would be the same, ever again.

It rained in the night. The next morning dawned shiny and innocent, the streets washed clean. I kissed Kenneth goodbye. The puddles winked at me. In the block of flats opposite someone opened a window, flashing a message to me. Or to him? Where was he going?

'Where are you going?' I asked.

'Liverpool,' he said, quick as anything. 'A shipment's coming in.'

From Ireland? I couldn't bear to ask him. By questioning him, I felt it was me who was doing the betraying, not him. Ridiculous, I know.

His hair was slicked back, dark and wet, from the shower. His signet ring caught the sun as he scratched the side of his nose. I put my arms around him and held him tightly; silently I said goodbye to the old Kenneth. I smelt his familiar scent of tobacco and Aramis.

'There, there,' he murmured, 'I'll be seeing you tomorrow.' He disentangled himself, glanced up and down the road and loaded his suitcase into the boot. I tried to help him, but he wouldn't let me and slammed the boot shut. He was slightly breathless.

He drove off and I went inside, slowly. I felt very old. Mrs Prichard, hurrying downstairs, looked as spry as a girl.

'Is he gone, that naughty boy?' she asked, waving the *Daily Express*. 'I was going to tell him his stars.'

That's the only bit *I* used to read, I wanted to reply. The horoscopes. Now I understand why I never looked at the other pages.

'He likes to know it before he flies,' she said. 'These airline pilots are very superstitious.'

Oh Lord, he had lied to her, too.

I closed my front door. My cats pressed themselves against my legs. They pressed against his legs too, they didn't know the difference. I tried to practise my postural meditation but for once I couldn't concentrate. Squatting on the carpet, I stared at myself in the mirror: cloudy black hair, square face. Velda Mathews, aged thirty-one. All these years I had gone to groups and cultivated my inner space, hoping to find something there. Buddhism, I had tried. Psychotherapy, oh years of that. I had sat on beanbags, sobbing on strangers' shoulders and saying I loved them, but in truth it had been one big void. Then along came Kenneth and suddenly I had come alive. Ironic, wasn't it? A man who spent his time blowing people to smithereens.

I switched on the radio. It was tuned, as usual, to Radio 3, but I fiddled around until I found some news.

'. . . a security alert in Central London . . . a soldier was shot dead in North Belfast . . .'

I switched it off, went into the bedroom and opened the wardrobe. His clothes hung there but I couldn't touch them. I didn't want to find anything out. I went to work in a daze and served a customer with gooseberry fool instead of guacamole. Margie, who ran the café, asked if anything was the matter but I didn't tell her because once I put it into words it would become real. Not only would I have to cope with her reaction – she adored crises – but I would have to decide what to do. Kick him out? Tell the police? Betray him, just as he had betrayed me? But maybe he had been protecting me, by his lies. You see, I didn't know how to react. My group told me how to cope with denial and rage and absence of self-worth, but nobody told me how to cope with a murderer. We weren't used to that sort of thing. Parental damage was as far as we got.

He came home the next evening. He looked exhausted. We went to bed and he fell asleep, his leg a dead weight on mine. *It's dangerous, out there.* Down in the street, a police car wailed. *A man, he makes a mistake maybe once in his life and then he's caught.* Maybe he had joined when he was young and foolish, and now he could never escape. He was theirs for life, caught in a spiral of violence.

He turned over, grunting.

'If you're ever in trouble . . .' I murmured.

He sat up. 'And what trouble might that be?'

Down in the street a woman screeched with laughter. A car door slammed. I remembered my suspicions – when was it, only a week ago? If only I could roll back time; if only we could start again from *there*.

He went back to sleep. It was unnerving, this body next to mine.

Suddenly I sat up. Yesterday morning, what had he been hiding from me, in the boot of his car?

I slid out of bed, wrapped myself in my kimono and crept into the hallway. I fished in his jacket pocket. How sharp and cold his keys felt, how solidly knobbly the St Christopher! Actually doing something, rather than har- bouring vague suspicions, is shockingly physical. I went outside. It was freezing.

I unlocked the boot and opened it. Inside, half-hidden by a blanket, was a long, bulky-looking bag. Like a bag for golf clubs, that long. Only I knew there weren't golf clubs inside.

'Can I help you?'

I swung round. A police car had drawn up beside me; I heard the crackling static of a radio.

'Just . . . forgot something in the car,' I stuttered, and slammed the boot shut.

The next morning, at seven thirty, the phone rang. I picked it up.

'Hello?'

There was no answer, just the sound of breathing. Down the line, faintly, I heard the sound of machine-gun fire. A muffled rat-a-tat-tat. Then the receiver was replaced.

Kenneth was sitting up in bed. 'Who was that?' he asked, sharply.

'Wrong number.'

Frying his bacon, half-an-hour later, I tried to be light-hearted.

'I don't know anything about you,' I said.

'And what sort of thing might you be wanting to know, my petal?' His voice was light, too. I felt we were caught in some conspiracy together.

'Anything.' I slid the eggs on to his plate. 'I don't even know your hobbies.'

'Oh, I like to pull the wings off little girls.'

I tried to laugh. 'Well, sports then. What do you play. Tennis, golf?'

He paused. 'Golf, I enjoy. Trouble is, the people you meet.'

What did he mean – British imperialists or something? Anti-republicans? 'Do you have a club?'

'Oh no, I play with my bare hands.'

'I mean, do you belong to a club?'

He tipped the ketchup bottle; red sauce slopped on to his plate. 'The Mountview. Why, my sweetheart?'

When he had gone, I looked up the Mountview Club in the Yellow Pages. It was out in Enfield. I dialled the number.

'Er, I want to leave a message for one of your members,' I said. 'A Mr Kenneth McTurk.'

There was a shuffle of paper at the other end. Somebody was obviously looking at a list. Finally the voice said: 'We have no member of that name.'

That morning explosives were found in a Ford Transit van, parked in Chancery Lane. I read about it in the *Standard*; I read the papers every day now. *Please be vigilant*, said the Head of the Anti-Terrorist Squad. *You, the public, are our eyes and ears.* There had been a spate of kidnappings in Derry, too; the latest had been a local supermarket manager and his wife. Shamefully, I didn't consider the victims in all this or the political rights and wrongs. Love makes us myopically self-absorbed. I just thought: does he really care for me, or is he using me for my flat, a place where he can lie low?

When I got home that evening, he was already there; his car was parked outside in the dark street. I let myself into the flat like a thief, like somebody who didn't belong there – criminality is catching. I paused outside my bedroom door. He was talking on the phone.

'What do you mean, *now*? I can't come now!' His voice was shrill; almost unrecognizable. 'Pipe down, will you! Get a hold on yourself! They'll hear what you're saying!'

I went into the kitchen and stared at the piled-up sink. Ludicrously, I thought: can't even terrorists help with the washing-up? My eyes filled with tears.

'Forgive me, my lovely.'

I jumped. He was standing in the doorway. He looked

terrible. His eyes were bloodshot and his tie was loose, like a drunkard's.

'I have to go out, see.'

'Why do you have to go out?' My voice rose. 'Why can't you tell me? Don't you trust me? Do you think I wouldn't understand?'

'I have no doubt whatsoever, my darling, that you wouldn't understand. Nobody in their sane mind would understand.'

He kissed me and then he left, slamming the door behind him.

I ran downstairs. His car was pulling away from the kerb, its headlight beams weeping in the rain.

At that moment I took a decision, a split-second decision; a cab was passing and I stepped into the street.

'Follow that car!' I said.

The stagey words made the whole thing unreal. I was sucked into the momentum of a thriller. I clutched my handbag to my chest, swaying as we rounded corners, jolting as we shuddered to a stop at intersections. At one point we nearly lost Kenneth, but one of his tail-lights was broken so I could spot him ahead. To calm myself I chanted 'Om, om' but it suddenly seemed silly. Had I shut the front door? Would the cats get out? Had I got enough money for the fare, wherever we were going? The driver said nothing. I watched the sturdy back of his neck; beyond it the slewing wipers and the wobbling blobs of red. They smeared, rhythmically, across the windscreen.

Half an hour passed, maybe more. Then the cab stopped. We were somewhere in the suburbs. Large, Tudor-style houses loomed up on either side. Was this IRA headquarters? I fumbled for the fare; the driver didn't seem the slightest bit curious. Ahead of us Kenneth's car had stopped; its tail-light was extinguished. I saw him climb out, open the boot and pull out the long, heavy bag. He paused in the rain, looked up at one of the houses and walked slowly towards its front door.

I got out of the cab. The driver drove off. A woman hurried past me, her head down. I stopped her.

'Excuse me!' I hissed. 'Who lives there?'

'There?' She looked at the house. 'An estate agent.'

'Estate agent?'

'And his family.' She hurried off. I stood there, sodden.

It's odd, how one reacts in a situation like this. One can't tell beforehand, simply because it never arises. I felt disembodied, floating. Adrenalin fuelled me, like some emergency engine humming into life. I understood what was happening. He was going to kill this estate agent. Or take him hostage.

I ran towards the house. Kenneth had gone in. I rushed round the back, pushing through some wet bushes. From the ground floor came the sounds of gunfire — rat-a-tat-a-tat, machine-gun fire. I tried the kitchen door. It was open. I went in.

Upstairs I heard him shouting, and a woman's voice. 'You bastard!' she cried, over and over. 'You bastard!'

Downstairs the gunfire had stopped. I ran upstairs, two at a time. Light blazed on the landing. I heard their voices through a closed door. I flung it open.

He was standing in the bedroom with a woman. They swung round and stared at me.

'Velda!' he gasped.

'That's *her*?' said the woman. 'What's she doing here?'

My knees turned to water. I sat down, heavily, in a chair. Two boys came into the room; one of them carried a gun.

'Fergus! Dominic!' he said. 'Go back to the lounge, this minute!'

The boys looked at me, their eyes wide, and went out. Clatter-clatter went the gun against the banisters as they trailed downstairs.

The woman sat down on the bed. She was bleached blonde, and very good-looking. 'So that's her,' she said. 'She's a big girl, isn't she?'

There was a silence. Downstairs the TV came on. Kenneth, his face red, fumbled for a cheroot.

'Don't smoke that in here,' she said, 'you know I hate it.' He put the packet back in his pocket. He hung his head, like a small boy in front of a headmistress. She was looking at me with dispassionate interest. 'I didn't know anyone wore kaftans any more.'

'Sally—'

He started to speak but she took no notice. She turned to me. 'You can have him. Do you know, Valerie or whatever it is—'

'Velda.'

'—I've actually been whistling around the house?' She flung herself back on the bed. 'Take him!' She gazed up at the chandelier. 'No more hoovering every day and keeping this huge bloody house nice, not that he'd notice, except he notices when it's not done, *and* trying to run my shop, not that I've had any support in *that* department . . .' Her voice grew dreamy. 'No more having to stop the boys fighting because it might disturb him, and clearing up their stuff but he says they should do it but if they did, it would never get done and then he'd get even more irritable, and letting them watch their ghastly videos . . .'

'I am *here*, you know,' he said.

'And he's getting so *fat*!' she said. 'It must be all those dinners he's eaten twice. First sitting chez moi and second sitting wherever you live.' She raised her head and looked at me. 'You obviously like your food too.'

'There's no need to talk to her like that!' he snapped.

She turned to him. 'I smelt a rat with that sudden interest in golf. You're such a lazy slob. Amazing I didn't guess. Tournaments in St Andrews, weekend championships God knows where. Coming back all muddy and shagged out. In a manner of speaking.' She started to laugh.

I turned to Kenneth. 'I didn't realize they were toy ones. The handcuffs.' I couldn't think of anything else to say.

'Take him!' cried Sally, tears of laughter streaming down her face. 'Take him! Make up your mind!'

A long, long moment passed. Finally, I looked at Kenneth, and made up my mind.

Ta for the Memories

Edith knew nothing about pop music. For a start, she called it pop music. Apparently, you were supposed to call it something else nowadays. Then there was the sight of people at pop concerts, swinging their heads round and round as if they were trying to get a crick out of their neck. Didn't they know how silly they looked? And the noise! Edith had a bicycle and a cat, both virtually silent. The only noise she made was singing in her local choir. Haydn's *Creation* was next on the agenda.

So the name Kenny Loathsome meant nothing to her. The girls in the office moaned. 'You lucky sausage!' said Muriel in Rights. 'You'll meet him! You'll touch him! Don't wash!'

The last book Edith edited had been *Signs and Symbols in Pre-Hellenic Pottery*. That was more her thing. The publishing firm where she worked was a family business, the last of the musty old outfits in Bloomsbury. They were attempting to drag themselves into the nineties – ill-advisedly, Edith thought – by putting some glitz into their list and had signed up this Kenny Loathsome to write his autobiography.

Muriel pointed a trembling finger at her magazine. 'That's him.'

Actually, Edith did vaguely recognize him. She had video-taped a programme about Schopenhauer and got *Top of the Pops* by mistake. With horrified fascination she had watched Kenny Loathsome snarling into a microphone – a tadpole-shaped man with disgusting hair. If *she* went on TV, she would wash her hair first. He was the lead singer, apparently, in a group called The Nipple Faktory. Obviously, spelling wasn't one of their strong points.

'He's had sex with nine hundred women,' breathed Muriel.

'One thousand two hundred,' said Oonagh from Reception.

'Hope they kept their eyes closed,' said Edith, 'and held their noses.'

So that was how she found herself flying to the Côte d'Azur, to the hideaway of a famous pop star. He called it a hideaway, apparently, but you could see it for miles. It was the colour of pink blancmange and was festooned with satellite dishes. A servant-type person ushered her into Kenny Loathsome's den, a dark room lined with antique guns. He sat slumped in a leather chair watching Arsenal play Sheffield Wednesday. For half an hour this was the only information she could prise out of him. When the match was over he bellowed, either with joy or rage, and drained his tumbler of Southern Comfort. She introduced herself.

'I've come to help you write your autobiography.'

'Yeah, darling. Trouble is, I can't remember nothing.'

It was the drugs that had done it. During dinner – caviar, hamburgers and champagne – he itemized the substances he had ingested over the past twenty-five years. He said he had been a walking chemist's lab. 'Acid, speed, coke, methadone, quaaludes, diazepam.'

'My head's reeling,' she said.

'Not as much as mine was, darling.'

'What was the point of taking an upper if you were just about to take a downer?'

He said they had totally nuked his brain and the past was all a blur. The next afternoon, when he emerged blinking into the sunshine, she saw that under the hair, his face was ravaged by the years of abuse. Not unattractively, actually. She had always been drawn to older men, but in the past they had been the professorial type. Back in her room she removed her glasses and put in her contact lenses.

They got down to work – well, she did. She took out her tape recorder and prodded him with questions – his childhood in Accrington, his spell as a delivery driver for a firm of wholesale butchers. 'Why are you called Loathsome?' she asked.

'Dunno.'

'Did your mum call you that and you didn't know what it meant?'

He paused and nodded. 'Except I didn't have a mum. It was me foster-parents.'

'Poor Kenny.' She thought of her sunlit childhood in Oxfordshire, Labradors and sisters and Marmite sandwiches. No wonder he didn't want to remember.

He sat there, his face furrowed with concentration. 'Think!' she ordered. 'Martial said "To be able to enjoy one's past life is to live twice."'

'Martial? What team does he play for?'

'You must remember something. What sort of delivery van did you drive?' she asked. 'Who were your friends at school?'

He spoke stumblingly. After her second glass of Rémy Martin she said recklessly: 'If you can't remember, make it up!' She was an *editor*. What was happening to her?

He kept depraved, nocturnal hours, getting up at noon and staying up till late. At three in the morning, yawning, she switched off the tape recorder. 'Could you ever sing at all? Did you have any talent whatsoever?'

He shook his head.

'Funny, isn't it,' she said. 'You can't sing and you're a millionaire. I've got a beautiful voice and I'm broke.'

He laughed his gravelly laugh, choking in his cigarette smoke. 'And who's the happiest little camper?'

A week went by and he didn't make a pass at her. What was wrong? She put up her hair but he didn't seem to notice; her eyes stung from her blithering contact lenses. She wasn't sure she wanted him to try but her pride was at stake. What was she going to tell them back in the office? He seemed to live in a state of amiable, alcoholic stupefaction. Whilst she transcribed her tapes, he watched satellite game shows or spent hours on the phone to his business manager. He was suing his band for some recording deal (note that she now said 'band' not group). He tussled with faxes about alimony suits and palimony suits. All the worry had given him a peptic ulcer. No, nothing happened. The most exciting event in her bedroom was when she dropped a contact lens and, blindly searching for it, knocked against the panic button and summoned a vanload of *gendarmes* from Nice.

The only things he really loved were his vintage cars. He took her into his triple garage where they slumbered under dustsheets. 'Feel that bodywork!' he said, stroking the sleek flank of an Alvis or something. 'She's, like, responsive, know what I mean? She don't want nothing from me – like, me house in Berkshire and half me assets. That's why I love her, see?' He sighed. 'Dynamite when she's warmed up. 'Cept I've lost me driving licence.'

'You could always get a bike,' said Edith briskly. She was beginning to suspect that his legendary conquests were as much a fabrication as the past they had been cobbling together in the gloom of his den.

In two weeks they were finished. As she waited for her taxi he ruffled her hair. 'Take care, darling,' he said. 'See you around.' Around where? Nowhere *she* went.

She arrived back in London looking radiant. That fortnight had changed her in a way nobody could guess. At the rehearsal that night her voice soared. Next day she met a breathless reception in the office.

'Your tan! You look great without your glasses! Go on, tell us. What happened? Did you . . .?'

Edith smiled mysteriously. She dumped her transcripts on her desk. She looked at the heap of paper. She had given him a past; she had created it for him. He was grateful to her and in a curious way she was grateful to him. So why couldn't he create a past for her? For didn't Alexander Smith say, 'A man's real possession is his memory. In nothing else is he rich, in nothing else is he poor' (*Dreamthorp* 1863)?

'Oh, it was extraordinary all right.' She sipped her Nescafé, gazing at the pairs of round eyes. She was Scheherazade, she was all-powerful. 'He was even better than all the stories.'

'How? What did he do? Did he, you know . . .?'

She nodded, she sipped, she took her time. 'We stayed up all night. We didn't get up till lunchtime.'

'What did he do?'

'He stroked my flanks, his eyes full of desire. He

murmured, "How responsive you are . . . when you're warmed up, you're dynamite!" '

They sighed, like a breeze through pine trees.

'We went up to my room. Our lovemaking was so intense that we rolled off the bed and I hit his panic button . . . half the Nice *gendarmerie* arrived . . . As George Dennison Prentice said—'

'Who?'

'In his *Prenticeana*: "Memory is not so brilliant as hope, but it is more beautiful, and a thousand times as true." '

She wasn't sure about this, but they didn't seem to notice.

Soon after that the firm was bought by a multi-national media conglomerate which owned six satellite TV stations and Edith was made redundant. Her tan had long since faded. She went to work for a professor of Middle English who was writing a book called *Courtly Love: Legend and Myth*. Which had she created – legend or myth? Did she actually know, or care? She only knew she was grateful to Kenny Loathsome and he would never know why. For he had made her happy with her two rooms in Peckham High Street, and besides, it was simpler to be loved by her cat.

The next September his book was published. She heard he was doing a signing in Harrods so she went there and queued. It was all women, nudging and giggling. When she finally got to his table he didn't recognize her. She knew he wouldn't. His head was bent down as he wrote, laboriously. She noticed, for the first time, that he was thinning on top.

'What shall I write, love?' he asked, without looking up.

She smiled, and pointed to the empty page. 'Just write "Ta for the memories." '

Stopping at the Lights

I saw Scottie today. I was stopped at some traffic lights and I saw his little face, quite clearly. When he grinned, that's when I knew. But there were cars behind me, honking.

I've still got the bit of paper from his dad. It's somewhere, I know it is. Tonight I'm going to have a really good look. Wigan, I think he's gone. I'm meeting this bloke tonight, 7 p.m. outside Garfunkel's. He's from Computer Dateline, so I bet I'll be home early. I'll look then.

Off and on all day I've been thinking about him. Scottie, I mean. He was such a gorgeous kid. Ginger hair, freckly nose. Racing around going vroom-vroom. He arrived with his mum four years ago and they moved into Trailer Three. They didn't have a car; they must have walked from the bus stop with their suitcases, the wind blowing off the fens like knives. His mum, Janine, was very young but she always wore high heels. Mottled, bare legs, but always a pair of slingbacks. Ankle chain, too. Looking at her face, you wouldn't think she was a goer. Mousy little thing, undernourished. It was like all the vibrancy had drained into her footwear. And into her son; he was bouncing with life.

I never knew where they came from, but that wasn't so unusual in those days. My husband, Jim, asked no questions. He didn't ask *me* many questions, either. To tell the truth, he didn't talk much at all, except to his budgies. He bred pieds and opalines; he played them Radio 1. He stood in their aviary for hours, squirting his champion hens with plume spray.

Graceland, that's what our place was called. After The King, of course. It was a little bungalow outside Spalding. There were ploughed fields either side, as far as you could see. It was dead flat. The road outside ran straight as a ruler. We had half an acre out the back, conifers fencing it in, and it was there that the trailers were parked. Seven of them. At night you could see the seven blue glows from their TVs. Sometimes, when I was feeling fidgety, I'd walk around at night; I could follow the story in *Miami Vice*, the actors mouthing at me.

I could hear the sneezes, too; the walls were that thin. And the rows, of course. There were always people coming and going, cars starting up in the middle of the night. That's why Jim insisted on rent in advance, and deposits on the Calor gas cylinders. Our tenants told me such stories about their lives and I always believed them. Mr Pilcher, who said he was just stopping for a week or so while a loan came through from the Chase Manhattan Bank. Mr Carling, who said the girl he was living with was his wife, though I heard her, quite clearly once, call him 'Dad'. The bloke who said he was a Yemeni prince before they took him back to the hospital. Sometimes the police arrived, Sheba barking, blue lights flashing around our lounge. When Mr Mason did a flit, for instance. He told me he owned a copper mine in Cameroon but when they opened up his trailer it was full of these videos. I nicked one; I thought it might re-activate our sex life, but I just got the giggles and Jim was shocked. He was much older than me, you see; he liked to believe I was innocent. He wouldn't listen to those stories of Elvis getting bloated either. Who was I, to tell him the truth? I was in a real mess when he took me in, he was ever so good to me. I loved Jim, I really did, though I did behave badly on occasions. But he always took me back, no questions asked. He didn't want to hear.

Janine was running away from something, I could tell, because she never got any letters. Nobody knew she was there. But then nobody knew that most of our tenants were there. It was as if we didn't exist.

'Know what we are?' I said to Jim one night. 'Lincolnshire's answer to the Bermuda Triangle. We're the place people disappear to.'

We were playing Travel Scrabble; he was trying to enlarge his vocabulary. 'FYRED', he put down, smoke wreathing up between his fingers. He had been a heavy smoker since he was fourteen, and ran away to join the Wall of Death.

'It's not Y,' I chortled, 'it's I.'

'I know it's you,' he said, stroking my cheek with his nicotine-stained finger. 'Every morning, I can't believe my luck.'

After that, I hadn't the heart to correct him.

Janine was a hopeless mother. At that period there happened to be no other kids around; Scottie was bored, but I never saw her playing with him. She sat on the steps of her trailer, painting her toenails and reading the fiction pull-outs in women's magazines. Sometimes she tottered up the road in her high heels and stopped at the phone box. Once she dyed a whole load of clothes mulberry and hung them up to dry; they flapped in the wind like whale skins. She hadn't a clue about cooking; then neither had I. Sometimes, suddenly, she decided to make something impossible like angel cakes. 'Can I borrow a recipe book?' she'd say, but I only had the manual that came with my microwave. Domesticity wasn't our *forte*. But surely, I thought, if *I* had a kid I'd be better at it?

Scottie liked wandering into our bungalow. He liked tapping on the aquarium and making the guppies jump. He liked inspecting Jim's trophies from the Cage Bird Society. He liked sitting on my knee, pulling bits of fluff out of my sweater and telling me stories. 'My dad's an airline pilot,' he said one day. The next time his dad would be a champion boxer. I'd be lying under my sun lamp and there he would be, staring at me with that clear, frank look kids have.

'Why're you doing that?' he said.

'Got to be ready for when the limo arrives,' I said, my eyes closed behind my goggles. 'It's a stretch, see. Cocktail cabinet and all. Got to be ready for Tom Cruise.'

One day he came in when Jim had got dressed up in his Elvis gear. It was the white satin outfit – slashed shirt, rhinestones, the works. Jim was going to the Elvis Convention in Coventry. I was embarrassed – I was always embarrassed when Jim looked like that – but Scottie didn't mind. Besides, he was togged up too, in his cowboy suit. I looked at them in their fancy dress: the six-year-old Lone Ranger and the fifty-year-old Elvis with his wizened, gypsy face and bowed legs.

'My dad's a famous pop singer,' said Scottie.

'Is he now?' asked Jim, inspecting himself in the mirror. He combed back his hair to cover his bald patch.

'He's so famous I'm not allowed to say his name,' said Scottie. 'My dad's got a Gold Disc.'

'Know how many he's got?' Jim pointed to the Elvis

medallion on the wall. 'Fifty-one. The most awards to an individual in history. Fifty-one Gold Discs.'

I laughed. 'Know what Jim's got? A slipped disc.'

They both swung round and stared at me. I blushed. I hadn't meant to say that; it had just popped out. Jim turned away. He knelt down and adjusted Scottie's bootlace tie.

I tried to make it better. 'He got it on the Wall of Death,' I said. 'Riding the motorbikes. You know he worked on it? He was the champion for years. They went all over – Strathclyde, Farnham. Till he did his back in.'

Neither of them replied. Jim was kneeling beside Scottie, re-buckling his holster belt. 'Wrong way round, mate,' he said.

Eight months passed. Scottie didn't go to school. Sooner or later, I thought, somebody in authority was going to catch up with him and his mother. She looked restless, laying out Tarot cards on her steps and then suddenly sweeping them all into a pile. Sometimes she tottered up the road and just stood there at the bus stop, looking at the timetable. I dreaded Scottie going. I loved having him around, even though he got up to all sorts of mischief. One day I caught him opening the aviary door. Luckily the budgies just sat there on their perches, the dozy buggers. They were that dim. God knows what Jim used to find to say to them.

At our place, see, people came and went; they never stayed for long. Eight months was about the limit, for us. I remember one evening, when I was waiting for my high-lights to take – I was wearing one of those hedgehog caps – I remember saying to Jim: 'It's like, this place, we're like traf-fic lights. People just stop here for a while, you never know where they've been or where they're going. The lights turn green and whoosh! They fuck off.'

I think he replied but I couldn't hear, the rubber cap was over my ears, but it was true. We were just a stopping place at some dodgy moment in people's lives, people who were trying to make it to London one day, when their luck changed. Or maybe they were escaping from London, from something in their past, and they fetched up with us. I had a friend in London, Mandie; she and I had this dream of setting up our own little hairdressing business one day.

People came and went, and there Jim and I were, grounded on East Fen Road with our broken cars. Jim had these cars out in the front yard, you see – Cadillacs and things, Pontiacs, American cars, the sort you saw in films with Sandra Dee in them, and despite his arthritis he spent all day underneath them, tinkering with their innards, while his beloved country and western songs played on his portable cassette recorder.

Scottie liked to sit in the cars too. He would sit there for hours, waggling the steering wheel and making humming noises through his lips. He was in a world of his own, he was going anywhere in the world. When he climbed out he wiped his hands on his jeans, like Jim wiped his hands on his overalls when they were greasy; his face had that set, important look blokes have when it's a job well done, that nobody else would understand.

In July there was a heatwave. Janine grew jittery, like a horse smelling a thunderstorm. I woke up one night and saw her standing in the dark, ghostly in her white nightie against the solid black of the cypress trees. The moon shone on her upturned face.

The next morning it was very hot. There was a tap on my back door and there she stood, thin and pale in her halter-neck top. She never got tanned, even in that heat, and even though I had offered her unlimited sessions under my lamp. Her face was tight; just for a moment I thought that something terrible had happened.

She said: 'It's Scottie's birthday today and he's set his little heart on meringues.'

'Why didn't you tell me? I want to get him a present!'

'Is Jim going into Spalding? He could give me a lift and I'll buy some.'

But Jim had removed the carburettor from the Capri, our only roadworthy car; bits of dismembered metal lay all over the yard. We were marooned.

So we decided to have a go at cooking the meringues ourselves. I phoned up my friend Gloria, who was trained in catering; she did the lunches at the King's Head, and she told me the recipe. Egg whites, icing sugar, easy-peasy but keep the oven really low, Mark One.

Easy-peasy it wasn't. Janine had run out of Calor gas, see, so we whisked up the egg whites and put them on a baking tray in my own oven. Just then we heard a bellow from Trailer One. Mr Parker's TV had gone dead. He used to sit in there all day watching TV, and it was in the middle of Gloria Hunniford when the electricity went off. We were always having power cuts.

Nobody else was home that day except Mr Parker. We couldn't use his Calor gas cooker. I'd only been in his trailer the once and, to put it mildly, hygienic wasn't the first word that sprang to mind. Besides, he was always trying to lift my skirt with his walking stick.

So know what I did? I put the tray of meringues into the Ford Capri. It was at least 120 degrees in there. I put the baking tray on the back seat and closed the door. 'Aren't I a genius?' I said, polishing an imaginary lapel. 'I'm wasted here.'

We suddenly got the giggles. Even Jim joined in.

'One oven, fully MOT'd,' I said.

'It's Meals on Wheels,' said Jim.

'Change into fourth,' said Janine, 'to brown it nicely on top.'

Jim was chuckling so much that he started one of his coughing fits. Scottie jumped up and down. Sheba's chain rattled as she ran this way and that, suddenly sitting down and thumping her tail.

While the meringues were cooking in the car I went indoors, to find Scottie a present. I went into the bedroom. All my soft toys were there, heaped up on the bed – teddies, rabbits, the giraffe from my twenty-first. I liked to cuddle them at night. I picked up Blinge, my koala bear, and paused. It was as if I was seeing them for the first time. They made me feel awkward, as if I was intruding on myself. They were too babyish for Scottie.

Just then Jim came in. He had recovered from his coughing fit and he was mopping his forehead. He opened the wardrobe and looked in. He always took his time. Then he took out his cowboy hat.

It was still wrapped in plastic. You should have seen it: palest tan, with a woven suede band around the brim. The genuine article. He had bought it at a country and western event in Huddersfield and it had cost a fortune.

'Oh Jim,' I breathed.

'Got any wrapping paper?' he asked.

We had a wonderful party, the four of us. Looking back,

maybe we all felt that something was about to happen. At the time I just thought it was the rush you get with a birthday, the jolt it gives you. The fridge had rumbled back to life and we drank cans of Budweiser and a bottle of German wine. Janine and Jim, who had hardly spoken all those months, even danced together to Tammy Wynette, crooning the soppy lyrics. Jim was supposed to be off the booze, but to tell the truth it improved him. Janine's sallow face was flushed. I danced with Scottie, the cowboy hat slipping over his nose. In the middle we suddenly remembered our meringues. We rushed out and opened the back door of the Capri. They hadn't cooked; they had just sort of subsided. It didn't matter. We gave them to Sheba, our canine dustbin.

When the sun went down we sat on the back porch. Janine put her arm around her son and squeezed him. She wasn't usually demonstrative.

'You're a big boy now,' she said, 'you're the man of the family.'

'He's not big,' I said. 'He's only a kid.'

She squeezed him tighter. 'You'll look after me. You'll see it's all OK.'

'At seven?' I asked. 'Give him a chance!'

There was a silence. From the trailers came the murmur of TVs, the rising laughter of a canned audience. Beyond the bungalow, we heard cars whizzing past on the road. Where were they going?

Jim spoke. He said: 'I wish to God I'd had a son.'

That was the first and last time he ever spoke of it.

The next morning I was standing in the kitchen, looking at the bowl of egg yolks. Six egg yolks; what was I supposed to do with them? I was standing there when the phone rang.

A woman's voice asked: 'Is there a J. Maddox at that address, please?'

'Nobody of that name,' I replied. It was so hot that the receiver stuck to my hand.

'Are you sure about that? Janine Maddox?'

I paused. Janine's surname was Smith. That's what she had told us, anyway. We got a lot of Smiths.

Something in the woman's voice made me wary. 'Sorry,' I said, 'nobody of that name here.'

A fly buzzed against the window pane. Outside, in the yard, Scottie was sitting in the Chevrolet. It was his favourite. I could just see the top of his head, at the wheel. Jim had managed to get the electrics working and Scottie was trying out the indicators. First the left one winked: that way it was London. Then the right one: that meant somewhere else, somewhere beyond my calculations. Somewhere only Scottie knew.

I suddenly felt sad. I went out the back. Janine had washed her hair. She sat on the steps of her trailer, her hair wrapped in a towelling turban, smoking. For once there was no sign of a magazine. I realized for the first time that she was ever so young – twenty-two, maybe. Twenty-three. Younger than me. I realized that I hardly knew anything about her.

'Someone just phoned,' I said, 'asking about you.'

Her head jerked up. 'Who was it?'

'A woman,' I replied. 'It's all right. I said I didn't know you.'

She looked down at her feet. They were bare today, but her scuffed white slingbacks were lying on the grass nearby. When her toes were squashed into them, Scottie said they looked like little maggots.

She blew out smoke, shrugging her bony shoulders. 'Thanks,' she said.

There was a thunderstorm that night. I lay next to Jim, listening to his wheezing breaths. His lungs creaked like a door, opening and closing. My koala, Blinge, was pressed between us; my giraffe, Estelle, lay on the other side. She took up as much room as another person. I could feel her plush hoof resting against my thigh.

Outside, the sky rumbled. It sounded like furniture being shifted. It sounded like bulky objects being dragged across tarmac. I lay there drowsily. I've always loved thunderstorms; when I was little I used to crawl into bed with my mum and smell her warm body smells.

Maybe, in fact, that noise *was* something being moved. At our place, things were often shifted at night. The thunder cracked. I touched Blinge's leather nose. 'It's all right,' I whispered, 'it's nothing.' I ran my finger over his glass eye; there was only one left. 'I'm here.'

Jim stirred in his sleep. He wheezed, and then there was a silence. It went on for an alarmingly long time. I held my breath, willing the noises to start again.

Finally they did; the creaking wheezes. I wrapped my arm around his gaunt chest. He muttered something in his sleep; I couldn't catch the words. Then he said, quite distinctly: 'You've got your life waiting.'

The next morning Janine and Scottie had gone. Cleared out. Their trailer was empty. We never knew who had come to collect them, moving their belongings in the night, or where they had gone. All that remained were small mementoes of Scottie: his sweet wrappers, swept into a corner of the trailer – Janine was surprisingly tidy, she wasn't like me in that respect. A criss-cross of knife marks in the trunk of one of the cypress trees, as if he were going to start a game of noughts and crosses, and hadn't found anybody to play them with.

Not long after that, a few months in fact, they demolished our place to build an out-of-town shopping mall. A socking great thing, with an atrium – they're all the rage.

Our property, where we lived, that's where the access road is now. They've put up traffic lights, too, it's that congested. So I was proved right. Graceland, and its accompanying trailer park, was just a brief stopping place for all concerned.

I got a job at The Rushy Shopping Experience. Jim was in hospital by then, and I visited him in the evenings, en route to my flat above one of Spalding's hot spots, Paradise Video Rentals. Sitting beside my storage heater I grieved for my husband, whilst the local ravers visited the premises below, hiring videos with Bruce Willis in them. The manager, Keith, watched the latest releases all evening, gunfire erupting through my carpet. It was as if Scottie was downstairs, shooting everything in sight. Then the shop went quiet, and I was alone. I thought of Jim, wheezing beside me in the night. I thought of him more than he ever believed.

I'll tell you about my job. I stood under the atrium bit, glass arches above me as high as a cathedral. One side of me there was a Next; the other side there was a Body Shop. It was nice and warm, that was something. Canned music played, to put people into the mood. It never rained there, and the wind never blew like knives. They had invented new street names and put up the signs: Tulip Walk, Daffodil Way. That was because Spalding is famous for bulbs.

I had to wear: Item One – a mobcap. Item Two – a gingham apron. The first day I felt a right prat. I stood at a farm cart in the middle of the mall, selling Old Ma Hodge's Butterscotch Bonbons. They were packaged in little cardboard cottages, with flowers printed on them. Actually, the bonbons were made in a factory in Walsall but who was I to tell? Maureen, who became my friend, she stood at an adjacent cart selling Country Fayre Pot-Pourri. Know them? Those things full of dead petals nobody knows what to do with. Both enterprises were leased on a franchise basis to a man we never saw.

I only worked there for a year, while Jim was holding on for longer than anyone had expected. He had always been stubborn. Now he couldn't speak so well, he suddenly seemed to have a lot to say. On my visits he told me more than I had heard in five years of marriage to him. It was mostly about his early days in children's homes. He spoke in a rush, kneading my fingers.

At work I re-arranged my wares, stacking up my toffee cottages and signalling by semaphore to Maureen, who was going through a divorce. She crouched behind her cart reading a book called *Life Changes – a User's Guide*. She said we were in the same boat, but I didn't agree.

I never knew what the weather was like outside, so I can't recall what season it was when the man came in. He wore a two-tone turquoise anorak, so maybe it was winter. He looked lost; he didn't look as if he had come in to do any shopping. We didn't get many single blokes there, except at Discount Digital Tectonics; most blokes were simply being towed along by their wife and kids.

I saw him approaching Maureen, at the next cart. She flirted with him and flashed me a glance. A man! He spoke to her for a moment, then she pointed to me. He came over.

'Douglas McLaughlan,' he said, extending his hand. He was a beefy bloke, not unattractive. Ginger hair and twinkly eyes. Sort of jaunty. Despite the name, he had a London accent. 'The charming young lady over there thought you might be able to help me.' He cleared his throat. 'I believe you have connections with a caravan park hereabouts.'

'Me and my husband ran it,' I said. 'It was right here, where you're standing. But they knocked it down to build this.'

He paused, taking this in. 'Ah,' he said. He offered me a small cigar. A woman passed, pushing a pair of twins in a double buggy. A group of schoolgirls came out of the Body Shop, linking arms. 'I'm looking for a young lady called Janine,' he said. Then he added casually: 'And her little lad.'

It was then that I realized. I looked at him, recognizing the likeness. The ginger hair, of course. He had Scottie's freckles, too, and his jutting lower lip. Scottie's lip had that determined look when he was concentrating on his driving.

'I'm sorry,' I said, 'I haven't a clue where they've gone.'

He smoked in silence for a moment.

'I'm sorry,' I said again. I felt awkward, and re-arranged the cottages.

'Had to do a bit of travelling,' he said, 'what with one thing and another. Thought I'd found them this time. Thought I'd hit the jackpot.'

I looked up. 'He was a gorgeous kid.'

'He was?'

I nodded. The man took out a piece of paper and wrote

something down. 'If you hear anything . . .' He said something about going to Wigan. Then he handed the paper to me. 'Funny old business, isn't it?'

We stood there for a moment. Then he pointed, with his thumb, at the little cardboard cottages. Sometimes, when I was bored, I arranged them into streets like a real village. He pointed at the display trays featuring the smiling face of Old Ma Hodge in her broderie anglaise bonnet.

'Don't believe a word of it myself,' he said. 'Do you?'

I drive a Sunbeam Alpine now; it's a collector's item. First thing I did, when I came to London, was learn to drive. I whizz all over London, fixing people's hair in their own homes. I started on my friend Mandie's hair, and some of the blokes at the club where she works, and the word got round. I'm quite good, you see. I tell my new clients that I trained at Michaeljohn and I believe it myself now. Jim believed he worked on the Wall of Death even though he only drove the equipment lorry. His real name was Arnold, in fact, but he re-christened himself after Jim Reeves, another of his heroes. I only learnt this near the end. With all the harm in the world, what's the harm in that? Scottie never knew his father; he can believe anything.

I was thinking this today, because I saw him. I told you, didn't I? I saw Scottie when I was sitting at the lights.

It was at a junction leading into the Euston Road. These two boys were there, teenagers really, washing windscreens. They started on mine before I could stop them. There was a lot of splashing and lather. I think they liked the car; you don't see many Sunbeams around nowadays. Anyway, I sat there, flustered, rooting around for a 50p piece.

They did it really thoroughly, there was foam all over the place. Then suddenly, as the lights changed, the windscreen was wiped clear and I saw his face. He was wearing a denim jacket and a red T-shirt; there were pimples on his chin, as well as freckles. I only realized who he was after I had wound down the window and passed him the coin. 'Cheers,' he said. His piping voice had broken.

The cars behind me were blaring their horns. I had to move on. I was helpless in the three lanes of traffic, like a stick in a rushing current, there was a socking great lorry thundering behind me.

It took me a while to get back to where I'd begun. It was the same place, I know it was – big office block one side, church the other, covered with plastic sheets and scaffolding. It was the same place, all right. But the boys had gone.

Not a trace. They must have picked up their bucket and gone. There was nothing left except some damp patches on the tarmac.

Gentlemen always sleep on the damp patch. I suddenly thought of Jim, and how he winced when I said something crude like that. I thought of how he had been a gentleman all his life, with nobody to tell him how.

The lights changed to green. I thought of how he never blamed me for the one thing I couldn't give him. Then the chorus of horns started up behind me, and I had to move on.

How I Learnt to be a Real Countrywoman

We were sitting in the kitchen, opening Christmas cards. There was one from Sheila and Paul, whoever they were, and one from our bank manager, and one from my Aunt Aurora which had been recycled from the year before. The last one was a brown envelope. Edwin opened it.

'My God!' he said. 'These bureaucrats have a charming sense of timing.' He tugged at his beard – a newly acquired mannerism. Since we had moved to the country he had grown a beard; it made him look like Thomas Carlyle. I hadn't told him this because he would think I was making some sort of point.

The letter was from our local council, and it said they were going to build a ring road right through our local wood.

Now Bockham Wood wasn't up to much, but it was all we had. It was more a copse, really, across the field from our cottage. Like everything in the country it was surrounded by barbed wire, but I could worm my way through with the children, and amid acres of ploughed fields it was at least somewhere to go, and from which we could then proceed home again. Such places are necessary with small children (eight, six and three).

It was mostly brambles, and trees I couldn't name because I had always lived in London. There was a small, black pond; it smelt like damp laundry one has forgotten about in the back of a cupboard. Not a lot grew in the wood, except Diet Pepsi cans and objects which my children thought were balloons until I distracted their attention. But I loved it, and now I knew it was condemned I appreciated its tangled rustlings, just as one listens most intently to a person who is going to die.

'A two-lane dual carriageway!' said Edwin. 'Right past our front door. Thundering pantechnicons!' This exploded from him like an oath. It *was* an oath. He went off to work, and every time the kids broke something that morning, which was frequently, we cried 'Thundering pantechnicons!' But that wasn't going to keep them away.

We live in a pretty, but not pretty enough to be protected, part of Somerset. People were going to campaign against this ring road, but the only alternative was through our MP's daughter's riding school, so there wasn't much hope.

That afternoon I drove off to look for holly. When you live in the country you spend your whole life in the car. In London, of course, you simply buy holly at your local shops, which is much better for the environment. I spent two hours burning up valuable fossil fuels, the children squabbling over their crisps in the back seat, and returned with only six sprigs, most of whose berries had fallen off by the time we had hung them up.

This was our first Christmas in the country, the first of our new pure life, and I was trying to work up a festive spirit unaided by the crass high-street commercialism that Edwin was so relieved to escape. Me too, of course.

Have you noticed how dark it gets, and how soon, in the country? When I returned home our wood was simply a denser clot against the sodium glow of our local town, the one whose traffic congestion was going to be eased at our expense. This time next Christmas, I thought, the thundering pantechnicons will be rattling our windowpanes and filling our rooms with lead pollution. It will be just like Camden Town all over again, but without the conversation.

That was what I missed, you see. Edwin didn't because he has inner resources. He's the only person I have ever met who has actually read *The Faerie Queene*. He has a spare, linear mind and fine features; nobody would ever, ever think of calling him Ed. When we lived in London, in Camden Town, he taught graphics. But then his art school was dissolved into another one and he lost his job. The government was brutish and philistine and London was full of fumes, so he said we should move to the country and I followed in the hot slipstream of his despair.

'Look at the roses growing in our children's cheeks!' he cried out, startling me, soon after we moved.

It was all right for him. He had people to talk to. He became a carpenter – sorry, Master Joiner – and he worked with two men, all of them bearded. The other two were called Piers and Marcus; they were that up-market. They toiled in a barn, looking like an illustration in my old *Golden Book of Bible Stories*, while Fats Waller played on their cassette recorder. They made very expensive and uncomfortable wooden furniture. Thank goodness we couldn't afford it. It was Shaker-style, like the furniture in *Witness*, which I had already rented three times from our visiting video van because all his other films were Kung Fu. The van came on Wednesdays and its driver, an ex-pig-farmer with a withered arm, was sometimes the only adult I spoke to all day, unless someone came to buy our eggs, which was hardly ever.

I talked to the hens, of course, and to the children. I had also become a secret addict of *Neighbours*, which ended just before Edwin arrived home each day, though he probably heard its soppy theme tune as he took off his bicycle clips. I never dreamed I would work out who all the characters were, they all looked the same, pan-sticked under the arc lights with their streaky perms, but to my shame I did, and worse, I minded. I even hummed its tune when I was standing at the sink, digging all the slugs out of our organic vegetables.

Perhaps, I thought, if I joined the anti-road campaign I could meet intelligent people like Jonathon Porritt. Perhaps they didn't all live in NW1. Most of them seemed to; that was the trouble. I missed Camden Town, where everyone worked in the media. At the children's primary school, where they had cutbacks, parents donated scrap paper and they were always things like shooting scripts for *The South Bank Show*. I used to read them, on the other side of the children's drawings, so I could startle Edwin when we were watching TV and I knew what Leonard Bernstein was going to say. Then there was the time when I could tell him who did the murder in a Ruth Rendell book, because I had found the last page in our local photocopier. Edwin thought all this was febrile, but Edwin had inner resources. I only had the children. You can't have both.

And then, on Boxing Day, I had a brainwave.

It was freezing outside and the cat had had an accident in front of the Aga. Well, not an accident; she just hadn't bothered to go outside. Edwin was clearing it up with some newspaper when he stopped, and read a corner.

'Listen to this,' he said. 'Leicester County Council is spending £19,000 on four underpasses, specially constructed for wildlife.'

At the time I wasn't listening. I was throwing old roast potatoes into the hen bucket and working out how long it had been since Edwin and I had made love.

'It's to save a colony of great crested newts,' he said.

We hadn't even on Christmas night, after some wonderful oak-aged Australian Cabernet Sauvignon. The last time had been Thursday week, when we had been agreeing how awful his mother was. This always drew us close. For such a pure-minded man he could get quite bitchy, when we talked about her, and this invigorated us. We had one or two such mild but reliable aphrodisiacs. Usually, however, our feet were too cold, or one of the children suddenly woke up or we had just been reading something depressing about the hole in the ozone layer.

Then I thought about the campaign, and as he started washing the floor, I caught up with what he had said about the newts.

It was such a simple idea, so breathtakingly simple that my legs felt boneless and I had to sit down.

I didn't know much about natural history when all this happened, last Christmas. I was brought up in Kensington and spent my childhood with my nose pressed against shop windows, first toys then bikes then clothes. Unlike Edwin, I have always been an enthusiastic member of the consumer society. If a bird was brown and boring, I presumed it was a sparrow. Frogs were simply pear-shaped diagrams of reproductive organs which we sniggered over in biology lessons.

Then Edwin and I married and we went to live in Camden Town. Its streets were be-dimmed with sulphuric emissions and we could only recognize the changing seasons by the daffodil frieze at Sketchleys (spring) and the Back-to-Skool promotion at Rymans (autumn). In our local park litter lay like fallen blossoms all year round. Edwin, waking up to a dawn chorus of activated car alarms, hungered for honest country toil and started buying books, published by Faber and illustrated by woodcuts, which told him how to clamp his beetroots and flay his ox.

A romantic puritan, he bemoaned the greed of our decade, saying that even intellectuals seemed to talk about house prices nowadays. He said London was so materialistic, so cut off from Real Values. We lived in a flat, and my contact with nature was to grow basil, the seventies herb, and coriander, the eighties one, on our balcony, digging them with a dining fork. I bought them at Clifton Nurseries, London's most metropolitan garden centre, where I liked spotting TV personalities pushing Burnham Woods of designer foliage in their trolleys to the checkout.

So I came to the country green, as it were. And after a year of organic gardening all I had learnt was how to drive into Taunton, buy most of the stuff at Marks & Spencer and then pretend it was ours. It's so tiring, being organic. Being married, for that matter.

The day after Boxing Day I walked across to the wood, alone. It was a still, grey morning and without its foliage the place looked thin and vulnerable; I could see right through it. Within its brambles was now revealed the

archaeological remains of countless trysts, date-expired litter from expired dates. But now I knew what I was doing I
felt possessive. We didn't own the wood, of course – it
belonged to our local farmer, Mr Hogben, and he wanted
the ring road because it meant he could retire to Portugal.

I took out my rubbish bags and set to work. It's amazing
how much you can do when you don't have three children
with you. In an hour I had tut-tutted my way through the
place, filled four black bags, and scratched my hands.

That evening I didn't watch TV. I looked through
Edwin's library instead. He was outside, in the old privy,
running off campaign leaflets on his printing press. Nursing my burning hands, I leafed through his *Complete
British Wild Flowers*. I had no idea there were so many
plants, and with such names – sneezewort and dodder,
purging buckthorn and bitter fleabane, maids bonnets
and biting stonecrop (or welcome-home-husband-though-
never-so-drunk). Poetic and unfamiliar, they danced in my
head as I gazed at the eternally blooming watercolours.
The book divided them into habitats, which helped. I took
note of the 'Woodlands' section, writing down the names
of the most endangered species. I hadn't learnt so much
since school.

When Edwin returned he was surprised I was missing
Minder. So was I.

'I want to learn more about the countryside,' I said.

He was terribly pleased. We started talking about his
youth in Dorset, where his father was a vicar and he a pale,
only child. He told me how he had wandered around with
a stick, poking holes in cowpats.

'I became an expert on spotting those in perfect

condition. Crusty on top, but still soft inside. A pitiful little skill, but something, I suppose . . .' He paused. 'Other people remember their childhoods as always being sunny. All I can remember is the rain. Sitting for hours at the window, looking at it sliding down the pane.' He looked at me. 'I wish you'd been there, I wish I knew you then.'

'Do you?'

'You'd have thought of lots of things to do.'

I was moved by this; it was the first time he had admitted to being bored. Unhappy maybe, but never bored. People like *me* were bored by the countryside. We talked about the treacherous nature of expectations. We talked about the years before graphics department politics, and children, and trying to find people rich enough to buy his tables.

'I wanted to be Edward Lear,' he said. 'I wanted to explore the world and find everything curious.'

'Not just cowpats,' I said. 'But wasn't he lonely?'

He nodded. 'But what an artist.' He paused, tugging his beard. 'Everybody has a time when they should have lived.'

'When's yours?'

'1890.'

'Think about how much it would have hurt at the dentist's.'

He laughed. 'When's yours?'

'Now.'

That night, despite our icy feet, we made love – the first time since that Thursday. He even licked my ears, something I had forgotten I adored. He used to do it quite a lot, in London.

Afterwards he said: 'I've been worried about you, Ruthie. Have I been dominating? Selfish? Bringing you down here?'

I shook my head. 'I'm liking it better now.'

Mabel Cudlipp had newts. She was a fellow mother. I had seen her at the school gates for a year now, but we had never really talked. To tell the truth, I thought the mothers here looked boring compared with the London ones, who arrived at school breathing Chardonnay fumes from Groucho lunches. But when the spring term began I started chatting, and it turned out Mabel Cudlipp had some in her pond.

'Great crested newts,' she said. 'They're very rare. In fact, they've been protected since 1981.'

'You couldn't possibly spare one or two?'

She nodded. 'They're hibernating now, but we can look when it gets warmer.'

So then we chatted about plants, and she even brought her daughter back for tea.

You might wonder why I didn't tell Edwin. The trouble was: his honesty. Once, he found a £5 note in Oxford Circus and took it to the police. They were as taken aback as I was. Nobody claimed it, of course, because nobody thought anyone could be that decent. Another time he drove twenty-two miles in freezing fog to pay somebody back when I had overcharged them for eggs. But that was when we were in the middle of a quarrel, so he could simply have been scoring a point.

Nor did I involve the children, for the same reason. Throughout the spring I worked away during school hours, accompanied only by Abbie, who was three and who couldn't snitch on me. She carried the trowel on our daily pilgrimage to the wood, which I now considered ours, its every clump of couch grass dear to me. When boxes arrived from obscure plant nurseries I told Edwin that I was really getting to grips with the garden. He was delighted, of course. He never noticed the lack of progress there; he hardly ever went into the garden, he was too busy. In fact, he didn't know anything about plants; he just had strong opinions about them in a vague sort of way. He was like that with the children.

While he battled against the bureaucrats – the Stop the Road campaign wasn't getting anywhere – I glowed, my cheeks grew roses, my fingernails were crammed with mud. I felt as heavy as a fruit with my secret; I hadn't felt so happy since I was pregnant.

I was also becoming something of an expert. For instance, on *Potamogeton densus* and *Riccia fluitans*. Latin names to you, but essential aquatic oxygenators to me. I bought them at my local garden centre, which had an Ornamental Pond section, and carried them to the wood in plastic bags. I had dug out the pond, and turfed its sides.

Then there was *Triturus cristatus*, or perhaps *i* because there were four of them, courtesy of Mabel. Perhaps you don't know what this is. It is the great crested newt. The male has a silver streak on the tail, and at breeding time develops a high, crinkled crest and a bright orange belly. The female, without crest but with a skin flap above and below the tail, is 16.5cm long overall, slightly longer than the male. *I* was feeling slightly longer than the male; more vigorous and powerful.

For good measure, and why not, Abbie and I planted some surprising plants in the wood too, garden plants, and some blue Himalayan poppies. I had to use my Barclaycard for most of this; the whole operation was costing a fortune.

And then there was my *coup de grâce*, the orchids. We planted the lady's slipper (*Cypripedium calceolus*), the lizard and the bird's nest (*Neottia nidus-avis*), all extremely rare, and purchased from a small nursery in Suffolk whose address I had found in the back of *Amateur Gardener*. I cut off all the labels, of course; I'm not a complete fool, I even went to university once. I planted them tenderly in the patches I had cleared amongst the brambles. Above us the birds sang, and the watery spring sunshine gleamed on the ivy which, lush as leather, trousered the trees. I even knew the trees' names now.

In all those weeks Edwin never visited the wood. He never had time. In the country people never have time to do things like that, unless someone comes to lunch. It's like living in London and never visiting the Tate Gallery unless some American friends arrive. Edwin was busy doing all the things that people who live in the country really do, like driving twenty miles to collect the repaired lawnmower, and then doing it all over again because the lawnmower still doesn't work. Like driving thirty miles to find some matching tiles for our roof, and discovering that the place has been turned into a Bejam. So he never knew.

They didn't build the ring road past us; they're building it through the riding stables. This is because our wood has been designated a site of Outstanding Scientific Interest. They've put up a proper wooden fence, and a sign. They are even thinking of building a car park. And instead of thundering pantechnicons we've now got thundering Renaults full of newt-watchers.

It's August Bank Holiday today and people have come from all over, it's been really interesting. They knock on our door and ask the way, and admire our cottage – botanists in particular are very polite. We're doing a brisk trade in eggs, too. Ours are guaranteed salmonella-free because the hens are fed on my organic bread, which is so disgusting we are always throwing it away. Sometimes the people leave their children here, to play with mine, while they tramp across the field to inspect the orchids. Danny, that's my eldest, has even started saying things like 'mega-crucial'. Now we have our own traffic jams I don't miss Camden Town at all.

What Edwin feels about this is best described as mixed. Still, his furniture business is booming because it's only two miles away and even he is materialistic enough to put up a notice, with a tasteful sepia photograph and a map, pointing them in the right direction. And so much has happened during the day that we don't have to talk about his mother any more.

This morning I decided to start doing teas. I'll buy Old-Style Spiced Buns at Marks & Spencer and throw away the packets. I've learnt a lot this past year, you see, about the *real* country way of doing things.

Family Feelings:
Five Linked Stories

1. Fool for Love

How do these things begin? What's the moment? For Esther, it was seeing the back of his neck – the sight of it, smooth and boyish. Brown hair curling against it as he bent over a parcel in the dispatch room. She had a sudden desire to lean towards him and smell it – the warm, biscuity smell of youth. Men of her age, mid-forties – various things were happening to their necks, none of them an improvement. To hers, too. And suddenly they had all bought glasses. The last time she had had dinner with her ex, one of their stilted, we're-still-friends dinners, when the menu had arrived they had both startled each other by producing a pair of spectacles. His were half-moon, professorial things that had aged him ten years but of course it was no longer her place to tell him so. They had talked, as always, about the children. A safe topic. Well, safeish.

Esther worked in an advertising agency. Owen was twenty-six. *Twenty-six.* He packed parcels downstairs with an old boy called Clarence who had been there for ever. Esther started bringing down stuff herself, instead of leaving it in her Out tray. She sprang downstairs to the beat of Capital Radio. At home she shouted at her children to turn the blasted thing down but here in the dispatch room she was suddenly skittish. One Friday she wore her daughter's Lurex top, glinting with silver, and Owen raised his eyebrows.

'You free lunchtime?' he asked. She nodded. 'Want to help me buy a Christmas present for me mum?'

He pulled some Sellotape; it hissed like indrawn breath. Her heart soared and sank. A date, yes! But did he just want the advice of a mature woman?

After two weeks' chatting in the dispatch room it was thrillingly intimate, to step into the outside world. Traffic roared down Regent Street; above them, angels blew trumpets into the drizzle. They gave up on the present, it was too wet, and ate kebabs in a plasticky café. Owen was slender and pale; she had a shamefully maternal desire to fatten him up. Maybe he was just a substitute son to replace her real one who had gone to Goa in his gap year and would soon be gone for ever.

She said: 'Toby, that's my son, he despises what I do, filling the world with consumer durables nobody needs. Huh, he can talk – you should see his bedroom!'

Owen gazed at her over his cappuccino. 'What about it?'

'Crammed with TVs and ghetto blasters and blooming consumer durables—' She stopped. You couldn't complain about adolescents to somebody who was practically one himself. 'He's in Goa,' she said. 'They all travel. They're so blasé nowadays. Popping malaria pills and telling each other they'll rendezvous in some Bengali flophouse. *See you in Beijing*, they say, *see you in Buenos Aires*.' She nearly said *in my young day we were lucky to go to Broadstairs* but she stopped.

Owen rolled a cigarette and grinned. 'You like dancing?' he asked.

And so it began, their affair. They went dancing in clubs which were so dark that nobody could see what an idiot she looked, clubs which pulsated to the jungle beat of her past. It had been so many years since she had fallen in love, since she had embarked on this adventure. Since she had mooned around in a dream, smiling at check-out girls. Since she had shaved her legs every single day. How exhausting it was, being attractive! She borrowed her daughter's clothes, picking her way like a carrion crow through the debris on Kate's bedroom floor. She spent hours in the bathroom, Kate rattling the door; she spent hours on the phone, Kate sighing loudly because none of her friends could get through. She yawned through work; like a student she never read newspapers and lost track of what was on the TV – she, supposedly a media person! Supposedly a mother, too. But one night she fell asleep at Owen's flat, the other side of London, and woke with a start at seven thirty. She grabbed the phone.

'Time to get up!' she said to Kate. 'Time for school! Remember your homework!' She rolled back, sighing, into Owen's slim young arms. So much for motherhood.

Two weeks passed. Various small milestones had been surmounted, various *first times*. She had woken up with a disgusting stye in her eye and Owen still found her attractive. She had lent him £10 – he never had any money – and he had paid her back: see, he wasn't using her! He had seen her snarl with rage at another driver and hadn't been repulsed. They had not yet encountered true triumph or disaster and seen if they treated these two imposters just the same, but each minor incident shunted them further into intimacy. She felt alternately very old and ridiculously young. Certain things made her feel her age: the awful music he listened to, the way he asked her eagerly if she had actually seen Jimi Hendrix live. By having to explain so many things to him she realized how much the world had changed since the sixties, how nothing remained the same – nothing except perhaps Marmite. Lying in bed one Sunday morning, in his flat, and feeling guilty that she wasn't with her daughter, she told him a joke (ah, to have a new person to hear one's jokes!).

She said: 'There was this boy who was always late for school. Finally the teacher made him stand in the corner, and not come out until he had answered a question right. It was a geography lesson and the teacher asked the class where the Rhodesian border was. The boy put up his hand. *I know where the Rhodesian boarder is*, he said. *He's in bed with me mum, that's why I'm always late for school.*'

Owen asked: 'What's Rhodesia?'

'Oh, of course – it's Zimbabwe now.' So much to explain, but how delightful to explain it while running her finger along his smooth young buttock!

The only other problem – no, not problem, discrepancy – was money. She lived in a house in Chiswick crammed with the consumer durables her son despised – even more so, it seemed, now he had arrived in Nepal and phoned her saying how spiritual it was to live unencumbered by material possessions, a phone call interrupted by Kate grabbing the receiver and yelling, 'Mum's got a toyboy!'

Owen had never travelled. He lived in a bare, squatter-type room in Leytonstone. He didn't even have a TV because he couldn't afford the licence and even his cassette recorder was broken. He lived off the sort of food, like tinned pilchards, she thought nobody ate any more except pensioners. Maybe the young did, but the only young she knew were her children's friends who ate *moules marinières* from Marks & Spencer because their parents were career people with large disposable incomes and no time to cook.

Owen came from a working-class family. His dream was to become a minicab driver, to be independent and work his own hours. The humbleness of this ambition humbled her. She thought of her own children, who had been given everything but who still complained, for adolescents have to complain about something.

The trouble was, Kate now had cause for complaint. She clomped about the house mulishly, in her great boots, slamming doors. She said her mother was never there, and there was never anything in the fridge. She said her Lurex top had never been the same since her mother wore it. Esther smiled dreamily and said she would buy her another one.

'What shall I buy Owen for Christmas?'

'A teething ring.'

'Kate!'

'A potty.'

'Shut up! Just because I'm a woman! Your friend Paula's father's married someone half his age and nobody thinks *that's* odd.'

'You're so *embarrassing*,' said her daughter.

'You should be proud of me,' said Esther.

'Anyway, it's not fair.'

It was true. There was her daughter, aged seventeen, primed up and ready for romance. A thousand magazine articles had told her how to tone up her thighs and always use a condom. Products, some of which Esther herself promoted, promised to bring her love if only she rubbed them into her hair and painted them on to her lips. The bathroom was full of bottles and tubes, including an oatmeal face gel for which Esther had created the slogan *Face the Muesli*. It wasn't fair.

'Don't you like him?' Esther bleated. They were having a rare evening alone together.

'He's just using you.'

'Kate! Why are you all so cynical, you young people?'

'He must be. Why else would he want an old bat like you?'

'I'm not an old bat. I'm an experienced woman. He says girls his age are too aggressive.' She looked down at her daughter's feet. 'And wear such hideous boots.'

'He *is* using you.'

'When there's an age difference people always think that. An old man with a doting young starlet – they think it's a trade-off. But all love is an emotional trading transaction.'

Kate jerked her head towards the stairs. 'I know he's using you. I've just been into Toby's room.' She looked at her mother like a schoolmistress at an errant pupil. 'I've seen what's happening.'

Esther fell silent.

Ten days before Christmas, Toby came home. Esther stood at Heathrow Arrivals. She didn't recognize him until a voice said 'Hi, Mum.'

She jumped. Her son's skin was burnished caramel, his scarecrow hair bleached yellow. His body, when she hugged it, felt bony – wasted by subcontinental digestive disorders. She felt a rush of maternal love – the same rush she had felt when she had first seen Owen.

'How was the flight?' she asked.

'A baby screamed all the way from Dubai but it was OK. I meditated.'

'You? Meditated?'

He rummaged in his rucksack and gave her a book – *The Radiant Truth* by Swami Somebody. 'Once you reach Nirvana you feel so light.' He staggered, loading his rucksack on to his back. 'So free. You, like, shed the material world.' He pointed to a page. '*Detachment is the deliberate renunciation of desire for objects seen or heard.*' He looked around. 'Why're we going this way?'

'We're taking the tube.'

'What's happened to the car?'

'I'll tell you later,' she said.

Back home, her son went into his bedroom and dumped his rucksack on the floor. He took out a framed picture and put it beside the bed. It showed a fat Buddha, his eyes closed. Toby took out two joss-stick holders and placed them on either side, like an altar. Then he stopped, and looked around.

'Where's my ghetto blaster?' he asked. 'Hey, where's my TV?'

Esther tore open his packet of joss-sticks. 'Shall I light one?' she asked.

'Mum, where are they?'

Kate appeared in the doorway. 'She's given them to her toyboy.'

'*What?*'

'Lent them,' corrected Esther, striking a match. 'You don't mind, do you?'

'And she's lent him your Walkman and your calculator and—'

'*Mum!*' bellowed Toby.

'Darling, they're just material possessions.' Dreamily, she watched the smoke unfurl from the joss-stick. 'Owen needs them more. I'm just helping you on the path to Nirvana.'

Kate fingered the row of studs in her ear. She looked at her mother. 'You told him about the car yet?' she asked.

Esther knew she was a fool – a fool for love. She knew this, but what the hell. She that tooketh from her children with one hand, she giveth to her lover with the other. For her own son was already loosening himself from her, as he must. Toby drove, shaved, was capable of producing his own children. His address book was filling up with unfamiliar names and when she spoke to him he rocked on the balls of his feet like his father did, as if he was getting ready to run. Soon she would be left alone, so who could call her a fool? Not her son. Nor her ex, because it was no longer his place to do so.

'You've *what*?' Toby stared at her.

She put on her new reading glasses and opened his book. '*When non-covetousness is firmly rooted the yogi knows his past, present and future.*'

'But I'm meeting my mates tonight,' he said. 'Like, a reunion. I've got to have the car!'

She read: '*The journey to enlightenment is a long one—*'

'I've got to get to bloody Muswell Hill!'

'I'll call you a minicab,' she said.

Ten minutes later the doorbell rang. Toby looked out of the window into the wintry night. 'That's our car!'

Esther nodded and opened the door. 'Hi, Owen,' she said, and kissed him. 'Meet my son, Toby.' She propelled Toby down the step. 'Here's your driver. You can get to know each other on the way. And he won't charge you; it's on the house.'

2. The Use of Irony

She called Barnaby the Barnacle. He was her little half-brother and he clung to everything. He clung to her leg when she was trying to get to the lavatory; he clung to her calf when she was trying to do her homework. He unthreaded the laces to her boots and then he couldn't – or wouldn't – thread them back again. If he were the cat she would kick him off.

'Can't you take him, Dad?' she pleaded. 'I'm trying to work!'

'So am I!' he bellowed, pounding upstairs. Paula's father was a writer. He wrote books about a detective called Norman who suffered from clinical depression. In each book Norman grew gloomier. Her father was very fond of his detective but as yet Norman had failed to grip the public, sell in vast quantities or be turned into a TV series. Her father slammed his study door; he had a deadline. But then so did she.

Paula was trying to write an essay entitled 'The Use of Irony in *Cold Comfort Farm*'. She had to finish it by the end of term but she hadn't even started it yet. Home was so chaotic, that was why. The house was so small with Barnaby in it. Simone, her stepmother, was training to be a psychotherapist and she liked to have quality time with Barnaby when she got home. This meant that Barnaby didn't get to bed till late and spent the evenings screaming around the house pretending to be a fighter jet. He liked launching himself from the settee and landing on Paula's stomach. Wherever she spread out her notes, the cat sat on them. Then there was her father, padding around because he had writer's block, making himself cups of tea and engaging everyone in conversation but scuttling away the moment Barnaby approached. Finally there were her step-mother's women friends who were all going through personal crises. They hung around in the kitchen drinking wine and blocking Paula's route to the fridge. Why did adults always fill up the kitchen when they had a sitting room to sit in? It meant that Paula couldn't get to the Pecan Nut Crunch without her stepmother spotting her and thinking she had an eating disorder.

Simone was much younger than Paula's dad – only thirty-two. She was beautiful in all the ways Paula wanted to be – like being thin, with masses of black hair that some-how looked sexy and wild, whereas Paula's just looked a mess. When she moved in, she said she didn't want to be a stepmother type of person, she wanted to be Paula's friend, her confidante, just girls together. She said if ever Paula wanted to talk, she would be there. She said *talk* in a spe-cial way, a capital letters way, that filled Paula with unease and somehow made the walls of the house close in around her.

The trouble with Simone was that she was too under-standing. She understood Paula's feelings about her mother, who had run away to Totnes with a man who made stained-glass windows. She understood about being plump because she said – unbelievably – that she too had once had a weight problem. She understood about being adolescent because she was still practically one herself, and besides, she had written a paper called 'Psychodrama and the Teenage Dynamic'. What she didn't understand was the main point of being seventeen, which was to be misunderstood.

'If only she was older,' Paula said to her friend Kate. 'I want her to be like a parent.'

'No parents are like parents any more,' said Kate bitterly. 'Even the real ones. Mum borrowed my leggings last night and spilt effing red wine down them.'

'Your shiny ones from Camden Lock?'

Kate nodded. Her mother had fallen for a young bloke called Owen and was making a complete wally of herself. 'Last night they started dancing to Rod Stewart. Rod Stewart! The curtains were open, anyone could see! And swigging Becks from the bottle. Mum doesn't even *like* beer. It's so sad!'

Their similar predicament had drawn them closer. Paula, from her years of experience, described the humiliating early days of her father's relationship with Simone, when he had grown designer stubble because he thought it looked trendy but at his age simply made him look like an alcoholic. Why couldn't they just grow old properly? Kate snorted. 'They behave like bloody teenagers. They'll be bringing home traffic cones next.' It was she and Paula who felt like the elderly ones, clucking and disapproving. Somehow there was no space for them; it was as if their parents were sucking out the oxygen of their own growing-up.

'There's no space at home,' said Paula. 'Simone wants to talk to me about boyfriends but I can't tell her I haven't got one. She'd say *do you want to talk about it?* Ugh!'

Kate said there was no space at home because Owen was always there, giggling with her mother or watching TV with his cowboy-booted feet on the coffee table. 'He's always staying over because she feels so guilty leaving me and staying with him. They take showers together in the morning! It's so pathetic!' It was worse now, apparently, because he had just left his job and become a minicab driver, using their car, and dropped in at odd times of the evening just when she was settling down to her homework.

It was ten days before Christmas. They were walking home from school. Along Chiswick High Street a mannequin Father Christmas beckoned them into the car wash. Despite his lopsided hood he looked wiser than their parents; his head nodded, as if he knew all the answers. Term ended soon and Paula still hadn't started her essay.

'Can't I come and work at your place?' she asked. 'At least your mother's boyfriend's grown up. At least he won't start bouncing on top of me.'

'Don't be too sure,' said Kate.

At least at Kate's house she would get some peace and quiet. Toby, Kate's brother, had just come back from India but he wouldn't be any trouble; he spent most of his time in his room smoking dope and reading *Viz*. Besides, Kate's house was bigger than hers and other people's fridges, like their bookcases, were always more interesting than one's own.

The next day, after school, she had a brainwave. Toby could be useful. 'Just dropping round to Toby's place,' she said casually. 'You know – Toby, Kate's brother. He's really nice.'

Her stepmother's eyes widened, luminously. Then she smiled. 'It's happened at last,' she said. 'I'm so glad.'

So Paula went round to Kate's house and, under the guise of having a boyfriend, started to tackle her essay. When she got home, Simone smiled at her in a twinkling, us-girls type of way. 'Is he nice?' she asked. 'Do you want to talk about it?'

'I'm a bit tired,' said Paula, who had been struggling all evening with her participles.

There was a problem. Though it was liberating to get out of the house, Paula found that she had only exchanged one set of distractions for another. The problem was Kate's mother and her toyboy. Owen was reasonably good-looking in a preeny, fancying-himself kind of way but his eyebrows met in the middle and *Just 17* said that showed he was not to be trusted. And his clothes! He wore, would you believe, a cowboy shirt, one of those sad things with bootlaces. No wonder he liked Rod Stewart. When he arrived at the door Kate's mother called down the stairs: 'Have him washed and sent up to my room!' Until recently she had been quite a dignified sort of person. When he wasn't nuzzling up to her, he engaged the girls in conversation, presumably to ingratiate himself – what were their favourite bands, that sort of stuff.

However, it was even worse when he wasn't there. Kate's mum mooned around the house, playing soppy music, and then would knock on their door when they were trying to work and fling herself down on her daughter's bed.

'Don't ever fall in love,' she sighed. 'Oh God, I ache when he's here and I ache when he's not here, I feel such a fool. This morning, when I saw he'd opened the window in the bathroom I just gazed at the catch, thinking *his* hand had touched it. Am I mad?'

'*I* opened the window in the bathroom,' said Kate. 'It was my hand.'

'I can't eat, I keep thinking how it can't last, how one day he'll have children with somebody else, somebody young like him. I can't work—'

Nor can I, thought Paula, gazing at her notes.

'I gaze at this poster campaign we're doing and all I can see is his face—'

'It's not love, what you've got,' said Kate. 'It's called limerence. I read about it in *Marie Claire*. It's a sort of intoxication, sort of madness, it lasts six months and helps you not get womb cancer.'

'I keep on thinking, is he using me? Because I've got a car, because I feed him up and look after him, because I'm taking him off on holiday after Christmas—'

'When?' demanded her daughter. 'Where?'

'Venice. When you're going skiing with your dad.'

'You never told me!'

'I'm so old! Look at my wrinkles. Look at my neck – soon it's going to be like a turkey's, I'm getting so flabby. When I run down the street to catch the bus—'

'Yeah – because *he's* got the car—' said Kate.

'When I run, I can feel the tops of my arms wobbling. He's so young! Maybe we've got nothing in common. He doesn't even know where Rhodesia is!'

There was a pause. 'Where is Rhodesia?' they asked.

When she had gone Paula said: 'You've got to get her out of the house. Tell her to stay over at his place—'

'She feels so guilty when she does that,' said Kate. 'Last

time she phoned to wake me up and I didn't hear it and missed school—'

'Please! Tell her you don't mind if she stays with him, you don't mind if she *lives* with him, we can look after ourselves. Go on! Your brother's here. We can have the whole house to ourselves!'

They went downstairs and began their campaign.

'It'll be so romantic,' Kate urged her mother, 'so sexy. You and Owen, alone in his little room. Just you and him. Breakfast in his sunlit kitchenette. You need time together, to get to know each other. It says so in *Cosmopolitan*.'

When people want to do something they don't need much persuading. Kate's mother agreed to stay more nights at her boyfriend's place. Paula went home, glowing with triumph. Three more days of term – at last she would get her essay done. Simone smiled at her as she came in the door.

'You look wonderful,' she said. 'How's it going? Do you want to talk about him?'

Paula sighed. 'When he opened the bathroom window I looked at the catch and thought: ooh, his hand's touched that.' She sighed. 'I ache when I'm with him and I ache when I'm not with him—'

Luckily she was interrupted by Barnaby shooting at her, rat-a-tat-tat, with his imaginary gun.

The trouble was, it didn't turn out as she expected. What does? You think you know your parents and suddenly they grow designer stubble. Or they start getting skittish and nicking your lipliner. You think you know your best friend and suddenly you realize that her motives were completely different from your own. How could you have misunderstood her so completely?

The moment her mother was out of the house Kate shouted to her brother: 'Get my phone book!'

Toby came pounding down the stairs, they started telephoning and within an hour the house was filled with their friends. 'While the cat's away . . .' laughed Kate.

They started rolling joints and cracking open cans of Heineken. Toby turned up the volume on the CD player. Paula tried to escape upstairs but Kate's bedroom was crammed with girls from school smoking Marlboros and giggling about who was getting off with who in the living room. Nobody noticed when Paula, clutching her notes, let herself out of the front door and went home.

Her house was quiet. Simone was out at her Inner Healing evening class. Her dad lay snoring on the settee, Barnaby asleep on his stomach. Now Barnaby was unconscious he looked so sweet she wanted to wake him up. Ironic, she thought. Then she pulled out the Shorter Oxford Dictionary to look up the word.

She sat down at the kitchen table and leafed through the pages. '*Irony:*' it said: '*A contradictory outcome of events as if in mockery of the promise or fitness of things.*'

Suddenly she was filled with a deep peace. She uncapped her Pentel and started to write her essay.

3. Rent-a-Granny

Munro had been married three times and by now he had been accused of everything. Three fierce and articulate women – between them they had covered most of the ground; that mud-churned battlefield. According to his wives his failings included: drinking too much, not being supportive, not noticing when they had got their hair done, the usual selfishness, egocentricity, unresponsiveness, laughing at his own jokes, repeating his own jokes, leaving the lav seat up . . . just being a *man*.

Then there were his children's accusations. His eldest daughter from his first marriage, Tabitha, accused him of being in denial – or maybe of putting *her* in denial, it was usually one or the other. She was thirty-two and had been in analysis for years. She accused him of setting up an abuse pattern which seemed to stem from him not turning up once for her school sports day. He had never been allowed to forget it. In his opinion, when somebody reached thirty an amnesty should be declared; they should lay down their arms and say they were grown-up now and nothing was their parents' fault any more.

Paula was his teenage daughter from his second marriage. In many ways she had been his loyal ally through rocky times, but even she accused him of smoking too much and foisting Barnaby on her.

Barnaby, his little son, accused him of being a wibbly-wobbly dumdum. Barnaby was only four and hadn't honed his arguments yet. Mostly he bounced up and down on Munro's balls and prodded him with his Sten gun – simpler weaponry than the women used, but painful all the same.

At the moment, in fact, Barnaby was his main problem. It was the week after Christmas and Munro was trying to work. It was prime working time – that hibernating period between Christmas and New Year, cold and grey, London closed down, a city under a spell, and everyone away. Christmas itself had been exhausting as usual, its festive spotlight pitilessly illuminating the cracks and fissures of his personal life. But it was over now, and he had a clear week to get on with his book.

Or so he thought. But then it turned out that Simone, his wife, was planning to spend the week attending a course. Held in some women's centre, it was one of her empowerment-type things called 'Freeing the Warrioress Within'. As if she didn't terrify him enough already. It always amazed him, how the fiercest women he knew went on courses that taught them how to be even more alarming. The timid ones, who might have needed it, never did.

Simone was only thirty-two, almost his daughter's age. She possessed the certainty of youth plus this new steeliness they seemed to be born with nowadays. How did young men deal with this current crop of women? It was exhausting enough when one was fifty-six, with a certain amount of experience under one's belt. A few years ago women were loud and demanding. Now it was much more insidious; they simply took it for granted that a bloke would be supportive of their work, of their parenting, be a new man and look after Barnaby.

Munro was a sociable chap, prone to padding around the house searching for somebody to talk to, welcoming interruptions because it gave him an excuse not to get on with his book. On his door he had pinned up a notice: *Please Disturb; Writer at Work*. But Barnaby's interruptions were of a different order. To be perfectly frank, he hadn't wanted to have another child, nappies, all that. He was getting too old for it. He had done it too often. But Simone had wanted a child and he had wanted to oblige her because it seemed so selfish otherwise. He loved his beautiful young wife. It was his third marriage and he had to make a go of it, or else people would start thinking there was something wrong with him.

The first couple of days were all right. He roped in his reluctant daughter Paula to help, but then she went away to stay with her mother in Totnes. Barnaby went to a playgroup in the mornings, but by the time Munro had taken him there, come home and settled down to work it was time to pick him up again. How short the days were, and how long the hours of darkness! What could he *do* with him? He needed, desperately, to have some time alone with Norman.

Norman was his detective, the hero of his three latest books, a gloomy man who lived in a bedsitter and was prone to long interior monologues. Munro's publishers were getting worried about Norman; they said the plots kept getting held up by Norman's bitter broodings about women. Munro said they weren't bitter, they were profound. His publishers said the books weren't selling because thrillers should have a plot, that was why people read them, and that Munro's stories were getting more meandering with each book.

Munro slotted in a Postman Pat video. 'Postman Pat!' he called, cheerily, to Barnaby.

His son came charging into the living room and flung himself on the settee. Munro tried to sneak away. 'Watch it with me!' yelled his son, grabbing Munro's leg.

After ten minutes Barnaby closed his eyes. Munro tried to extricate himself again, but Barnaby was too quick for him. He gripped his hair – or what was left of it. 'Watch this bit!'

Munro sat there, mute. If his eyes strayed from the screen Barnaby sensed it, by radar, and jerked his head back. Trapped, Munro watched the little red van bounce over the green hills. Postman Pat had a plot. Things got delivered. What worried him was that he had started this book without any idea how it was going to end. The general gist was child-kidnapping – wishful thinking, no doubt – but he was simply hoping that if he went on writing, something would work itself out. He had always found stories difficult. In one of his maudlin moments, when he was thinking how much sooner he would die than Simone, he had said to her: 'I know what you must put on my tombstone: *A Plot At Last.*'

He tried to reassure himself by thinking of Raymond Chandler, who apparently got in such a muddle he couldn't work out who was supposed to be killing who. Raymond Chandler had done all right, hadn't he?

At two o'clock Tina, their cleaner, arrived. She had been coming to them for a couple of months and Munro liked her because she was the sort of woman they didn't make any more, at least amongst his acquaintance – a woman who dressed for men. She had dyed blond hair, shiny red lipstick and, most cheering of all, a little gold chain around her ankle. His spirits always lifted when she tap-tapped into the kitchen and inspected herself in the glass of the microwave.

'Tina,' he said, 'I'm desperate. When you've finished, could I pay you for another hour to take Barnaby out?'

'Where?'

'Anywhere. Anywhere but here. Just an hour,' he wheedled.

She agreed. They would be back by six. Munro went upstairs and sat down at his computer. Norman was having trouble meeting his alimony payments; Munro could write this from the heart.

The problem was, an hour was so short. Munro's eyes strayed to his pile of stationery. He picked up a packet and read: 'The Ivy range of self-adhesive labels. For almost every need.' Almost every need? What about hunger? Loneliness? Could you use self-adhesive labels for that? Could you use them for sticking Barnaby to the settee?

An hour seemed to have passed. It was six fifteen and they hadn't returned. Munro went downstairs and poured himself a whisky. Simone would be back at six thirty – they must be home before she arrived. Why? Why shouldn't she find out? What was wrong with paying one's cleaning lady to look after one's child?

Because it would be an admission of defeat, that he couldn't cope. That he couldn't even manage a few days of bonding with his son. That he would rather entrust Barnaby to a flighty young woman whose address they didn't even know. Simone would – oh God – want to *talk* about it. He looked at the leaflet for her course. '*During our workshops we learn to recognize the warrioress within, set her free and develop true empowerment.*' He wailed silently: she's empowered enough already! She frightens the life out of me!

The doorbell rang. It was Tina and Barnaby. His mouth was smeared red. As she ushered him in she said: 'Sorry. See, I had to get my legs waxed and it took ages. I bought him a lolly.'

'Er – what about tomorrow?'

'Can't.' She winked at him. 'I'm meeting somebody. Hence the wax.'

'So where's your husband then?'

'In Wokingham.' She smiled. 'In fact, if I don't come in next week, can I use you as an alibi?'

He stared at her. What was the world coming to? 'An alibi? Then I'll have to do my own bloody cleaning too!'

She giggled. He bundled Barnaby away to wipe the red stuff off his mouth. For some reason, it looked adulterous.

The next day, Tina the cleaner rang. 'There's an old dear upstairs called Oonagh. She'll take your son.'

So that was how Munro rented a granny. Oonagh was the real thing – cosy, dumpy, grey-haired, looking as if she had forgotten what sex was like forty years ago. In fact, Munro realized with an unwelcome jolt, she was hardly older than him. Her own grandchildren were scattered across Britain and Canada; she missed them, and took to Barnaby on sight. 'What a duck!' she said.

He considered keeping it a secret from Simone but he had visions of his warrioress-wife spotting her son in the high street hand-in-hand with this elderly child abductor and giving chase. Besides, Barnaby was bound to spill the beans so he got in first. He decided to make a joke of it. 'Maybe I'll give up the writing and start a business called Rent-a-Gran,' he laughed. 'A sort of inter-generational introduction agency. It suits both sides, see. There's so few bona fide grannies left – most of them are having HRT and running their own companies. Look at your own mum.' Simone's mother was the PR for a rock band and currently having an affair with the bass guitarist. Catch *her* crocheting beside the fire.

Simone poured boiling water on to her herb tea. 'So this woman's going to come three hours a day?'

'I need three hours, otherwise I can't get down to anything. Just till life begins again – his school and such.'

'Till life begins again – what a curious phrase. You mean life without our son.' She dredged out her teabag and flung it into the bin. 'Maybe I should cut this course and stay home myself.'

'Don't make me feel guilty!'

'No. *I* feel guilty.' She sighed. 'I chose to have him.'

Munro felt a steel clamp tightening around his temples. Oh, sticky labels, help me now! Help me stick together my marriage!

'I think we should talk this through,' she said.

'Not yet! Not till I've finished my book!'

He won – if anyone wins these things. Oonagh the surrogate granny ensconced herself downstairs and peace descended on the house. Oonagh wasn't empowered. No warrioress, she. Oonagh wasn't in denial; in fact she was completely unreconstructed.

'Little boys should only speak when they're spoken to,' she said, knitting needles clicking. Barnaby, stunned, sat obediently at her feet rewinding her wool.

Upstairs Munro gazed at his computer screen. Sounds drifted up, sounds from his own childhood. A past when grannies were grannies, roast on Sundays, a golden age. A world of security before women were empowered and cleaning ladies committed adultery. He closed his eyes; Proustianly, he could almost smell his father's pipe smoke.

Suddenly he pressed the delete button. *Delete document?* Yes. *Delete backup disk?* Yes. He fished out a piece of paper and wrote 'Chapter One'.

Forget the thriller. Real life was much more thrilling. Forget Norman the detective. Enter Norman the real man.

'Page One.' He would write a novel – a real novel, from the heart. A long, Joycean monologue, brooding and profound, bitter maybe, but funny too. It would be the story of his own life, a voyage into the interior. Forget police tactics; emotional tactics were much more interesting. A great, literary sponge, his novel would sop up the mess of his life and spin it into gold. And with mixed metaphors like that, who knows? It might even win the Booker Prize.

Munro picked up his Pentel and, just as his daughter did, two weeks earlier, he began to write.

4. Sex Objects

What was the national average – two-point-four times a week? No, that was children. How many times a week, max, after you had been married a couple of years like he had? Trouble was, you never knew what other people got up to, bedroom-wise, you never knew if you were, like, a normal sort of bloke. Nobody told the truth. In the pub, of course, they bragged. Take Robbie, their panel-beater. He claimed that last summer, on Paxos, he had done it minimum four times a day with a girl from Barclays Bank. But Robbie was a Glaswegian.

Desmond's wife Tina was a beautiful girl with strong appetites. He should be the luckiest man in the world. He *was*. He loved her vigour and her animal spirits. He loved the way she sashayed down the street, tossing her head when scaffolders whistled at her. She could whistle back through two fingers – something he had always admired and longed to be able to do himself. The energy of the woman! She cleaned people's houses, she waitressed for a catering company, she worked out at a gym, arriving home luminous with libido and pouncing on him like a panther. He must be the envy of every red-blooded male in London.

That was the problem. He knew he was lucky. That was what made it worse, his recent but unmistakable feelings of reluctance when it was time to go to bed. He knew the sounds so well – the rasp of the match as Tina lit the candle in the bedroom, the click of the stereo as she inserted her get-ourselves-in-the-mood cassette. This was currently a Motown compilation called *Night is the Time for Love*. He knew, by the length of time she was in the bathroom, that she was inserting her diaphragm. Before she got into bed she puff-puffed herself with perfume, ready for action. The stage was being set for his performance and of course he was willing but sometimes, just sometimes, a man had to get a good night's sleep. Or even catch up on his reading. Desmond had left school at sixteen and was trying to work his way through the classics, but for weeks now he had been stuck at page thirty-six of *Moby-Dick*.

Then there were the weekends. Dozing, exhausted, in front of the TV, he would be woken by her nimble fingers unbuttoning his shirt. 'Let's have a quickie,' she would breathe into his ear. Only last week he had been making himself a cup of tea in the kitchen and found himself pinioned against the units. 'They can see us opposite!' he protested, indicating the window. But she just wiggled her fingers over his shoulder. 'Hi there!' she called. He went to pull down the blind and knocked over the geranium pot on the window ledge, scattering earth on the floor, but even that didn't deter her. The next day he had had a throbbing pain in his lower spine, from where it had been pressed against the fridge door.

Sunday mornings were the other time. Waking drowsily, he would hear her purposefully brushing her teeth in the bathroom. This meant that when she climbed back into bed she could kiss him properly – in her opinion it was only in films that people made love in the mornings with their mouths all frowsty. So then he would have to get up and brush his teeth too, and bang went his lie-in.

Putting it this way sounded unromantic but sometimes, to be perfectly honest, this was how he felt. His wife was becoming so impersonal; it seemed as if she were reading a manual over his shoulder. Sometimes he felt he was simply part of her work-out routine, a piece of gym equipment she was using to shape up her thighs and flatten her stomach muscles. He felt *used*.

Desmond worked at a garage called Chiswick Lane Autos. It was the week after Christmas, a busy period due to the number of silly buggers drinking and driving on the icy roads. Two major prangs were towed in on the Wednesday, a Mazda and an Escort GTI. He worked hard all day. When he got home, Tina snuggled up and put his hand on her shin.

'Go on, feel!' she said. 'I've just had them waxed.'

'Give us a moment,' he said, slumping on to the settee.

'Don't then. Some people'd give their right arm to feel my legs.'

He stroked her bare skin with one hand, and picked up the mail. Amongst it was a brown paper package addressed to Mr Murphy, who lived in the maisonette next door. The paper was torn; a video cassette poked out. Tina grabbed it and wriggled it out of the parcel.

'The dirty bugger!' she giggled. 'I knew he was funny! The way he looks at me when I take out the rubbish!' She held up the video. He glimpsed the word *Lovers* and *Adults Only*. She lunged towards the TV. 'Come on, let's put it on!'

'We can't,' he said.

'Why not?'

'It's not ours.'

'Des!'

How could he explain to his wife that the thought of watching a pornographic video with her filled him with exhaustion? More than that – with a sort of cosmic despair? He got up. 'I'm going to make a cup of tea.'

'Typical!' she said, and added ominously: 'Some people I know would jump at the chance.'

He went into their little kitchen and gazed at the units. He suddenly felt lonely. What's it all about? he asked himself. Any of it?

He took the next day off to visit his mother in Wokingham – his yearly Christmas duty. Tina wasn't coming; she said his mother was boring. His mother probably *was* boring for all he knew, but he knew her too well to use that sort of word, and was obscurely disappointed that Tina did.

He said goodbye to his wife, who was plucking her eyebrows in the bathroom. She was humming. After their spat last night, she seemed surprisingly cheerful.

He took the video with him. Just as he was poised outside Mr Murphy's letterbox, about to post it through, he heard footsteps and sprang back. Mr Murphy came out. 'Morning,' Des mumbled, and retreated to the car. He couldn't possibly let Mr Murphy know that *he* knew; he would post it back later, when the coast was clear.

When he got back that evening Tina was in the bath, humming again. 'You been in there all day?' he joked, peering around the door.

She jumped; the water sloshed. Then she shook her head. 'Been working flat out all afternoon, at Mrs Whatsit's and then at that other place, you know, took hours. I'm totally shagged out.' And she slid under the foam.

The next morning, he was under the bonnet of a Citroën CX when he heard a rattling, grinding sound. A car drew up in the forecourt and shuddered to a stop. It was a badly damaged Volkswagen Passat; its side panel was caved in, part of the bonnet as well, and two of its windows were shattered. He recognized the vehicle – he had recently MOT'd it – and its driver, Mrs Wakeman. She had been coming here for years.

She climbed out. She looked pale; when she gave him the keys her hand trembled.

'You OK?' he asked, wiping his fingers on a rag. 'You just done this?'

'Not me,' she said. 'My boyfriend. He crashed it last night. *Ex-boyfriend*.' Suddenly she burst into tears.

Desmond sat her down in the office and passed her some kitchen roll. 'You mean he's dead?'

Mrs Wakeman shook her head. 'Wish he was.' She blew her nose. 'Oh, I could *kill* him! He's just been using me. Oh, I'm such a fool!'

'Want a cup of tea?'

'He was using my car for minicab work. I lent it to him, my children've had to stand freezing at bus stops – how could I have been so besotted? It's called limerence.'

'What?'

'A sort of madness. My daughter read about it in *Marie Claire*. My own children are wiser than I am! You got kids?'

He shook his head. Tina didn't want them yet; she didn't want to get stretch marks.

'There was a girl with him, you see,' said Mrs Wakeman. 'Sitting in the front seat.'

'Was she hurt?'

She shook her head. 'But she was in the front seat, don't you see? She wasn't a paying bloody passenger, she wasn't sitting in the back. She was a *girlfriend*. Anyway, he confessed.' She started sobbing again. 'I'm sorry. I shouldn't be telling you all this, but everybody else is going to say *I told you so*.'

He looked through the window, at the car. 'You contacted your insurance company? Looks like a write-off to me.'

'The whole thing's a write-off,' she said. 'We had nothing in common but I fooled myself into thinking we had. You meet somebody, you lust after their body, and from then onwards you make yourself believe you're soulmates, you try to mould them into being what you want, you sort of re-invent them for yourself and then, once the scales fall from your eyes, you realize you've invented somebody who doesn't exist, that it's all self-delusion. I should know. I work in advertising.' She wiped her eyes. 'Are you in love?'

He poured water on to the teabags. 'Well, I'm married.'

She laughed, shakily. 'That's no answer.'

'Sugar?'

She shook her head. Rummaging inside her handbag, she pulled out a video. 'You don't want two tickets to Venice, do you?' She put the video on the desk and pulled out her cigarettes. 'I'm supposed to be going there with him next week. That's the video from the travel agents. We were going to watch it together tonight.' She offered him a cigarette. 'Don't you want to go to Venice? It'd be so romantic.'

'Can't,' he said. 'We're off to Florida next month.'

'Gosh. Doesn't everybody get around nowadays!' He knew what she meant – by *everyone* she meant *even garage mechanics*. She blushed. 'I mean, my son's friends,' she jabbered, 'they're always munching malaria tablets and whizzing off to Togoland. *See you in Guatemala!* they say. In my day we were lucky to get a week in Bognor Regis.'

'It's a different place now, the world,' he said. Then he added, surprising himself: 'Like, it used to be women who were sex objects. Now it's men.'

She smiled. 'Maybe that's what Owen felt. My boyfriend – ex. Sometimes I felt I was banging on a closed door, trying to get through. More and more desperate.' They paused for a moment. From the workshop came the *thwack-thwack* of Robbie, panel-beating. 'Still, it was fun while it lasted,' she said.

When she left Desmond felt strangely stirred. He thought of Tina, and their first holiday together in Portugal. How the sight of her tenderly peeling shoulders had brought tears to his eyes. Why didn't he tell her how much she moved him? 'You never talk!' Tina said, accusingly. Was that what she had been doing, these past few months – banging away at him to get his attention?

He packed up early, at five. As he got into his car he had a strong sensation of danger – so strong that it blocked his throat. Those baths, that leg-waxing – how could he be such a fool? He thought: I've got to do something now, before it's too late.

When Tina arrived home he led her to the settee. He turned off the lights and lit a candle.

'What's all this in aid of?' she asked.

He passed her a glass of wine and slotted in the video. He pressed *play* and sat down beside his wife. 'Let's feel those shins,' he murmured.

'I've got my tights on.'

She lifted up her bottom and he pulled them off. 'Mmm, nice and smooth,' he whispered, stroking her leg.

She pointed at the TV and laughed. 'So we're going to watch it?'

He nodded. 'It's called *A Place for Lovers*.'

The video came on. Sunlight shone on a row of gondolas, bobbing on the water. A voice said caressingly: '*Let us explore together the most romantic city on earth, a city for lovers . . .*'

'This is it?' she asked, surprised.

'*Time has etched its mark on her face but it can never erase her ageless beauty . . .*' said the commentator.

He stared at the TV. 'I brought home the wrong video,' he said. 'This is a thing about Venice.'

'*Let us stroll across St Mark's Square, bustling and cosmopolitan, and be serenaded by the plangent notes of a violin . . .*'

She paused. Then she snuggled up against him. 'Oh well, never mind,' she said. 'This is a lot more romantic.'

And, as it turned out, it was.

5. I Don't Want to Know

Lara sat at the window, gazing at the cows, and wondered whether to go to her ex-husband's party. She had always been a creature of impulse. It was on impulse that she had run away from him in the first place, eight years ago. She wasn't used to weighing up the pros and cons – should she go, shouldn't she? – but it was New Year's Eve and that made it significant, particularly now Jupiter was in conjunction with Saturn.

Lara was a jeweller. She lived in Totnes with a man called Flange. His real name was Gilbert but only his intimates knew that and he didn't have many of those. None, in fact. Flange was a solitary, bearded man who made stained-glass windows. He didn't believe in New Year's Eve. He said that a truly spiritual person should treat every day as a new year. And he certainly didn't believe in parties.

Outside it had started to rain. The drops tattooed on the corrugated iron of the outhouse. Within it, Flange would be working in his customary silence.

Lara jumped up and looked at the timetable. There was a train to London at eleven thirty.

'You've invited Mum?' Paula stared at her father.

The wine for the party had arrived. Munro was uncorking

a bottle, purely for tasting purposes. 'I feel expansive,' he said. 'Did we buy any Twiglets?'

'She'll never come all this way anyway.'

'Why not?' he said. 'She might be curious.'

'Curious? Mum?'

'I know your mother's not overly interested in others, but even *she* might want to see if success has spoilt me.' He smiled smugly. 'Has it?'

'Yes,' said his daughter. 'If you play that video of yourself on *The Late Show* one more time I'll scream.'

Munro's novel had just been published to rave reviews. Strange to think that a year ago he had been gloomily struggling with a tinpot detective story. As he had told the *Independent*, his novel had come to him in a burst of inspiration and he had written it in three months flat. Now he was the darling of the literati, some of whom were coming to his party tonight. 'Shall I leave some copies of my book around, just casually?'

'No!' said his daughter.

'Wonder if your mum recognizes herself in it.'

'She probably hasn't read it.'

He nodded. 'In Totnes they only read Tarot cards, don't they? Promise to deal with her if she gets embarrassing.'

'Dad, I've told you! I won't be here. I'm babysitting. It's triple-rate on New Year's Eve.'

Motherhood had changed Tina. Desmond's feisty young wife had been transformed overnight into a demure, contented – well, *mother*. Her face, innocent of make-up, looked bare and vulnerable. Once the life and soul of the party, she now stayed at home reading baby magazines and nursing their three-month-old son Bruce. When Des said: 'It's New Year's Eve, I'm taking you up West,' she had stared at him as if he'd suggested a trip to the moon.

'We can't leave Bruce!'

'We'll get a babysitter.' He laughed. 'Seems funny, *me* having to persuade *you* to come out for a night on the tiles.'

She burped Bruce and laid him in his carrycot. They gazed at him. It was hot in their little maisonette; Tina was terrified their baby might catch a chill. Bruce's carrot-coloured hair was plastered to his forehead.

Desmond had dark-brown hair and Tina's, now the blond had grown out, was revealed as mouse. When their red-headed son was born Des had been startled. For a mad moment he had thought that all babies were born red-haired, like rabbits were born blind. Tina had said nothing. When a few weeks had passed and the hair remained red he had said it must be inherited from his great-aunty Dottie, who he had heard was definitely gingery on top. That must be the explanation. Tina had nodded wordlessly. The next day she had bought Des a beautiful leather jacket. 'What's all this about?' he had asked. She hadn't replied.

They got a babysitter – Paula, the daughter of one of Tina's old employers. At eight o'clock a minicab arrived to take them to Leicester Square where they were going to have an Italian meal. The driver, a young bloke in a cowboy shirt, asked if they liked country and western music and slotted in a cassette.

'. . . *your cheatin' heart*,' crooned a man, '. . . *I been a fool . . . to trust you . . .*'

Des lit a cigarette and gazed out of the window.

Munro's party was in full swing. Barnaby, his little son, barged through the crowd and spilt Ribena down the leggings of the *Guardian*'s fiction critic. Munro mopped her up. 'Thank God you've already written your review,' he laughed. He had a growing suspicion that he was drunk; he had a sudden, clear memory of telling the same story twice. No, three times.

He looked across at his ex-wife, Lara. He hadn't seen her for years. She was ageing surprisingly well in a hippyish, patchouli sort of way. She was gazing fixedly at a woman called Esther, the mother of one of his daughter's friends. A lifetime ago, when he'd first met Lara, he hadn't realized why she had gazed at him so intensely; it was because she was too vain to wear her glasses. He had thought, erroneously as it turned out, that she was actually interested in what he was saying.

The minicab was driving through Hammersmith. A car slewed across the road in front of them. Their driver slammed on his brakes.

'Dickhead!' he shouted. He turned to them in the mirror. 'A year ago some drunken berk wrote off my car. Well, not *my* car. Side caved in. Girl I was with, one more inch and she'd've been dead.'

Desmond gripped his wife's hand. He thought of chance, of a few inches, of the fragility of life as the year rolled on its axis. The music crooned as they drove up Knightsbridge.

'. . . *all you do is tell me lies . . .*'

'Isn't life amazing,' said Des to his wife. 'Like, pot luck. Like, if someone had pulled out a different raffle ticket I wouldn't have won that holiday in Portugal, I wouldn't

have fallen in love with you, there wouldn't be a baby lying
in his carrycot—'

'Des—' she said.

He stopped her mouth with his finger. 'I just mean –
accidents can happen. Or not happen. Either way it's, like,
out of our hands.' He lifted up the champagne bottle. 'After
dinner we'll take this to Trafalgar Square.'

Esther was still talking to Lara. She had to shout over the
noise of the party. 'I used to work in advertising but I've
just given it up. You see, this time last year I went to Venice
with a woman friend and suddenly felt this lump. I
thought – typical! I'm staying in the most romantic city in
the world and I have to feel my own breasts! Anyway, they
took the lump out and it was benign but the whole thing
shook me up, shook up my priorities, and advertising
seemed . . . so trivial somehow . . . and I'd made some disastrous mistakes in my personal life . . .'

Lara, gazing at her, suddenly had a vision of Flange. He
would be standing in the corner looking mutinous, itching
to leave. He would be gazing at all these people and thinking *chatter-chatter, yackety-yack, what fools they look*.
Lara gazed at the party guests and thought they looked a
lot more interesting than the woman who ran the post
office and why did it always rain in the country? Then she
thought, with blinding clarity: Flange is boring. I'm bored
to tears.

Esther was saying: 'What I really want to do is sell up
and move to the country.' She gestured around. 'I'm tired
of all this yackety-yackety media gossip. I want to move
somewhere quiet and do my own thing . . . painting . . .'

'Jewellery,' said Lara automatically.

'. . . jewellery. That'd be so creative. Funny they call *advertising* creative . . . huh . . .' She sighed. 'I know what *my* New Year Resolution's going to be. Move to the country and change my life.'

'I know what mine's going to be, too,' said Lara. She moved away. 'Just going to find my daughter.'

Paula was looking after four babies. Once the word had got around, several neighbouring couples had grabbed at the chance of leaving their infants with her and going out to celebrate. She sat in Tina's lounge, the TV on low, surrounded by carrycots. Their inmates slumbered. She had never liked New Year's Eve parties; it was so embarrassing, being kissed by people she had never seen before. That the event should be significant, and never was, made it worse. She worked out how much money she was earning and felt at peace.

At ten to twelve the doorbell rang. Her mother stood there, clutching a bottle of champagne.

'I pinched this from the party,' she said. 'I had to see the new year in with my daughter.'

The doorbell had woken up two of the babies; they started to cry. 'Now look what you've done,' said Paula.

'Goodness, a crèche!' Her mother lifted up a yelling baby and vaguely joggled it up and down. 'Listen, I've made a New Year's Resolution. I'm sure it's in my stars. I've been thinking about you so much, my pet. I'm going to move back into London and be with you, where I belong. Mother and daughter together.'

'It's a bit late for that,' said Paula. 'I'm eighteen. I've

finished school, remember? I'm going to Thailand next month. Oh hell!' The two babies had woken up the other two. They struggled to a sitting position in their carrycots, whimpering, limbering themselves up to scream. Her mother was trying to uncork the champagne bottle with one hand. Suddenly furious, Paula pointed to the babies. 'How can you talk about mother and daughter! These parents have only left their kids for one night. *You* left *me* for eight years!'

'Darling, don't be so unforgiving!'

Paula hoisted a baby on to her hip. She went into the kitchen to heat up some milk. Her mother followed.

'Why did you leave me?' Paula demanded. 'You've never told me. I want to know.'

'Oh, it's a long story. Your father . . .'

Her voice was drowned by yells. 'Quick, take this bottle!' said Paula.

Back in the lounge the noise was deafening. Paula only caught a few words. '. . . your father . . . selfish . . . unresponsive . . . no idea of my needs . . .' her mother raised her voice over the din. 'Then he started drinking . . .'

'Pass me that bottle,' yelled Paula, 'and that dummy!'

'. . . he was like a *child* . . .'

'Pick that one up! Can't you even change a nappy?'

The noise grew louder. Suddenly Paula looked at her watch. Gripping a baby, she lunged to the TV and turned up the volume. Big Ben started striking. The screen showed Trafalgar Square; the crowd roared.

'SHUT UP!' Paula yelled – to the babies, to her mother. In the sudden silence she grabbed the champagne bottle and took a swig. 'I don't want to hear,' she said. 'I *can't* hear.' She passed the bottle to her mother. 'Happy New Year anyway,' she said.

It was twelve thirty. Des and Tina sat in a taxi, travelling home. Their throats were sore from shouting greetings to complete strangers. For one magical moment, at midnight, Des had felt part of a huge family thousands strong. His own seemed so small, and besides, Tina thought they were boring. Problem was, you couldn't choose your own parents, just as they couldn't choose you. Easier with strangers.

'Hope Bruce is OK,' Tina said.

'Don't worry. I'm sure he's fine.'

Tina picked a streamer off her coat. 'Des,' she said. 'There's something I've got to tell you. About Bruce.' She paused. 'A year ago—'

He put his hand to her mouth. 'Don't,' he said. 'Honestly, truly – I don't want to know.'

For the rest of the journey they didn't speak. When they arrived home, Tina had torn the streamer into bits. They lay scattered on her lap and fell off when she got up. When Des put the key into the lock, she nuzzled his neck.

In the lounge the TV burbled on, unwatched. The babies lay asleep in their carrycots. On the settee slumbered their babysitter and an unknown, messy-looking woman wearing a lot of jewellery.

Des inspected the carrycots, one by one. 'Which one's Bruce?' he joked, gazing down at the babies. He smiled at his wife. 'Hey, does it really matter?'

Tina held his gaze for a moment. 'They've left some

champagne,' she said finally, picking up the bottle. She fetched two glasses.

Des leaned over Bruce's carrycot. He planted a kiss on the baby's treacherous red hair. He whispered: 'Happy New Year to you too, mate.'

A Pedicure in Florence

Be honest. Look into your heart. Do you prefer to get a postcard saying 'Having a wonderful time', or one saying 'Holiday a total disaster, wish we could come home'?

Helen, shamefully, felt a small rush of pleasure from other people's misfortunes. Perhaps she wasn't very nice at all; perhaps that was why Alan had divorced her. But then holidays with Alan had always been a strain; to compare them with others' non-successes was some small consolation, she supposed. Events conspired to irritate him – her map-reading, the children's bleary refusal to get up early and seize the day, the presence of other British people in some remote and inaccessible location where he thought himself and his family alone and speaking the language like natives. She always remembered his bellow of pain when, staying the night in a chai house in the middle of the Hindu Kush, he had opened the visitors' book and found the names of Denise and Donald Waterman, the couple who lived opposite them in Ealing.

Such a strain, keeping him happy, silently urging the children to ask enquiring questions about Romanesque architecture rather than moaning that their Walkman batteries had run out. But all that was over now; she was a single woman again. After twenty-two years she and Alan had parted. Mysteriously, marriage itself seemed to have been the *coup de grâce*. They had met in that long-lost golden age when everyone was hanging loose, hanging out, whatever they all did then. After seventeen years of living together and bringing up a family their increasingly muti- nous children had rebelled. 'We keep on having to explain to people!' they moaned. Finally, they delivered their own *coup de grâce*. 'It's so *seventies*, not being married.'

That had done it. Stung, she and Alan had gone to a register office and got married. Things had started disinte- grating and within four years they were divorced.

Alan-less, the summer holidays approached. Welling up beneath her sense of panic and failure she was aware of an exhilarating new feeling – freedom. The children were almost grown-up; she was forty-four. She could go any- where; do anything. She would do what she had always wanted to do: rent a house in Italy and not do anything cultural. She would swim and sunbathe and drink litres of red wine. She wouldn't visit any museums and churches at all – not unless she felt like it. Alan, laden with guidebooks, had always insisted they did these things thoroughly; he could even pronounce 'Ghirlandaio'.

She went with her friend Xandra, a cheerful, accommo- dating woman who was also man-less, though a veteran of two marriages and a recent disastrous liaison with a young motorbike messenger who worked at her courier firm. Helen was fond of Xandra, but the real basis of their bond was their two daughters, who were best friends at school and the only ones of their various children who had conde- scended to come on holiday with them.

'Four women in Italy!' chortled Xandra, snorting smoke through her nostrils. 'Two young, two old – three thin and

one –' prodding herself '– fat. We're going to have a ball!
They won't know what's hit them.' She laughed her laugh
that sounded like dried beans rattling in a glass jar.

It started off all right. 'How romantic!' Helen cried as
they drove up a gravel track. It climbed miles up a hillside
above Perugia. The undercarriage scraped over a rock; they
laughed. How grateful she was that Alan wasn't here to
wince at the scraping noise, to hear the girls' complaints
that it was miles from anywhere, to have heard Xandra's
ribald and explicit assessment of the local talent lounging
outside the village shop – or, as she put it, resting on their
Zimmer frames.

The house stood at the top of the hill – a handsome stone
building complete with pool and a wonderful view. 'Look
at the wonderful view!' cried Helen. The German couple
who owned it lived in an apartment on the ground floor.
The man, Hans, a bronzed, overweight bull in tiny trunks,
was fiddling with the filter in the swimming pool.

'They *live* here?' hissed Annie, Helen's daughter. 'How
am I going to take my top off?'

'Look at the swallows!' cried Helen. 'Look at the flowers! Oh look – a darling little lizard!'

They had forgotten to buy bread so Helen drove back
down the gravel track to the village. It took twenty minutes
and just as she arrived she saw the shutter crash down on
the shop. She banged on it and after a moment an old
woman with a flourishing moustache appeared and jabbered rapidly in Italian.

'*Aperto? Aperto?*' asked Helen. An old retainer sitting
outside the bar held up four fingers. Watched by the row of
geriatrics, she climbed back into the car. Half of her

thought: I'm glad Alan's not here; *we* don't mind. We'll eat biscuits. The other half thought: if only he were here, he would have remembered that the whole country closes down from one to four.

When she returned she heard girlish laughter and splashes. Her spirits rose until she saw that it was not their two daughters jumping into the pool; it was a small girl wearing water-wings. Annie and Abigail sat fully clothed on the terrace, looking mutinous and scratching their mosquito bites. Charcoal smudges on the concrete floor betrayed where they had been stubbing out their Marlboros.

'There's somebody else staying with the Germans!' they hissed. 'An Australian woman called Binkie!' They pointed to the little girl. 'That's her daughter!'

Binkie turned out to be a talkative, pear-shaped woman who was blithely unaware of their territorial rights to the pool. Like many single parents of a single child, she devoted herself to her daughter's development, informing her at some length about her every move. Her daughter was called Mena and over the next couple of days they learnt to stiffen as Binkie approached the pool. 'Now Mena, Mummy's going to take you for a swim and then you can have an ice lolly and then we'll lie in the sun with these nice people . . .' Presuming anyone who was reading had to be bored, she would look at their books. 'Oh, *The Age of Grief*, Helen, is that a sad book?'

'She's always *here*!' hissed the girls. 'She's always talking! She's so boring!'

It seemed churlish to object to a small child playing in their pool – after all, like them, Binkie was a single mother. Helen's irritation sprang partly from her own suspicion that she herself was being petty. So she smiled sweetly – so sweetly that Binkie stopped asking if she could use the pool and ensconced herself on the best lounger, the only one with a mattress.

The other problem – no, not problem, they did *live* there – was the German couple. Hans was always at the pool-side, fishing out insects with his net or fiddling with a complicated tangle of filters and hoses. The girls tried to find a secluded place to sunbathe but then his wife came out there to hang up her washing and ask them what they felt about the Royal family. The girls retreated to the house.

'Look, we're still white! We've got to get brown, to show our friends! They're sitting on our terrace. They're using our barbecue!'

'They did ask,' said Helen. 'They've got friends coming round tonight.'

'Why didn't you say no?'

'I couldn't.'

Trapped by their own cowardice, they cowered indoors. Helen thought: if Alan were here – if any man were here – he would have made our territorial rights politely clear at the beginning. Women are so feeble. We are trapped by our eagerness to be liked. That evening, to avoid their hosts, they forsook the terrace with its swallows and its wonderful views over the Umbrian hills and drove down to the village where they sat in the small, concrete bar. Lit by a strip of fly-bespattered neon it was a quiet place, its clientele the geriatric men who spent the rest of the day sitting outside the shop. One of them cleared his throat and spat into a handkerchief. The girls gazed at the pensioners and stubbed out the cigarettes their mothers no longer had the strength to stop them smoking.

'When I was your age,' said Helen, 'I went on holiday with my parents to Malta and the first night I went out with a waiter and got love bites all over my neck. For the next whole week I had to wear a scarf. My parents kept saying *aren't you hot? Why don't you take it off?*'

Annie snorted. 'Huh. The only things biting us are effing mosquitoes.'

Abigail looked around. 'None of this lot have got any teeth anyway.'

Xandra, chuckling, leafed through her phrase book. '*Questi sono difettosi. Me li potrebbe cambiare!*' She looked up. 'These are faulty. Can I have a replacement!'

It took them a week to admit, openly, that their holiday was a disaster. Abigail had constipation, then diarrhoea, and spent a great deal of time in the lavatory, which abutted the kitchen. To spare her embarrassment they kept away from the kitchen, the walls were so thin, and just darted in to grab some food. How small the place seemed, and how many of them in it! Annie wrote long letters to her friends bemoaning the lack of men and wishing she were home. Xandra's period was late and, terrified that she had been impregnated by her toyboy motorbike messenger, she drove down to the village to phone him up but couldn't get through. Her daughter, who had overheard this from the lavatory, emerged and snorted: 'You're not pregnant. You're getting the menopause.' At this Xandra burst into tears and drank a bottle of Chianti. At midnight she staggered into the bathroom and threw up. 'I must be pregnant!' she wailed.

Helen, to escape, tried to go for a walk but unlike Xandra the countryside proved impregnable. Walking down one gravel path she arrived at a rubbish dump and walking down the other she was stopped by a gate saying STRADA PRIVATA. Walking back to the house she reflected upon the illusions of liberty. Now she was here, how free seemed her life in London! In Ealing she could walk anywhere. Unchained from the domestic grind she could shop anytime, rather than be in thrall to the siesta. Best of all, she had the personal liberty of her own privacy and didn't have to wait, behind a window, for the moment to dart out to the pool, and spend the rest of her time trying to find a tin-opener or gazing at someone else's hideous furniture. Outside the German invasion was gathering pace and several more house guests had arrived; they lay around the pool, grilling themselves. Xandra said: 'I feel like pricking them with a fork.'

Trapped in the house, Xandra and the two girls began to get on Helen's nerves. They still had a week to go. In desperation she finally suggested a cultural expedition. They drove to Arezzo to see the Piero della Francesca frescoes. Sweltering in the heat, they parked in a tow-away zone and hurried into the church with ten minutes to go before it closed. In the gloom they could just make out a wall covered with flapping plastic sheeting and a sign saying IN RESTAURO.

When they got back the girls flung themselves on their beds and said they had finished their books and what on earth were they going to do now? They lay there sulkily, counting their mosquito bites. Helen was gripped by the same panic. What *does* one do on holiday?

So when the girls, exasperated by the lack of local talent, said they were going to take a day trip to Florence, she felt secretly relieved.

'You're only seventeen!' Xandra protested.

Abigail snorted: 'At seventeen you got pregnant with Ben.'

'Exactly,' said her mother. 'That's what I'm worried about.'

But after a short tussle the teenagers won and at an unearthly hour – unearthly for the girls – they were dispatched on to the train for Florence.

Can you sense these things? As a mother, can you sense them? At seven o'clock Helen began to feel uneasy. Xandra was trying to get her out to the terrace for a drink before the Germans emerged from the house. 'If we're sitting there already, maybe they won't talk to us,' she whispered – they had taken to whispering. After a week the Germans, encouraged by the women's feebleness, had presumed their company was always welcome and engaged them in long conversations about the British parliamentary system when they were trying to read their books.

They carried out their wine, willing Binkie not to join them with the latest instalment of the saga of Mena's tummy upset. They drank, unmolested. The girls were due back at ten-ish; they were going to take a taxi from Perugia station.

'What'll I do?' wailed Xandra. 'I can't have another baby! I'm forty-three!'

Helen, gazing at the sinking sun, thought of the hot bonds of motherhood, how one was never free of it, not until one died. How when even a grown child was absent a terrible scenario played over and over in one's head; increasingly lurid, it ceased only with the child's return. How could one start again with all that?

At ten o'clock she said: 'Do you think they're all right?'

At a quarter past eleven Hans appeared. 'Phone for you!' he bellowed.

It was Annie. They had been robbed. 'We were sitting on these steps outside the whatsit, the Duomo,' she sobbed faintly, 'and these boys came up to us and we thought they were so nice . . .' Her voice broke. 'We've only got this phone card and it's running out . . .'

Helen, her bowels churning, shouted: 'Check into a hotel, one that takes Visa cards! Wait for us there!' The line went dead.

The next morning Helen and Xandra drove to Florence. The girls had phoned with the name of their hotel and by noon they had found it – a leprous-looking pensione up a side street near the railway station. At the reception desk a man jerked his head, indicating upstairs. A fan lifted and lowered his newspaper.

In Room 26 the curtains were closed. It was a narrow cell, smelling of last night's cigarettes. The girls, who had only just woken, lay in bed watching an Italian game show on TV. Around them lay scattered the empty contents of their minibar. 'We've lived off it,' said Annie, as Helen hugged her. 'There isn't room service and we missed breakfast.'

With some pride, Abigail pointed out the empties to her mother. 'Coke, Kronenbourg, Sanpellegrino Aranciata, J&B, Campari soda, a bag of peanuts and that funny liqueur even *you* don't drink.'

Xandra's face froze. She looked at them all and then darted into the bathroom. Behind the closed door they heard a yelp.

'It's started!' she called. 'Blimey, my period's started!'

Helen pulled open the curtains; the sun blazed in. Suddenly they all burst out laughing. Strange, wasn't it? Imprisoned in their cell, they were filled with joy. Why? Because they had found their girls? Because they were alone, at last? Because when they were supposed to be enjoying their holiday they weren't, and now they weren't, they were? Helen felt an airy, shuddering sense of liberation. Freedom is a Visa card, she thought. Freedom is not being pregnant. Freedom is not being married, for it seemed suddenly very simple to be four females alone in this squalid room. Nobody to blame them, nobody to know. Nobody to chastise the girls for being bored, for being uncultural, for being robbed. To celebrate, they shared the last bottle – Asti Spumante, which the girls hadn't touched because they thought it was champagne and too expensive. See – despite their mulishness they were nice really.

Later they sat on the rim of a fountain and ate pieces of pizza in smeary paper napkins. Junk food for tourists, according to Alan, but Alan wasn't here. And after lunch Helen didn't visit the Uffizi or the Pitti Palace or the Santa Maria Novella. She stopped somebody and, using the phrase book, asked: '*Dove il piu vicino* . . . er, *istituto di bellezza?*'

Never in her life had she done this before. Never in her life had she had a pedicure. She went into a scruffy little beauty parlour and sat in an airless cubicle whilst a chain-smoking beautician clipped her toenails and pushed back her cuticles. The only culture she saw was a view of Venice on the heaped ashtray, and a scorched reproduction of Botticelli's *Birth of Venus* printed on the lampshade.

She gazed at her toenails, freshly painted crimson. She smiled at the woman. '*Bene!*' she said. She thought: freedom is doing exactly what I've always wanted to do. For the first time since her divorce – no, since way back in her marriage – she felt truly grown-up.

And later that day she wrote postcards. 'Having a terrible time,' she wrote, 'robberies, stomach upsets, boring Germans.' She wrote that because happiness made her generous.

Summer Bedding

I was planting the summer bedding when he talked to me. I was bending over, rump in the air. I was planting white begonias, red geraniums and an edging of verbena – well, *I* didn't like the colour scheme either. I was working in St James's Park and Big Ben chimed in time with the thrust of my trowel. Being so near to parliamentary decisions made me feel vigorous and participatory. It made significant the packed, cylindrical roots of the plants I inserted into their new home, the old earth. In the Commons they were debating some law about press intrusion and I wondered if such a measure would ever take root.

Anyway, I straightened up and saw this trim, neat man. Grey beard; grey silk suit. Dapper. I wiped my hands on my dungarees. He asked me where he could get a cup of tea and I told him. 'I am so very obliged,' he said. So polite, but then he *was* foreign. He looked at me and sighed. 'Ah – Silvana Mangano.'

That dates him – dates me too. I was too young to have seen *Bitter Rice*. He said: 'She stood like you stand – I thought, never have I seen such a magnificent creature.' He smiled. I felt the heat spreading into my face.

Later, he came back. I was sitting on a bench drinking tisane from my thermos. Big Ben chimed five. He sat beside me and talked about movies. I said that when I came home,

I was so exhausted I could hardly switch on the TV. Note that I didn't mention my husband. This omission made me blush again. He lifted my arm. 'Your elbows,' he said, 'how charming they are!' He gazed at them. My skin prickled. Nobody has ever noticed my elbows before. Gavin had never remarked on them. But then I had never said anything about Gavin's elbows either. In the silence a pelican flew up from the island, clattering and prehistoric.

He came back the next day. I was putting in the verbena – magenta, horrible colour. Somebody had left a *Sun* on the bench and I read that a scandal was brewing – a cabinet minister had been spotted canoodling with a comely young researcher. He sat down – his name was Bertrand – and said that in his country there was a *modus vivendi* for affairs of the heart, and to him the scandal was that it obscured the real scandals and removed able men from office. Didn't we all need romance in our lives?

He asked me to take a glass of wine with him. 'My hands! My clothes!' I cried.

'We will wash your hands,' he replied. 'As for the rest – you look the most radiant young woman in London. Others have to buy the colour of your cheeks in a little container.'

So that was how it began. That was how I, a married woman, became the mistress of a married man. My own summer bedding took place in a hotel room in Victoria. It happened during the lost hour after work. Down in the street, beyond the double-glazing, traffic flowed soundlessly. It was their rush hour, but we took our time. My dungarees lay, guiltily empty, over a gilt chair; afterwards I washed myself with his complimentary shower gel.

He was Belgian, and something to do with the European

Commission, but he didn't want to talk about that, it was too boring, and I certainly didn't want to hear. I never said a word about Gavin, either. His name, spoken aloud, would have felt too shocking. Bertrand and I existed in another dimension, disconnected, sealed in with its own adulterous air-conditioning. Is it always like this? I had never done it before, you see.

Back home Gavin would be hunched over his computer. For three years now I had been supporting us while he studied quantum mechanics – a subject that, like my liaison, existed on another inexplicable plane. We lived in a small flat in Kilburn – draughty, freezing in winter – and the real reason we didn't go to the cinema was that we had no money. We were saving up for central heating. Gavin and I were chums. Are chums. He calls my breasts 'boobs'. With Bertrand I became another creature – a woman. A real woman, the old-fashioned kind for whom doors are opened and whose breasts, not boobs, are worshipped. Who is given gifts.

Oh yes, he gave me those. And what gifts! The first was a bracelet with little jewels in it. Not my thing at all but that made it all the more arousing; I felt like a kept woman. There is something very sexy about being politically incorrect. A few weeks later he gave me a necklace with little blue stones in it. The next day I wore it under my T-shirt while I heaved sacks of manure. That he was paying for my body made it delightfully precious; I bloomed for him. All these years I had been paying for a man and now a man was paying for me! These gifts were the jewelled equivalent of our love affair – utterly unlikely and disconnected to anything familiar. As old-fashioned as having a continental lover, as unlikely as the pelicans in St James's Park and almost as prehistoric. I told nobody; not even Janice who had trained with me at Wisley and who at the last count had slept with twenty-seven men. She would have found it hysterical. So I just wrapped the little boxes in brown paper and hid them under a loose floorboard in the bedroom. This hiding place seemed appropriately stagey, too – easing up the board made me feel as if I were acting in one of Bertrand's beloved Inspector Clouseau films.

So the summer passed. The cabinet minister resigned. Another scandal brewed; I read about it in a copy of the *Daily Express* that somebody had left in a litter bin. An MP was spotted coming out of a gay video club; a week later he was found dead in his fume-filled Ford Granada. And in October Bertrand went back to Brussels.

He was charming to the end – courteous and regretful. I guessed that he had done this often before, but curiously enough I didn't mind. I felt like the last in a line of mistresses that stretched back not just through his life but back into history – kept women, *Mistresses*. A species that, like coracle-builders, must be almost extinct. We said 'au revoir' over a half-bottle of champagne from his mini-bar and I slipped out, into the rush hour, into normal life.

In St James's Park I pulled up the summer bedding. The plants came out easily. The packed earth beneath them was still pot-shaped; they had hardly rooted at all. It was a drizzly October; the next week we planted bulbs there and you would never have known the summer arrangement had existed. The House of Commons reconvened after its ludicrously long summer recess with two of its number replaced. The old, sexually disgraced ones were Tories; the new ones were Lib-Dem. And Gavin announced that we had saved enough to install the central heating.

Which is how I came home one day, aching from double-digging, to discover him in a most un-Gavin-like state of excitement. He dragged me into the bedroom. 'What, *now*?' I said. 'But I'm filthy.'

I stopped and stared. Three of the floorboards had been removed, to install the radiator. Gavin held out a parcel wrapped in brown paper. 'Open it,' he said.

I opened it.

'Say something,' he said.

My throat closed up.

'Well?' He gazed at me. 'Well, Angie? Are we going to be honest?'

I paused. 'Honest?'

'Like, tell anyone. It must be someone's. Someone who lived here.'

I took a breath. 'Of course we won't tell. They don't belong to anyone we know.' I looked at my husband. 'We don't know anyone like that. Nobody like that would live here.'

So he sold the jewellery – they were real sapphires and real diamonds – and came home with £2,500. I got dressed up in my cheap Indian bangles from Camden Lock and we went out to dinner.

A curious thing happened. Over the following months Bertrand entered the bloodstream of our marriage. All summer he had been separate but now, for the first time, he came into our lives. He was there in the insouciance with which we bought a microwave, just like that; in our carefree lack of hesitation when we decided to go out to the movies;

he was there in our flushed cheeks and heightened merriment when we drank a bottle of vintage Bordeaux. He was even there in our subsequent, wine-flushed lovemaking.

Our marriage did have roots, you see. We're still together, five years later. It did have roots, but my bearded, old-fashioned, middle-aged little Belgian – he helped it to flower.

Smile

We had to wear these SMILE badges. It was one of the rules. And they'd nailed up a sign saying SMILE, just above the kitchen door, so we wouldn't forget. It's American, the hotel. Dennis, the chief receptionist, even says to the customers 'Have a nice day', but then he's paid more than I am, so I suppose he's willing.

I was on breakfasts when I was expecting. Through a fog of early morning-sickness I'd carry out the plates of scrambled eggs. The first time I noticed the man he pointed to the SMILE badge, pinned to my chest, then he pulled a face.

'Cheer up,' he said. 'It might never happen.'

I thought: *it has.*

Looking back, I suppose he appeared every six weeks or so, and stayed a couple of nights. I wasn't counting, then, because I didn't know who he was. Besides, I was on the alert for somebody else, who never turned up and still hasn't, being married, and based in Huddersfield, and having forgotten about that night when he ordered a bottle of Southern Comfort with room service. At least I'm nearly sure it was him.

I was still on breakfasts when I saw the man again, and my apron was getting tight. Soon I'd be bursting out of my uniform.

He said: 'You're looking bonny.'

I held out the toast basket and he took four. Munching, he nodded at my badge. 'Or are you just obedient?'

It took me a moment to realize what he meant, I was so used to wearing it.

'Oh yes, I always do what I'm told.'

He winked. 'Sounds promising.'

I gave him a pert look and flounced off. I was happy that day. The sickness had gone. I was keeping the baby; I'd never let anybody take it away from me. I'd have someone to love, who would be mine.

'You've put on weight,' he said, six weeks later. 'It suits you.'

'Thanks,' I said, smiling with my secret. 'More coffee?'

He held out his cup. 'And what do you call yourself?'

'Sandy.'

I looked at him. He was a handsome bloke; broad and fleshy, with a fine head of hair. He wore a tie printed with exclamation marks.

I've always gone for older men. They're bound to be married, of course. Not that it makes much difference while they're here.

When he finished his breakfast, I saw him pocketing a couple of marmalade sachets. You can tell the married ones; they're nicking them for the kids.

When I got too fat, they put me in the kitchens. You didn't have to wear your SMILE badge there. I was on salads. Arranging the radish roses, I day-dreamed about my baby.

I never knew it would feel like this. I felt heavy and warm and whole. The new chef kept pestering me, but he seemed like a midge – irksome but always out of sight. Nobody mattered. I walked through the steam, talking silently to my bulge. This baby meant the world to me. I suppose it came from not having much of a home myself, what with my dad leaving, and Mum moving in and out of lodgings, and me being in and out of Care. Not that I blame her. Or him, not really.

I'd stand in the cooking smells, look at my tummy and think: You're all mine, I'll never leave you.

When she was born, I called her Donna. I'd sit for hours, just breathing in her scent. I was always bathing her. It was a basement flat we had then, Mum and me and Mum's current love-of-her-life Eddie, and I'd put the pram in the area-way so Donna could imbibe the sea breezes. Even in our part of Brighton, I told myself, you could smell the sea.

I'd lean over to check she was still breathing. I longed for her to smile – properly, at me. In the next room Mum and Eddie would be giggling in an infantile way; they seemed the childish ones. Or else throwing things. It was always like this with Mum's blokes.

I'd gaze at my baby and tell her: You won't miss out. You'll have me. I'll always be here.

Behind me the windowpane rattled as Mum went out, slamming the door behind her.

I went back to work, but in the evenings, so I could look after Donna during the day and leave her with Mum when she was sleeping. They put me in the Late Night Coffee Shop. It had been refurbished in Wild West style, like a saloon, with bullet holes printed on the wallpaper and fancy names for the burgers. The wood veneer was already peeling off the counter. Donna had changed my world; nothing seemed real any more, only her.

I had a new gingham uniform, with a frilly apron and my SMILE badge. I moved around in a dream.

One night somebody said: 'Howdee, stranger.'

It was the man I used to meet at breakfast.

He put on an American accent. 'Just rolled into town, honey. Been missing you. You went away or something?'

I didn't say I'd had a baby; I liked to keep Donna separate.

He inspected the menu. 'Can you fix me a Charcoal-Broiled Rangeburger?'

It was a quiet evening, so we hadn't lit the charcoal. Back in the kitchen I popped the meat into the microwave and thought how once I would have fancied him, like I fancied the bloke from Huddersfield, like I almost fancied Dennis in Reception. But I felt this new responsibility now. Why hadn't my parents felt it when I was born? Or perhaps they had, but it had worn off early.

When I brought him his meal he pointed to my badge. 'With you it comes naturally.' He shook salt over his chips. 'Honest, I'm not just saying it. You've got a beautiful smile.'

'It's added on the bill.'

He laughed. 'She's witty too.' He speared a gherkin. 'Somebody's a lucky bloke.'

'Somebody?'

'Go on, what's his name?'

I thought: Donna.

'There's nobody special,' I said.

'Don't believe it, lovely girl like you.'

I gave him my enigmatic look – practice makes perfect – and started wiping down the next table.

He said: 'You mean I'm in with a chance?'

'You're too old.'

'Ah,' he grinned. 'The cruel insolence of youth.' He munched his chips. 'You ought to try me. I'm matured in the cask.'

Later, when he finished his meal, he came up to pay. He put his hand to his heart. 'Tell me you'll be here tomorrow night. Give me something to live for.'

I took his Access card. 'I'll be here tomorrow night.'

During breakfasts he'd paid the cashier; that was why I had never seen his name.

I did now. I read it, once, on the Access card.

Finally, I got my hands to work. I pulled the paper through the machine, fumbling it once. I did it again, then I passed it to him.

'What's up?' he asked. 'Seen a ghost?'

That night Donna woke twice. For the first time since she was born, I shouted at her.

'Shut up!' I shook her. 'You stupid little baby!'

Then I started to cry. I squeezed her against my nightie. She squirmed and I squeezed her harder, till her head was damp with my tears.

Even my mum noticed. Next day at breakfast she said: 'You didn't half make a racket.' She stubbed her cigarette into her saucer. 'Got a splitting headache.'

I didn't answer. I wasn't telling that last night, I'd met my father. I couldn't tell her yet. She'd probably come storming along to the hotel and lie in wait in his room.

Or maybe she'd just be indifferent. She'd just light another fag and say: *Oh him. That bastard.*

I couldn't bear that.

The day seemed to drag on for ever. Overnight, Brighton had shrunk. It seemed a small town, with my father coming round each corner, so I stayed indoors.

On the other hand, Eddie had grown larger. He loafed around the flat, getting in the way. I needed to talk, but nobody was the right person. Just once I said to him, raising my voice over the afternoon racing: 'Did you know I was called Alexandra?'

'What?'

'My mum and dad called me that, but when I was twelve, I changed it to Sandy.'

'Did you then?' He hadn't turned the volume down. Then he added vaguely: 'Bully for you.'

I didn't know how to face him. On the other hand, I would have died if he didn't turn up. I waited and waited. I nearly gave up hope. I had to wait until ten thirty. I felt hot in my cowgirl frills.

He came in and sat down at the table nearest my counter. I walked over with the menu, calm as calm. I didn't think I could do it.

'I thought you weren't coming,' I said.

'Me?' His eyes twinkled. 'You didn't trust me?' He took the menu. 'Oh no, Sandy, you give me a chance and you'll find out.'

'Find out what?'

'That I'm a man of my word.'

I couldn't answer that. Finally I said: 'Oh yeah?' in a drawling voice. 'Tell us another.'

'Honest to God, cross my heart.'

I looked at him, directly. His eyes were blue, like mine. And his nose was small and blunt, a familiar nose in his large, flushed face. I wanted to hide my face because it suddenly seemed so bare. He must be blind, not to recognize me. I was perspiring.

Then I thought: why should he recognize me? He last saw me when I was four. Even my name is changed. Has he ever thought of me, all these years?

Taking his order into the kitchen, my mind was busy. I stood in front of the dead charcoal range, working out all the places I'd lived since I was four . . . Shepperton, Isleworth, Crawley . . . There was nothing to connect me to Brighton.

SMILE said the sign as I walked out.

'You travel a lot?' I asked, putting his plate in front of him.

'A conversation at last!' He split the ketchup sachet and slopped it over his chips, like blood. He nodded. 'For my sins. So, what's my line of business, Sandy?'

'You're a rep.'

'How did you guess?'

'Your hands.'

He looked down with surprise and opened out his palms. There were yellowed calluses across his fingers.

'You're an observant lass. Do I dare to be flattered?' He put out his hand. 'Here. Feel them.'

I hesitated, then I touched his fingers. The skin was hard and dry. I took away my hand.

'You've always been a salesman?' I asked.

'Well . . .' He winked. 'Bit of this, bit of that.'

'Bit of what?' I wanted to know.

'Now that would be telling.'

'You've been all over the place?'

'It's the gypsy in my soul,' he said. 'Can't tie me down.'

There was a pause. Then I said: 'Eat up your dinner.'

He stared at me. 'What's got into you?'

'Nothing.'

There was a silence. I fiddled with my frills. Then I went back to the counter.

When he paid, he said: 'I know you don't like old men but it's Help the Aged Week.'

'So?' I put on my pert face.

'You're off at half eleven?'

I nodded.

'Let me buy you a drink.' He paused. 'Go on. Say yes.'

The bar had closed. Besides, it was against the rules for me to go there. You're only allowed to smile at the customers.

But who knows where a smile might lead? It had led me here.

He had a bottle of Scotch in his room, and he ordered me a fresh orange juice from room service. When it arrived, I hid in the bathroom, so nobody could see me.

His things were laid out above the basin. I inspected them all: his toothbrush (red, splayed), his toothpaste (Colgate), dental floss (so far, unused), electric shaver, aftershave (Brut, nearly finished). I wanted to take something home but that was all there was. The towels belonged to the hotel so there was no point. I wondered where he kept the marmalade sachets. But they weren't for me.

'Welcome to my abode,' he said, pulling out a chair.

I sat down. 'Where is your abode?'

'Pardon?'

'Where do you live?'

He paused. 'You don't want to hear about my boring little life.'

'Go on,' I said, giving him a flirtatious smile. 'Tell me.'

He hesitated, then he said shortly: 'Know Peterborough?'

'No.'

'Well, there.' His tone grew jaunty. Eyes twinkling, he passed me my glass. 'A fresh drink for a fresh young face. How old are you, Sandy?'

'Nineteen.'

'Nineteen.' He sighed. 'Sweet nineteen. Where have you been all my life?'

I tried to drink the orange juice; it was thick with bits. There was a silence. I couldn't think what to say.

He was sitting on the bed; the room was warm and he had taken off his jacket. The hair was an illusion; he was thinning on top but he'd brushed his hair over the bald patch. Far away I heard a clock chiming.

I wasn't thirsty. I put down the glass and said: 'What do you sell?'

He climbed to his feet and went over to his suitcase, which had a Merriworld sticker on it. He snapped it open.

'Let me introduce Loopy.'

He passed me a rubbery creature dressed in a polka-dot frock. She had long, bendy arms and legs and a silly face. He fetched a pad of paper, knelt down on the floor and took her from me. Her arms ended in pencil points. Holding her, he wrote with her arms: TO SANDY WITH THE SMILE. Then he turned her upside down and said: 'Hey presto.' He started rubbing out the words with her head.

'Don't!' I pulled his hand back. I took the paper, which still had TO SANDY WITH, and put it in my apron pocket. He looked at me with surprise.

Then he put Loopy away. 'Rubber and pencils all in one. Wonder where the sharpener ought to be . . .'

'What?' I asked.

'Just my vulgar mind.'

'Where do you take these things?'

'Ramsdens, Smiths, that big shopping centre,' he said.

I knew all the places; I tried to connect him with them. I'd bought Donna's layette at Ramsdens.

He took out a clockwork Fozzie Bear, a Snoopy purse and a magnetic colouring book.

'So you sell toys,' I said.

'It's the child in me,' he said. 'I'm just a little boy at heart.'

'Are you?'

'Happy-go-lucky, that's me.'

'Anything for a laugh?'

'No use sitting and moaning.' He poured himself another drink. 'Got to enjoy yourself.'

I gazed at the scattered toys. 'Just a game, is it?'

'Sandy, you've only got one life. You'll learn that, take it from me.' He shifted closer to my legs.

'Anything else in there?' I pointed to the suitcase.

He leaned back and took out a box. 'Recognize it?'

I shook my head.

'Ker-Plunk.'

'What?'

'You were probably still in nappies. It's a sixties line, but we're giving it this big re-launch.' He patted the floor. 'Come on and I'll give you a game.'

He took out a plastic tube, a box of marbles and some coloured sticks. 'Come on.' He patted the floor again.

I lowered myself down on the carpet, tucking my skirt in. This damn uniform was so short.

'Look – you slot the sticks in, like this.' He pushed them into perforations in the tube, so they made a platform; then with a rattle he poured the marbles on top, so they rested on the sticks.

'Then we take it in turns to pull out a stick *without*' – he wagged his finger at me – 'without letting a marble drop through.' We sat there, crouched on the floor. 'If it does, you're a naughty girl.'

I pulled out a stick. He pulled one out. I pulled out another.

'Whoops!' he said as a marble clattered through the sticks.

'Bad luck!' he cried. 'I'm winning!'

Sometimes his marbles fell through, sometimes mine. I won.

'Can't have this,' he said. 'Got to have another game.'

He poured himself some more Scotch and settled down on the floor again, with a grunt. We collected the sticks and pushed them into the holes, then poured the marbles on top.

I didn't want to play, but then I didn't want to leave either. We pulled out the sticks; the marbles clattered down the tube.

He slapped his thigh. 'Got you!'

Outside the window the clock chimed again. Sitting there amongst the toys I thought: Why did you never do this with me properly? At the proper time?

'Your turn,' he said. 'Stop day-dreaming.'

I pulled out a stick. My throat felt tight and there was an ache in my chest.

'Whoops!' he cried. 'Bad luck.'

I felt a hand slide around my waist. The fingers squeezed me. He shifted himself nearer me, so our sides were touching.

'Silly game, isn't it?' he said.

I moved back, disentangling myself. 'I must go.'

'But we haven't finished.' He looked at me, his face pink from bending over the game.

I climbed to my feet. 'Mum'll be worried.'

'Come on, you're a big girl now.' He held up his hand. 'Come on, sit down.'

'No.'

He winked. 'Strict, is she?'

I shrugged. He climbed to his feet and stood beside me. We were the same height.

'What about a kiss then?'

I looked into his eyes. Then his face loomed closer. I moved my head; his lips brushed my cheek. I felt them, warm and wet. I bent down and picked up my handbag. My hands were shaking.

'Must go,' I said, my voice light.

He probably blamed my reluctance on my age. He saw me to the door, his hand resting on my hip. 'Can I see you home?'

'No.' I paused. 'I mean, no thanks.'

He opened the door. 'I'm leaving tomorrow, but I'll be back next month. Know what I'd love to do?'

'What?'

'Take you down to the pier. Never been to the pier. Eat ice-creams.' He squeezed my waist, and kissed my cheek. 'Know something?'

'What?' I whispered.

'You make me feel years younger.' He paused. 'Will you come?'

I nodded. 'OK,' I said.

He buttoned me into my coat, and smoothed down the collar. He stroked my hair. 'You're a lovely girl,' he murmured. 'Tell your mum to keep you locked up. Say I said so.'

I couldn't bear to wait at the lift, so I made for the stairs. As I went he called: 'Tell her it's my fault you're late, that you're a naughty girl.' His voice grew fainter, 'Tell her I'm the one to blame.'

Six weeks took an age to pass. I had looked at the ledger in Reception; he was booked for 15 April.

Donna was sleeping better, but for the first time in my life I slept badly. I had such strong dreams they woke me up. I would lie there next to her calm face and gaze at the orange light that filtered down from the street. I had put his piece of paper under my pile of sweaters. That was all I had of him, so far. I said nothing to my mum.

On 15 April Eddie knocked on the bathroom door.

'You're planning to stay there all day?'

I was washing my hair. 'Go away!' I shouted.

At seven o'clock prompt I was on station in the Coffee Shop. They had redecorated it on a medieval theme and I wore a wench's costume. It pinched.

Time dragged. Eight . . . eight fourteen . . . Each time I looked at my watch only a minute had passed.

Nine thirty. The doors swung open. It wasn't him. Business was slow that night; the place was nearly empty.

Ten thirty. The last customer left.

Eleven . . .

At eleven thirty I closed up and took the cash to Dennis in Reception.

'Not got a smile for me?'

I ignored him and went home.

When I got back Mum was watching the midnight movie. I was going to my room but she called: 'Had a flutter today.'

I nodded, but she turned.

'Don't you want to see what I've bought?' She reached down and passed me a carrier bag. 'Put it on Lucky Boy and he won, so I went mad at Ramsdens.'

I stared at her. 'Ramsdens?'

'Go on. Look. It's for little Donna.'

I went over, opened the carrier bag and took out a huge blue teddy bear.

'Cost a bomb,' she said, 'but what the hell.'

Next day I made enquiries at Reception. He'd checked in, they said, during the afternoon as usual. But then he had come back at six and checked out again.

Later I went to Ramsdens and asked if the Merriworld representative had visited the day before.

The girl thought for a moment, then nodded. 'That's right – Jim.' She paused to scratch her earlobe. 'Sunny Jim.'

'So he came?'

She pursed her lips. 'Came and went.'

'What do you mean?'

She looked at me. 'What's it to you?'

'Nothing.'

She shrugged. 'Dunno what got into him. Left in a hurry.'

He had seen Mum. He'd seen her buying the bloody teddy bear.

He didn't come back. Not once he knew she was in Brighton. At Ramsdens, six weeks later, there was a new rep called Terry. I checked up. Not that I had much hope; after all, he had scarpered once before.

But Donna smiled. It wasn't because of the teddy; she was too young to appreciate that, though Mum would like to believe it.

And it wasn't wind, I could tell. It was me. She smiled at me.

The Wrong Side

They were stuck behind two French lorries, an English caravan and one of those grey corrugated Citroëns you always get stuck behind. Exhaust fumes blew around their windscreen. It was hot. They had the windows open and Bach playing, telling them about order and patience.

'Well?' Leonard asked, at the wheel. He steered out a little, so she could look.

'Yes, fine,' she started. 'No.'

Leonard swerved back into line.

'Sorry,' she said.

Bach stopped; with a click the machine stuck out its tongue.

'Other side?' she asked, taking out the cassette.

'We've just had it.'

'Ah.' She leaned to the side, peering out. 'Try again.'

He drew out.

'Now!' she said.

He changed gear; they roared past the Citroën, the caravan and two lorries. She gradually unclenched. Years ago, on another holiday, Leonard had compared French roads to chronic catarrh: 'That slow build-up of phlegm, then a good cough and a spit and you're clear, ah but it's only temporary.'

They were driving south. They had left behind those

drab, straight towns lined with telegraph poles. Now the farmhouses looked crumbly and baked. On the walls, barely visible, were faded ads for SUZE. They were passing the first fields of sunflowers; even today they lifted her heart. Their dark discs were all turned the way that she and Leonard were going. 'And half the United Kingdom,' he said, 'is going too.'

They slowed down behind a lorry heaped with tyres. Leonard leaned her way.

'*Now!*' she said.

He swerved out. She felt a frisson of power, being in the passenger seat. For that split second, he needed her. They shared a fear for their lives. One of the few things, it seemed, that remained for them to share.

A worse fear was that at some point he would put this into words. It was not a fact until he did so. To herself she could pretend it did not exist – to herself she could pretend anything. (Just another of the traits he found so irritating.)

'Where after Doué?' He changed down.

They were driving through some suburbs. DOUÉ said the sign. SA PISCINE. SES EGLISES. She scrabbled for the map, which had fallen to the floor. One holiday, they had applied this criterion to England, noting the passing sights. '*Sa Tesco monumentale*', '*ses car-parques multistoreys*', with the children mute in the rear seat. It had lasted from Mill Hill to Rugby.

'Doué . . . Doué . . .'

Anxiety made her flustered. She had folded the map wrong, of course. Red N roads to Rouen, to Travaine, ran in all directions like blood veins.

'. . . Hang on . . .'

They had reached the centre of town. Leonard pulled up. Behind, a car hooted. He jerked forward, drove the car around the corner, and stopped. He took the map from her and shook it out, slapping it with his hand. It was ridiculous, of course, that the driver should have to do the map-reading. In Leonard's place, she would be annoyed too. *Doué. Ses anglais chauds et irrités.*

'Thouars. We go to Thouars.' He kept his finger on the map, like a schoolmaster, as he passed it to her.

They drove out of Doué. Once, long ago, he had found her map confusions endearing. That holiday in England, the mad, leisured spiral of their conversation, the married inconsequence of it. *Rugby. Ses anglais heureux.* Here in France, as they drove down the wrong side of the road, their children having grown up and vacated the rear seats, she thought how subtly the right side changes to the wrong. A process, indeed, that could take twenty-three years of marriage and be acknowledged by neither of them. Once upon a time, her optimism had cheered him. Once he had compared it to sap, moving up and warming his heart. 'You call a bottle half-empty,' she had said to him once, 'and I call it half-full.' He shook his head. 'You, my dear, call it three-quarters full.'

At some point, his word for this charming trait had changed. Perhaps, for fairness' sake, she should not call it the wrong side – just the other side, like a photograph slowly turning back into a negative, the blacks turning to white and the whites to black. Now he called it 'fudging' or 'fooling herself' and implied that such anxious brightness was less fetching in a woman of forty-three. Which increased it, of course.

Anxiety was the taste of her days. Here, on holiday with the gourmet Leonard, it was anxiety that the restaurants should be neither too full, too empty, nor too populated with the English. That her reactions should be as he predicted, yet not predictably dull. That, when they picnicked, the mosquito should bite not Leonard but herself. She never paused to consider the restaurant itself, or whether the bite hurt. She had not thought of this for years, what with Leonard and the children. Which of course had made her duller. Sometimes she felt eroded into a shell of anxious acquiescence. Hollow, and forty-three, and getting fat.

Leonard had not put on any weight. He was tall and gaunt, with the drained good looks that handsome men achieve beyond their prime. Giscard had just been defeated in the elections; Leonard had the same air of ruined distinction. In his case, though, it was not through dealing in politics but in second-hand books.

She looked at his profile. He drove efficiently. Their car was a white Rover. In England he enjoyed the deference of short-sighted motorists who mistook them for a police car; it made overtaking so easy. Here in France, of course, this did not work. They were taking the D routes to avoid, with limited success, the lorries and the English. They were travelling down to the Lot valley, the one further south than the Dordogne, to avoid the English too. Half London, he said, was in the Dordogne now, its villages full of Volvo station-wagons and children with bad manners and Rubik cubes. He reacted to British cars as if discovering a slug in the salad of France. His dread was to enter some wayside café and find it full of puce rucksacks and Birmingham accents. She had asked: 'What about them finding it full of us?'

Like herself – one day she might dare tell him – like herself, the English were on the wrong side. An English car driving too fast was foolishly reckless and insensitive to rural *calme*; a French car doing the same just displayed Gallic verve. Mysteriously, French caravans were OK; he was charmed by such dedication to *la vie urbaine en plein air.* Identical English caravans, however, were just suburban. She felt some sympathy for her fellow Brits; besides, like them, her French was not as good as Leonard's.

'Now!' she said from her position of power. Leonard overtook the van. It was midday. Their white bonnet dazzled her. She kept her finger on the map and said: 'We're getting near the crease.'

'Tecreese? Where's that?'

Had he forgotten? 'The crease in the map.'

After all, it was five years since they had been to France. During holidays they had always stopped, for a celebratory drink or picnic, at the place halfway down France where the map folded, like travellers pausing at the equator. On their old Michelin map this could be, depending on the route south, just below Mirebeau, Châtellerault, or several other places she had now forgotten. After the crease, one felt it was downhill all the way. Leonard had once suggested that the local *départements* should install morale-boosting placards: VOUS AVEZ PASSEZ LE FOLD in five languages.

'Ah,' he said. 'You mean it's time for lunch.'

They had already bought the picnic; the car smelt of ripening cheese and warm upholstery. She started watching out, as inevitably the road became verged with hypermarkets called *Monsieur Meubles.*

'*Now,*' she said. Then as he slowed down: 'Perhaps not.'

Everyone dithered over picnic sites, she had once pointed out with spirit. Finally, miles further south than the fold, they found a canal. It was lined with poplar trees which in England depressed Leonard, reminding him of being bullied on the school rugby field, but which he liked in France, being so French. They drove over a bridge, which meant they could picnic on the other side from the road. There was nobody else about.

Leonard stopped the car. They opened the boot and unpacked the old tartan picnic rug. Leonard searched in the dashboard for the corkscrew. She laid things out. Behind them was a bush; under it she caught sight of scrumpled rubbish and old Evian bottles. She willed him not to notice them – at least not until it was time to leave. Holidays made her so tense. There was this pressure for everything to be all right. Whereas, as she knew, happiness could not be ordered on time. It swept over her at the least expected moment – not during the candlelit dinner but after it, with the striplight glaring, when they bumped into each other with some joke, and damp tea-towels. When was the last time that she and Leonard had been happy? When had she not been anxious?

They spread out the rug and sat down. Leonard had just uncorked the Corbières when a car stopped on the other side of the canal. She felt Leonard straighten beside her. A man, woman and two children climbed out and began to set up their picnic on the opposite bank.

After a pause Leonard said: 'We must move.'

'We can't. We've just got everything out.' Across the water the children called to each other in high London whines. 'Anyway, it would look rude.'

They did not move. They unwrapped the pâté and ate in silence. They were sitting in the shade of the poplar. Opposite, the English family sat in the sunlight. She did not resent them. Across the water she heard the man, quite clearly, tell the little boy not to put his fingers in the yoghurt. Munching her quiche, she envied them the simple complications of their lives. She envied that era when her own children were small; when she had actually complained about being needed too much by all three of them. Once, years ago, they had gone camping. Leonard had sunbathed on the new lilo they had bought and for one whole afternoon had walked around with a sticker on his back saying DO NOT OVER-INFLATE. In the end the children had told him, spluttering with giggles. In those days she had not been afraid of his reaction.

Across the water the children laughed, and then started squabbling. Oh, those days when the children were young, when their future lay ahead, when anything was possible. She thought of Anthea and John. Leonard found them both deeply dull, his own children.

By late afternoon they had reached the Périgord, *région gastronomique*. The light was softer now and the countryside itself seemed sunk into repletion. Leonard, a convert to *la nouvelle cuisine*, had inspected his *Gault Millau* guide and planned stops for tonight's and tomorrow's meals. She still felt full from the picnic, but she knew she would eat a heavy meal tonight. Tomorrow they were going to the most acclaimed restaurant for hundreds of miles, *Le Beau Rivage*. Eating out used to be a shared celebration, but in recent years the pleasure had drained from it . . . him testing, her tense. The less they had to say, the more elaborately they ate.

Billboards stood beside the road. ICI! PÂTÉ DE FOIE GRAS. Giant wooden geese cast their shadow upon prefabricated huts with their wayside car parks. Poor geese, force-fed. Stuffed and stuffed, unable to escape. Leonard and she had a drink in a café, before dinner. She shuffled through the postcard stand. Amongst the slyly captioned pigs, the costumed peasants and the Dordogne rustics drinking wine out of soup bowls there was a photo of a goose, jammed by the neck in a wooden box.

She gazed at it. 'I won't eat pâté again. Darling, it's so cruel. Look, they've even got a postcard of it.'

'Their unsentimentality,' he said, 'is refreshing. Look over there.' He gestured out of the window. Outside, at the crossroads, signs pointed in all directions including ABATTOIR.

'Ugh. Not before supper.'

'Oh Anna, fudging again.' He sipped his kir. 'My dear old Anna. Don't you ever *think*?'

She wanted not to think. Then she would realize how frightened she was.

The fear had been growing for months. It was worse now he had decided to take her alone on holiday, like this. Usually they shared a villa with Tim and Margot, or she accompanied him on buying trips around Britain and visited her nieces and long-lost families who once lived next door. It was more than the routine anxiety – she had grown used to that. It was fear – fear that he had brought her here to talk.

Their hotel was in the *grand confort* category. She did

not want him to talk; she did not want to hear. It was a large room overlooking the back alley, jammed with cars. Dustbins glinted in the evening sun. If it's another woman, she pleaded, don't you understand? I don't want to know. Haven't we even that understanding left? You have every opportunity; you stay away nights, you travel all over the place. I am soft and fat and empty. Let's stuff ourselves with food; unlike the geese, we have a choice. Two chef's hats, this hotel has in the *Gault Millau*. Let's not put anything into words. Either that there is somebody else or, perhaps worse, that there isn't. Let's go downstairs and eat that truffle thing you told me about, followed by their fishy thing for which they are so famous.

Leonard had a shower. The heavily upholstered room seemed to be waiting for an answer. She went to the window. Down there, a man lay spread-eagled on a car bonnet. It was a young man; his eyes were closed. His white apron was smeared with blood. After the first shock she realized he was just one of the chefs, snoozing in the evening sun. How wonderfully simple he looked.

'Plenty of Dutch,' she said the next day. 'No Brits, but plenty of Dutch.'

'Foreign, yes. But slow.'

It was nearly midday and they were driving along the Lot valley. The road twisted alongside the water; to one side rose thickly wooded banks topped by cliffs. A dangerous road for overtaking.

He pointed towards the roof. 'Up there lies our lunch.'

According to the map, and Leonard's description, *Le Beau Rivage* restaurant was built on the cliffs above them, overlooking the river. Last night's place had two chef's hats in black; today's lunch, however, was superior, for its two hats were red. Even Leonard, not a mean man, had admitted it was expensive. He had eaten lunch there earlier this year, when he had been down on a swift business trip – an English recluse had died and his château, with some rare first editions, was being auctioned.

Leonard swerved out.

'No!' she cried. A blind bend lay ahead. The road dipped and twisted; queues of cars crawled along it. She knew she should feel pleased, that he wanted to repeat his gastronomic treat with her. He had talked so much about this place, and now he wanted her to share it. But she felt uneasy. Leonard placed such emphasis on style. She had the feeling that he was going to fill her up with wonderful food and then say something shattering.

'Quick!' she cried. 'Now!'

He swerved out. There was a corner ahead. Her stomach shifted. The engine roared as they slipped in front of the line of cars. He turned to her; sunglasses hid his eyes, but his mouth twitched.

According to Leonard, you could tell the best restaurants by their atrocious décor. *Le Beau Rivage*, built in a small hilltop village, was set into the cliff. It had panoramic views and picture windows. Inside, a good deal of effort had been made with the furnishings: turquoise sateen chairs, lime-green paisley wallpaper, and much wrought iron – *décor rustique*. Over the violent colours hung an air of hushed good living. The restaurant was half-empty – or, as she would put it, three-quarters full. For Leonard's sake, she saw with relief just one other British family sitting far away from where they themselves were placed. Also with relief, she saw that the head waiter recognized Leonard, without being over-effusive about it.

They sat next to the drop. Below, the river glistened in the sun. The road curled snake-like around its bends. The black twiddly balcony pressed against their window.

'Do you mind eating alone,' she asked, 'on your trips?'

Leonard took off his sunglasses. 'It concentrates the mind wonderfully,' he said, 'on the food.' He lifted the menu. 'One can be an object of fantasy, or at least speculation, to the other diners.'

She warmed to him. 'Last time here, did you present your left-side profile? The car one?'

'What?'

She must relax. This morning, in preparation, she had put on her nicest dress, the one with the red poppies that Leonard approved of – he always gave a detailed judgement on her clothes. By her standards it was a bold, modern print with its splashes of red. She was sitting next to the window; the sun heated her arm.

The menu made her helpless. She still felt full from breakfast. She did not say so, of course; she let Leonard order for her. An *omelette aux cèpes*, he proposed for her, followed by *le turbot clouté d'anchois à la rhubarbe*. This was what he had eaten last time, he said, back in April. He was starting with the *pâté de foie gras*. She glanced up sharply; is he telling me something? But his face had no expression.

Leonard was spreading his pâté when the fat man came in. The man was indeed immense – perspiring in his pale suit, and his face was the colour of luncheon meat. He was just being shown a table when he noticed Leonard, paused, and came over. Leonard stood up; both men smiled, shook hands and said *comment ça va*? She was introduced, though Leonard had obviously forgotten the man's name. Another smile and nod, and the fat man was seated at the next window table.

'Who's he?' she whispered.

'Oh, just a fellow diner,' said Leonard shortly.

'You chatted with him last time?'

He nodded, sliced a piece of pâté and spread it on his toast. She felt awkward about continuing the subject; perhaps Leonard was hushing her because of the man's proximity. But at least it would have made a subject for conversation. They ate in silence. The whole room was quiet; the murmurs and clinks were so low that she did not like to clear her throat. Even the British family, with two boys, was inaudible. Leonard had finished; a smear of pâté remained on his plate. He put down his knife. She tensed, waiting for him to speak.

'Is that nice?' He indicated her omelette.

She jerked into life, nodding. 'Delicious.' She went on eating; there seemed so many mouthfuls to be got through and yet, each time, so much remained.

What are we delaying? she thought. She had shredded her napkin; in her lap it was scattered over the poppies. That man sitting opposite, eating his *loup de mer*, he is my husband. Why does he fill me with fear? Perhaps I'm just dizzy in the sun. Perhaps we will just continue like this, making the occasional remark about the heat, and how far we will drive before evening. Perhaps there is nothing to happen.

They finished the meal. Leonard asked for the bill and

then got up to go to the lavatory. Beyond his empty chair sat the fat man, dimmed in cigarette smoke.

'*C'était bon?*' asked the man. 'It was good?'

She nodded, smiling.

'Cigarette?' he asked.

She shook her head. '*Non, merci.*' She gave him another smile.

They were sitting just too far apart for conversation, in the holy quiet of this place. She decided to wait for Leonard outside. Many people had now paid and left.

She picked up her handbag and stood up, dusting the napkin off her dress. At his table she hesitated. Having refused his cigarette, some cordiality was necessary.

'*La belle vue,*' she said, gesturing at the window.

'*Oui,* very beautiful.'

A pause. He gestured around the room. 'It is pretty, yes?'

'Oh *oui,*' she lied.

Another pause, and then she had an idea. She pointed to the fancy balcony at the window, and then to the wrought-iron brackets that held the wall-lamps.

'*Ma fille,*' she started. 'My daughter . . .' Curious how one felt compelled to explain it in English. '*Elle travaille avec les choses comme ça.*'

'*S'il vous plaît?*'

She had forgotten the word for 'blacksmith'. She pointed to the fireplace. It was hideously edged with brick, and inside it stood an ornate, empty grate, a Gallic version of the sort Anthea made.

'*Elle travaille avec . . . les trucs en feu.*' Was that right? *Iron things?*

He sucked on his cigarette. '*Oui madame. J'ai remarqué*

son intérêt. She was liking them ... *elle les aimait beaucoup.'*

Elle les aimait. He must mean – what was it? The subjunctive. She had done that at school, a thousand years ago. *She would like them.*

She worked it out and said eventually: *'Oui, elle les aimerait.'*

'Le feu,' he said. *'* . . . The fire, it was lighted. It was very pretty.'

She remained standing. The heat rose slowly to her face. She did not know how long it was before she spoke. He appeared to notice nothing unusual.

'Elle était . . . sitting . . . *assise, ici?'* she was saying. *'Ici, dans le restaurant?'*

'Là-bas. There, that place.' He indicated another table. 'My congratulations, madam. You have a very beautiful daughter.'

Time must have passed. She must have said something polite to him before she left. It was probably 'thank you' in English.

Now she seemed to be outside in the car park. How hot it was. The poppy dress chafed her armpits. The bright windscreens hurt her eyes.

So that's that, she thought, over and over again. So that's it. So that's that. My husband, and a girl young enough to be his daughter.

She was standing beside the Rover. She looked at its cleft, dusty tyres.

Behind her somebody was whistling.

'Know what?' said a voice.

She turned. It was the English boy from the restaurant. He was leaning against a car.

'Know what this is?' he asked again. 'Guess.'

He made snatching gestures in the air.

'What?' she asked stupidly. 'What do you want?'

'Guess,' he said patiently. 'Guess what this is.'

He snatched again, grabbing the empty air. She must be going mad.

'What is it?' she asked.

'Give up?'

'Yes.'

'It's God, trying to catch a Smartie.'

'God what?'

'God, trying, to catch, a Smartie, dum-dum.' He paused. 'He can't, you see.'

'Can't?'

'Can't. Because of the holes in his hands.'

It was then that her throat shrank and she knew she was going to be sick. She had managed to get inside the corridor now, pink striped walls buzzing and jarring, and now she was kneeling at the lavatory. Below her the porcelain spattered. She watched it, and the words bounced around her head. *It's not God, you stupid, stupid boy, it's Jesus.* The words bounced round in rhythm. *It's Jesus, Jesus.* All that food splashed out, all of it, the months of it, years of it. She knelt, holding the bowl in her arms.

Leonard blamed it on the *cèpes*. They were driving down the zig-zag hill, back to the main road. Her head was wedged with a cushion. He was talking about *cèpes* and *girolles* and rubbish like that. She did not bother to hear him. She felt oddly relaxed. For the first time in years she did not bother to respond.

He turned the car into the main road. Lorries thundered by in the opposite direction. They were driving towards Cahors. He said something about Cahors having a splendid bridge with turrets. She said nothing. She did not mind what he thought. She felt the car slowing down but her eyes were closed. I did not know what I feared, she thought. Not then.

'Buck up.' Leonard's voice, spoken to the car in front. 'Buck up, sonny boy.'

She opened her eyes. They were stuck behind a caravan. Leonard, Leo, my husband. Do you know what I was afraid to admit? Shall I mouth the words in the air?

That I no longer love you. That I no longer even like you. That I haven't for years.

Face up to it, you said. *Anna, you fudger. You never face the truth, my old dear, do you?*

You are cold and snobbish and faithless. Never mind about the girl; you've been faithless for so long now and she is not important.

'Anna, could you have a look?' That voice, so familiar. Tense with irritation, waiting for her to do something wrong. 'I mean, if you feel better.' He did not care if she felt better. A click, as he slotted in a cassette. Music flooded the car.

She opened her eyes and leaned to the side.

'Wait!' she said. He swerved back.

Trees pressed against the road one side; the river's railings pressed against the other. You are locked inside marriage. It has to stop you seeing those things. You don't dare face the truth.

The road twisted and turned, with its blind corners. Her stomach felt light, after its emptying. The traffic was travelling fast, but he wanted to go faster.

She gazed at the back of the caravan, with its GB sticker. The violins were leaping and spiralling upwards.

'Try again,' she said.

Leonard drew out. She leaned to look.

Her chest clenched. On the other side of the road, approaching fast, loomed a lorry. It was a big one; a pipe stuck up into the sky, with black smoke pouring from it.

'*Now!*' she shouted.

Making Hay

I worked, the next day. Well, what else could I do – book one of those round-the-world cruises? Throw a party?

Mind you, I'm not ruling those out. There's months to go, they told me, and I won't be ruling anything out. But I'm telling you about that particular day, the day after I'd heard, when the sun was blazing through the windscreen, heating me up. It was a perfect June morning; you don't get many mornings like that. The sky was the colour of that bird's egg – I've forgotten what sort, but it was like a pure blue dome above me. Bloody beautiful.

I sat in the coach, waiting for my passengers. Though the door was open, there was this glassed-in silence around me. I was double-parked on Haverstock Hill; behind me, cars hooted and queued, then revved up as they drove past. What's the fuss? I thought. What's the bloody fuss?

At the delicatessen, this little bloke was pulling out the awning, just like he must always do; just like this was a normal morning. A woman dragged her squatting dog away from a lamp-post. I thought: let him. Let the bugger relieve himself.

The trees threw dappled shadows on the pavement. I told myself I must notice this; why hadn't I had the time before? People were crossing the road as if it was important where they had to go. There was a man with a briefcase who danced back, with a hop and skip, when a car drove past. He shouted some words that echoed, far away. I watched him mouthing them.

Everything seemed sharp as crystal, that morning. Yet I felt sealed-off, as if I was in this aquarium and the whole city was coming alive outside my glass walls – people going to their offices, answering phones, painting yellow lines in the road. I suppose it was because the news was just beginning to sink in.

It's unexpected, little things you think of when you're in my position. Sitting there in the sun, I thought irritably that it had to be some little creep in a white coat, a complete stranger, who'd told me. I couldn't even remember his name. But he was half my age, and he had acne.

Then I watched some blossom float down from a tree planted outside the cinema and I thought: I don't even know the name of that tree. This made me depressed. I made a resolution to find out, and then I thought: what the hell.

I hadn't told Doriza. That's my wife. I hadn't told her all the night before; I hadn't said I'd been to the hospital. She's highly strung, you see.

Eight thirty. People were wandering towards the coach. More were coming out of Belsize Park tube station, in ones and twos. They were all women – I'd been warned about that – and some of them had pushchairs with babies in them.

'Is this the coach?' one of them asked.

'Oh no,' I said. 'It's a Morris Minor in disguise.'

'You know what I mean.' With a half-smile, she swung herself on board. Other women climbed in, unstrapping their babies. You can always tell a middle-class bunch of passengers because they get on the coach without waiting for somebody to tell them what to do.

I climbed out and went round the back to load the push-chairs into the boot. I'd already lost some weight but you wouldn't have believed it to look at me. 'All British beef,' Wally had said at the depot the week before, punching me in the ribs. Well, he didn't know, did he? Nobody did, except that bloke with the skin problem.

In the back window they'd already Sellotaped up a plac-ard saying CND, and another one saying WOMEN AGAINST THE BOMB. Most of them were loading their stuff themselves. They looked muscular; they were dressed like garage mechanics. I glanced wistfully at a girl passing by, wearing a floaty summer dress. But she was going to work, and disappeared into the underground.

'You've a nice day for it,' I said to one of them. I jerked my head at the blue sky. 'Not a cloud.'

She looked up, frowning. 'Not yet.'

'I heard the weather forecast. Set fair.'

'I'm not talking about the weather forecast.'

Blimey, I thought. We've got one here.

I usually like it, once I'm out on the open road. Foot down, radio playing, steaming along the fast lane at 70 mph. That's the best thing about this job – the independence. They've usually all gone to sleep by this time . . . It's just you and a dreaming coachload, heads nodding, and that wide motorway with the fan blasting cool air into your face and a few dawdlers to flash at. It made a change from home, what with all the little jobs that needed doing – fixing the guttering, decorating the kitchen; well, I wouldn't be doing them now.

And another thing. Doriza likes the heating full up. She says she feels the chill in her bones; it must be her coming from Eastern Europe, and what her family went through in the war. But it makes the house so stuffy; it makes the rooms feel so small. And her leaning across the table asking me don't I like her goulash; is that why I'm not finishing it? And her needing me to hear her complaints about the neighbours; she's always squabbling with them. And why had I forgotten our wedding anniversary; did I mean I don't love her any more? Her voice, it's like the wrong tune on the piano played over and over.

It's the speed and the solitude I enjoy. But that day it didn't feel like solitude, it felt like loneliness. I told myself it was all those women, forty-five of them, and what chap wouldn't feel separate?

Someone behind me lit a cigarette. I turned round and wagged my finger at the notice, underneath the cartoons and my St Christopher, which said NO SMOKING.

'But *you* are,' she said, pointing to my smouldering fag.

'I'm different.'

'You're different because you're driving?' She shrugged – I saw her in the mirror – and grimaced at her companion. 'That's not fair.'

'You're right about that.' I drew on the cigarette. That morning I needed it.

I thought: all these years I've been a forty-a-day man; all these years I've been trying to give it up.

I looked up at the vast blue sky ahead of me. Somebody up there had a sense of humour.

'*All things bright and beautiful, all creatures great and small . . .*'

A few of the women were singing in high, reedy voices. I remembered the hymn from when I was a lad; I thought, how nice they're teaching it to the kids. But then I realized they'd altered the words.

Instead of '*The Lord God made them all*', they were singing '*And we destroyed them all.*'

I looked in the mirror. Through the perspex roof, lurid orange light bathed their faces and the bowed, sleeping heads of their children.

'Jesus Christ,' I said to myself.

It didn't sound like an oath; it sounded like a conversation-opener. I turned up the volume on the radio.

I'd been warned about the traffic jams, but this rally lark was even bigger than I'd expected. I'd turned off the M4 near Newbury, and the lanes were choked with traffic and people tramping along on foot – men, women and children – and DIVERSION signs. The air-conditioning had broken down and the coach was sweltering. My shirt stuck to me, it felt like I was wrapped in cling-film. But nobody seemed to be complaining. Behind me the women pressed their noses to the window and exclaimed about the turn-out. The hedges were grey and dusty from the traffic. Beyond them, in a lush green field, black-and-white cows were munching, unconcerned. I thought: nice to be a cow.

The coach park was a large field. I sat while they filed out. I was tired; nowadays even driving tired me. Now there was a word for my exhaustion, it seemed worse. Trapped in my seat, I felt that echoing, glassed-in sensation again . . . that everything was happening a long way off, and separate. Yet crystal-sharp, as if I'd never seen a line of coaches before, or the deeper-green clumps of thistles amongst the worn grass. I realized, too, that I hadn't listened to what the women said, or stored up their daft conversation as jokes for Wally. A bunch of dungareed peace women – what a subject! He would have enjoyed that. Why hadn't I bothered to take it in? I felt panicky.

They trudged off across the field, looking purposeful. I opened the boot; the mothers took out the pushchairs. Then I leaned against the coach. Over the far side of the field there was a coffee stall. A crowd of drivers stood there; they looked as small as insects and shimmered in the heat. I knew I should go over and join them, for my own sake. I'm a sociable bloke, you see, and if I started behaving out of character, I'd give myself the creeps.

I stayed, leaning against the coach, my eyes closed. I heard the murmur of the crowd, way beyond the field, and the muffled booming of a loudspeaker. It seemed to come from another year. My passengers had all gone. I told myself I was reassured by the smell of warm metal and the diesel fumes from another coach that was just parking in front of me. Trouble was, nothing smelt familiar. Or rather, it felt only too familiar but it was out of reach. It was like the first day at school, when you're closed off in a classroom and you hear the noises in the street outside but you can't get at them. Like that, but worse.

I was thinking about Doriza, and how I'd have to tell her. Sooner or later, I'd have to. 'Why don't you finish it up?' she'd been asking me recently. 'You don't like my cooking?' Our kitchen seemed so cramped with her in it, fussing me. I suppose most marriages aren't as happy as people hoped, if we're being truthful about it. (I was telling myself the truth that day, for the first time. You would too, in my position. The truth, it rears up and stares you in the face.) Fifteen years ago, when we first met, we had this fiery relationship. I'd met her at Paddington Station and she'd been what they'd call voluptuous. Wally would say big tits, but it was more than that, she seemed soft and scented and foreign. Mysterious. But mystery's the first thing to wear off, isn't it?

If we'd had children, it would have been different. She's always seemed so dissatisfied. She's always asking me if I love her. If I get up to go to the toilet, she asks me where I'm going. If I'm reading the paper, she asks me to read it out loud. Sometimes I feel my head's going to burst. Don't get me wrong, I'm still fond of her. We're probably no worse than most people. Maybe if we'd had kids we'd have had more in common.

Dolly (I call her that), *Dolly, I've got something to tell you . . . Know how I've been feeling not quite the ticket? . . .*

A skeleton climbed out of the coach opposite me. Well, it was somebody wearing a skeleton suit. He or she loped off down the field, amongst the crowds of people.

I closed my eyes; the sun beat down on my face. I imagined Doriza smothering me in her arms – she's a big woman – and soaking me with her tears. I imagined us having to be loving to each other, all the time. After this, we'd never be able to lose our tempers. I imagined the house hushed, and hotter, and closing in around me. I thought of Wally and Dave, my partners, shutting up when I came into the depot office . . . shuffling their feet and stopping their jokes.

*

I went to lock up the coach. There was somebody still sitting in it.

'Hello,' I said. 'We've arrived.'

'I know. I felt queer. Ill.' She paused. 'It must be the sun.' She was sitting in an aisle seat, near the front. 'I felt awful on the motorway,' she said. 'I thought I was going to be sick.'

'On my new velour? You wouldn't dare.'

She looked pale, but then she was one of those redheads, with that white skin. Nearer to, I could see she was covered with freckles. Her hair was bushy; in the orange light it was like a halo around her face.

'Yes, you do look peaky,' I said.

'Great. Thanks.'

'Sorry.'

'I'm not marching. I'd probably faint and let everybody down. I'll just stay in the coach.'

She didn't. She climbed through a fence with me; we walked across two fields until we came to a little triangular meadow where they'd been cutting hay. Woods closed it in on two sides; there were bales stacked up all over the place. We sat against a pile of them. Above us there were larks singing – well, I think they were larks – and the occasional clackety-clack of a police helicopter.

She was young enough to be my daughter. You should've seen her hands; they were so small, with faint bluish veins at the wrists.

'I feel better,' she said. 'I'm a bit anaemic, that's why.'

We sat there for quite a while, in silence. She seemed to think it was perfectly natural, just to sit there with her coach driver. I didn't mind. I didn't mind anything, that day. It all seemed unlikely. I'm not in the habit of sitting in fields.

She closed her eyes. Most women feel they have to talk all the time, but she didn't seem afraid of the gaps.

For the first time since I'd heard the news, I felt peaceful. I suppose it was the countryside, and the fact that she didn't ask any questions. She was a stranger, and I didn't have to tell her anything. Just because of that, I felt she was the only person I could tell.

Before I could speak, she opened her rucksack.

'Want a sandwich?'

'I've got some in the coach.'

'Have one of mine.' She passed me a doorstep of brown bread, packed with cheese and pickle and cucumber, and started wolfing hers down. For such a frail girl she had quite an appetite.

She paused, with crumbs on her lips. 'You don't want any more?'

I gave her back the other half. 'You finish it.'

'Why?'

'I'm not that hungry.'

'You'll waste away.'

I looked at her sharply.

'Only joking,' she said, prodding my solid chest. That decided me not to tell her.

She ate in silence, tearing at the crust. It did me good to watch her. Finally, she swallowed the last mouthful.

'Got any kids?' she asked.

I shook my head. 'Nope.'

'All those kids in the coach, they made me feel so sad.'

'Why?'

She paused. 'Actually, I suppose they just thought it was a day out in the country.' She was silent, staring at her toes. She'd kicked off her plimsolls.

'I'd have liked to have kids,' I said.

She swung round and stared at me. 'Would you?'

'Yes,' I said, realizing just how much. 'Why not?'

She gestured at the field, then up at the blue sky. 'What, bring them into this world?'

'Looks beautiful to me.'

She made an impatient sound, and turned away. What was the matter with her? A young girl like her, who'd eaten her sandwiches with such relish, greedy as a child, she shouldn't be talking like this. I looked at her horrible baggy khaki trousers, and her T-shirt the colour of mud. A lovely-looking girl like her ought to be wearing something bright, instead of drab colours. Something pretty, that would do her justice.

She turned back. 'What's your name?'

'Frank.'

'Listen, Frank, don't you understand?' She stopped and sighed. 'Oh, I wish I'd gone on the march.'

'What's your name?'

'Tessa.'

'Tessa . . .' I mulled over the name, fitting it to her. Then I grinned. 'I know why you didn't. So you could sit here with me.'

She frowned. 'What?'

'Only joking. Don't mind me.' I paused. 'I mean it – you've made me feel a lot better.'

'I couldn't have.'

'No, honest.'

She flung back her head. 'It wouldn't have done any good anyway.'

'But I just said – it has.'

'I mean going on the march. Just a bunch of people.'

'Well, you've done *me* good. One person.'

She squinted at me, the sun in her face. 'But what the hell are you and me? What can either of us do?'

She had a small, flat, hard voice. I wondered how she'd sound when she was laughing. She ought to be laughing – a beautiful girl like her, on a beautiful day like this. And she shouldn't be wearing those depressing clothes.

I wondered how her hair would feel – soft or wiry. I imagined picking wildflowers and putting them into her hair. She'd probably slap my face. Anyway, the hay was cut and there was only stubble left.

Beyond the woods, a helicopter clattered. Suddenly she turned and grabbed me. Before I could do anything, she pulled me towards her.

'Frank, I'm frightened.'

'It's only a chopper.'

She pressed her face into my chest. She repeated in a low voice: 'I'm frightened.'

I put my arms around her. She felt even more frail than she looked. I held her against me, feeling her sharp shoulder blades and the knobs of her backbone. I pressed her bushy hair against my chest, bending my head and smelling her. She smelt of soap, and warm skin. She smelt young.

I said: 'Not as frightened as me, love.'

We clutched each other, rocking. The hay bales bumped

our sides. Far away I heard the hooting of cars in the endless traffic jams, and the sound of a tannoy.

Then she disentangled herself, and in one violent movement she pulled her T-shirt over her head. She bent over to unbutton her trousers. For a mad moment I thought she was going to sunbathe. Then she swung round, tossing back her mass of hair.

'Come on.' Her voice was flat.

'But—'

'You afraid? Who cares?' She gestured at the woods. 'Life's too short.'

'But—' I started again, and stopped. To be honest, this sort of thing doesn't happen to me that often. Like, never. But wasn't she going to smile or something?

She moved her face towards mine. I looked at her white, freckled skin and her dry lips. She searched my face, seriously. Then we kissed. I hadn't kissed anybody for a long time. She started unbuttoning my shirt and I tried to help her, with my clumsy hands, but before we'd finished, she pulled me down on top of her, and wrapped her bare legs around me, holding me fast.

Greedily she wanted more. She gripped me; there was something impersonal and determined about the way she did it. She kissed me, her tongue pushing into my mouth; she ran her lips down my neck, but when I drew back to speak she twisted her head away and just pulled me towards her again. Once she bit my shoulder, hard.

At last she lay back, panting. Her skin was shiny with sweat. She was very thin; her breasts were so small they were barely there – just soft, pale nipples and a freckled chest. I wanted to hold her in my arms, but she was lying absolutely still, gazing up at the sky. She hadn't smiled, once.

There was a silence. Then she said: 'Make hay while the sun shines.'

'What about "Make love while the sun shines"?' I said, trying to be friendly.

'Love?' She turned, and squinted at me. Then she said, in that flat voice: 'I'd call it despair.'

I parked the coach outside Belsize Park tube. There was this golden evening light across the parade of shops. Above the delicatessen the awning was still out; it seemed unbelievable that the shops had been open all this time, and that it had only been one day.

I missed her. By the time I'd opened the boot, she'd got out of the coach. When I straightened up and turned, I saw her disappearing into the tube; she was hitching the rucksack over her back.

I drove home from the depot and sat in the car outside our front gate. I knew what I was going to say; the words had been rolling round my head since the night before.

Dolly, I've got something to tell you. I'm not just off-colour . . . As a matter of fact, I've got leukaemia.

I've got leukaemia and I'll spend the rest of my days, short though they are, here in this overheated house with you, pretending we've always been happy. I'll have to behave like a saint because nobody, you or Wally or anyone, will let me behave like a jerk.

Life's too short. That's what she'd said.

Doriza was in the lounge, eating marzipan fancies. I paused at the door, and opened my mouth.

Then the words came out.

'Dolly, I've got something to tell you.' I walked in and stopped in front of the gas fire. The words were different to what I'd meant. 'Today I met this girl, this bird . . .'

Suddenly I felt airy inside, and lighter. The words came out in a rush.

'See, we went into this hayfield . . .'

Dolly stopped munching and stared at me.

I watched her expression change.

Lost Boys

My husband Ewan once shouted: 'Don't you realize I had a deprived childhood?'

It sounded a wonderful childhood to me, compared to my own upbringing in safe and leafy Kent. His mother was a painter called Lily Frears. You might have heard of her; she was a great success in her day, and she was a part of so many lives that she's in the indexes of all those biographies one reads on the train. She'd been a beautiful girl with ruddy skin and bold gypsy eyes. She'd modelled for Augustus John. More than modelled, I suspect. She'd been through two marriages, one to a young sculptor and the other to Ewan's father, a Swiss businessman and patron of the arts. He'd been bemused by her, besotted with her, and had finally died – I said from unrequited love, but Ewan says from pancreatitis. Throughout her husbands and lovers, she'd kept stubbornly to her original name, her independence, her subtle, dappled paintings and to hand-rolling her own cigarettes from pipe tobacco.

I imagined Ewan, a small boy, perched on the corduroy knees of the eminent painters of the past, most of whom, at some point, had been in love with Lily. In fact, I was half in love with her myself. Another thing Ewan once said, only partly joking: 'You married me for my mother.'

'Lots of people loved her.'

He replied: 'The only things she loves are her cats.'

'But you're her son. She must love you.'

'She's vaguely surprised by me now. That she produced this enormous man.' He paused. 'When I was young, I just got in the way.'

He said she forgot he was there. Those evenings I imagined – oh how I imagined them, with coarse red wine and passionate beliefs – he remembered just as boring and smoky. He said he'd crawl under the sofa to sleep and the next day he'd miss school. I thought it sounded marvellous. Sometimes she took him to France, or to Tuscany for the summer. Once they lived in a hotel in Cairo for a year; he never knew why.

I called her romantic. He called her untrustworthy. She sent him to boarding school in Sussex. Suddenly she'd turn up during chapel, swathed in a Kashmiri shawl; as he filed out, she'd whisk him down to the beach to search for shells. But sometimes on real visiting days he would stand at the gates, all smartened up, and wait, and wait . . . when we were quarrelling, he'd tell me this story to make me sorry for him.

She lost him frequently, he said, quoting Oscar Wilde about losing twice seems like carelessness. We live in Hendon (a suburb she always found vaguely comic – she could never remember the number of our house and would send postcards to the wrong address). Above our lounge fire is one of her paintings. I love it. There's drenched green bodies, all naked, sitting under the trees. He remembers when it was painted.

'We'd rented a cottage in the New Forest, and a lot of the grown-ups went swimming, naked, in a river. Afterwards she sat down and painted the others and I wandered off.

She forgot me. I was only five. I wandered down the stream and fell in and nearly drowned.' He paused. 'All for that painting. What would you rather, that painting or me?'

'But I've got both.'

He sighed. 'That's just what she would say.'

When I first met Lily, she was still lovely – old and bony, but with those large, vague eyes: a face with a Past. Even if she didn't wear her fringed dresses and crimson stockings, people would have gazed with admiration in the street. She lived in a cluttered mansion flat opposite the British Museum and ate in the sandwich bar downstairs. She still taught, part-time, at the Central School of Art, where she had become mythologized in her lifetime, the last of an era. When I was first married, I used to visit her and sit for hours, eating salami rolls and listening to her as the day darkened outside and neither of us wanted to break the spell and switch on the lights.

Anyone less like a mother-in-law would be hard to imagine. In fact, I felt older than her – the sober, sensible one who voiced objections and wanted her to get the dates right.

Ewan visited her too; not as a treat, however, but as a duty. One day I looked at him: he was thirty and already thinning on top. It was harder nowadays to imagine him as a child.

I said: 'You didn't appreciate her. She's such a free spirit.'

'I didn't want a free spirit,' he said. 'I wanted a mother.'

It all changed, as everything does, when we had children. Alexis arrived, and then Cassandra (the arty names were my choice). I became closed into our house in Hendon and I couldn't get up to London to see Lily. When I did it was not the same. The children sucked the paintbrushes and tripped over the cat litter trays. Lily bought them charming presents, like a second-hand railway engine, that were far too old for them and had to be put into the cupboard, amidst shrieks, when we got home.

She was always Lily, never Granny. She wouldn't let them call her that because she felt the wings of mortality brushing her face; she said this, touching her rouged cheek.

My own parents' house was, as always, more comfortable and appropriate than Lily's flat. We'd go down for Sunday lunch and the children could toddle across the safe green lawns of my childhood. They loved my mother's fridge, which was always crammed. I thought of Lily's, empty but for a tin of Kit-e-Kat and a half-bottle of gin (I said she was too poor to buy a whole bottle, but Ewan said she was too stingy).

At Lily's, the only roast beef came in a cellophane roll, but at my parents' there was a proper Sunday lunch with gravy. Ewan always got on well with my parents – better than I do myself – and during the talk about What We're Doing to the House (a perennial topic) I found myself disloyally yearning for Lily, who'd never owned anything in her life.

When Alex was three, he tried to sip the sherry, and when reprimanded he said: 'Lily lets me.'

My mother looked at him. 'Well, Granny doesn't.'

By the time Alex was four, a small, grave boy and the image of his father, and Cassie was eighteen months, Lily had become distanced into a golden ideal of freedom. It seemed as hard to reach that as to walk into her green, forest painting above our mantelpiece. Ewan thought I was a wonderful mother but then he didn't know what domesticity was like, he only came home to it. Arms full of damp Babygros, sometimes I sat down and screamed.

What was I like; where had I gone? I felt emptied, an empty vessel, drained by others' needs. I wanted to be myself, like Lily.

Ewan said: 'She should never have had me. She wasn't a natural mother. You are.'

I said sharply: 'How do you know?'

Mentally I added up the weeks – yes, weeks – since we had made love. And then how had it been? Functional, courteous.

Dull.

I thought: life's passing me by. It never passed Lily by. She *lived*.

One hot June day, on impulse, I took the children up to London and rang Lily's bell. Kissing her papery cheek, I realized how strongly I'd been missing her.

'You say you like surprises.'

'My dear girl,' she said. 'We shall go swimming.'

We took a taxi up to Hampstead Heath and walked along a grassy path, through a meadow. The grass and cow parsley were taller than Alex. Bees murmured, or was it the drone of cars? The city seemed far away as we walked along our enchanted path. Hendon dwindled. I hadn't been to the Heath for years; I didn't realize it was so wild. I felt drunk with the scent of flowers.

Finally, we arrived at a hedge, fenced with railings. In front of us was an open gate.

'I've been coming here for ever,' said Lily. 'First, I'd swim, then I'd draw the bathers. It's ladies only – the Ladies' Pond.'

The Ladies' Pond . . . even the name sounded mysterious. Behind the hedge I could hear faint laughter: I could see a glint of water. I never knew such a pond existed; the splashings through the hedge had the charmed inevitability of a dream.

We only had Lily's costume – an odd, shiny, red garment – and besides, children weren't allowed, so one of us had to wait in the meadow with them. Lily picked two grass-heads and I drew out the short one, so she disappeared first through the gate – a tall, striding figure, despite her age. She wore a straw hat and a faded orange dress. She looked so young from the back that it was a shock when she turned to wave.

She seemed to be gone for hours, but that afternoon time had no importance. Cassie had fallen asleep in the push-chair. I sat with Alex amongst the tall grasses, nibbling sorrel leaves and trying to persuade him to take off his T-shirt. Like his dad, he preferred to be fully dressed.

'We used to swim naked here,' said Lily, sitting down beside me and passing me the swimming costume. 'Or did I just imagine it?' Her face looked damp and bare and old with the make-up washed off.

'Will you be all right?' I asked, looking at them as I left. 'Try to take Alex's clothes off.'

What followed was the most beautiful half-hour I think I've ever spent. Slipping into the water, warm and murky as soup, was like slipping into one of Lily's paintings. The heavy horse-chestnuts cast a dappled shade, and on the banks lay sunbathing women, some bare-breasted. No cocksure, competitive men, no loud boys showing off, no children with their whines and needs . . . Just silence as women swam lazily to and fro, each alone, each free. It was hard to believe we were just a few miles from Leicester Square; it could have been the New Forest. I could be Lily, swimming twenty years before . . .

I swam slowly, gazing at my bare arms, blurred and yellowed in the water . . . The water weeds brushed my legs, like drowned women. Far above, a plane passed. It made no noise, it was irrelevant. I imagined it packed with businessmen. Ewan was taking the Glasgow shuttle that day – like his mother, Ewan is in paint; in his case, however, it's the Marketing Division of ICI. I thought that of all the people I knew, only Lily would have brought me here.

I dried myself luxuriously, taking my time. Then I got dressed and walked barefoot down the cinder path towards the gate. I remember my exact sensations during that walk. My damp hair tickled my shoulders; my limbs felt refreshed and elastic, my body felt alive for the first time . . . oh, for years. I wondered how I'd feel if I had a lover whom I could tell these things, and who wouldn't think I was being self-indulgent. No – who wouldn't need telling – who would know.

Through the hedge I could see the orange blur of Lily's dress. The last thing I remember thinking was: the children are quiet.

Lily was sitting still. It took me a moment to realize she had an open pad and she was drawing Cassie.

I walked nearer and looked down, over the henna streaks of Lily's drying hair, at the delicate lines of my child's face on the paper.

'Can't get that waxiness,' murmured Lily. 'Not with a pencil.' She paused. 'Such exquisite little objects . . . I've always preferred them asleep, don't you?'

I smiled, then I looked around. 'Where's Alex?'

Silence. Lily was just shading in the mouth.

'Hmm?' she said. 'He was here a minute ago.'

'Where is he?' The sharp note in my voice frightened me.

'Oh, I know. He said he was looking for bottle tops.'

'Was it just a minute?'

I straightened up and looked around. To one side was the hedge. On all the other sides stretched the meadow, full of tall grass. Far away stood some trees, with people walking and picnicking.

'Alex?' I called.

I waited. Silence, except for a splash in the lake.

'*Alex!*'

Nothing moved except the breeze, which blew gently over the meadow, silvering the grasses. Swathes of them rippled, and then were still. I waited. The breeze blew again, chilling me. The grass moved, the cow parsley swayed, its white heads bobbing and bouncing, and then was still.

'*Alex!*'

I swung round. 'Lily, you go that way.' I pointed in one direction, then I tried to unbuckle Cassie. She woke with a yell. My hands wouldn't work; I fumbled with the pushchair buckle. Finally, I wrenched it open and grabbed her. I bundled her under one arm and plunged into the grass, in the opposite direction to Lily.

The meadow was so huge; I'd never realized Hampstead Heath was this size. It was bumpy, too; it was difficult to run, stumbling over the hidden potholes with Cassie bouncing and shrieking.

'*Alex!*'

The sun had slid behind a cloud and the Heath looked sinister. How could I have believed in the happy freedom of my swim? How could I have been so foolish? Why had I left an old, vague, self-absorbed lady in charge of my most precious possessions? How could I?

Tears blurred my eyes as I struggled through the weeds – they were weeds, wicked weeds, trying to trip me up. As I neared them, the trees looked loomingly black and heavy.

People stopped to stare. 'Have you seen a little boy?' I screeched. They shook their heads and I hated them for being in the wrong place; but I hated myself more.

Far away I could see the orange blur of Lily. I thought: you stupid old woman.

If this has ever happened to you, then you know those pictures that crowd your head and that you'd never allowed yourself to see. You'll know how time literally ceases.

How long it took I'll never remember. But when I saw that small, blue and white figure, he was standing beside the gate, right back at the place we'd left. He was standing waiting for us, my lost boy, and his face was red.

Lost boys. I pictured Ewan, a little boy in his school blazer, waiting at the school gates for a mother who never arrived.

Ewan once said: 'I never had a childhood. Know why? Because *she* was the child.'

I never told Ewan what had happened, though Alex in his usual matter-of-fact way said that he'd only found two bottle tops. But after that, for the first time in his life, he slept for fourteen hours solid.

Eight years have passed since that day. Lily's dead now. But I remember it because this morning Alex, now twelve years old, asked me about the drawing of Cassie we have in the lounge, above my desk. (I run my own small business now, oh yes, I've done something.) It's a beautiful drawing and I like looking at it when I'm working out my VAT . . . That sleeping, waxen face from a past era, years that were suffocating, and often painful, but which I'll never forget.

Alex asked me, and I told him about that day and what happened. He couldn't remember anything about it. And for the first time I tried to tell him exactly what Lily was like. I said that in fact she was not such a famous painter, just an artistic woman who had some doting patrons. That she wasn't a living legend at the art school, but that they'd kept her on out of kindness. That when I first met her, I resented my parents and compared them to her in a way that did justice to neither. That idolizing her hurt my husband, because he knew the truth. (I doubt if Alex took this in, but I went on in a rush.) That people sometimes giggled at her in the street, but that I was sure others saw the ruined, striking beauty of her face.

That she was utterly herself, a true original; that she had time for me when nobody else noticed I needed it. And that there was nobody I would rather see walking through the door at this moment.

I said all this, and more, because I wanted him to know her. To idolize anyone is the worst thing one can do, because then they are lost to us.

Then I said that for the price of that drawing of Cassie I might have lost him. But he pushed me away. He's like his father; he hates soppy stuff.

Snake Girl

Everyone liked Johnnie. Always a smile, and first with the drinks at the Sind Club bar. Last to leave, too, but then he lived alone and where else would he go?

He would horse around with the kids, as well, at the Sind Club pool. His jokes were sometimes of a robust nature, for down in the bazaar he knew a supplier of plastic masks. Mothers liked him because they could dreamily give themselves up to the sun. Their children called him uncle and chased him, whooping, through the verandas. Turbaned bearers stepped aside. 'He's never grown up,' parents said, as they sipped lime sodas under the dusty palms. 'He's a child himself.' Sometimes, when they were posted elsewhere, as they inevitably were, they told their children to send him a postcard. Sometimes they remembered.

Nobody knew when he had come to Pakistan. He was simply one of the fixtures and fittings: a lean man in a beige bush-jacket, who could tell a newcomer where to buy the best Baluch carpets and who knew all the reels for Burns Night. This happened once a year at the Consulate; he was paired off with career secretaries of uncertain age and American divorcees who chomped on menthol cigarettes and sometimes, unsuccessfully, asked him back to their place. There was Johnnie, blurred in the corner of a hundred snapshots, caught for ever in a lost episode in people's lives – before Washington, before London again, before their divorce and the dispersal of their growing children. 'Isn't that him?' they'd point. Fixed, his face, eager to please in the blinking rabbit glare. Passingly, they felt curious.

He had an ageless, leathery look, from decades in the sun. He was a bachelor, and one of those innocents who survive surprisingly well. How old was he: forty-five? Fifty-five? He wasn't secretive; it's just that if one does not offer information there are others more ready with their own, busy selves. Johnnie was a spectator, and one of that rare breed: a truly modest man.

He was British; a pilot with PIA. Few people knew his real name; he had been nicknamed Johnnie Walker on account of the whisky, which in those days cost Rs 300 per bottle on the black market. At his shindigs there was always plenty of that, what with his airline connections and his legendary generosity. And plenty of homemade beer, which he brewed in buckets and called hooch. His cronies slapped him on the back and called him 'old chap'.

Why had he never married? Jokingly he said that he'd missed his connection and the flight was never called. Besides, he was always somewhere else – Frankfurt one day, New York the next, standing the crew a drink in the bar of some intercontinental hotel. He wore the glazed bonhomie, the laundered pleasantness, of the permanently jetlagged. He returned with perfume for the plainest girls at the British Consulate, who thanked him wistfully. If people paused to wonder, they decided that his true love was planes – after all, the flight deck of a DC10 was simpler than any woman. And what could beat the romance of flying – lights blipping, that vast blue space above, arriving only to depart, the sweet angst of loss flavouring every encounter? He adored his job, that was plain; just look at his flat.

You had to duck to get into the living room. This was due to the model planes suspended from the ceiling. Hurricanes, Spitfires, Mosquitoes – civilian and military aircraft, revolving slowly in the breeze from the fan. Otherwise his flat had a transitory air. It was situated on the new beach road outside the city: Route 43, that so far led nowhere. Apartment blocks had been built along it but in those days, the mid-seventies, they had not yet been completed; most were still concrete cells with electrical wires knotted from the ceiling, and a view of the sea. The parking spaces in front were edged with oil drums, from each of which drooped a bougainvillea bush.

Hot wind blew, sand against concrete. Behind the flats stretched the grey desert.

'One day,' he joked, 'this'll be the Third World's answer to Malibu Beach.' People asked him if he felt lonely, living with the few other pioneers in Phase One, and he replied: 'Me, lonely? With the best view in Pakistan?'

He said the sun setting over the Arabian Ocean was beautiful, but most sundowns he was to be found at the Sind Club bar.

Then in 1975, to everybody's surprise, Johnnie married. Gossip buzzed in the Sind Club bar; after all, there was little else to gossip about. 'Young enough to be his daughter.' A nudge and a wink. 'He's landed on his feet,' said Mr Bashir from Cameron Chemicals. 'Has he?' asked Kenneth Trimmer from Grindlays Bank. What did she see in him, and he in her? She was a tiny Pakistani girl, seemingly sprung from nowhere. But then Karachi was used to arrivals and departures; the airport road was the busiest in the city.

Another nudge and wink. Above, the ceiling fans creaked. Along the walls, bearers stood like waxworks. Beyond, the tree frogs whirred; beyond them, beyond the beach route and the apartment blocks, the hot wind blew in from the sea.

She had indeed sprung from nowhere. At least, she was new to him. Music thudded from his lounge, where his guests gyrated under the swaying aircraft. There she was in his kitchen, buttering a slice of bread.

'You look starving,' he said.

She gazed up at him. She had large black eyes and shiny lipstick. 'Someone said there was smoked salmon.'

'All gone.' A plate lay there, scattered with lime wedges. 'I brought it back from London.'

'You're the pilot then?'

He nodded. He wanted to feed her up. He opened the fridge but by this stage in the evening everything had been eaten.

'Jam?' he asked. She nodded. She was wearing jeans and a yellow T-shirt with spangles on it. Despite the make-up, and the indolent way she pushed her hair behind her ear, she looked so young. She ate greedily.

Her name was Aisha and she had come with Farooq and his crowd – young bloods who drove their daddies' cars and went to the Excelsior Hot Spot. They knew the location of parties by a kind of radar.

And Aisha disappeared with them, with honking horns

from down below and a slewing of tyres. Johnnie was left
amongst the ashtrays, and when he moved to the window
there was nothing but a huge moon silvering the sea. A
string of streetlights led to Karachi. He thought of flying,
of cities laid out below like winking puzzles that sometimes
made sense; he thought of his own back which was starting
to ache whenever he leaned over. He picked up a glass and
straightened with a grunt.

The next flight to London he brought back a packet of
smoked salmon and put it in his fridge. And a few days
later he found her.

It was in downtown Karachi. Through a haze of exhaust
smoke he spotted her outside the Reptile Emporium. Air
crews bought shoes and handbags there; she was looking at
the window display. He wanted to buy up the shop; he
wanted to please her.

Nearby, a pavement kiosk sold cigarettes. But also, for
those who knew, copies of *Vogue* and *Penthouse* could be
produced from under the counter. He asked to see the selec-
tion. Inspired, he knew just what she wanted: a glossy copy
of the Harrods Christmas catalogue.

They sat in an open-air café behind the Metropole Hotel.
Against the white glare of the sky a sign stuttered for *7-Up*.
She drank through a straw and pointed to photos of ostrich-
trimmed nightgowns. 'Ooh,' she gasped.

The next page was a festive table, laden with food; it
glowed in the candlelight. 'Look,' she pointed. There were
two brushed children and their parents gathered around a
pile of presents, which were wrapped in ribbon. Behind
them an olde-worlde window was speckled with snow.

'I want to go to England,' she sighed.

He smiled. 'It doesn't really look like that.'

Two street urchins came into the café and held out their hands. 'Baksheesh!' they demanded. She shooed them away. Johnnie, however, gave them Rs 5 each – far too much. They sniggered and ran off. Today he felt foolish; he felt young.

Two months later they were married. He had never been so happy. Aisha sat on his knee and he told her about Singapore and Sydney. Her eyes widened; she stroked his cheek.

She liked jokes, too. One evening she put on a small black moustache.

Startled, he asked: 'What's this – Hitler?'

She knew nothing of the Second World War. She replied: 'Look, I'm Charlie Chaplin!' She loved the movies and could see the same ones again and again.

In their high apartment they gazed out at the sea; they ate smoked salmon and Bendick's Bittermints. Some other windows were lit now, and sweetmeat sellers had set up their stalls on the sand. With his wife on his knee, his flat became his home. He was no longer seen at the Sind Club; she thought it fuddy-duddy, with its shrouded billiards tables and relics of the Raj. She preferred the beach. Young men from the city drove out nowadays, their car boots clanking with crates of Bubble-Up and their radios blaring. The place was being developed into a seaside resort of a minor nature. Fairy lights had been strung around a chicken-tikka café. Bold couples parked their cars and necked.

His own bearer had left, disapproving of this plump young woman who had bewitched his master. Neither

Johnnie nor Aisha could cook, so the two of them went down to the beach café and sat on mismatched plastic chairs. They drank sweet tea while car radios played film music and the vast sea sighed. Young men ogled her; she shouted back at them – Urdu oaths which even Johnnie, an old trooper, couldn't understand.

Once, he asked her about Farooq, who had brought her to the party, but she just shrugged. Farooq's family was in favour with the Bhutto government and involved in developing the beach; they had landed the contract to build a casino. One evening he and his friends arrived and dragged Aisha, squealing, to the water's edge. They sauntered back, their cigarettes glowing in the dark. Later she showed Johnnie the mark on her wrist where Farooq had gripped her. He was angry, but she shrugged. 'Stupid Rooqi,' she said, with one of her baffling smiles. He felt pain, first for her and then for himself.

'In England she'd be called a scrubber,' said Shirley Trimmer, 'but I like her.'

They were driving home from a Sind Club dinner-dance. 'Not top drawer,' said her husband Kenneth. 'But then, if one thinks of it, neither is he.'

It had been a stifling evening – an elderly band playing Frank Ifield tunes; polite wives in saris. She glanced at Kenneth. His nose was peeling. He had never been as pompous as this in England, but then in England he had never been a sahib.

She sighed and looked out of the window. Something was caught in the glare of the headlights. It was a camel, bedecked with beads. It turned its head slowly, like a puppet. She felt a rush of pleasure – the first, and last, of the evening.

Like her husband, Aisha was a lost soul, an orphan. Sometimes she talked about the past, but it was always the far past, when she was a child. Her father had been the assistant clerk of an irrigation scheme up in the north, in the Punjab. She talked about the ditches filled with brown water, the banks moulded like putty. She didn't use those words, but Johnnie pictured it.

He stroked her hair as she sat, curled in the armchair, and told him how she had adored her father and how she had followed him along the canals. He didn't know she was following him; he would have been angry. One day she lost him; she remembered looking down and seeing the water moving with snakes. Long, shiny snakes, they had coiled and knotted themselves in the water which was as warm as soup.

Johnnie tilted her face towards him; her jaws worked as she chewed on her gum. He was filled with such tenderness that his limbs felt boneless.

'My serpent of old Nile,' he said.

'Pardon?'

'William Shakespeare,' he replied.

She smiled and turned the page of *Movie Secrets*.

'My snake girl,' he said.

She shivered. 'Ugh! I hate snakes.'

Kenneth and Shirley Trimmer came out of the Reptile Emporium. It was May, and the suffocating weather just beginning.

She was carrying her new snakeskin shoes. 'You shouldn't have bargained!' she hissed.

'They respect you for it,' he replied. 'You should understand by now, my dear.'

'Don't be condescending.'

Only recently had he started calling her dear. She looked at him coolly. The subcontinent was turning him into the housemaster of a minor prep school. She should have suspected it.

Ahead she spotted Johnnie and his wife; Aisha wore luminous pink salwar-kameez and red high heels. She clung to his arm as they hailed a taxi.

'Don't they look happy,' Shirley said.

'Who?' He was not an observant man. She pointed them out. He said: 'Obvious, isn't it? She's looking for a father and he's looking for a daughter. Won't last.'

There were damp semi-circles under his arms. She turned away and thought: But will we?

When Johnnie flew, he flew for his wife. Planes simply became vehicles to shorten the distance until he held her again. In foreign hotels his heart ached. He only found peace browsing in the gift arcades.

Sometimes he managed to get through on the phone – the lines to Pakistan were erratic – but often there was no reply. On his return he never asked her about this; he was too old to want to know the answer.

He returned, laden with gifts. Once, when he came home from a long haul and the phone had never answered, she gave him a present.

He unwrapped the box. It was a Mark V Spitfire,

ready-assembled. In fact he had one already, suspended near the kitchen door, but though she had tried to learn the difference between his planes she had never succeeded.

'Do you like it?' she asked. 'There is a toy-wallah in Bohra Bazaar. I told him to make it for you.'

Deeply moved, he hugged her. How could he explain that the fun was in doing-it-yourself? For her, the fun was not-doing-it-yourself.

She didn't understand him. But what did that matter when in some obscure way, he could never find the words for it, they were two of a kind? He loved her all the more.

One day Shirley bumped into Aisha in Bohra Bazaar, the main bazaar of the city. Along the alleys, saris hung like flags; village women shuffled past, shrouded in burqas; a legless beggar sat on his trolley and the air smelt of incense.

'I'm going to London soon,' said Aisha. 'I'm going to Oxford Street.'

Shirley grimaced. 'It's awful. Tacky and crowded.'

Aisha gestured around. 'But this is dirty and crowded.'

'No,' smiled Shirley. 'This is romantic.'

Aisha wrinkled her nose. 'You English people, you must be mad.'

He wanted to show her the world; on the other hand, he wanted to keep her safe. For the first time in his career he thought of hijackers and metal fatigue. He blamed this for his reluctance.

But how her eyes would widen at the England she desired so fiercely: acres of separates at Marks & Spencer; fairy lights not over a tikka café but looped high around Harrods; clean, moneyed streets.

He himself had lived abroad for so many years that by now this was his England too. He too saw it from an air-conditioned transit bus; he had become an outsider. London was where you bought gift-wrapped jars of marmalade and where people still sometimes said *I'm sorry*. If you move from one scentless hotel room to another, cities blur. They become a fast flip of picture postcards, a forgotten memento at the bottom of your suitcase.

He fixed them a holiday in London, for two weeks in October. He booked her a direct flight; he himself would be arriving from New York. They planned to meet in the hotel. 'It's our honeymoon,' he told her, though they had been married a year. He booked a room overlooking Hyde Park, so that when she opened the window, for the first time in her life she would smell autumn. He pictured the two of them, laden with carrier bags, walking beside the lake and kicking the leaves. He hadn't kicked leaves since he was a boy, and seldom then. He had been raised in an orphanage. He hadn't kept this a secret; it was just that nobody asked. It was his wife who fifty years later was giving him back his childhood. For this he would give her the world, which he had crossed so many times alone. If not the world, at least he would give her London.

He was leaving two days earlier than Aisha. He hugged her. Ridiculously, his stomach churned. He had never before suffered from flight-nerves.

'Look after yourself,' he murmured. He pressed her glossy head to his chest. She gripped him. 'Fly to me safely.'

'You always say it's the safest way to travel.'

'But you're different,' he said.

'Why?'

'You're precious.'

When he left, a gust of wind blew through the apartment. Doors slammed; the planes rocked.

All that evening a gale blew in from the sea. Sand dimmed the sunset; drifts half-buried the café chairs. Down in the city, dust swirled.

Shirley, emerging from a business function at the Metropole Hotel, saw Aisha climbing out of a Mercedes. Giggling, she was smoothing down her loose lurex slacks which billowed in the wind. Another girl followed her, and three men. Cigarettes glowing, the men propelled the girls downstairs into the Excelsior Hot Spot.

Shirley climbed into her own car and sat next to her husband. She thought: Aisha is an innocent. Not as nice as Johnnie, but an innocent too.

Now why did she think that? The words jostled in her head; a puzzle she hadn't the will to work out. Let them get on with it, she thought recklessly. Tonight she was tipsy. She had drunk a great deal of Rs 300-a-bottle imported gin.

Perhaps, when he returned, Johnnie would hold one of his shindigs. Ah, she remembered, but by then she and Kenneth would be back in London; his contract finished at the end of the month.

At that moment, as they drove through the dusty street, palm trees swaying in the headlights, Kenneth clearing his throat beside her – at that moment, with the crystal clarity that alcohol can bring, she knew that once she returned to England she would leave him.

In the subcontinent, the most beautiful times are dawn and dusk. Johnnie had often remarked upon this. The sky was pearly-pink as Aisha sat in the car with Farooq. The storm had passed; the sea glinted, swelling like oil. It was the early morning. Across the world, across time zones, her husband slept. Or maybe he was eating lunch. Who knew? Painfully, she wished she did.

Farooq kissed her forehead. 'You'll adore Yasmin,' he said. 'She's a terrific girl.' He withdrew his hand from inside her blouse and reached into the back seat. 'Remember, Thursday morning. Where?'

'The Kardomah Café,' she repeated.

'And where is that?'

She closed her eyes. 'In Oxford Street.'

'Where in Oxford Street?'

She paused, and said dreamily: 'Opposite Marks & Spencer.'

He passed her the parcel. It was a box, wrapped in ribbon. 'No peeking,' he said. There were drops of perspiration on his forehead.

'It's her birthday present?' she asked again.

He nodded. 'Snakeskin shoes from the Reptile Emporium.'

'Snakeskin.' She shivered.

'My sister adores it, and it's damn expensive in London.'

She closed her eyes again. 'I'm going to Harrods and Marks & Spencer and Selfridges—'

'Yasmin'll take you. She knows simply everybody and everywhere. Shops, nightclubs, you name it.'

'Johnnie and I don't know anybody.'

'Trust her. Have a sooper-dooper time.' He took her arm and folded it around the parcel. 'And don't forget this, will you?' He kissed her lightly. 'Sweetie.'

She flew overnight. Below lay the glittering grids of cities; around and above, black space. Whimpering, she pressed the airline pillow to her cheek; she felt rigid with fear. She had never flown. Surely the plane would fall? Surely Johnnie would not be there?

The cabin bucked. Everyone else slept blamelessly. 'Just a little turbulence,' the stewardess told her, as Aisha gripped her hand.

She clenched her eyes shut. She tried to rub out the thought of Farooq's hand between her thighs. She knew she was wicked, and that she would be punished.

They didn't believe her. Who would believe an overdressed Pakistani girl, who reeked of cheap perfume and scratched the customs officer with her crimson fingernails? She yelled that the box wasn't hers, it was given to her by a friend. Who? Called Farooq. Farooq who? She didn't know. She had never known his surname but he was a good friend, his father knew the President. What sort of friend is that, they asked, that you don't know his surname? Where did he live? She didn't know.

The packet was laid out on the table: small, white and smug. There were now four officers in the room. She struggled; the policewoman held her down.

She screeched: 'He said they were shoes!'

'Yes, dear.'

'Snakeskin shoes!'

By now she was hysterical. She twisted in the policewoman's arms; she spat like a cat. She was pregnant, she yelled, she was ill, she wanted her father, he was a very important person, he was a personal friend of President Bhutto. She started swearing in Urdu. They frowned, looking at the flimsy walls; people would think they were beating her up.

The mascara ran down her cheeks, her voice rose higher. She wanted her husband, he was very important too, he knew everybody, all the places to go. Her mother was sick, her mother was dying, she had to get out. Where did her mother live? they asked.

She tried to struggle free. 'At Harrods!' she shouted.

An hour later Johnnie arrived, breathlessly. They were trying to take a statement from her; she had jammed shut the lavatory door and was yelling for her husband. He heard her shrill voice; his heart shifted.

It only took him a moment to realize what had happened. It all made the most painful sense, but he didn't want to think about it. He only knew that she meant everything to him, and that the world was senseless without her. He stood, swaying with fatigue, staring at the creamy walls.

For cocaine smuggling she would get at least a year in prison, his darling wife. Or maybe they would deport her and she could never visit Britain again, all her life.

He heard her voice approaching as she was dragged out of the toilets. She sounded coarse as a fishwife; he had learnt some of the oaths by now, but he would always love her.

He cleared his throat and addressed the police officer.

'I did it,' he said. 'I put it in her suitcase.'

He was given a short prison sentence. Remarks were made about a man in his position, a senior pilot, and how he had abused a job that demanded the utmost trust and integrity. Regrets were expressed that a man with such a distinguished wartime record could end his career on such a note of disgrace. More abominably, that in doing so he had tried to corrupt a simple-minded girl who was young enough to be his daughter. What were the British coming to?

In his absence the Sind Club members learnt more about Johnnie than they had ever learnt when he was there. His real name was James and he had been decorated for bravery in action during the war; he had been a fighter pilot, flying Hurricanes, and one had been shot in flames from beneath him. As a child he had lived in institutions; once grown up, he had restlessly moved from place to place, living at one time in Australia and then Canada. Finally, in the forties, he had moved to Karachi. Until now his record had been blameless.

'Well, well, so he's a crook,' said Mr Khan, who that morning had slipped Rs 30,000 to his good friend Habib sahib at the Port Authority, to facilitate the importation of some air-conditioners in which he himself happened to have an interest. 'I always said there was something odd about this chap Johnnie, he was so nice to everybody.'

*

It is the next summer, 1977. At the far end of the beach route the casino remains uncompleted. It is simply a concrete shell, a monument to the corrupt Bhutto regime which is now ending. There will soon be bloodshed. In July Bhutto himself will be thrown into prison and executed. Martial government and strict Islamic law will be introduced; gambling will be forbidden and drink no longer available even on the black market. No more shindigs.

Farooq and his family, having Bhutto connections, are now out of favour and have fled the country. They were last heard of living in Knightsbridge.

Aisha had unwittingly told the truth, the previous October; she was indeed pregnant. This summer she gives birth to a boy. The baby's skin is surprisingly dark but this is never mentioned either by herself or by Johnnie. Neither wishes to. He dotes on the child.

He is no longer employed by PIA, but then he says that he always wanted early retirement. Flying has lost its importance; he prefers to be at home sweet home. Phase One is now finished and a small bazaar has sprung up between the apartment blocks. Aisha shops there, ordering aubergines and onions to be piled into her increasingly frail Harrods carrier bag. When she passes the cars, parked facing the beach, she rolls her eyes at the young men. Nothing will change her, but Johnnie has always known that.

One evening, unused to the heat, June and David drive out to the beach. They are new arrivals; he is Kenneth's successor at Grindlays Bank. To mark his status as sahib and branch manager he is trying to grow a small moustache.

There is a café on the beach. Johnnie and Aisha are

sitting there. Johnnie holds the baby in one arm while with the other he passes a model aeroplane to and fro above its head. He makes aeroplane sounds.

David turns to his wife. 'Isn't that the chap who went to prison?' he asks. 'Unlikely looking couple, aren't they?'

June sighs, but so softly her husband doesn't hear. She watches them for a moment, then she says: 'They do look happy.'

Vacant Possession

Some people call us cynics. Us, being estate agents. With a chortle they quote our advertisements: '*Studio Flat*,' they read. 'You mean a bedsit. *Easily maintained garden*. You mean four square yards of concrete.'

I'm not a cynic. In fact, I'm the opposite. I'm a romantic. I see the possibilities in the meanest property. I don't just see it; I believe it. For instance, I don't tell myself that a garden is surrounded by buildings, I tell myself it's secluded. If a flat overlooks Tesco's loading bay I tell myself it's convenient for the shops.

And to my surprise it works. If you're blind to the disadvantages, you pull other people along with you in the warm slipstream of your vision. Next time you're in the Fulham area, drive around and have a look at all those boards up saying *For Sale: Prewitt, Cudlip & Little*. Cudlip's me.

Oh yes, this optimism has got me a long way professionally. In my private life, however, it's been a different matter. Only the most foolish of romantics, the blindest of fools, would believe that a married man, working for the Department of the Environment, with three teenage children, would ever leave his wife.

Nigel was going to, of course. But not quite yet, because Vicky was doing her O-levels and he'd never be able to forgive himself if she failed. Because his wife was depressed

309

after her hysterectomy and he couldn't bear to upset her just yet. Because, because.

They had gone on for four years, these becauses, and meanwhile I'd see him once a week or once a fortnight, when I was known as 'a conference in Southampton' or 'a meeting in Hull'. I'd been every major town in the British Isles. Once, for a couple of days, I was actually a summit meeting in Brussels.

Work is easy, isn't it, compared to everything else. I would sit in my beige office with its warbling phones and its window display of dream houses which I passed from one stranger to another. I would drive around in my shiny Metro, making valuations on the properties of Fash Fulham. I worked out percentages on my calculator; how cool those numbers were, how simple the soft bleeps of my sums.

If you want to know what sort of properties we handle, then Marcus Tanner's house was typical. I'd already acted for several clients in Foster Road, a street once occupied by the humble. A few still remained, with their net curtains and polished front steps, the chrysanths carefully staked in the gardens. But they were a vanishing species, outnumbered by the middle classes who knocked through their ground floors, called to each other in fruity, confident voices and filled up the street with their double-parked Renaults.

It was a morning in May that I went to Marcus Tanner's house to make a valuation. I guessed the reason for selling when I saw that the tubs on each side of the front door were choked with weeds. After six years in the house trade, I can recognize a divorce.

'Think you can shift it?' he asked. 'Quick?'

I nodded. 'No problem. These houses always sell. They're
so sweet.'

'You mean small.'

'I mean sweet. Bijou. Perfect for—' I stopped.

He sighed. 'It was.'

Blushing, I gazed around the lounge. It was a typical
late-seventies job – open plan; William Morris wallpaper;
corduroy sofa; pub mirrors; Maggie Thatcher candle.

I paced the carpet. 'Hold this, will you please?' I gave
him one end of the tape measure. 'Immaculate through-
lounge,' I murmured.

'Immaculate?' He raised his eyebrows. 'Looks a bit
battle-scarred to me.'

I ignored him. 'Period features retained.'

'You mean these grotty old cupboards?'

I looked at him. 'You want to sell this house or not?'

He grinned. 'For a moment I thought you were a
romantic.'

'Oh no. I'm a businesswoman.'

We went into the kitchen. 'Compact,' I muttered.

'You mean it's a cupboard. Hey, don't lean on those
shelves, I put them up.'

'Everything within reach,' I said, measuring it.

'Shall I tell you about the dry rot?'

'No.'

We went outside.

'Even you can't pretend this is a garden,' he said.

'No, but it's a suntrap patio.'

He paused, picking a weed out of the wall. 'I'll miss this
place. It's full of single-parent actresses. On Sundays you
hear them learning their lines. And then there's the Sloane

girls who've been bought their houses by Daddy. On summer evenings you can hear the pop of Waitrose hock bottles and the rustle of After Eights.'

'Now who's sounding romantic.'

'No. Just over-sexed.'

We went inside.

'It's an up-and-coming area,' I said.

He sighed, and inspected himself in the passage mirror. 'Look at these period features.'

He looked all right to me: a tall chap, I would say in his early forties. A lived-in, humorous face. I seem to have a weakness for older men. He wore a tired-looking jacket and corduroy trousers.

We went upstairs. Halfway up, I paused and looked out on to the extension roof. There was a flowerpot there, with shrivelled foliage.

He asked. 'What are you writing?'

'Roof terrace.'

We went into the bedroom. To me, the outsider on the inside, entering their lives at a moment of stress, they divide into two sorts. The ones who say nothing (men) and the ones who say too much (women). But Mr Tanner, unlike most men, wanted to tell me about it.

'Spacious fitted cupboards throughout,' I murmured, writing it down.

He opened one. It was full of dresses. 'She's coming for them tomorrow. It'll look even more spacious then.'

'What about the carpet?'

'Oh, get rid of the lot.' He paused, gazing at the bed. A cat lay curled there, its fur lit by sunlight. 'Looks peaceful, doesn't she?'

I gazed at the cat nestling on the daisy-patterned duvet, and nodded.

'She left me for her T'ai Chi instructor.'

'What?'

'Chinese martial arts.' He shut the cupboard with a snap. 'Spiritual self-defence. She was taking classes.'

'So he's Chinese?'

'No. From Tufnell Park. Between you and me, a bit of a wanker. But then I'm biased.'

There was a moment's silence. We stood in the bedroom, listening to the far strains of Radio 1 coming from the opposite house, which was being done up. No doubt another couple was moving in there, full of hope. I thought of the wheel of fortune, turning. Couples rising, and the casualties fallen by the wayside. Him, for instance; and me. I was not becoming a cynic.

'Enough maudlin talk,' he said. 'How much can we ask?'

'Sixty-eight,' I said briskly. 'Are you open to offers?'

He grinned again. 'Depends who's offering.'

He worked at the BBC, so he was out all day. Over the next week I showed prospective buyers around the house. After all these years I still feel intrusive, letting myself in through somebody else's front door. Particularly when that person lives alone; their solitary possessions seem vulnerable when exposed to strangers.

I showed round young couples who lingered, arm-in-arm. 'Lime-green!' said one girl. 'What a ghastly colour for a bathroom.' In the kitchen, an officious young man prodded the shelves. 'What a wally job. Wonder who put these up.'

I felt prickly. I told myself it was simple jealousy. These

people were couples, and they were actually buying a house. They would walk down a street together, arm-in-arm, in broad daylight.

I looked at the bowl of half-eaten Weetabix and wondered if Marcus Tanner always ate his breakfast standing up in the kitchen. I wondered how he passed his evenings. In the lounge one day, while the floorboards above creaked with yet another couple, I found an open *Time Out* next to the phone; various cinemas had been underlined. He'd been doodling in the margins, and he'd drawn specs on Helen Mirren.

The cat, disturbed from her bed, came downstairs and rubbed herself against my legs. I fetched a tin and fed her. Even though I didn't know her name, I felt at home then.

It was Thursday. That evening I was expecting a visit from Nigel. We were going to a suburban cinema, where we couldn't be spotted, to watch *Gandhi*. I realized how I had been changing recently. Once I would have resented *Gandhi* because it was three hours long and that meant three hours missed when I could have had Nigel to myself, in bed. Now I just wanted to see the film. I thought: I'm curing myself. The cure is working.

But in the end, it was immaterial because he phoned up with his call-box whisper, and said he couldn't come because his son had been sent down from Oxford for possessing cannabis and they had to have a family confrontation.

So I went to *Gandhi* alone, at my local. At least I didn't have to travel all the way to Orpington. The next morning, he sent me a bunch of roses in apology. I shoved them into the swing-bin, jamming down their heads in a crackle of cellophane.

When I went to Marcus Tanner's house that morning there were two empty wine glasses on the table. In the kitchen I found two coffee cups; it wasn't his usual Nescafé, he'd made proper coffee in his cafetière. Two breakfast plates, with toast crumbs. Irritably I thought: what a mess. How's he going to sell his house if he leaves it like this?

I was called upstairs then. The people wanted to know if the blinds went with the house. I answered them, gazing at the bed. Beside it were two glasses and a half-empty bottle of Calvados. And his Maggie Thatcher candle, burnt down to a pair of sloping blue shoulders. She must have been important, for him to have burnt his candle.

'Pardon?'

'I said,' the man repeated, 'is the seller open to offers?'

I replied: 'Apparently.'

A week later an offer was made, and accepted. I spoke to Marcus Tanner on the phone.

'Come out and celebrate,' he said. 'Say you will.'

'You only got sixty-two thousand.'

'I knew you were an optimist. A romantic.'

'I'm a businesswoman.'

'Forget business,' he said. 'I'll give you a meal.'

He took me to a Fulham Road bistro. The evening got off on the wrong foot when one of the waiters looked at me, then winked at him.

'I see you're known here,' I said.

'Oh yes,' he said blandly. He was wearing a red shirt and

a bright blue tie. In the candlelight he looked caddish; a divorced man on the loose.

'Have you found somewhere else?' I asked.

'I'm looking. A flat in Barnes, I thought. Lots of BBC people in Barnes.'

'Lots of actresses.'

'Lots.'

I looked down and ordered veal, the most expensive thing on the menu.

The wine arrived. He said: 'Glad I didn't get Prewitt or Little.'

'Watch it. They're my partners.'

'But they're not as pretty.'

'They're blokes.'

'I don't go for blokes.'

'I've gathered that.'

He laughed. My neck heated up. I sipped my wine and thought of the breakfast coffee cups, and despised myself. Why shouldn't the chap enjoy himself?

I thought: catch me becoming another melted portion of Maggie Thatcher. Blushing harder, I thought: What on earth am I thinking?

We ate our antipasto. For a while it went all right. He wanted to know how I'd got into the business and I told him about my flat, and my brother's awful wife who hoovered under his lifted feet, and what I'd thought of *Gandhi*. I hadn't talked so much for ages; he made the words come into my head. I found I was entertaining even myself.

Then he said: 'Who is he?'

'Who's who?'

'There must be some lucky bloke, somewhere.'

I paused. 'Well . . .' I speared an anchovy.

'Go on. I've been longing to ask.'

'It's all . . . well, rather difficult.'

'Ah. That sort of difficult.'

I glanced up sharply. 'No!'

'Jesus,' he said. 'What a waste.'

'It's not!'

'How long has it been going on? Do you mind me asking?'

'Yes. No.' I ate a green bean. 'Four years.'

'Four? That's appalling.'

'It's not appalling. It's . . . difficult.'

'So you sit by the phone, and when it rings there's that pip-pip-pip?'

I said coldly: 'You're obviously speaking from experience.'

He ignored me. 'And all weekend you wash your hair, and hear the hours ticking away, and watch the families in the park—'

'Marcus, shut up!'

'And he keeps promising he'll leave her, and sometimes he even breaks down and cries—'

'Look—'

'—a grown man, and that makes you feel even worse.'

'Marcus—'

'And so you throw yourself into your work, and sublimate—'

Furious, I shouted: 'What a stupid, sexist remark! You wouldn't say that if I were a man.'

'I wouldn't feel like this if you were a man.'

I pushed an olive around my plate. 'It's none of your business.'

We fell silent. After a while we started talking politely. It was Wimbledon fortnight and we discussed McEnroe, but the zest had gone.

Outside he offered to drive me home, but I said I would rather walk. I thanked him for the dinner.

He took my hand. 'Sorry.'

'It doesn't matter.'

'It does.' Lorries rattled past. He was gazing at me, frowning. 'Four years is a long time. I just feel . . . you ought to be more honest with yourself. Not such a roman-tic.' He paused. 'You should face up to reality.'

'I do!'

He smiled. 'You and your suntrap patios.'

On the way back I stopped outside the office. We were doing so well that we'd had it refurbished. In the window, each photo was mounted in a plastic cube, lit from within . . . glowing from the heart. *Charming period house . . . Delightful garden maisonette.* Beyond them I could see the shadowy room and my dark desk.

I thought of Marcus's words. Why was he such an expert, when he'd made such a mess of his own life?

I worked harder than ever the next couple of weeks. Houses move fast in July; people are restless.

I was restless too. I felt hot and cramped in the office. I spent a lot of time in my car, driving clients around and visiting new properties. Once I drove to Holland Park, just to see if I could pass down Nigel's street without my stom-ach churning. I stopped outside the house. The blinds were down; he had taken the family on holiday.

I knew that, of course. For the first time in four years, however, I didn't know where they had gone. Or even how long they would be away. I hadn't asked him.

I gave the house a long, honest look. I saw it for what it was: an imposing, terraced mansion with a pillared porch. There it stood, large and creamy. A family fortress.

I drove away. I had three appointments that afternoon, meeting prospective buyers at various empty properties.

Two of them passed without incident. At five o'clock only the last remained. It was not until then that I fished the third key from my bag, and found the piece of paper, where my secretary had noted down the person's name.

He was waiting outside in the street.

'It's you,' I said stupidly.

He grinned. 'It's me all right. I'm glad it's you.'

'What?'

'Not Prewitt or Little.'

'No. It's not them.'

We stood there by the front gate. Trying to collect my thoughts, I fiddled with the gate-latch. There was a moment's silence, then he pointed up at the house.

'Which floor's the flat?'

'The second. Didn't you know?'

'I just saw the board up, with your name on it. So I phoned.' He picked at the blisters on the fence. 'On impulse.'

I felt hot. I said: 'Thought you were looking in Barnes.'

'I looked. Everyone's married.'

'Even the actresses?'

'Even them.'

We stood there. He popped the blisters in the paint. He wore his tired-looking jacket.

'Didn't you go to work today?' I asked.

He shook his head. 'Went round looking at your boards.'

I moved towards the door. 'You won't like this flat.'

'Why?'

'Just being honest.'

We went upstairs. The flat was a new conversion. It had been flashed up with magnolia paint and woodchip wallpaper.

'Cowboy job,' I said.

'You are being unromantic today.'

We stood in the empty room.

'Vacant possession,' he murmured.

'Oh yes, it's that all right.'

He looked at me. Then he said: 'How are you, Celia?'

I gazed at the floorboards. 'All right.'

'How's things?'

I looked up at him. 'Oh, they're over.'

'Are they?'

I nodded. There was a silence.

Later we had a meal. Not at the bistro place; somewhere else. He said: 'I don't want that flat.'

I shook my head. 'No.'

'It's cheap and nasty.'

I nodded. 'Yes.'

'Are we both telling the truth now?'

'Yes.'

Afterwards we sat together in my Metro. The car shook as lorries rumbled down the Cromwell Road.

I said: 'You feel so warm.'

'Oh yes,' he replied. 'I'm fully central-heated.'

Charming garden-level flat. That's what he bought, and it means a basement, of course. It had a *country-style* garden which meant full of nettles but I've been seeing to those.

It is charming, too. I'm not just saying it. I've come to know every corner, over the past few weeks. It charms me.

Some Day My Prince Will Come

I was woken up by Tilly prising open my mouth. They'd had the school dentist yesterday, that was why. She was smug because they had found nothing wrong with her.

'Wider,' she said. Small ruthless fingers pushed back my lips, baring my gums. I was lying in bed and she was sitting on top of me. 'There's these bits here ... yellow bits ... round the edges of your teeth.' Her calm eyes gazed into my mouth. 'It's called plaque,' she said. 'You should brush your teeth gooder.'

Beside me, Stephen grunted. 'Seen the time?'

Tilly was now yanking down my lower jaw. 'Ooh, look at all your silver stuff.'

'Half past six,' said Stephen, and went back to sleep.

'You've got lots of holes, didn't you,' she said.

Most of them, I thought, when I was pregnant with you. I lay, mute as a cow, under her gaze. She was only five and already she made me feel inferior. She would say things like: 'You shouldn't smoke.' I hadn't the heart to reply: I didn't, till recently.

Tilly settled down to deeper inspection. I was going to say: go and look at Daddy's teeth. Then I thought: better not, he had a hard day yesterday, at the office. A long day ahead, too. It's Saturday, Working on the House Day. Every Saturday and every Sunday ... weekends of the whirring

Black & Decker, and fogs of dust, and muffled curses from the closed door behind which he toiled . . . of tripping over the plumbing pipes, and searching for one small sandal in the rubble, and keeping out of Daddy's way . . . So much of the time I spent protecting Stephen from his children.

Tilly got bored and padded off in her nightie, sucking her thumb. From the back she suddenly looked terribly young. Outside I heard a thud: she had knocked down a roll of wallpaper.

'Hey!' Stephen's head reared up. Where his tools were concerned his reaction was so sharp. I swear he could hear a chisel shifting in its box three rooms away. Funny how he could sleep through all the children's noises – crying and squabbling, the thud as *they* rolled over and fell out of bed.

However, this seemed a churlish waking thought, with a weekend ahead. I ticked myself off, running through the litany to make myself a more loving wife: Remember, Stephen's slaving away just for us. Wasn't it me who wanted this house, such a lovely one right near the common, and we could never have afforded a done-up one in a street like this. And I bet he would rather spend the weekends playing football and watching the telly and drinking cans of lager . . . He would probably even prefer to spend them striding over the common with Tilly on his shoulders, like fathers did in building society advertisements. He had never done that. He said: there's so much to do.

Did your character change when you had children? Mine did. Trouble is, it's crept up on me so gradually and by now I simply can't remember what I was like before . . . What *we* were like. What did Stephen and I do, those three years of long, child-free weekends in our flat? What does one do?

Did we actually sit and talk, and read books unmolested, and wander off to the cinema on impulse, go anywhere on impulse, go to pubs . . . And dawdle in shops unembarrassed by clumsy infants and cold, shop-girl stares, and make love in the afternoons? That bit I do remember . . . I remember that.

Anyway, that Saturday I got up, and fed the children, and peeled off their Plasticine from Stephen's hammer before he saw it . . . Really, compared to the rest of the week, weekends were such a strain . . . And pulled a nail out of Tilly's plimsoll. She made such a fuss that I tried to shut her up by telling her the story about Androcles and the Lion, but I couldn't remember what had happened. Didn't Kirk Douglas play Androcles? By this time Tilly was wearing her school-mistress look. And Adam had just fallen down and was shrieking so loudly that Stephen could hear him over the electric sander.

After lunch Stephen went out. He had all these errands to do on Saturdays, like getting his hair cut and the car repaired, and things mended that I had forgotten to do during the week or that I had been too busy to fetch – he can't understand that I'm busy, when there's nothing to show for it. No floors re-laid, nothing like that. And he has to go to all those proper little shops with old men in overalls who take hours; he refuses to go to the big help-yourself places because he says they're soulless.

It's taking ages, our house. It's like one of those fairy stories where Mrs Hen won't give an egg until she's been given some straw, and Mr Horse won't give any straw until he's been given some sugar. You can't plumb in the bath until the skirting's fixed, and you can't fix the skirting until the dry rot's been done . . . I told this to Stephen and he gazed at me and then he said: 'That reminds me. Forgot the Nitromors.'

It was two thirty and raining outside. Do you ever have those moments of dulled panic: what on earth can one possibly do with the children until bedtime? The afternoon stretched ahead; Adam was staggering around, scattering wood shavings. Then I looked in the local paper and saw that *Snow White* was on.

So I wrote a note to Stephen and heaved out the double buggy and spent 23½ minutes searching for their gumboots and gloves . . . I actually went to college once, would you believe, and I can still add up . . . 12½ minutes to find my bag, and the teddy that Adam has to suck.

I pushed the children along the street – at least, Adam sat in the buggy (he's just three) and Tilly walked beside me because she only sits in the buggy when she's sure not to meet any of her friends.

'Does Snow White wear a beautiful pink dress?' she asked. 'With frillies?' She's obsessed with pink.

'Can't remember,' I said. 'I was your age when I saw it. I loved it more than any film I've ever seen.'

'Snow White gets deaded,' said Adam.

'She doesn't!' I cried. 'She's only asleep.'

'Deaded in a box. Seen the picture.'

'She isn't! She's just sleeping. And do you know how she wakes?'

'Got worms in her.'

'Shut up. She wakes up when the Prince comes along,' I said.

'Why?'

'He kisses her.'

When did Stephen last kiss me? Properly. Or when, indeed, did I last kiss him?

The Prince just touches her forehead, or is it her lips? Just a peck, really. Just like when Stephen comes home from the office.

No, not like that at all.

'Mummy! I said what happens after that?' Tilly's addressing-the-retarded voice. 'Does she get a baby? Does she get married?'

'Oh yes, they marry all right. He takes her off to his castle in the sunset, on the back of his big white horse.'

We arrived at the cinema; a peeling brick cliff, its neon lights glaring over the grey street. How could such buildings house such impossible dreams?

Inside I saw him. I saw him straight away; the place was half-empty. But I would have spotted him, I bet, in a crowd of a thousand. He was flung back in his seat, in that abandoned way he had, with his hair sticking up like it always had. He had never taken care of himself. The lights were still up; if I'd dared I'd have looked longer.

I had sat next to him in fifty cinema seats . . . Him beside me, flung back in that restless, tense way, never settled . . . his arm lying along the back of the seat. But now his arms were flung each side of his children.

'Let's go here!' Tilly demanded.

I pulled her away.

'Mummy! We can see over the edge!'

'Come on. This way.'

'Don't be silly! There's all these seats.'

'Silly bum-bum,' said Adam.

I dragged the buggy further away.

'Wanna sit here,' cried Adam.

'Ssh!'

I sat them down at last, pulling off their anoraks and trying to shove the buggy under the seat. The cinema darkened.

'Gimme the popcorn!' said Adam.

I rummaged in my carrier bag. While I did it, I stole another look. A red point glowed . . . She hadn't stopped him smoking, then.

'You said half!' Tilly hissed.

'Have a handful each.'

'S'not fair! He's—'

'Ssh! It's starting.'

Snow White was washing the steps, scrubbing and singing, the birds cheeping. I thought: forgot the Daz, and now I've missed the shops.

'When's the Prince coming?' hissed Tilly, her mouth full of popcorn.

'Hang on,' I replied. 'Don't be impatient.'

'Will he come on his horse?'

'Of course.'

He'd had a motorbike, an old Triumph. I'd sat behind him, gripping him with my arms, my face pressed against the leather. Ah, the ache, that his skin was hidden . . . The physical pain, that I couldn't get my hands on him. I wanted him all the time. Where did we go? Transport cafés at four in the morning. The glare of the light, the suddenness of all those strangers, after we had been alone for so long . . . He'd take off his gloves and hold my hand; I stroked his hard fingernails, one by one, and then the wider nail of his thumb.

Afterwards, driving oh too fast – he had a death wish all right – driving just for the heck of it . . . Then back to my digs, lying naked on the twisted sheets, the sun glowing through the curtains and the children down in the street whooping on their way to school – they seemed a hundred miles away . . . And me missing my lectures.

I wish you had met him. You'd probably think he was wildly unsuitable, far too neurotic. My parents did. They were terrified that I would marry him. And I didn't, did I?

I wonder if you'd have thought him beautiful. I wondered if he still was. It was too dark to see. All I'd heard was that he had married a social worker and had two children. She was called Joyce. I'd pictured somebody with a political conscience and thick ankles, who would care for him and see that he ate. Well, that's how I liked to picture her. Today she must be staying home, making flans for the freezer. Did he write her poetry, like he had written for me? Did anybody, once they got married? Joyce . . . not the dizziest of names.

'*Mirror mirror on the wall, who's the fairest one of all?*'

The Dark Queen was up on the screen, with her bitter, beautiful face. The light flared on her.

A hand gripped mine. 'She's horrid!' said Tilly.

'She's jealous,' I whispered.

'I hate her.'

'Ssh.'

Where did he live? It must be around here. On the other hand, on a wet Saturday afternoon he might have crossed London to see *Snow White*.

I would follow him home. I'd find out where he lived and press my nose against the window and gaze into his life, his lamplit family life all unknown to me, where I was not needed . . .

'Ugh!' The hand squeezed. 'She's turning into a witch!'

'Look at her horrid nose!'

'Isn't she ugly.'

'I don't like her!'

Tilly said in her posh voice: 'It's because she's got ugly thoughts.'

She took away her hand and sat there primly. She was wearing her kilt that she'd chosen herself, and her awful orange plastic necklace, and her *I've Seen Windsor Safari Park* badge.

Snow White was in the forest now; it was blacker than Windsor Park and the trees were swaying and moaning, warning her of danger. I thought that Tilly would be frightened here but she didn't show it. I had a sudden desire to grip my growing, wayward girl, so cool and so young. I wanted to grip her and protect her from what lay ahead. But she disliked shows of emotion.

Snow White had arrived at the dwarves' cottage and, little housewife that she was, she was clearing up, dusting, polishing, a song on her lips (well, she had about twenty squirrels and rabbits to help). I looked round. He was getting up.

I felt panic. But he was only carrying out one of his children, down the aisle. They must be going to the lavatory. He passed quite close, gripping the child. He was wearing a pale pullover and he held the child so tenderly. Ten years later and he looked just the same, whip-thin. I thought how easily that child could have been ours. It could have been us sitting there, and no Tilly. No Adam. Or a different Tilly . . .

'Mummy, you're hurting!'

I had been squeezing her hand, so I took mine away. But then she groped for it – both of them did – because the witch was knocking on the door of the cottage.

I feared for his remaining child, left alone. But I stopped myself. It wasn't my child to worry about. Besides, there he was, his hair haloed by the screen, bowed so he wouldn't block the view of this terrifying, powerful film.

Snow White let in the witch. As she took the apple, the audience sat absolutely still. All those children – not a sweet paper rustled. Nothing.

When she bit the apple, Tilly hid her face. My cool, superior Tilly. I pressed my hand against her eyes.

'It's all right,' I whispered.

'I want to go.'

'It's all right,' I said desperately. 'I told you – the Prince will come.'

He came, of course, as you knew he would. He rode up on his muscular white horse. Tilly took away her hand; she sat there, calm as ever. She knew it would turn out all right.

The Prince knelt down to kiss Snow White. And then she was in his arms and he was lifting her on to the back of his horse. Not a motorbike – a stallion with a thick curved neck, and the sun cast long shadows between the trees as they rode off, and ahead lay the castle, radiant.

Businesslike, Tilly was rummaging in the bottom of the popcorn bag. I sat limp; I felt her busy concentration. She knew the Prince would come, she believed it. Every girl must believe it, because wouldn't life be insupportable if they didn't?

'Come on.' She was standing up.

Every girl . . . Every boy too. All those young, believing children.

'Where's your hanky?' I muttered.

She had this hideous little diamanté handbag that Aunt Nelly had given her; she carried it everywhere. I took the hanky and blew my nose. The lights came on.

'Don't be soppy,' she said. 'It's only a story.'

I saw him ahead of us in the foyer. He had sunk down in front of his child and was zipping up its anorak. He was speaking but I couldn't hear the words.

Outside it was dark, and still raining: a soft November drizzle. I saw him quite clearly standing at the bus stop on the other side of the road. His children looked younger than mine.

I wanted to follow him. I couldn't face meeting him but I wanted to see where he lived. I wanted to set him into a house and give him a locality. I would be able to dream about him better then. All these years he had just been the same set of memories, stale and repeated; his present life was a vacuum. I hungered even for the name of his street.

'I'm wet!'

'Wanna Slush Puppy!'

'I want to go home.'

I wonder if you would have followed him.

I didn't. It was cold out there, and dark, and fumey as people revved up their cars. The warmth of the cinema, the dreams, they had vanished like that castle into the raw air of this South London road. Really, what was the good? Besides, the person I was seeking belonged to somebody who no longer existed.

They both sat in the buggy, they were so sleepy. I gazed

down at their two anorak hoods, lolling, brown in the sodium light. Some day, I thought, will your Prince come? If you get lost in the dark wood, as you will, and I can't always be there to protect you . . . If you get lost, will somebody find you? Will you be happy?

Twenty minutes later I was walking up our street. The cardboard eye of our bedroom looked at me blankly. It said: *shouldn't have gone, should you?*

Our car was outside and the house lights were on. Stephen must be home. The rain had stopped but I wiped my face on my sleeve. Besides, he would just think my face was wet from the rain. If, that is, he ever noticed anything about me.

I went into the house, with its naked lightbulb hanging down. The light shone on a lot of planks, propped against the wall; they made a forest of the hallway. He had been to the timber merchant.

Adam stirred and started to whine. Tilly climbed out of the pushchair and they went into the living room. A burst of canned laughter; they had switched on the TV.

Stephen didn't come out of the kitchen. No buzzing drill. I hesitated. Could he feel my thoughts? In the sitting room the advertisements came on; I heard the jingle for the Midland Bank. The children call it the Middling Bank.

Then I thought: he's made me a surprise.

I stood still, the realization filling me, through my limbs, like warm liquid.

You know how, just when the children are driving you insane, when you can't stand another minute . . . You know how, suddenly, they do something terribly touching? Like drawing you a card with *I Love Mum* on it or trying, disastrously, to do the washing-up?

Stephen had made the supper. Hopelessly, because he couldn't cook. But he had cleared the table, and bought a bottle of wine and lots of pricey things from the deli. He had realized how I'd been feeling lately.

I opened the door. But this wasn't a story. Life is not that neat, is it? No fairy tale.

There sat Stephen, with a can of beer in front of him and the lunch plates still piled in the sink. Packets were heaped on the table: not exotic cheeses but three-point plugs and boxes of nails.

'Hello.' He looked up. 'Didn't hear you come in.'

'Exhausted?'

He nodded. Fiction is shapely. A story billows out like a sheet, then comes the final knot. *The End*. Reared up against the suffused, pink sky there stands a castle, lit from within. The end.

A silence as he poured the lager into his glass. The froth filled up; we both watched it. He said: 'The end is in sight. I think I can finally say I've finished this bloody kitchen.'

List of Stories and
First Publication Details

All stories may have been slightly amended since previous publication.

The following stories were previously published in book form in *Smile* (William Heinemann Ltd, 1987):
'Smile'
'The Wrong Side'
'Making Hay'
'Lost Boys'
'Monsters'
'Snake Girl'
'Vacant Possession'
'Some Day My Prince Will Come'

The following stories were previously published in book form in *Changing Babies* (William Heinemann Ltd, 1995), and first published or broadcast as detailed below:

'Changing Babies' – first broadcast on Radio 4, then printed in *Telling Stories* and *Best Short Stories 1991*
'Suspicion' – first broadcast on Radio 4, then printed in *Good Housekeeping* and *Telling Stories 3*
'Ta for the Memories' – published in the *Daily Telegraph*
'Stopping at the Lights' – published in *New Writing 2*

'How I Learnt to be a Real Countrywoman' – first published in *The Times*, then broadcast on Radio 4 and published in *Telling Stories 1*

'Family Feelings: Five Linked Stories' – first broadcast on Radio 4

'A Pedicure in Florence' – published in *Freedom* (Red Cross anthology)

'Summer Bedding' – published in *Marie Claire*

All other stories were first published in book form in *Fool For Love* (Tinder Press, 2022).

If you enjoyed *Fool for Love*, discover
more unputdownable books from
Deborah Moggach . . .

Pru's husband has walked out, leaving her alone to con-
template her future. She's missing not so much him, but
the life they once had – nestling up like spoons in the
cutlery drawer as they sleep. Now there's just a dip on
one side of the bed and no-one to fill it.

In a daze, Pru goes off to a friend's funeral. Usual old
hymns, words of praise and a eulogy but . . . it doesn't
sound like the friend Pru knew. She's gone to the wrong
service. Everyone was very welcoming, it was more
excitement than she's had for ages. So she buys a little
black dress in a charity shop and thinks, now I'm all set,
why not go to another? I mean, people don't want to
make a scene at a funeral, do they? No-one will challenge
her – and what harm can it do?

Available now from

TINDER
PRESS

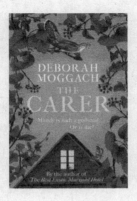

James is getting on a bit and needs full-time help. So Phoebe and Robert, his middle-aged offspring, employ Mandy, who seems willing to take him off their hands. But as James regales his family with tales of Mandy's virtues, their shopping trips and the shared pleasure of their journeys to garden centres, Phoebe and Robert sense something is amiss.

Then something extraordinary happens which throws everything into new relief, changing all the stories of their childhood – and the father – that they thought they knew so well.

Available now from

TINDER
PRESS

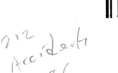
p 28 - 34
p 39 peem
p 40 Equip
p 45 Camp

p 12
Accidents
p 236
req

p 47 stress

p 39
What
they did

p 50
Train

p 53 girls
& boys

p 55
Train

p 113
Charcoal

p 114
some

p 163
camps

p 206
health

About the Author

Joanna grew up in Surrey, the most wooded county in England, loved to climb trees as a girl, and was often outside working on things with her father. She studied Psychology at Hull University and spent two years in France snowboarding, surfing and living in Les Landes, one of the largest pine forests in Europe. Inspired by an interest in organisational behaviour and gender issues at work, after several years as a PR consultant she studied for an MSc in Occupational and Organisational Psychology at Surrey University.

After raising two daughters, Joanna discovered the Lumberjills while working for the Forestry Commission. With a wild, adventurous spirit and a passion for forests, she felt a connection with their story. Few people had heard of them, so Joanna travelled the country to meet them and tell their story. Joanna worked with the *Daily Mail*, *Woman's Hour*, *Wartime Farm*, *Countryfile*, *How We Won the War* and *The Great British Menu* to increase recognition for their war work. She then concentrated on writing a novel that eventually turned into her debut history book – *Lumberjills*.